Prologue
London – 1985

He had to calm down; focus; concentrate. Concentrate on the target. He had almost been caught twice in the last half hour! Imagine – him, John Kelly, the IRA's top operative in the UK, almost getting caught by an ordinary bobby in the street!

He couldn't explain it. He had been the guy who had done all the big jobs – the Para's barracks; the booby-trap bomb in the Police Commissioner's car – done in broad daylight posing as a mechanic; the attack on the Home Office Government Minister – in his own home, for Christ's sake! All jobs had been meticulously well-planned, nothing left to chance. So much so that Kelly had been in and gone long before the police could react. No trace of evidence was left; oh, the police and military knew who was responsible, all right, but it could never be pinned down – never traced to Kelly. He was good, they all acknowledged that, and each job he undertook seemed to make him better and even more aloof.

But today – what the hell was it? Was he getting old? Christ, he was only 32! Was it a portent of what was to come? A warning? Was it the target? No, it had been meticulously researched as always, though not by Kelly; but the kids who did the work were good. He knew that. All were in their teens or early twenties, most highly intelligent, dedicated to the cause. Recruited on the back of the hunger strikes in '81 when Prime Minister Thatcher's stubborn refusal to grant political status to IRA prisoners led to probably the best PR campaign the organisation could have hoped for – the sympathies evoked by the sight of men being prepared to die for a principle leading to the best recruitment drive the IRA ever had. Young men were prepared to join up in droves – they could even afford to be selective in who they took! An organisation that conducted a terrorist campaign needed quality, not quantity.

Was it because the target was indiscriminate? Ten pounds of Semtex to be left in one of London's busiest department stores. No, he had done indiscriminate before – that raid on the pub in Belfast in '75 – the early days. Oh, they had known it was a Prod pub, and there was every likelihood that there might be UVF members or sympathizers inside, but it was indiscriminate nonetheless. The body count had been twelve with at least twice that number injured. There was no evidence that any of the dead or injured had been there for any reason other than to enjoy a quiet drink. Nonetheless, this did not bother Kelly or the boys in the organisation – a legitimate target was a legitimate target and that was that.

Somehow, this was different though. For a start, it was London. Oh, Brits were Brits and all that, but Kelly was far too intelligent to believe that sort of Provo bullshit. He had killed before, many times, but perhaps the thought of blowing innocent lunchtime shoppers to bits for a cause most of them wouldn't even be aware of, never mind have any involvement in, was a step too far? Still, he had gotten the order and that was that. He followed orders.

The larger problem, or at least part of it, was that John Kelly was a believer. He hadn't joined the organisation out of the bitterness of a bad experience at the hands of the Brits or the Unionists or the empathy with friends or neighbours who had. He had actually had a sheltered enough upbringing – his parents were upper middle class; his mother a primary school teacher from Coalisland, his father a clerk with the town Council in Omagh. He had had an excellent education and enjoyed all the benefits of the British National Health Service and other parts of the Welfare State bequeathed by successive Labour Governments since the war.

While not directly affected himself, he had always been aware of the divide, the "us and them." He knew that his family was privileged and that most of his fellows had been discriminated against in one way or another. Education and employment were available to all, in theory, but every society had its networks, its connections, its series of nods and winks; it was who you knew rather than what you knew. Societies that were composed mainly of one major ethnic group worked fine this way, but when there were two polarized groups with one having a stranglehold on power, it was a recipe for disaster. He had seen, from an early age, the powder keg that was building in Northern Ireland. He watched things deteriorate from the civil rights marches of the late sixties into the brutal savagery that followed and felt, in all conscience, that he had to take a stand. Deep down, he was, or at least he told himself, committed to peace and justice but the only way he ever saw his people gaining that justice was to fight for it. Unfortunately that involved some very unpleasant tasks and he was at the cutting edge of that.

He had joined the IRA in 1975 and was initially shocked by the lack of professionalism and inability to organise. They were a raggle-taggle bunch in those days, but they had learned, and now posed a greater threat to the security of Britain than at any time in their long history. The driving force and direction was provided by the new pseudo-politicals, thinly disguised as a political party; Sinn Fein. The military wing was now a finely tuned killing machine, organised in tightly knit cells that were almost impossible to penetrate. Even if one was caught or penetrated, it caused the minimum disruption to the rest of the organisation. There was no need for a stepped hierarchy; they weren't in the business of taking over the country – just in the business of creating terror, havoc and chaos. The cells were spread throughout both parts of Ireland and, more significantly from an operational viewpoint, the mainland of the UK. At the forefront of the military campaign – in fact, one could say, its cutting edge – was John Kelly.

Kelly's cell was based in London, though not in the traditional Irish enclaves of Kilburn or Notting Hill. He lived in an apartment in Ealing and, to his neighbours, was just another successful young professional reaping the rewards of the boom that was taking place in the city. The English were a placid and generally un-inquisitive race, so no one questioned the young man who left for the city each morning and normally didn't return until long after nightfall.

If someone had bothered to follow him, they would merely have had their suspicions confirmed. He did work in the city. He seemingly worked hard and had continuous consultations and meetings with all manner of business associates. Had someone scrutinized these associates in detail, they would have discovered that there was frequent contact between John and three particular associates – two men and one woman – but never at the same time. These meetings invariably took place in the myriad of pubs, coffee shops and restaurants available in Central London, or were held in some or other public place. However, to the untrained eye and even to most trained eyes, nothing untoward or suspicious ever transpired.

But John Kelly and his "associates" were constantly planning. Only he knew what the instructions were and who his controller was. There was no need for the others to know. In the unlikely event of his capture or death, the controller would know where to contact one of the others. In this way, even if a cell member were identified, captured and tortured by the British, they could provide very little information. While John Kelly and his group were constantly reconnoitering possible targets, they were only aware of one – the next one – at any one time.

They had been aware of this one for two weeks now. Kelly himself as the bag man, who would actually place the bomb, had only visited the place on one occasion and that fleetingly. He was very much aware that each frame of videotape from each security camera would be studied in minute detail afterwards and he had no wish to appear as the special guest in any of those videos. He had only visited the store after one of the others had checked it out and gauged the position of the video cameras. Thereafter, they were avoided. Very detailed plans had been drawn up of the layout. The precise path from the underground had been mapped. The distances had been stepped. He would be in and out of the store and half way across London before the bomb would detonate.

Then why was he so bloody nervous? One thing he was certain of: it was he who had noticed the policeman on the way in to Earls Court tube station; not the other way round. But he had broken the golden rule: never make eye contact – never draw attention to yourself. Yet he had looked into the eyes of that young bobby. He kept asking himself why? Was he losing his nerve? Did that young fresh face represent something? Did he see something there – some hope, something that he had once had but had now lost forever?

Yes, maybe that was it – but no, wait; this was John Kelly. He didn't notice things unless they needed to be noticed. Was there a trap? Was it a set-up? Couldn't be – not now. No one knew; just the controller and the cell members, and they had never let him down before. Was there a bigger agenda here that he was not privy to? He had heard murmurings about ceasefires and fellows getting soft, but there were always stories; it was part of the game – wasn't it?

He was thinking so frantically that he walked straight into the second policeman, this time a transport cop, and almost knocked him down. Jesus, this was the beginning of a disaster – it was like all his good fortune had deserted him and his bad luck was all arriving on the same day. Whether or not the first cop at Earls Court remembered him, he was certain the second guy would. He had even dropped the briefcase, for Christ's sake.

The transport cop had picked it up and handed it back seemingly un-suspiciously – "Careful there sir, don't want to scatter our lunch all around the platform, do we?" For a split second Kelly hesitated and then training took over and he laughed heartily at the remark. The transport cop had accepted the incident as seemingly innocuous but he would remember it when the remains of the briefcase were analyzed and he would remember what John Kelly looked like. For a man whom British Police only vaguely knew existed and had no photograph of, this was worrying.

He thought of aborting, but this one was crucial; he had been told from HQ. Make sure you carry this one through. Why, he couldn't figure. After all, it was indiscriminate. A jumble of thoughts swam in his head and competed for his attention. Had the boys warned the British that unless concessions were given, something like this would happen? Were they on the lookout for it? Had there been a leak? Was he being sacrificed on the basis of a ceasefire deal? No; surely not their top operative? He *was* the top operative – wasn't he?

The IRA had targeted the same store two years before. Although a warning had been given, due to the bungling of the police, six people had died. This time there wouldn't be a warning. Perhaps that was why Kelly had been chosen to do the job. They trusted him. They knew he was a hard bastard; a dedicated one. The best and the worst kind, depending on your point of view. How many would die? Or would there be a warning after all – damn it, had it already been phoned in? His head was spinning and he had difficulty concentrating.

Calm down, calm down for Christ's sake – this isn't the correct demeanour for a cool assassin. What does it matter if I'm ten minutes late? I am in control here! The bomb was timed to detonate at half past one, right in the middle of lunch hour, when the department store would be at its busiest; but he could always readjust the timer. It was now 12.50 and he had less than a five-minute walk. Hell, he had to take time out – he could have a coffee and calm his nerves and still be in and out of there by one o'clock. The bomb was fine; Semtex was stable. Don't worry.

He chose a 7-11 store rather than a café; self service coffee; more impersonal. The key point was that no one should remember him as anything other than a normal young business executive like the thousands of others going about their daily tasks.

Coffee – milk – no sugar – hands shaking – count to ten – hands calm – drink coffee – scald mouth – damn it – more milk. Has anyone else noticed – noticed what, for Christ's sake? There's no one in here apart from you and a bored-looking Pakistani behind the counter; will you get your act together!

And then it was gone and he was John Kelly again. Cool, professional, together. The panic had subsided. He finished his coffee, nonchalantly discarded the paper cup in the bin provided, stretched, picked up the briefcase, and left the shop. He strolled casually down the street, eyes straight ahead, relaxed but focused. It was a beautiful day in London. He now noticed the bright sunshine for the first time. Just like any other young executive out for lunch; four hundred metres to the corner, left, two hundred and fifty to the pedestrian traffic light, wait for the green, and then in through the side door of the department store; the one which didn't have a video camera! A few quick steps up the stairs. Not the escalator. Apparently, a detonation on the first floor was most effective – it would cause maximum damage on that floor and might even bring down the floors above, causing the whole building to implode. Browse casually through menswear and place the briefcase between the racks of coats at the far end. Place it between the very large sizes; rarely disturbed. People hardly ever looked at coats in summer anyway, and given the day outside, chances were practically nil that the briefcase would be discovered in the short time it would rest there.

Everything went as planned. In fact, there hadn't even been a shop assistant in that section of the menswear department. He walked casually back downstairs, very briefly browsed in the jewellery department and exited the same door he had come in through, less than five minutes earlier. He glanced to his left and there it was, C349XJK, the pre-arranged black taxi. He donned the dark glasses and sat in. He spoke just one word – go. Then he sat back and relaxed for the leisurely drive to Heathrow. No way was he hanging round for the aftermath of this one.

Police Constable Alan Williams had been close to the end of his shift when he had made eye contact with Kelly at Earls Court Station. It had been a normal morning, without incident, and he was looking forward to getting out of his uniform in this heat and a well-earned afternoon on the golf course. It was strange; almost as if Kelly's eyes had sought him out rather than the other way round. For just an instant, he had detected that vaguely guilty, panicked look, and then it was gone.

It was probably nothing, and he really should be getting back to the police station, but he nonetheless decided to follow at a discreet distance. Difficult enough when you are in full uniform on a hot summer's day. Still, he witnessed Kelly's collision with the transport officer and his suspicions were redoubled. The man seemed to be unsettled. But what should he do? He couldn't follow him on a tube train – he would stand out like the proverbial sore thumb. His only option was to report to base.

He watched the train doors close as Kelly headed east on the Picadilly line. He thought of reporting it to base and clicked his radio but then hesitated. What was he going to say – he had seen a man acting suspiciously with a briefcase? He'd be the laughing stock of the station for months!

"And what did this man do then, PC Williams?"

"He got on a train, sir."

"And where was this train headed to, Constable?"

He could hear the guffaws of laughter and the derision already. And yet, doubts persisted. He decided he'd contact his best mate in the Metropolitan Police, who happened to be working the same shift. Damn it, one call wouldn't hurt. He was a conscientious policeman and he was going to do his job.

He clicked the radio. "Control, this is PC Williams. Can you connect me with PC Mortimer?"

"Stand by one moment please, Constable Williams. You are connected, go ahead please."

"Dave, this is Alan. I'm up at Earls Court, what's your location?"

"Hi Alan; I'm at Knightsbridge, just finishing up. What's happening?"

"Probably nothing, but a guy just got on the Picadilly line here heading in your direction and, well, I dunno, there was something suspicious about him. I mean, he was dressed as a businessman, he carried a briefcase, but he just didn't look like a business man to me; know what I mean?"

"I copy that Alan, what you want me to do, jump on the first train that comes through and arrest him?" Dave Mortimer had trained with Alan Williams and they were best mates but he was familiar with Alan's often-unfounded suspicions, which had sometimes resulted in wild goose chases. The ribbing back at the station had been cruel, but Alan had persisted and was determined to follow up on every minor detail, no matter how seemingly insignificant. While Dave ribbed him as much as the others, he knew deep down that Alan was a good policeman and that he would go far, probably very soon to Detective division.

"Ok, ok, only joking mate. Tell me what he looks like and I'll keep a look out."

"Cheers Dave, we'll probably never see him again, but for what it's worth, he's wearing a dark grey suit, he's white, about five eight-five nine, slim build but wiry. He appears to be strong and fit, looks like he works out a lot; short brown hair, fair complexion, brown eyes, I think. He's carrying a black briefcase, standard size, gold combination locks."

"Wonderful, Alan, you just described half the businessmen in west London; but don't worry, if he comes by here, you'll be the first to... hold on. Wait, Jesus, I think I've spotted him. Leave it with me; I'll get back to you."

P.C. Mortimer discreetly observed Kelly as he took the underground exit furthest from the department store and then strolled down Knightsbridge like a man without a care in the world. He watched as he had coffee in the 7/11 and then walked the few hundred metres to Harrods Department Store. Still nothing to worry about really; a businessman stopping for a brief lunch, then deciding to drop into Harrods for a spot of shopping. Once inside, the guy could easily disappear or could exit through half a dozen different doors. Dave's shift had already ended and he would now be late for his tee-off time with Alan. If they missed their slot, bye, bye golf game. Ah, bugger, he'd give it another few minutes.

But wait, there he was, exiting through the same door; or was it him? Yes, yes, it was; and sweet Holy Mother, he was missing the briefcase. He watched as Kelly jumped into a waiting taxi; but wait, there was something not right about this. The taxi rank was at the front of the store. Taxis only dropped off at the side entrance. Shit, the taxi was already 100 metres away. He quickly memorized the registration plate and dashed into the store. He grabbed the first clerk he found.

"Hey, that guy, the man in the grey suit who just left. He had a briefcase when he came in. Where did he go? What department was he in?"

The clerk and her colleagues gave him a bemused but disinterested look. "Sorry officer, but I have no idea what you're talking about." He suddenly realised he was sweating profusely. It was 13.01.

Sir Charles Wrixon, Metropolitan Police Commissioner, had just finished a briefing with his anti-terrorist chief, Detective Chief Superintendent Roger Devon. They had met, at Sir Charles' insistence, at Devon's office at Scotland Yard, as Wrixon wanted to meet some of the troops and not be the faceless man his predecessor had been reputed to be.

It had been an good meeting and he was looking forward to lunch. Both men enjoyed an excellent relationship and he had invited the Chief to join him. They were winning the battle with the terrorists as Whitehall had finally realised the threats that existed and had given both them and MI5 the necessary funding.

As both men strolled casually towards the exit, an out-of-breath and apparently stressed policewoman dashed towards them. "Sir, we have a report of a suspected terrorist incident in progress at Harrods."

"Thank you, Constable. Sir Charles, if you can excuse me?"

"Certainly, my dear chap. Keep me fully informed, won't you?"

Devon walked briskly back to the central control room to be briefed. As they walked, the WPC, Sally Young, explained. "It's quite straightforward sir. We have a report from a PC Mortimer, who is in the store now, and thinks a man has planted a bomb there. Another Constable, PC Williams, confirms that he had seen the man acting suspiciously earlier this afternoon."

"Well done, PC Young. Can you get me Mortimer on the phone?"

They arrived in the control room, which was already a hive of activity. Devon changed his mind and immediately sought out DCI Roger White, who was sitting with his feet up on the desk, smoking a cigarette, apparently relaxed about it all.

"Full sit-rep please, White," said Devon.

"I was just waiting for your go-ahead, sir. Emergency Response and Army bomb disposal units on stand-by, ready to go. Hospitals are alerted, ambulances on stand-by, but hopefully it won't come to that. I have a very nervous PC Mortimer with the General Manager of Harrods trying to clear the store quickly and without panic. I didn't wait for your okay on that one, sir; felt

14

we had to act. For the record, we used the 'suspected gas leak' ploy. We've alerted all units to be on the lookout for our man's black taxi. We do have the number plate, but as you'll appreciate, sir, there are rather a lot of them in the city."

"Yes indeed, excellent, Chief Inspector. Now, if you can tear yourself away from that chair, I want you to come with me. I have a feeling about this one."

White was slightly more cautious. "Sir, you do realise that this may just be a copper's hunch and lead us on a wild goose chase?"

"Yes, of course I do, but we can't afford to take the chance. Now come along. There's a good fellow." It was 13.10.

The Chief Super's chauffeur-driven Granada swept to the curb and Devon and White jumped in.

"Harrods please, Jenkins, and we'll have full lights and siren, good man. Oh, and hand me the radio please."

The car tore down Broadway to Victoria St and must have been doing close to 70 mph going round by the Palace. At this rate, they would be in Harrods in a few minutes.

The car's police radio crackled to life. "Sir, Clegg here in control; confirmation that the Army bomb disposal unit have arrived at Harrods and the premises appear to have been cleared of all members of the public, over."

"Message received, Constable. Should be there in about four minutes, over."

It was 13.13.

The radio crackled to life again.

"Sir, London black taxi, reg no C349XJK has just been spotted in Acton. Car contains white male driver and white male passenger fitting the descriptions supplied by PC's Williams and Mortimer. Unit tried to intercept, sir, and the cab took off at high speed. Two units giving chase sir, over."

"Thank you Constable, excellent news."

Bloody marvellous! Devon felt this was going to be a good day. Now, if this was for real, it would more than likely be Kelly, and he wanted that bastard badly. He made an instant decision; he grabbed the radio and pressed down the send button.

"Constable Clegg, this is DCS Devon, come in please, over."

"Clegg here, sir, over."

"Change of plan, Constable. Advise all units that we are diverting to Acton, repeat, diverting to Acton. Please patch me in to officers in pursuit of black taxi, over."

"Certainly sir, doing so now. Just informing you sir, that is an open frequency, over."

"Acknowledged Constable, and do keep us updated on the Harrods situation if you would. Over and out for now."

It was 13.15.

PC Dave Mortimer was frantic. Alan Williams had arrived a few minutes before, and along with the bomb squad and reinforcements from the Met, had been systematically searching behind displays, in corners, dustbins, toilets; anywhere the suspect could have left his briefcase. A brief moment of terror shuddered through Dave as he realised that he might have overreacted and sparked an enormous false alarm! What if the guy had met someone and just given him the briefcase? What if he had been returning it? They hadn't had time to check and the staff were gone. What if he had gotten it wrong and it had been another guy he saw leaving the store? What if Alan had got it totally wrong too? He could see both their careers going up in smoke.

But no, no, wait, don't panic. He had definitely seen the man enter a taxi that was not at an official rank. But the taxi could have been waiting for him – no, he had arrived by Tube.

Then the news came through that the taxi was being pursued by two police cars in Ealing or Acton or somewhere, and he breathed a sigh of relief. It was short lived though as the search resumed.

Dave realised they were not thinking straight. He wished some of the big guns had gotten here; they'd know what to do. It was now almost twenty minutes since the suspect had left the shop, and surely if he had primed a bomb explosion, twenty minutes was more than adequate to get well away. Dave hoped the guy had been conservative. He needed to think.

He bumped into Alan again, this time in the front lobby. "I think we'd better take our leave of here, mate, we're surely out of time."

"For sure, but let's give it one last throw. Where would you place a bomb if you wanted to do maximum damage but not have the device discovered?"

"Any one of a thousand places, and we've looked in them all."

"No, think mate, think. He can't put it in the toilets or the restaurants; it's too likely to be discovered. He has to be sure. He has to put it somewhere no one is likely to go, but where is that? This bloody shop is enormous."

It was 13.21.

Ralph Thwaites, the frightened General Manager was standing outside well back from the store where a perimeter cordon had been established. Alan suddenly got a brainwave and ran the hundred yards to him.

"Ralph, I need you to think very, very carefully. On a day like today, in high summer, which department would be least busy?"

"Why, that's relatively easy, sir: menswear, of course."

"Ok, ok, good, now, menswear covers about an acre in there. Is there any section of it that might be quieter than the rest?"

"Why that's even easier, sir; men's overcoats, of course. We are the only store that keeps them in stock year-round, to facilitate our overseas visitors from different climes."

But Alan was gone, back up the street, through the lobby, shouting at Dave and the bomb disposal team to follow him, taking the stairs four at a time. Turn left, into the menswear section – overcoats, where were the bloody overcoats – at the far end.

Alan dashed at breakneck speed but in his frantic rush, tripped over a protruding cash register cable. He went headfirst into a Burberry display, coming to rest gazing up at Giorgio Armani's latest creations. As he scrambled to regain his footing, he saw it; the soft leather resting on the ground between the overcoats.

"Sweet Mother of Jesus, guys, come down here."

It was 13.23.

If the police were frantic, Kelly was now as cool as a cucumber. Mind you, he knew a lot that they didn't. First of all, the black taxi was no ordinary cab, but a heavily modified vehicle capable of speeds of 140mph and with all sorts of other adjustments from all-round disc brakes to reinforced suspension, wider tyres and supercharged engine. His driver had been practicing in London's streets for months and was a highly skilled operative. Yes, the boys were a slick, organised unit now for sure.

He had two other advantages. It was often said that London was not a city at all but a whole series of villages, with the denizens of each knowing their own "manor" intimately, but practically nothing about the rest of the city. This was true of many police drivers also who might not have the knowledge of the vast maze of back streets, lanes and alleyways which were a feature of each borough of the city. In fact, because of traffic difficulties, most taxi drivers rarely used main routes, and it was this tactic that Kelly's driver was using now.

Finally, he was aware that the Metropolitan Police was a largely unarmed force, apart from Special Branch, and he felt sure that none of those guys were likely to be in pursuit. Even if they were, they were highly averse to gunfire, particularly in London's streets. Kelly was unarmed himself, as was his driver. A technicality, but safer in a culture where guns were the exception and possession of one carried serious sanctions.

The one thing that bothered him was how he had been detected at all, but he assumed it must have been due to his misfortune at the underground station and his own subsequent reaction. Still, that was past. The concentration now was to sit it out and outrun these guys. If he could manage to get near another underground station undetected, he might be prepared to make a run for it, but he was close enough to the safe house to stick with it for now. He was confident in his driver and there was nothing else he could do, so he might as well just sit back and relax.

PC Mike Lyons had just come on duty when he had gotten the BOLO message about the black cab. He couldn't believe his luck moments later when he spotted it stopped at traffic lights at the junction of Bath Road and Bath Avenue. He was accompanied by

WPC Gill Merson and immediately advised her to hold on as he swung the police car in a U-turn, simultaneously switching on his overhead blue lights.

His misfortune was that the BOLO message had not said what the suspects were wanted for so he never anticipated the wide sweep that the black cab made as it reversed and U-turned back in the direction of Acton town. A London cab could turn on a sixpence so he lost vital seconds before he could pursue it.

Gill got on the radio. "Control, this is Lyons & Merson, suspect cab no C349XJK spotted on Bath Road, heading towards Acton; attempted to intercept and approach but no response from driver of cab; currently undertaking pursuit; request support of all units in the area, over."

"This is control. We copy that, Constable, please leave your channel open; all units, please converge on area around North Circular Road."

The cab driver may have been good and his car modified, but so was Mike, although in an inferior vehicle. He had learned to drive on the narrow back roads of County Wicklow when he was fourteen years old, so London's streets presented no great challenge.

The cab headed through Acton and onto the North Circular Road. Mike gained a little and then saw the other police car coming from the opposite direction. Now we have him, he thought, only for the cab to veer off into the group of back streets around South Ealing. He had to brake hard to even make the turn and he lost the cab momentarily. The other police vehicle had to U-turn to pursue and he thought he had lost him.

Gill got on the radio again. "Control, this is Merson, still in pursuit of black cab – its performance suggests it may be modified. Again request support of all units but advise to approach with caution. We think suspect may be trying to lose us in the back streets. He keeps going in a circuitous pattern and may be trying to get on to the M4."

The response startled her somewhat. "You're doing fine, Constable Merson. This is DCS Roger Devon of Special Branch. Continue pursuit and try to box in our suspect, but don't approach unless you have to. We have reason to believe that the man in this cab is a wanted terrorist. I have authorized closure of the East and West bound ramps of the M4 so don't worry; he isn't going to get to the motorway today. We're going to get this bastard."

Easy for you to say, thought Mike Lyons; where in hell has this guy got to? Then he spotted him, just as he again emerged from the maze and turned on to Uxbridge Road. Mike clipped the curb, momentarily losing control and barely missing a pedestrian as he swung hard on the Rover's steering wheel to arc back on to Uxbridge Road. Gill could feel the imprint of the seat belt cutting into her shoulder as she was continuously shunted back and forth.

"Control, this is Merson again, suspect now heading back towards the city on Uxbridge Road. Suspect travelling at very high speed, continuing pursuit."

The bomb squad wasted no time, initially satisfying themselves that there were no booby trap wires, then surrounding the briefcase with anti blast screens. They quickly determined that it was just a standard briefcase and highly unlikely to explode if moved. After all, the suspect had been carrying it around central London, so he was hardly going to take that chance.

Clive King, the senior disposal man, with over 20 years experience in the squad, had dismantled bombs in Cyprus, Northern Ireland and even once, a little-known one in Gibraltar. He hadn't told the police this, but he knew the suspect had left the store at 13.00 and he reckoned that still left him five to six minutes. Too risky to attempt to defuse, but he would try to get it out of the store. To do this he would employ the remote control device to roll into the lift, descend to the ground floor and exit. Alan, Dave and the team stood off and left him to it. He keyed the remote to begin the process.

The last thing Alan felt, before he blacked out, was an enormous whoosh of super-heated air. He vaguely detected a set of lift doors flying in his direction but thankfully he had already been knocked over and they flew above his head.

He came to, some moments later, to a scene of total bedlam. He crawled out from under a huge pile of ripped and torn clothing to discover there was no menswear department any more. Neither were there stairs or lifts or escalators. There was a huge hole in the ceiling and the upper floor seemed to be hanging precariously. Every window was gone; every display, counter, rail; everything had been flattened. There was dust everywhere and it was difficult to breathe. He was bleeding profusely from numerous cuts. None seemed to be life-threatening although he wasn't sure, as he couldn't think straight.

While it was probably only a matter of seconds, it seemed like hours to him before the ambulance men arrived. He was very quickly lifted on to a stretcher and brought down the back stairs to the street.

"You'll be alright mate, just some cuts and bruises and severe shock," said the paramedic as he quickly attached an I.V. line. It was only then that Alan realised what had happened.

He grasped the paramedic's arm in a vice-like grip. "Dave, where's Dave? And the bomb guys, did they make it?"

"Easy there matey, I dunno. Gotta get you off to hospital, though"

"No." Alan gripped his arm again and tried to rise. "Can't go till I check on me mate."

"Ok, ok, give me a second."

He rushed away and came back moments later with a guy Alan recognised from his training as some big wheel in Special Branch.

"PC Williams, I believe?" Alan nodded. "DS Collins, Special Branch. You're a very brave man, Constable."

Alan knew then, but he had to ask. "And Dave and the other guys?"

Collins gently shook his head. "I'm really sorry mate, they didn't make it."

Alan thought, what have I done here? Why did I start all this? Then he lay back on the stretcher and wept.

By now Devon and White had reached the chase area and were attempting to co-ordinate the operation. Both felt sure it was just a matter of time. More and more resources were poured into the area and streets were closed off, barriers were erected, and the net was tightened.

"Clegg here again sir. DS Collins has reported explosive device located at Harrods but unfortunately detonated before it could be defused. First reports suggest casualties."

Devon was furious; why the hell didn't they leave the bloody thing be when they found it? Buildings could be replaced, coppers couldn't.

It made him even more determined to get this bugger once and for all. He had outwitted them more than once but not this time, me boyo, oh no; we have you.

"PC Merson, it's DCS Devon again. Please confirm suspect car is still in sight, over."

"Just about, sir, but he seems to know the area even better than our units. We believed we had him trapped in dead-ends on two occasions but he found alternative escape routes, over."

"Keep suspect in sight at all costs Constable; don't give him the chance to run for it. Keep me continuously posted on the movements of the suspect. I want to apprehend him as quickly as possible."

"Copy that, sir."

It was getting tighter. The driver had been up and down these roads now for well over half an hour and still couldn't shake off that guy in the Rover. They were now in Hammersmith. Central London wasn't an option – afternoon traffic was a nightmare. Heading west again, they were likely to encounter roadblocks.

Out of the corner of his eye, he just saw the blue flash as yet another patrol car cut across their path, but his driver was good. Just a quick flick of the steering wheel to the left to avoid the collision, slam on the brakes, then a flick to the right that just caught the tail end of the police car and flipped it over nicely. Another one down! But there would be more, and matey in the Rover had gotten closer.

They screeched down Holland Road, cut straight across the traffic and then doubled back on to Addison. Matey couldn't turn fast enough and they gained considerably on him; but wait, shit, there was another police car blocking Addison Road. The driver turned left, heading for Holland Park, allowing Mike and Gill to gain on him slightly again.

It was then that Kelly spotted the black Granada emerging from the side street. He immediately ordered the driver, "Head for the park."

The British were so civilized about their parks, he thought. Unlike most European capitals, they allowed you to drive through most of them, albeit subject to speed limits and speed bumps; but that wouldn't be a problem.

The cab tore through the park, once again pursued by Mike's Rover. "Ok," said Kelly, "on to the grass and try to avoid the folks, if you can. Good man."

Football players, joggers, sun worshippers and afternoon strollers dived for cover as the driver expertly carved a path through them. They hit a patch of clear ground and they were finally losing matey in the Rover so the driver was mildly surprised when Kelly gave his next order.

"OK, now, wheel right round and ram him."

Even if he had slight misgivings, the driver obeyed instantly as his job was to drive, not to question.

Mike was nearly exhausted. He had been chasing this guy for almost an hour at speeds of over 100 mph and he was knackered. His car was good but he had to constantly compensate for the other car's superior performance. When the cab had entered the park, Mike thought the guy had lost it. Now it seemed like he was doubling back again.

Gill was constantly sending reports; "Now pursuing suspect through Holland Park. Suspect has crossed football pitch. Having to slow to take evasive action to avoid injury to civilians; continuing pursuit."

"Copy that, PC Merson, we are very close to you." This from DCS Devon. Mike had never played chicken, but it looked like his opponent wanted him to try now. He had turned and headed straight for the Rover, and Mike hadn't been prepared to give way. He assumed the cab would swerve at the last minute, leaving him with a difficult manoeuvre on grass to get back in pursuit, but he didn't.

"Sir, suspect has turned round and seems to be attempting to ram us."

The crash, when it came, was devastating. Both cars came to a juddering halt and the occupants of both were momentarily stunned. But all had expected the impact and all had been wearing seatbelts. Both cars seemed to be badly damaged.

Kelly was first to emerge but Mike, struggling to clear his head, was after him in a flash. He had perhaps a twenty-yard start but Mike was young, very fit, and confident of gaining on his quarry. He strained every muscle and sinew and gained a yard, two yards, five yards.

Kelly was also very fit and began to gain again. Mike's advantage was waning as they ran up a small hill. Then, as Kelly just crested the brow of the hill, the black Granada emerged from behind the trees.

Kelly was going too fast, was too committed and couldn't avoid the collision. He went headfirst over the hood and landed dazed at the other side. He struggled to get up again but two of the occupants of the Granada had quickly emerged and subdued him, slapping a pair of handcuffs on instantly. Mike stopped, exhausted. Gill arrived, panting, both lost for breath.

"Constables Lyons and Merson, I presume," said the tall man in the black suit. "Excellent work indeed. DCS Devon and DCI White. I'll arrange for one of the other cars to pick you up. Well done Constables, we won't forget this; got to get this man into custody immediately."

"Of course, fully understand, sir. Thank you."

Kelly was handcuffed and placed in the back between Devon and White, and the Granada headed off at high speed.

"Well done, Mike," Gill said, "great driving. I believe this guy was the main man."

"Well done yourself Gill and sorry about the bumps and bruises. Oh, what about the cab driver?"

"Out of it, I'm afraid. Doubt he's going anywhere for a while, but just to be safe, I handcuffed him to the steering wheel."

"Excellent, great result! I'm surprised that the brass didn't take him too, but he's probably small fry. Not to worry anyway, we've got a truckload of offences to charge him with."

They walked back down the hill together, a deep sense of satisfaction overcoming their fatigue. As the adrenalin rush of the chase faded, it struck Mike that there was something not quite right with the whole scene. Why had the driver decided to ram them? Whatever, no point in musing over it now; it had been a good afternoon's work.

He and Gill were a good team. Although he had only been on the force for a little over a year, the Met had recognised his driving skills when he had volunteered for a defensive driving course, and he had been the star performer on view. His days as a foot patrol officer were numbered after that and he was now doing the two things he had always wanted to do – drive and be a police officer. The fact that he was getting paid to do what he loved was an added bonus.

His only regret, albeit a slight one, was that he had had to leave his native land to realise his ambition. There had been nobody hiring anyone during the depressed Ireland of the early 1980's, so Mike had tried his hand in London. After six months working in bars, he had seen the ad for the Met and thought, why not? It's what I want to do so why not here?

Despite the fact that there were elements in his country that were, literally, at war with the British, he himself had never encountered any bias or prejudice. He was now an accepted member of the force and his future looked bright. After his heroics today, who knew where it would lead?

As he and Gill arrived back at the scene of the wrecked taxicab and police car, the mild concern at the back of his mind heightened when a black Ford Granada skidded to a stop beside the wreckage. Two middle-aged men in grey suits emerged.

"Good afternoon, officers. Detective Chief Superintendent Devon and this is Detective Chief Inspector White. Well done this afternoon. Now, where have you hidden our suspects?"

Concern gave way to panic with Mike. "But, we've already given... who are you... I'm terribly sorry, sir, but could we see some identification?"

"But of course; but what the devil are you playing at, Constable Lyons, isn't it?" said Devon as he and DCI White produced their badges and Scotland Yard I.D. passes.

"Yes, sir, it is, but…" Mike seemed to visibly sag in front of the two senior men as the awful realization dawned. Panic now gave way to dismay as the impact sank in.

"Oh Jesus sir, I think we've made a dreadful mistake."

"What the devil is it, man, what have you done?"

"Well sir, there were two…"

That was it; now it was clear. He knew what had been wrong with the scene, what had been bugging him. The two men in the other Granada had been far too young to have reached the ranks of DCS or even DCI.

He struggled for composure. "Sir, we apprehended the terrorist suspect but two other men arrived. They said they were you, sir, and the Chief Inspector and, I'm sorry to say sir, they took the terrorist suspect with them."

"Compose yourself, man. Where did they go? Which direction? What type of car did they have?"

"I'm not sure, sir; they had a black Granada, sir, same as yours."

"Did you get its number, Constable?"

"No sir, sorry sir, I didn't think it was…"

DCI White ran to the Rover and grabbed the radio. "All units, this is DCI White; suspect involved in chase in Holland Park has escaped. He is believed to be travelling in a black Ford Granada, no details of registration plate at this time."

The radio crackled vaguely but there was no immediate response. Realistically, this was hopeless. Mike was slumped over in despair. White re-emerged from the car.

"Sir, profuse apologies, my mistake entirely sir, but we still have the drive…"

Mike glanced at the wrecked taxi-cab. For a moment he thought his eyes were playing tricks on him, but no; the driver was gone too.

"You blundering idiot Constable. Do you realise how many fucking black Granadas there are in London?"

Part One
June 2011

Chapter 1 – The Council

The reservation in the Gulf Hotel in Bahrain had been made in the name of a corporation. As it was high summer and the outside temperatures were touching 50C, most tourists had been scared away and the hotel was relatively quiet. It was Saturday morning, the first day of the week. Most of the occupants of the spacious lobby were local businessmen meeting colleagues and taking an Arabic coffee or a glass of water in an attempt to gain a brief respite from the suffocating heat.

The suite on the sixth floor had been chosen carefully. It could be approached discreetly by an elevator that was easily accessed through a side door. The recent protests and effective uprising in Bahrain had heightened security and a special pass was required to even access the compound in which the hotel was situated, but as these were produced by the drivers of the limousines which delivered the guests, anonymity was assured. Protestors did not arrive in chauffeur-driven Mercedes or Bentleys; not in Bahrain, anyway. The seven occupants of these gleaming air-conditioned vehicles were hidden behind heavily darkened smoked glass, and even when they emerged from their air-conditioned havens were cloaked in robes and formal headdresses. All wore dark sunglasses.

Sheikh Abdullah bin Sama al Khadira had arrived well ahead of his guests. He was the youngest of the senior members of the organisation, and it was he who had requested the meeting. It had been excruciatingly difficult to organise, given the secret locations of all the participants. When he did manage to make contact, there had been strong objections to the meeting, given what had transpired the month before. Abdullah had anticipated

29

this and had painstakingly engaged with each member, explaining to them that even if the infidels discovered that something was afoot and even if they could identify the location of the meeting, they were hardly going to try to take out the group on the territory of one of their key allies in the Gulf. There was also an element of daring in meeting just a few short miles from one of the enemy's key military bases.

He felt that something had to be done. After an initial stunning victory against the Great Satan, they had grown complacent. Yes, millions of young men had been inflamed and had risen to the cause, but what had happened? For the most part they were disjointed, poorly organised, easily detectable and quick to become disheartened. The security resources of the infidel were seemingly bottomless, and with the advent of ever more sophisticated technology, it was becoming increasingly difficult for their soldiers to make any impact. London? Madrid? Yes, they had driven terror into the heart of the West, but there had been a massive response. Instead of the goal of disrupting and eventually destroying the sinful and decadent ways of the West, the response had, if anything made it stronger and more resilient.

He felt that perhaps their strategy had been wrong after all. Terror that would kill hundreds or thousands hit deep into the psyche of their enemies, but they remained far from defeated. Perhaps killing a smaller number would have had a far greater impact, provided the targets were chosen more carefully.

As he mused over what he might say to the gathering, his first guest arrived. Although the meeting was scheduled for 11.00, he knew the Afghan would arrive early. This man trusted no one. He had already checked with Abdullah numerous times and when he arrived at the hotel, his driver and personal bodyguard were first dispatched to the suite to check it out. When this had been done to his satisfaction, he entered the building and proceeded to the sixth floor.

There had been a discreet knock on the outer door of the suite and he had been ushered into the boardroom. The Afghan was the least popular of the entire group. Apart from being extraordinarily difficult to deal with and paranoid about security, he was extremely rude and humourless, communicating mainly in a series of grunts. He rarely seemed to wash, and his personal body odour was a heady mixture of sweat and bad breath.

Still, his attention to detail and his paranoia about security had served him well, and he was the oldest member of the group, having survived numerous upheavals and changes of leadership; not to mention a few assassination attempts. While no one would admit to it, Abdullah was sure that the smooth and dignified arrival of the six others to the suite was due to the fact that they had checked and had been assured that the Afghan was already there. Formal greetings and fond embraces were exchanged between all men. Abdullah offered refreshments, Arabic coffee, cold drinks, dates and sweets but most declined. It was agreed that Arabic would be the language used to communicate. Abdullah knew that each of these men, despite their rugged exterior, had been highly educated and could just as easily have conducted the meeting in English.

By the time all were settled, it was almost time for the midday prayer and the Saudi, as was his privilege, requested that in their prayers today, a special thought be offered to remember the great Leader, so brutally struck down just the month before. There was total silence and reverence and then the Saudi led them in prayer.

When they resumed, there was a general discussion on how each member was faring, polite enquiries about family and friends and general small talk. There was a brief break when Abdullah's manservant served more refreshments. When the meeting resumed, the Pakistani went on all out attack.

"We must kill the infidels in their thousands; rivers of blood, seas of gore – the great Leader must be avenged."

The usual rhetoric, Abdullah thought. Great for motivating young hyped-up rebels; useless as a strategy. The Yemeni was far more introspective.

"Before we do anything, my friends, we need to know who our friends are. Who betrayed our great Leader? Who can we trust now? We cannot recommence our Jihad until we know for sure that our organisation has not been infiltrated."

"Nonsense," said the man from Baghdad, "the Americans are not that clever. It is clear that someone was careless and gave away the location of The Great One inadvertently.

"How do we know that?" thundered the Yemeni. "Allah be praised, we could all be signing our own death warrants. The infidels are putting more and more resources at the disposal of their security people. I never expected this type of response."

"I am afraid, my dear friend," said the softly-spoken, heavily Arabica perfumed man from Iran, "when we set out on this path, we agreed that it was to the death. We cannot relent until we defeat the enemy and completely destroy his way of life. He has grown fat and decadent. He will respond, of course, but we will hit back stronger and strike ever deeper. We will not slay the dragon with one lunge. We must be patient, we must be careful, we must be strong; but above all, we must act. There has to be a response. Something must be done, and soon."

"I agree," said the Egyptian, who had not spoken at all before this. "We have highly-trained units ready to strike fear into the towns and cities of Europe and the United States. I propose we proceed to strike back and not let the enemy enjoy his brief victory."

This man was nominally their new leader, and had already issued many statements claiming the Jihad would continue. However, all were equal in this gathering, and as it had been rumoured that neither the powerful Afghan nor Pakistani wings had approved the appointment, he was as yet keeping a low profile until he was sure all in the organisation were behind him. A wise course of action, surely, thought Abdullah, wondering if he should make so bold as to say what was on his mind after all.

But then there were murmurings of assent and Abdullah, who had called the meeting in the first place, felt he was losing control. As the youngest member of the group, in deference to his elders, he rarely spoke. He now decided though that it was time for an intervention.

"My dear friends," he began, "if I may be allowed to comment. Our learned friend is correct. The Americans and the British may well have infiltrated us."

Uproar followed and many tried to speak. The Afghan, who up to then had taken no part in the discussion now thundered, "Shut up and let him finish."

"Thank you my dear friend," Abdullah acknowledged, now feeling far more confident that he had the attention of the Afghan. "I hasten to clarify that there is absolutely no question that any of us at this gathering is anything other than 100% committed to the cause. But I think we will not defeat the infidel by our present methods. We killed over 3000 in 2001, and what did we achieve? We killed many more in our previous and subsequent attacks. And what did that achieve? The enemy became stronger and hit back at us, invading our countries and killing many more of our own people. At the same time, they committed enormous resources to internal security. With the greatest respect my dear friends," he said, gesturing to the Iraqi and the Pakistani, "I believe that even now, as we speak, practically all our cells and our operatives are being monitored and that their every move is being documented by the enemy. They don't publicise this any more, so we can't and don't know whether we are safe until we make a move. You are all familiar with the failures of the recent past. It is my firm belief that we will never win this way. Even if we were to acquire a nuclear device and kill a million of them, they would still come back at us. No, my friends, I firmly believe that we must take a different path."

"Firstly, we must be more selective with our targets. Killing thousands and spreading blood on the streets is dramatic, but is it effective? I say no! The effect only lasts briefly; then they get on with their decadent lives. No, we must hit them where it matters – where it will be most effective. We must hit their morale, injure their pride, destroy their faith; show them the way they have chosen is wrong; bring them to their knees!"

There were widespread sounds suggesting agreement and Abdullah suddenly realised that he had been shouting, and sweating profusely.

"Forgive me, my friends," he said, pausing for effect and to take a sip of ice water. "If I may continue. Secondly, we cannot do this ourselves, with our own people, willing and numerous as they are now. No, my friends, fanaticism is useful but professionalism will defeat it every time. Forgive me if I am speaking heresy but the only way to defeat the enemy is to use his own people against him!"

The Chechen entered the discussion for the first time.

"But surely this will take too long? It would be many years before we can convert enough of them."

Allah help us all, thought Abdullah, if this is the level of thinking at the top.

"My friend, with the very greatest and deepest respect, I think you misunderstand me," he replied. "I mean that we should use their own people, hired people, to hit the targets that our group nominates. There are men available, my friends, mercenaries, who will betray their own countries for a fee and will perform any acts we want with complete discretion. I believe these men, despite their despicable trade, are highly professional and untraceable. They will not be caught because they know how to use the system and have been doing it for many years. We can strike many blows and the enemy will be helpless to respond. They will look increasingly incompetent and stupid and we will then strike again, when they least expect it. Thank you for listening to me, dear friends. I will of course follow what the will of the majority wish."

A long protracted discussion followed, which took Abdullah through an array of emotions; from hope, to joy, to doubt, to elation, to despair, and back again to confidence. He noticed that the Afghan took very little part in the discussion and appeared totally disinterested, constantly checking his watch. Abdullah wasn't fooled, though. He had seen the man in action before.

When there was a brief lull in the discussion, the Afghan spoke in a strong and clear voice. "Can I enquire of our learned friend from Bahrain that if these mercenaries are untraceable, how does he propose to contact them, and how does he propose to guarantee his anonymity?"

This was the break Abdullah had been waiting for. He felt relief surge through his body.

"If I may be permitted to respond, friends," he said, to quiet the noises of confusion. "I know of a man who has a long history of undertaking these types of operations. No one knows his name or where he comes from. He can only be contacted through a series of cut-out contacts, but I have acquired the knowledge of how to enter this chain."

"I presume this man will be expensive," said the Iraqi. "How can we be sure we know we are contacting the right person, and how will we be sure he will carry out our wishes?"

"We cannot be sure," said Abdullah, "and yes, he will be expensive, but I think we must try. If he fails, then we can try another. I beg of you to let me try this strategy, for the good of our Jihad and in the name of Allah."

From the Egyptian, "It is my belief that these mercenaries are reliable and dependable. I support our learned friend's proposal."

The Afghan nodded silently and made eye contact with the Saudi. Abdullah knew he was home. There appeared to be widespread agreement throughout the room and only a few doubting looks.

The Saudi then made the key intervention. "I agree also that we should try this path. It seems to me that it might offer a quicker and more effective method of finally bringing the enemy to his knees. Whatever funding you require, it will be provided."

Within minutes, brief farewells had been said and the participants had been escorted to their cars and had dispersed; the Saudi to drive back over the Causeway, possibly accompanied by the Egyptian, and the others seemingly planning to enjoy the Kingdom's hospitality for a day or two; discreetly, obviously, but who knew what roundabout way they had chosen to return to their own countries? Abdullah could only speculate.

Only he and the Afghan remained now.

"You know I nominated you to our ruling council because I felt you were the future of our organisation?"

"Yes, my learned friend, and I am forever grateful for your wisdom and support."

"You will have noticed we failed to discuss or even mention a replacement for our dear departed Leader?"

"Yes, but I thought – ah yes, of course. It would not be right; too premature."

"I can tell you, my friend, that if your little scheme is successful, I will be nominating you as our new Leader. As far as I can see, you made more sense here than any of the rest."

Abdullah was visibly shocked and tried to recover his composure. It had been the longest conversation he had ever had with the Afghan. He eventually offered, "You can depend on my complete and utter dedication my good friend and let me give you my pledge that I will not let you or the organisation down."

"For your sake, I certainly hope not," mumbled the Afghan gruffly.

They embraced and Abdullah showed him to the door and then collapsed into his chair. He briefly reflected on the Afghan's words and he felt a cold chill run through his body as he pondered on what he had promised and committed. Failure would not be embraced and could not be considered, not for an instant. Still, he had to go forward; there was no going back now and there was important work to be done. He felt sure he was on the right track, felt sure he would succeed. He fell to his knees to thank Allah for inspiring him and assisting him to his initial success and to pray for guidance and victory.

Chapter 2 – The Emissary

Abdullah now carried the weight of expectation on his shoulders. At 42, he was still young by the standards of his fellow ruling council members. The fact that they had entrusted him with planning the next phase of the Jihad was encouraging, but it also showed the lack of thinking – the laziness, almost – that had set in. The organisation had never been well-run or properly-coordinated anyway, and was full of maverick groups. In the beginning, this seemed like one of its strengths. Many groups spreading chaos and terror throughout the western world; systems breaking down; technology destroyed; blood on the streets; eventually bringing the infidel to his knees.

As time passed, Abdullah realised that this was useless rhetoric. The west was getting stronger, not weaker. Yes, the financial systems had collapsed, but this had been due to their own greed and avarice. In terms of undermining them, it had possibly had a greater effect than any of his organization's attempts; but still they survived. Their security systems grew stronger. In the U.S.A., between the NSA and Homeland Security, many cells had been discovered and neutralized. In the U.K., MI5 had done the same. Nowadays, their operatives couldn't use landline phones, mobile phones or even e-mail without some security organisation picking it from the ether. How they did it, he could not fathom. These systems seemed to work by magic. While Russia and the old communist regimes might have seemed to be the most policed states on earth, at least visibly, that honour now certainly lay with the U.S. and Europe. The crucial difference was that it was invisible policing; but it was there nonetheless. It was becoming increasingly difficult to launch any attack and their operatives were becoming disillusioned.

Six months earlier, on a visit to London, he had spent an evening drinking and whoring with some old colleagues. Deep into the night, one of his companions, who was very drunk, had started to boast of a man he knew about, an American apparently, who was available for hire. The man, though not a member or even a confidante of the organisation, seemed to think this American might be the solution to everyone's problems. Abdullah gave no reaction but next day after breakfast, he sought the man out discreetly and asked if he had remembered what he had said the night before. The man was still drunk and said:

"Of course I remember, Abdullah, old son; why, are you thinking of getting rid of one of those wives of yours?" and he roared with laughter. Abdullah continued to speak quietly and after a while, his friend realised that he was deadly serious.

"Do you know how to contact this man, Hakim?"

"All I know is that he is very difficult to make contact with. No one knows his name. No one knows his location. If he likes a job, he will take it. If he doesn't, he won't. So it is said about his reputation."

"But Hakim, my dear friend, how can one contact this man?"

"Sorry, Abdullah, all I know is something about a Dutch tobacco trader; but I will ask my friend and see what I can do to help you."

"Thank you, my friend," said Abdullah, as they embraced, "no doubt it will come to nothing, but it is useful to know."

They parted and some days later, a servant arrived in Abdullah's Dorchester Hotel suite with a sealed letter from his friend. Upon opening it he found a name and address in the city of Amsterdam and a plea from his friend: *Please memorize and destroy, for Allah's sake!* He consigned both to memory and set fire to both the paper and envelope in the ornamental fireplace grate. He then gathered the ashes and flushed them down the toilet.

He cast the incident to the back of his mind and thought no more about it. The Great Leader was still alive and running the organisation then, and Abdullah had no intention of interfering with that situation. But when disaster struck in May and the organisation was in crisis, the thought returned. Now, buoyed by his success at the Council meeting, he had drawn up a brief plan.

His first task was to prepare a sealed letter and send it by emissary to Amsterdam. He could not risk the journey himself. Now that he was a full member of the Council, any travel to the west had to be undertaken only in the gravest emergencies and with maximum security and using his own private jet. He was fairly sure that the infidels did not yet know of his membership of the Council, but if there was a chance they did, it didn't bear thinking about. He knew this was a crucial task, but he trusted Walid; and after all, he was only delivering a letter. He felt a low-key approach would attract far less attention, so Walid had been booked on the Monday afternoon KLM flight to Amsterdam. He knew, too, that Walid was not involved with the organisation, so would not be on any international database or wanted lists. His trip was sure to be trouble-free.

Walid Al Ghannam was 33 and had been Abdullah's devoted secretary now for almost ten years. They had developed a close bond and a deep friendship and in some ways, Abdullah felt guilty about using his good friend in this way. He thought about this now as he watched him come up the driveway of his luxury Manama town house. He had mentored the young man and had guided his career path. But Walid was innocent in many ways and not wise in the ways of the world. Should he use him for this task?

He realised he had to as Walid was his most trusted servant and after all, it was for the good of the cause and the good of all and done in the name of Allah, so it would ultimately lead to greater glory. Walid was the ultimate in discretion and would never ask what was in the letter. The young man was perfect for the task. His only query was to ask if Abdullah expected a reply, and he was told that he did not. They embraced and Walid left for the airport.

It was around 5.30 in the evening when the KLM 747 landed in Schipol. Walid had no difficulties clearing Immigration as his visa was in order and he was dressed impeccably in a bespoke three-piece Saville Row suit, with matching tie and accessories. He was six feet tall, strikingly good-looking with his very dark skin and smouldering deep brown eyes. Like all Arab men, he affected a moustache but was otherwise clean-shaven. He attracted no attention as his passport was returned to him and he thanked the officer with a smile. It was now six o'clock and by the time he had collected his bag and reached the city, it would be close to seven. He realised that it was pointless trying to deliver the letter today, as surely offices would be closed by the time he got to the city. He was here for three days anyway and while Abdullah had said the letter was important, he hadn't said it was urgent.

He had never been to Amsterdam before but he was booked into the five star Krasnapolsky hotel, right in the city centre, so he was going to enjoy himself. When he arrived at his hotel, he realised that it was close to Amsterdam's famous red light district. Perhaps he would enjoy himself even more! But no, he was on an important mission and like the good professional that he was, he would complete his task first.

Next morning when Walid arrived at the address written on the letter he had been entrusted with, he thought at first that he had made a mistake. There was no office and no indication of any business; nor was it a private house where he could deliver the letter. The property at the address he had was a small bar, a particularly seedy one, by the look of it, and it was not yet open for business. In fact, given its run-down state, he wondered if it even did business any more.

He thought that perhaps Abdullah had gotten the address wrong; but no, his patron had assured him that this was the address and that it was crucial that he delivered the letter to the man in person. He suppressed the desire to call his boss there and then to re-check, as he did not wish to appear stupid or inefficient. There was nothing for it but to come back later. Meanwhile, he would enjoy the city. After all, it was a glorious morning.

He shoved the letter back into his inside pocket, flagged a passing taxi and ordered him to return to the city centre. Perhaps the Royal Palace in Dam Square?

His cultural tour completed, Walid returned to the address in the early afternoon. There now appeared to be some life to the place. A man of far-eastern origin was setting up an awning on the pavement in front of the bar. He then commenced to bring out small tables and chairs and laid them with condiments and ashtrays. Walid proceeded to take a seat at one of the tables, having first examined it closely to ensure it would not stain his finely cut suit. He was somewhat nervous, as he seemed to be completely out of sync with his surroundings. The bar man looked at him and said something unintelligible out of the corner of his mouth.

Walid coughed politely and stated, "I don't wish to disturb you, but would it be possible to get some coffee?"

The man looked him over slightly menacingly and replied in a rapid fire manner in words that he couldn't fully grasp. He did however hear the words "in ten minutes", and he nodded his satisfaction.

True to his word, ten minutes later, the bar man deposited a small cup of espresso on the table, accompanied by a dog-eared, grubby, plastic coated menu, which Walid immediately declined.

"Thank you very much. Perhaps you can help me. May I ask if you speak English at all?" Walid politely enquired. The bar man appeared irritated. This was obviously an establishment where you ordered your drinks, paid for them and kept conversation to a minimum.

"Yes, of course I speak English, vat is it?"

"I am not sure if I have the correct address. I need to contact a Mr Rolf Van Henkel. Can you tell me if this is his bar or if he is a customer here?"

Walid thought he saw a momentary flicker of recognition pass across the bar man's eyes but he replied in the negative. "Sorry, never heard of him."

The address must be wrong! Now he was in a panic, what could he do? There was nothing for it but to call Abdullah and recheck the address. Better not use his cell phone; his boss had said this was highly confidential, so he decided to wait until he returned to his hotel. He finished his coffee, leaving a five-euro note and left the bar.

He was not looking forward to the phone call. His patron was a kind man but he *was* demanding and did not suffer fools easily. He had never failed him before, but now, what could he do? He could feel his anxiety levels rising. He was so distracted that he never saw the man emerge from the alley. He felt a heavy blow to the back of his neck, and then – darkness.

Walid awoke with a blinding headache. He had no idea where he was or how much time had passed. He was in almost total darkness, apart from a small chink of light that seemed to come from a nearby doorway. The air was thick with a vague sickly-sweet smell; what it was, he couldn't quite place. He felt for his watch and the Cartier was still in place. His first thoughts had been that he had been robbed but this could not be so, as surely the $10,000 Cartier would have been the first thing to go?

He tried to raise himself from the floor but this made his headache worse and sent flashes of light through his head. His mouth was dry and although he could see very little, he felt his clothes had been ruined and he was dirty. At times like this, the mind races and comes up with a million possibilities. Had he been kidnapped? He was not wealthy himself, but his patron certainly was. Would Abdullah pay a ransom? Would it even help? Would he be killed anyway? Was it some extreme right-wing terror group that had taken him? He had heard there were many of these groups operating in Europe and their chief targets were Muslims. Would he be tortured? Surely not that.

He said a quick prayer and it helped to fight off the rising panic. Then he thought of the letter; where was the letter? Why had he been so selfish, only concerned with himself? He had completely forgotten his mission.

He checked his inside pocket but it was there; he sighed with relief and again offered thanks to Allah. Almost as an afterthought, he checked his other suit coat pocket. His phone was there but his wallet was missing. Perhaps it was a robbery after all? No, don't be stupid; they would have taken the watch and they would not have kept him locked up. No, it was becoming clearer to him now, it was surely a kidnapping. They had taken his wallet to confirm his identity and ensure they had the phone number of his mentor to deliver the ransom demand.

With rising trepidation, he struggled to his feet and tried to check his surroundings. He seemed to be in a small storeroom surrounded by cleaning materials. Was that the smell? No, it was something else. The room was about six feet by twelve, a small storage area for sure, but obviously with the facility to lock down tightly. He suddenly realised that he needed to use the toilet and in the very limited light he could not find one. Well, that was it; he still had his dignity and his pride and he was not going to piss on the floor for anyone!

He banged loudly on the door and shouted for all he was worth, "Let me out of here, whoever you are, I need to use the toilet."

He was surprised at the almost-immediate response. It was like they had been waiting for him. He heard bolts being slid back and a key turning. The burst of artificial light blinded him and he immediately shielded his eyes. A large, muscle-bound man took him by the elbow, firmly but not roughly, and guided him down a long narrow corridor. He spoke not one word but opened a door at the end, which contained an old, grubby toilet.

Walid entered and closed the door. The smell wasn't great but he was nonetheless grateful for the release. He scanned the walls of the small cubicle. Needless to say, there were no windows and no skylights through which an escape attempt could be made. There always are in western movies, he thought sadly, which he supposed was really what they were; fantasies.

Having finished his business and flushed, he re-emerged into the corridor. His eyes had now adjusted to the light and he noticed that his captor was masked and wearing gloves. Was this a good sign? If they showed you their face, then they had to kill you, didn't they? He hadn't seen anyone at all yet but perhaps that was just a precaution. Allah alone knew what fate awaited him. Once again he fought off rising panic as his captor guided him towards the other end of the corridor. He was sure they had passed his little prison; and yes, they had. The guard opened yet another door and guided him inside.

He spoke one word – "Sit." The room was small and stuffy, about 12 by 15 feet, and contained a desk, a chair, a file cabinet and two couches. The light was poor but the walls seemed to be a vague blue colour. Walid took a seat on one of the couches. If they were going to torture him, surely they wouldn't start like this; but perhaps they were playing with him – who knew?

After a few moments, another door opened directly behind the desk and a man entered. He was of medium height, rugged, strongly built although with a growing paunch. His face was slightly pockmarked. It was impossible to detect anything else about him as he wore very dark wrap-around sunglasses. Also, he was dressed from head to toe in black. He sat down and nodded to Walid.

"My sincere apologies, Mr Al Ghannam; forgive the rudeness of my colleague. He is not as trusting as me and he wished to, shall we say, check you out first. We have now established your bona fides and are willing to converse." The man smiled, showing tobacco-stained teeth. That was it, Walid thought - that was the smell; raw tobacco.

He was confused. "I'm sorry but I don't understand, what do you want with me?"

"On the contrary, young man, we have no wish to see you at all; but I understand you expressed a wish to see me." Then the realization dawned on him and he felt stupid. Abdullah had said that Van Henkel was a tobacco dealer. Relief flooded through him like a giant shot of adrenalin and he almost collapsed into the couch. He was so relieved that he had not been kidnapped, and that he now appeared to finally be in a position to be able to carry out the task for his patron, that he forgot all about the circumstances of his arrival and made no complaint. Instead, with a broad smile he said, "I am sorry; please forgive my confusion. So you must be Herr Van Henkel."

"I might be, but it depends on who is asking?"

"Sir, I have been entrusted with a letter from my esteemed patron, whose name I cannot reveal to you. All I know is that I must deliver the letter personally to Herr Van Henkel. Can you prove to me that you are this man, or can you arrange for me to meet with him?"

The man seemed to hesitate for a few moments, then opened a desk drawer, withdrew a laminated identity card and slid it across the desk. Walid studied the card closely and compared it to the man seated behind the desk. Even with the sunglasses, he was clearly the man in the photo. The ID card said Rolf Van Henkel.

"Ok, sir, thank you, I am satisfied." He withdrew the letter from his inside pocket and passed it across the table. The letter was in a plain white manila envelope and was not addressed to anyone. This was possibly why whoever had searched him had ignored it.

Van Henkel took a silver letter opener from his desk and slit open the envelope. Inside was a type-written note and another sealed letter. He briefly perused the note, nodded, and put the other envelope into his desk drawer. He then hit a concealed intercom button behind the desk and said, "Rudi, you can take Mr Al Ghannam back to his hotel now. Thank you, young man; rest assured you have completed your mission and tell your boss that his letter will be forwarded to where he intends. And, once again, my sincere apologies for the inconvenience. Indeed, I do frequent that bar, but I am not in the habit of meeting young men in three-piece suits there in the middle of the afternoon. Enjoy the rest of your time in our city."

Walid breathed a deep sigh of relief. He stood and they shook hands. "Thank you too, sir."

The large man called Rudi then drove him back to the hotel, where he immediately went to his room, shed his clothes and spent about twenty minutes in the shower. Despite his rollercoaster of a day, he felt a sense of exhilaration and deep-seated relief.

He decided to treat himself to a drink from the mini-bar. It was against his religion, for sure, but he occasionally indulged, as did most of his countrymen. Unlike most Muslim countries, alcohol was freely available in Bahrain, and attitudes were far more tolerant. If he had only known the message he had just delivered and its potential consequences he might have thought again as to whether his land was that tolerant. Still, he had a large Chivas Regal from the bar and then decided to treat himself to another one. It was still only five thirty in the afternoon but he was hungry as he had skipped lunch. He decided on an early dinner. His task accomplished, he felt sure he would treat himself to more of Amsterdam's pleasures later tonight.

Chapter 3 – The Dutchman

Rolf Van Henkel was quite a successful, legitimate, and cautious businessman. He never knowingly broke the law, although some of his dealings might be described as questionable. His trade was in tobacco importing, mainly from the United States. He worked with the smaller cigarette and cigar producers, of which there were still – despite the big multinationals – very many in Holland and elsewhere. Because of the free availability of soft drugs like marijuana, hashish and cannabis in the Netherlands, Van Henkel had long been suspected of having a peripheral role in that trade. He had been searched on numerous occasions on trips abroad and his warehouse had even been raided once.

The truth was that he had no involvement in the narcotics business whatsoever, apart from occasionally delivering a letter on behalf of someone who may have had. In addition to being a businessman, he was a part-time courier.

Back in the recession of the 1980's, Rolf had overextended himself and was stuck with large amounts of tobacco leaf that he could not sell. Through a combination of the poor economic situation and the growth of anti-smoking propaganda, his business was in serious trouble. His creditors were ready to foreclose on him when he received an offer that seemed to be the answer to all his woes.

The letter that had arrived was unsigned but it offered him a substantial amount of money if, on his next trip to Virginia, he would deliver a letter to an address, of which he would be advised. If he agreed, he was to call a number and after he heard a message tone, merely say one word – yes; and give his bank account number. While he was suspicious that this might be attempted fraud, there was no money in his bank account anyway so no one could steal from him. He called the number and fulfilled the instructions. It certainly solved his cash flow problems.

Within days, a large cash deposit arrived in his account and he was able to hang in until the market turned and he could dispose of the stock. His benefactor also seemed to be aware of when he was travelling to the U.S. as the letter he had agreed to deliver arrived a few days beforehand, sealed in a letter to him marked "personal and confidential". A lot of people knew he was travelling and if the guy writing the letter did too, well frankly, that did not bother him.

Over the years he delivered many of these letters to a whole series of addresses without ever once having a hitch. He never met the people on whose behalf he was delivering, but he felt sure there were a lot more people involved than the person from whom he had received the original request. Each time he completed a delivery, a sum of money magically appeared in his account a few days later. Many of the messages he was asked to bring arrived by mail to his office, sealed within other letters. On occasion, he was approached in the little bar where the Arab had sought him out. He was known in the bar and as it was convenient to his warehouse, he liked to have a few beers there in the evening. He never conducted business there though, certainly not with stand-out men in three-piece suits. When the Arab had enquired about him, the barman had called Rolf. He was suspicious but curious and had immediately dispatched Rudi to intercept the man. Unfortunately, Rudi's interpretation of interception was a bit crude; but, all-in-all, the Arab – or the Bahraini, as he was – hadn't suffered too much inconvenience.

Rolf travelled the world with complete confidence, and although he knew there may have been some suspicion that he was involved in narcotics, he knew he was clean as a whistle. They could search him all they wanted but he couldn't be arrested for possession of a letter!

He pressed a button on his intercom and asked, "Maria, can you get me a ticket on tomorrow evening's flight to JFK? Oh, and can you get hold of Mr Jackson from Richmond for me? I need to set up a meeting with him." Best to get the task out of the way as soon as possible, he thought, although none of his Principals (he assumed there were many) had ever told him to hurry or given him a deadline. He had no idea what these requests were for; he had his suspicions but best to leave them at that. He supposed that anyone who was prepared to send a letter half way across the world hand-delivered was in no great hurry, particularly given the instant communications that were available today via the internet.

His phone buzzed. "Pete Jackson for you," said Maria.

"Hey Pete, how is it going? How is the crop this year?

"Lookin' good so far, Rolf, y'all thinking of coming over to take a look?"

"Yeah, I sure am, Pete. How are you situated for a visit in, say, two days' time? Maybe on Thursday?"

"Sounds good to me, Rolf. Maybe you'll stay over the weekend and come down to our place for barbecue?"

"That sure is tempting, Pete, but I don't want to put you to any trouble."

"It will be a pleasure, Rolf, my friend; believe me, Darlene has been asking me to invite y'all down for ages. Now don't you go booking no hotel or nothing either, you're staying right here with us."

"Gee Pete, that's awfully kind of you. So that's a definite then; see you on Thursday around lunchtime. Will you pick me up at the airport as usual?"

"For damn sure I will, Rolf, see you then. Safe travelling."

He replaced the receiver and buzzed his secretary again. "Maria, can you get me a Delta connection to Richmond on Thursday morning, returning next Monday, and the overnight KLM back home Monday evening?"

"For sure, Mr Van Henkel, it shouldn't be any problem."

"Oh, and book my usual hotel in New York for tomorrow night, won't you?"

"It's the very next thing on the list, sir."

He touched down at JFK the following evening from a brilliantly blue, totally cloudless sky. The flight had been trouble-free, as was his smooth passage through Immigration. As a regular visitor, with numerous stamps on his passport, he barely merited a glance these days. He collected his bag and strolled through arrivals to the taxi rank. As usual, there was an abundance of yellow cabs, driven by guys from every nation on earth. The driver of his car appeared to be of far eastern origin, but he couldn't quite place him; Vietnamese, perhaps?

The driver jumped out and threw his bag in the trunk. Rolf asked if he would take him to the Crowne Plaza in Times Square. He settled back to enjoy the trip with a deep sigh of satisfaction. He loved New York; always had, from that first time he had visited many years ago and had emerged from the subway to view those impossibly high buildings. They still gave him a thrill, even thirty years later. There was an atmosphere about the place that set his pulse racing. It was almost as if the whole city was alive, vibrant and welcoming. He always spent at least two nights in the city on his trips to America – it was almost like a renewal for him. Sure, Amsterdam was a beautiful city and he had a nice lifestyle there, but New York was where it was at for him. He thought it ironic that it had originally been named New Amsterdam but for him there was symmetry about this, logic. It was as if every time he visited, he left the old world behind and embraced the new. As the tour guide had said to him once, "here in New York, we have everything, the good and the bad – you take what you want from our city but remember to enjoy it." That had been always his philosophy. Some people said the city had lost some of its magic after 9/11 but not for him.

He always stayed in the same hotel, as he liked to be right in the centre of things. He could take in a Broadway show, visit any one of the city's other numerous attractions, or just simply dine in the bewildering variety of restaurants. Then there were the bars; not like those in Europe, which were, to his mind, more sedate. No, New York bars were noisy, brash, with a clash of sounds from the TV blaring out the basketball, baseball or football game, depending on the season. There always seemed to be some exciting sporting event happening. Then there were the guys playing pool or shuffleboard or just the chatter of the customers trying to speak to each other over the din. He loved all of it and despite the noise and general mayhem, bars were welcoming and friendly. New York bartenders were personable and would even chat to you when they weren't busy. He had spent many a pleasant evening in these establishments and he looked forward to another. Had he known the importance of the letter he carried in his briefcase, it might have dampened his mood, but the contents were not his concern. He was merely the courier.

He was up early next morning and was back at JFK by 09.00 leaving time for a leisurely check-in for his 11.00 flight to Richmond. He had had a wonderful evening, dining at a little Indonesian place he knew, then walking for miles just soaking up the atmosphere, and finally finishing the evening with a few beers. The city was so clean and safe now, not that it had ever worried him; but it was comforting that it was now safe for everyone, which added even more to the atmosphere. He was looking forward to the weekend with his friend and business partner in Richmond. Barbecue wasn't exactly his style but Pete was a great guy and he knew he would be treated royally.

At the last bar he had called to on the previous evening, he had had occasion to use the men's room. He had previously placed the Bahraini's letter in a waterproof package, which he then taped to the underside of the cistern lid. An old-fashioned hiding place, perhaps, but it had always proved reliable and extremely unlikely to be discovered, apart from by someone who was expecting it to be there.

It wasn't his favourite letter drop; that had probably been the library. He had visited it many times and had always placed the letter between the covers of a very obscure book tucked away at the end of a row of shelving. He didn't know if the person collecting the letter knew him by sight and quite frankly, it did not concern him. He had never met the next person in the chain and he had no wish to.

He had wondered why the drop location had changed. Perhaps the librarian had retired or become untrustworthy. Whatever; this was the new method, and that was fine by him. Whether it was a regular customer or the bartender in the place who collected the letter was of no consequence.

He realised he had been daydreaming as the plane bumped gently on to the runway at Richmond. It was another beautiful summer's day and the flight had arrived precisely on time at 12.55. Just in time to have lunch with Pete.

The guy who checked the cistern in the Men's Room that morning was not a customer or a bartender. He was the bar's owner, and had even less knowledge of what was going on than Van Henkel. He did not know from where the letter had come or where it was going. All he knew was that he had received an offer a few years previously that had allowed him to clear his gambling debts and keep the small bar which was his livelihood, provided he took delivery of an occasional package and delivered it to an address he was given.

He dispensed with the waterproof sheeting and tucked the envelope into the back pocket of his jeans. Luckily, his most reliable bartender would be working today, which would allow him to complete his task.

His thoughts were interrupted; "Morning, boss, you got here early."

"Hey, morning Wayne, my man. Had to catch up on a few orders. Good takings last night, well done."

"Sure, boss, no sweat."

"I gotta run today, Wayne, think you can keep her going until around ten tonight?"

"Not a problem, that's cool."

He grabbed his jacket and left the bar, hailed a yellow cab, and said, 'La Guardia please." He had been advised to vary his schedule and he did where possible but there was one way to do this run that was so easy that he tended to repeat it, albeit using different carriers. Cost was not a factor, as apart from his monthly payment, he was given a healthy bonus to cover his expenses whenever he had to make a delivery. Whoever was running this show sure had it organised.

Traffic was light now that the early morning rush was over. It was just after 11.30. The cab would shoot through the Midtown Tunnel, take the Long Island Expressway to the Grand Central Parkway going toward the Triboro Bridge, roll past Shea

Stadium, and he'd be at the airport in 35 minutes. Allowing for traffic, it could take an hour, but as he planned to get the 14.17 Delta to Charleston, he had lots of time. The flight would get him there by 16.30. He would have plenty of time to make his delivery and be back at the airport for the U.S. Airways shuttle at 19.05. A relaxing day lay ahead, all done at a leisurely pace, and he'd be back in the bar to take over from Wayne by ten. He lay back and relaxed.

When he got to Charleston, he went through his usual, well-rehearsed routine. He used a payphone in the arrivals hall to call the usual number. A voice answered on the fourth ring and he said, "Hi, is that Martin's?"

"Sorry, wrong number." He replaced the receiver. Last time it had been, Lewis's, next time maybe Norton's or whatever, provided it was the next number in the alphabet. This was the cue for his contact to meet him at a pre-arranged bar. The bar changed every time. There were plenty of them in downtown Charleston; it was just a question of checking and picking the next one on the list. He had already double-checked this on his copy of the local yellow pages. He then ambled out towards the taxi rank and took the first in line.

"235 East Bay Street, please."

"Sure thing, bud."

He probably should have picked a nearby street and walked, but ah hell, it was a hot day; and anyway, who was looking or following? The bar changed every time and he wasn't doing anything illegal. He often thought the whole routine was ridiculous, but as he was getting paid good money to carry it out, it sure must have had some purpose, and he wasn't gonna question it. The one thing he was wary of was taxi drivers, particularly nosey ones. He had a spiel worked out for when one of them got too inquisitive but he tried to remain as normal and friendly as possible. Taxi drivers remembered people, particularly difficult ones.

"You in town for business or pleasure, bud?"

"Ah business, we're in the bar trade, having a look at some possibilities down here."

They arrived at the bar, "Molly Darcy's Irish Pub", in no time. The waitress offered a menu but he wasn't hungry so he just ordered a Bud. The routine was always the same. He would call the number and go to the bar, usually taking a seat at the end furthest away from the door. He would order a beer or some food, finish his drink and go to the Men's Room. The corner cubicle was always the one chosen. The envelope would again be sealed and taped to the underside of the cistern. He would return to the bar, pay his tab and leave, catching a cab back to the airport in plenty of time to catch his flight back to La Guardia.

At precisely 17.15, when he was on his way back to the airport, the next contact would enter and take a seat at the other end of the bar. Happy hour ran from 17.00-19.00, or sometimes 16.00-19.00, so the bar was usually crowded and neither man would attract attention. The second man would also have a beer or a soft drink and then go to retrieve the envelope. The next contact man was always dressed in jeans and a leather jacket and always wore dark glasses, giving the appearance of a biker. He had a neutral expression and people rarely gave him a second glance.

The contact man was indeed a biker and he was ideal to complete the last phase of the journey. He was not from Charleston but from a nearby town in South Carolina. He was a free spirit who worked occasionally but mainly enjoyed life. The $3,000 that was lodged to his bank account each month helped and the fact that he had to do so little to earn it meant that he guarded the secret jealously. Like all the others in the chain, he had never met the ultimate addressee; nor did he know how many links were in the chain, or what its purpose was. He didn't need to know. He had been doing this run for three years now – not often, a few times a year – and he finally had the lifestyle that he had always aspired to.

He could be on I95 in ten minutes and in Orlando in four hours; well, maybe five if he kept to the speed limits. After he had delivered the letter to the pre-arranged mailbox in a remote part of rural Florida, he was a free man. He would be unlikely to be called on again for at least three months, although he would check his phone every day around 4.30 just in case. He was a free spirit but a careful man. All he had to do was make the delivery, send the pre-arranged text next morning, and then he could spend the summer in Florida. He thought of the beach, the beers, and the babes! He gave a deep sigh of satisfaction as he hit the on ramp of I95.

Chapter 4 – The Analyst

Paul Lincoln was a happy man as he sat enjoying breakfast in his home in the city of Falls Church with Barbara, Caitlin and little Pete. Two more days to go and they were off to Disney World. The children had been looking forward to this for what seemed to them like forever!

He'd lost count of the number of times Barbara had asked him if he were sure he'd be available. It had been a tough few months in Homeland Security, but last week they'd gotten a vital break. One of the terrorists they had suspected had panicked, having had no contact with his fellow conspirators for weeks, and had risked a phone call. It was brief and very little was said but it was enough. They had managed to triangulate the location within a minute. Very careful surveillance followed culminating in a lightning raid – this had been undertaken by the SWAT team from Capitol Police, with Paul's role officially that of an observer.

However, he had been involved in the case from start to finish. Hundreds of pounds of explosives, together with a large cache of automatic weapons, had been discovered. Paul didn't know what the targets were, or when – or even if – an attack was being planned, but hopefully this would be revealed through interrogation in the coming weeks.

The operation had been conducted entirely in secret and there had been no publicity. It was just one more successful operation against – he had to assume Al Qaeda, although this had not yet been confirmed. If the public knew how many screwballs there were out there planning to blow things and people up – right wing, left wing, fundamentalists, supremacists; the list was endless and could be frightening if one spent the time contemplating it or worrying about it. Thankfully, most of these idiots were poorly-organised, and left clues that made Paul and his team's job somewhat easier. A small number were very well-organised but the security services were winning the war. A huge number of looneys, not to speak of fundamentalists, had been discovered and the threat from them neutralized. The Government preferred to "eliminate" threats like this with the minimum of fuss and publicity and this suited Paul and his guys just fine.

One of the big problems that had beset U.S. Security and Law Enforcement Agencies in the past had been inter-agency competition, jealousy, and bickering, resulting in a lack of information sharing and co-operation, which had sadly resulted in many criminals slipping through the net. But that had all changed after 2001. Now, there were nearly 200,000 people in Homeland Security, assigned to various agencies. Much of their work was technical and involved complex IT analysis, so all had to have strong technical and analytical skills. But at the same time, they were expected to not forget that their primary calling was to be policemen and women, and all were expected to be in top physical condition. This suited Paul just fine. He was a wizard at technology and he had always been superbly fit, still working out at least three times a week.

Today, all he had to do was to meet this English guy and hold his hand for a few days. He didn't know who had suggested that it would be useful to get lectures from the English on counterterrorism, but the guy boasted a good CV, and Paul was prepared to listen and give the guy a chance. Who knew? He might even learn something. After all, the Brits had been dealing with terrorists on their home patch long before anyone attempted anything similar in the U.S., so they must know something.

He had initially delegated the minding duties to his second-in-command, Robert Weitz, but as the latest group of would-be assassins were safely under lock and key, and as Paul was the senior covert counter terrorism operative, he felt it would not only be correct protocol but also good manners to give Bob the morning off and go to meet the British guy himself. The proposal was that they would take the best from the British program, marry it to their own, and get this guy to talk to groups of people in small units. But all Paul had to do was work out the detail. The British would prepare the program and it would start up in around a month's time.

Paul was ecstatically happy with his life. He was 45 and had given over 20 years as a cop, first in the Washington P.D; and since 2002, with Homeland Security. He had been wounded twice in his days as a patrolman but not seriously. He was six feet two in his stocking feet, and at 190 pounds he was still in great shape. He worked hard but still found the time to work out. He had always been ambitious and for many years, colleagues said, married to the job. But that had all changed when he met Barbara.

Prior to this he had never been a player in the love game, just content to drift along with the occasional brief relationship, which usually ended when the woman discovered that he was far more interested in his career or basically in law enforcement than in her. This never bothered Paul and he saw himself as being permanently happy in this mode. He had seen far too many of his colleagues' relationships break up with the resultant heartache and effect on their performance. He had also, on a few occasions, been the unfortunate cop who had had to deliver the bad news of the death of a colleague in action to his broken-hearted widow. No, this was not for him. He felt his concentration and performance would surely be affected if he had a wife and family to worry about as well.

But Barbara had changed all that. She was ten years younger than Paul, almost a foot smaller, and was absolutely stunning. They had met, typically enough, on a case he had been working. Barbara taught P.E. at a high school in Rockville and when some disturbed student had barricaded himself in a classroom there during the summer of 2001 with a sawn-off shotgun and an attitude, Paul was in the first response team. He had, quickly and without fuss, arranged for all the students to quietly and efficiently vacate the premises and had then calmly talked the poor guy out of the locked room. The student had been one of Barbara's charges and as she felt personally responsible, she had refused to leave the premises until the crisis had been resolved.

Paul had immediately sensed the strong chemistry between them but in typical fashion did nothing about it. He politely and professionally thanked Barbara for her help in talking the guy down and commended her on her bravery. Then he got out of there before he did something he would have thought foolish. In the following days and weeks, Barbara occupied his every waking moment and much of his sleeping time too. He was distracted, irritable, edgy, giddy, the whole gamut of emotions. This went on for about three weeks until one Friday evening, Tom Dempsey, who had been Paul's boss seemingly forever, insisted they go for a beer. Paul rarely drank and when he did, it was just a couple of beers or a glass of wine. But with Tom, it would be OK. He was one of the very few people Paul would confide in, so he reluctantly agreed.

Tom ordered the Buds and launched straight in:

"So, who is she, Paul?"

He was taken aback. Paul was incredibly shy in matters of the heart and was reluctant to talk about it but even he could see the game was up. "Who is who, what you talking about?"

"Come on buddy, you ain't getting away that easy. You've been acting like a frickin teenager these past weeks, so there's gotta be a girl involved."

Paul decided that it was useless to argue. "That obvious, huh?"

'You bet, buddy, so come on; come clean?"

Paul wasn't reluctant but was slow to respond. "Well, to be honest, it isn't anyone I know; or, I mean, I haven't met someone. There's just this girl that was down at the school siege, you remember? I mean, shoot, I've never done anything like this before. Anyone I've ever met has been through someone else or at a function. I mean, would it be OK to call her? What do you think?"

"There's only one way to find out."

"Yeah, but jeez, I've never done anything like that. I mean, what if she says no?"

"Yeah, I see what you mean, and you've got it bad buddy. Hey, have another beer and leave it with me. I think Joe Liebowitz's kid goes to that high school."

They continued drinking and for once, Paul had way too many. They both ended up in Tom's den at seven in the morning toasting undying loyalty and friendship. Tom's wife, Marjorie, found them comatose when she rose around 10.00 on the Saturday morning. She was confident enough in them both, and loved Tom far too much to complain anyway, but she knew that if Paul had gotten drunk, there had to be something serious afoot.

Tom was as good as his word. Within a few days, he had gotten Marjorie, Joe Liebowitz and Joe's wife Sally on the case and through clever utilization of the parent-teacher school network had managed to get a message to the beautiful blonde P.E. teacher that a certain patrolman whom she had met during the school siege would like to take her to dinner. The response was a definite affirmative. Paul knew nothing of this until he received a call.

"Can I speak to Officer Lincoln, please?"

"Yes, speaking."

"Hi Officer, this is Barbara O'Brien, you probably don't remember me, but we met at the school siege a few weeks ago."

"Ah, wha, who?" he coughed

"Hello, are you there?"

He was struck dumb, eventually managing a croaked "yes." His heart must have been doing 180!

"OK, I was thinking, you know, that was a very brave thing you did in our school, and we never really got a chance to thank you. Would it be OK if we invited you back to talk to the kids?"

Oh, slight disappointment, heart back to 120. He managed a hoarse, "sure, I'd be delighted to oblige, ma'am."

"That's great, officer; do you think maybe we could meet to discuss it?"

Heart back to 160 and rising, "why sure, ma'am, and it's Paul."

"That's fantastic. How about tomorrow evening, say at Mario's around seven? And it's Barbara. Do you know Mario's, Paul?"

"Sure, ma'am; ah, I mean Barbara."

He wasn't sure what time he made it to Mario's, but it was at least as early as 6.30. When she eventually arrived, bang on seven o'clock, he thought his heart would burst through his chest. She was just magnificent; short casual black dress, oval-shaped face, perfect skin with very light make-up, and minimum understated jewellery. He managed a perfunctory hello.

The waiter arrived with menus and Barbara immediately launched into a recall of the school incident. Paul listened intently but heard not one word – he was too busy looking into her haunting green eyes and examining her cute lips and her fabulous smile and trying not to stare at her perfect figure. She must have been speaking for several minutes when the waiter returned to find neither of them had touched their menus. Both apologized profusely and began an intensive examination of the menu, all the while seeing nothing.

Eventually, Barbara broke the ice and said, "Are you as nervous as I am?"

"Far, far more, I think."

They both laughed and their hands briefly touched and that was it basically. He had never met anyone remotely like her before. He still couldn't remember what they ate. He had a vague recollection of a half-finished bottle of wine before hurriedly paying the bill and jumping into the nearest taxi. They just about made it to her apartment without losing it completely before struggling with the keys and fumbling for a light switch. There was no pretence of coffee or polite conversation. They were both too far gone.

In the dim light of a fading summer evening in Washington, they hungrily explored each other until both were spent. Afterwards, as they lay exhausted with the moonlight peeping through the windows, Paul knew, they both knew, that they would never again need anyone else.

They married within a month and a year later Caitlin arrived. Three years later, little Pete arrived and their world was complete. Their working careers also blossomed. Barbara continued to teach and was steadily promoted and she was now the school's principal. He had moved to Homeland Security after 9/11 and was now one of their most senior operatives in D.C.

As he sat finishing his breakfast, he still couldn't believe how lucky he had been. He never thought about his previous fears as a policeman, partially because the thought of losing her or anything disrupting his little paradise was too horrendous to even contemplate. He had continued to be a good cop, though, never shirking the risks to which his job was bound to expose him. Strangely, though, this never bothered him. It was as if his bond with his family had made him so much stronger. It was almost as if he had nothing before, and now had it all.

His musing was interrupted by the sound of small footsteps on the stairs as his children bounded down to meet another day. Barbara had already laid out their breakfast and there was no fuss, no panic. She seemed to glide through life and never got flustered or rushed. He could count on the fingers of one hand the number of fights they'd had and he doubted any of them had lasted longer than a half hour before he either phoned her or rushed to meet her to apologise and to say what an idiot he had been. But it had never even been necessary – to him she was the most loving, forgiving, caring creature on earth.

He thought of this again now as she arrived in the kitchen, still looking as stunning as ever and dressed to perfection.

"Gotta go, Dad," said Pete, "school in ten minutes, see ya later."

"Love you, Dad," this from Caitlin.

Barbara came round and kissed him briefly but tenderly. "Till tonight honey," she said, "oh, and bring that guy you're meeting round for dinner if you like. It *is* his first night in Washington." And then she was gone. Typical, he thought, that lady thinks of everything! He sat back and thanked his God for one more fabulous day with this woman. He still had hours to kill before his guest arrived at Ronald Reagan International so he decided to treat himself to one more coffee.

Chapter 5 - The Assassin

Carl Walker also woke that morning very happy with life. He had lived in the idyllic Lake Mary suburb of Orlando for over 20 years and things just seemed to get better and better for him. He had lived in the United States now for over 25 years and was a model citizen and a contributor to both political parties. He was active in Orlando society, although his role was usually a passive one and his primary concentration was as support for his wife in her numerous charitable pursuits and resultant society gatherings. He was officially a Financial Adviser who worked mainly from home. He had very few clients and usually only advised people who, while not quite in Forbes territory, were more than comfortable. He never actively sought clients and only took someone on by referral. He was, nonetheless, very good at his job and was very astute at managing assets for his clients, the most important of whom was himself. He operated with absolute discretion; none of his clients knew each other, and no one but him knew how many clients he actually had.

The person who probably knew least about his business dealings was his wife, Cindy, and that suited Carl just fine. He had only married Cindy ten years previously when he finally felt it was safe to take a full part in society and not just live in his large neo-colonial mansion by himself. He was not a legitimate U.S. citizen, although he carried a perfectly legal United States passport; in fact, he had several! The one he used when travelling with his family was in the name of Carl Walker, but if anyone had investigated how he had acquired that passport, and indeed the others that he used from time to time, his idyllic lifestyle might be disrupted somewhat. But of course nobody ever did because he was far too clever and intelligent to leave any tracks.

He had met Cindy over ten years ago when he was 47 and she a fresh-faced 27. She had been the classic American dream girl; blonde hair, blue eyes, hourglass figure, and she had been spoiled from birth. She had been an only child and when he met her, she had been lost, trying to recover from the tragic death of her parents in an automobile accident. She was perfect for him, as he had been looking for someone who was bright – but not too bright – with no connections. The last thing he needed was some clever Daddy checking out his prospective son-in-law.

He picked her initially for a combination of her stunning looks and her family situation. The fact that she was outstanding in the sack did her no harm either. However, he found that he, cynical to the core and the ultimate manipulator when he met her, had fallen in love with her. They had had two little girls; Abigail was eight and Paige was five, and he doted on them to distraction. Cindy may have been spoiled when he met her and difficult initially, but she had matured and was a fabulous Mom. She was also immensely popular and was forever being invited to this and that function or party or coffee morning or whatever. He gave her free reign and only accompanied her when she insisted it was for all their benefit or when she wanted to show him off to her friends.

He was almost 58 now and while at 38, she could still model if she wished to, she was immensely proud of her husband. He was still the same weight as when they had met, helped by a very careful lifestyle and furious workouts in his home gymnasium. He still had all his hair and could probably pass for 45. She loved him deeply and she had never been unfaithful to him; not that he knew of, anyway, and he prided himself that he *would* know. His skills extended beyond financial advice; but that was another story. He knew she loved him deeply and was warm and caring.

His only doubts were on the rare occasions that she looked into his eyes and seemed to see something that she didn't like or seemed to register some doubt. If he asked her what was wrong, she always passed it off as nothing, nothing at all, and was immediately loving and passionate. Due to a combination of suspecting what she might have seen and not ever wishing to face the reality of it, he never pushed her any further.

He worked mainly from home but several times a year, his work did involve him in travelling to look at investments or to attend various conferences or business meetings. These were mainly in the U.S, but occasionally he also travelled to check out investment possibilities overseas. All very plausible and easy to explain away to his wife or their friends or anyone else who took an interest. He always returned when he said he would, and almost invariably, any new investments he took on seemed to be successful and added to his wealth. His wife spent freely and he never complained even though their living expenses were quite substantial.

He was, in fact, a model husband; he was caring and attentive and he never once seemed to be tempted by any of the flashing eyes or knowing looks that he encountered over the years. Cindy was in no doubt that she had hit the jackpot with this man. He never spoke much about his own background, other than to say he grew up in Wisconsin but was orphaned at an early age and spent time in various orphanages and halfway houses. It was a part of his life that he preferred not to talk about and Cindy was just fine with that. They had made their own paradise and she was quite happy to live in it.

But of course Carl Walker had other reasons to lead a quiet reserved lifestyle when he was at home in Orlando, because he lived an entirely different persona when he left his little enclave. Carl, or whatever he called himself on the various passports he possessed, was in reality a hit man, an executioner, a killer-for-hire; call it what you will.

He had fallen into the trade quite by accident when he needed to "disappear" for a while after a bungled operation many years before. He had been involved in violent death from an early age, but initially it had been for a cause in which he had passionately believed. When he had failed in one of his missions all those years ago and had almost been captured by the police, the organisation remained loyal to him and hid him. However, he had eventually heard whispers from a few of his close contacts that some of the senior people felt that he had lost it and was damaged goods. He set high standards for himself, and given the mistakes he had made in that job, even *he* felt they might have a point.

He didn't wait around to find out. Not for him the quiet "disposal" that had been the lot of some of his predecessors, who had outlived their usefulness but knew too much and so were too hot to leave around. No; he decided to make a clean break. He was already highly skilled in methods of disguise and he had documents of which the organisation had no knowledge.

Initially, he went to Holland, where he alternated between Amsterdam and Rotterdam, carefully frequenting and working the waterfront bars, never saying much but all the while listening, waiting for his opportunity. He had heard of a vicious drugs feud between warring Italian families associated with the 'Ndrangheta of Calabria and the equally violent Camorra from Naples. Apparently, family members from both sides were being brutally tortured and murdered in a seemingly never-ending feud over control of the massive amounts of illegal narcotics that were being shipped into Europe's biggest port. Neither were nice people and the message was clearly to stay away. In those days, Carl (although he wasn't called Carl then) had been somewhat naïve, as he had always thought there was only one Italian organised crime organisation, La Cosa Nostra from Sicily. So much for watching Hollywood movies!

Late one night in a small bar, he fell into conversation with one of the Italians. The man was very drunk, whereas Carl had only had three or four beers. As was his wont, he let the Italian speak and the man got increasingly agitated. As the night wore on, he raved and screamed about the treachery of the other side. It was difficult to actually ascertain which side this guy was on but with more shots of aquavit and gentle urging, he eventually figured it out.

All the while he was listening, a plan was forming in his mind and as they eventually called it a night as dawn was breaking over the oily waters of the harbour, he said to the Italian, "I think I may know a man who can help you solve your problems once and for all. If you think you or your bosses might be interested, meet me here again tonight at the same time. If not, forget me and we will not meet again."

He returned that night, not really expecting to meet anyone as the man had been so drunk that he surely would have forgotten. He positioned himself with his back to the wall, close to the rear exit. He didn't really expect violence but better to be prepared. At around 11.30, the Italian was back, this time with another older, more serious-looking man. They nodded at each other and the Italians joined him at his table.

The older man was impeccably dressed in a dark suit, white shirt and red tie. He had deep furrows in his dark brows and looked like a man who had seen a lot of what life had to give and possibly a lot of the bad side of it as well. He looked about eighty but was probably in his mid sixties. His companion was, as on the previous night, scruffily dressed, small, and squat, with deep impenetrable eyes.

After some small talk, the older, more serious looking man stared straight into his eyes and said, "I believe you may have a proposition to put to us."

Carl had already calmly worked it out in his head. He maintained eye contact with the senior man, at this stage totally ignoring the drunk from the night before.

"My friend," he began, "I have heard of the nasty dispute in which you have become embroiled. I have heard that many of your people have died and even some of your immediate family have been badly tortured and killed. This is tragic and has to end. It seems to me that if you go on like this, both organizations will eventually be weakened and ineffective. Have you considered a compromise and a division of territory?"

He already knew the answer he would get but he was surprised at the strength of the Italian's response. He almost levitated as he exclaimed, lips foaming:

"Never ever, not as long as there is a breath in my body will there be a compromise with such scum!"

Carl didn't react, but continued coolly, "Fine, then the only other option is to take out all their key people; and I mean all of them."

"Don't you think we know that? We have tried but we cannot get close enough."

"I understand; you may not be able to, but I could."

"But how? We have tried."

He considered carefully before he made his response. "Well, I am here with you two now and I am close to you. I know who you both are and I could probably have taken you out at any stage this evening."

Both Italians recoiled and seemed to reach under the table. He could see this going bad. He was bluffing, of course. He only had a vague notion of whom he was talking to. He tried to defuse the situation by placing both hands on the table in clear view.

"Just an example, gentlemen; please forgive me. I am an honourable man, just discussing a business proposition."

The older man seemed to consider for a long time, then he nodded to the younger man who withdrew a large packet from his inside pocket.

The older man spoke again. "You may know who we are my friend but we know who you are also so don't forget that. Take them all out for us and I'll give you five times what's in that packet."

He affected to consider the offer and then replied. "I will need names, addresses, and photographs if you have them; habits – where they eat, where they drink, what sort of security they have. Where they go, what they do – everything about them. I need to live their lives, get into their minds."

The older man said, "Antonio will provide you with what you want if you give him your phone number. Good luck to you." They both stood and left the bar. Carl was shaking as he stood up to leave, but not with fear; more exhilaration. He had pulled it off, but what to do now?

When he got back to his apartment, he discovered that there was $50,000 in the packet, a huge sum then. He decided that if they knew who he was, his secret was out, so he might as well go ahead.

He received most of the data he needed the following day from Antonio. He then did some of his own research. He bought weapons, which were freely available. He used the advance he had been given and did not skimp. If he needed information he was prepared to pay for it. He prepared thoroughly and then he was ready.

He wouldn't have called it child's play, but for someone who had once done a British Cabinet Minister, it was not difficult. The fact that all the key men were in the city at the same time and could be tracked relatively easily was the key. With speed and ruthlessness, he sought his quarry and within a few hours, there was only one Mafia family in the city.

There was no drama, no hail of bullets, no machine gun shoot-outs, just a quiet and stealthy operation, with each target receiving two bullets from a silenced Glock. Only one of the men had seen it coming and even he didn't have time to cry out. There were a number of different locations involved but he had practiced the route over and over. This was also done in the days before mobile telephones so even if someone had discovered the first or second set of bodies, they would have been powerless to warn the men in the third location.

The police immediately dragged in all the usual suspects from the other side but all had rock solid alibis. The case was never solved and after a time was quietly closed, the police glad that peace had been at least partially restored to their city.

He kept a low profile for a few days until eventually Antonio called him.

"Tonight, ten o'clock, same bar."

He was there ahead of schedule, and at precisely ten, the old Italian walked in, again accompanied by Antonio. Few words were spoken but a large briefcase was placed on the table, momentarily flicked open so that he could inspect the cash inside, and then snapped shut again.

"I am very grateful, my friend; you have done very well and you deserve your reward. Stay in touch with us and we might have more work for you at some stage."

He thanked the man profusely and they parted. He decided there and then that word would eventually filter out about the Irishman; people talked, even in tight crime families. After all, that was how he had gotten the job in the first place – through Antonio's drunken indiscretion. He reckoned Rotterdam was too hot, and he'd spend his dollars where they had originated.

He used some of the false papers he had acquired earlier to gain access to the U.S. It was a lot easier in those days. Once he had become established there, he had effectively never left, other than for business. Acquiring a legitimate U.S. passport was also relatively simple. Using what would nowadays be called identity theft, he acquired several, all in different states and all for completely different personas. He had kept in touch with his patron from Rotterdam and, true to his word, the man had provided him with many assignments.

He had worked for governments of all types and hues, organised crime, drugs syndicates, big industrial corporations, and even a few private individuals. The word had gotten round that he was available. With more success, it was recognised in the underworld that he was good and useful to be aware of, and eventually, as the years rolled past, he became recognised as the best in the business.

He usually operated to the same M.O. His employers were requested to provide a driver, when he had finalised his preparations. The driver was to be told nothing; just that he had to collect a very important person and drive him to a location. He would be told the minimum of information, and only when it was necessary. He would then be told to wait or circle or whatever was required, then to collect the man again and to drive him to his safe haven, whether that was the airport, bus or train or underground station. He would be richly rewarded, provided he kept his mouth shut – it was made very clear to him what would happen to him if he spoke about it. No one ever did!

Walker found this so much easier than driving or having to hire a car and leaving a trail. He still drove himself some times when complete anonymity was required but he was very careful about it. He held numerous credit cards, all in legitimate names, all arranged on the basis of online billing. In the old days, he had used post office boxes. He had never been caught, but operating nowadays online guaranteed complete anonymity. All the cards were untraceable but were used on a regular basis anyway so as not to arouse suspicion.

He was the ultimate professional because he viewed his work as just doing a job, like any other. His planning and execution were always meticulous. He prepared, got in quickly, did the job, and always had an exit strategy. He was purely an assassin. He never did messy stuff like kidnap or torture work; not his thing – too messy. He was a killer and he did it quickly and cleanly.

He was careful in choosing his jobs and he had by now acquired the financial security to be able to do so. He liked a challenge but he was very careful in whom he worked for, where he operated and whom he liquidated. Carl liked his freedom. He loved the United States. He liked living in the land of the free and he wouldn't sacrifice this for anything. Not for him to seek asylum in some stinking hellhole in South America or some remote outpost. No; he intended to stay right here in Florida and eventually retire peacefully.

As he was having his breakfast, he was thinking that he hadn't worked now for nearly six months when his i-Phone beeped twice. Hmm, incoming text at 08.30 in the morning, the agreed time. He sipped his coffee and finished a piece of toast, looking out over the heart-shaped swimming pool and the beautifully manicured gardens to the tree line. His wife had just left to take his two girls to school. Like most mornings in Orlando, it was gloriously sunny and warm, with just the gentlest of breezes. He finished his breakfast, brushed a few stray crumbs off his dressing gown and stretched.

"Will you be requiring anything else Mr Walker?"

"Not at all, that was lovely Lateecha, thank you," he said to the lady who had been serving him for nearly twenty years. "It's a lovely day, I think I'll take the Harley out for a spin."

"Sure, ok sir, but you be sure to be careful now, you hear?"

He assured her that he would, lifted the phone from the table and pressed the 'read' button.

Chapter 6 - The Policeman

Mike Lyons was looking forward to working in Washington D.C. He had visited the U.S. a number of times but had never been to the capital. He had been born in Ireland but had spent most of his life in the UK. Still, you never lost your roots, and while he was perfectly happy living in London, he was a regular visitor to his birthplace in County Wicklow. His parents were still alive and well and he took great pleasure in heading back and spending a few days on the old farm, pottering around, mending a fence or doing a bit of gardening or any of the numerous little tasks his Mother seemed to store up for him every time he came home. Although he often came back physically tired, he was always mentally refreshed and ready to again apply himself to attempting to solve Britain's increasingly complex crimes.

Initially, he had had a successful career in the London Metropolitan Police for over ten years. He had very quickly progressed to the Detective Division and was steadily moving up the ranks when the offer came to join MI5, the British Government's Internal Security and Anti-Terrorist Service. He was sad to leave the Met but couldn't forego the opportunity to apply himself at a higher intellectual level. There were a few raised eyebrows initially because he was Irish and, at that stage, Britain had been engaged in anti-terrorist operations in Northern Ireland for almost 30 years, and probably even before that. But by the time Mike joined, those operations were being scaled down and peace was at long last on the way to that troubled part of the world.

In any event, he never became involved in Irish operations, but soon proved his worth with some spectacular successes on the domestic scene. He had a particular ability to adapt to every new circumstance or each new terrorist threat that surfaced. Some of his greatest challenges had come in recent years with the growth in support for Islamic fundamentalism on Britain's mainland, which culminated in the 7/7 bombings in 2005. He had worked ceaselessly to put a framework in place that would prevent a recurrence, and the apprehension of the members of many other similarly-minded cells had been largely due to the implementation of his strategy. He was now recognised as one of the foremost experts in anti-terrorism.

He loved his job but had no wish to keep doing it indefinitely. There were lots of other things that he wanted to do and as he had accumulated over 27 years of service between both forces, he could retire on full pension. In 2010, MI5 had encouraged a large number of older staff to go as they wished to recruit a younger generation who were more computer-literate. A generous early retirement package had been offered. Mike was as skilled with a PC as the next man, but he knew what they meant, as many of his colleagues were not.

Most of MI5's counter-terrorism work focused on Islamic extremists, many of whom made sophisticated use of the internet and other computer technologies to prepare and co-ordinate their plots. Much of MI5's successes at discovering these plots and apprehending the terrorists in recent years had been through the use of technology. At any one time, MI5 had over 2000 individuals under surveillance and this was increasing so sophisticated use of technology was imperative.

Mike applied for the exit package and his application was reluctantly accepted. His immediate superiors realized that he had many other ambitions, and that they could not hold on to him, so they agreed but asked him if he would be available to assist in certain areas or to provide help and co-operation with their allies, as a sort of part-time consultant. He readily agreed and formally left early in 2011.

He had no regrets whatsoever. He had had a great career in the services; he knew he had been highly regarded, and they had continuously assured him that he wasn't one of the ones they needed to let go. His mind was made up, though, as he had always wanted to travel, for pleasure as well as for work. He was not married and had no family ties in the UK. He hoped to do some other consultancy work in law enforcement, and he had already had a few offers in that regard. He knew as much or more about anti-terrorism as anyone else so there were bound to be lots of opportunities. But first he wanted to relax and spend a long vacation with his parents on their farm. Then he would start his travel plans.

His first destination was going to be the U.S. so when he was asked to do some sessions with Homeland Security, it suited him ideally. The plan was to fly to Washington, meet with a number of the agencies, then come back and draw up a program that would be mutually agreed. Mike would then lead the sessions in D.C. His initial contact was to be with a Paul Lincoln of Homeland Security. He had checked Paul out before he left. He got a sense that they might be kindred spirits and he was confident they would get on well.

Compliments of the Americans, he was flying in Business Class on British Airways and he was going to enjoy it. He chose his in-flight meal and ordered a glass of Chablis. Then he adjusted his seat and lay back like he hadn't a care in the world. In fact, if the truth be known, he hadn't. The guys in the service had often joked about the Irish guy who never seemed to get stressed. He did, of course, as much as anyone else, but his way was to keep calm and work through it. He had also always had the ability to switch off when he left work, to compartmentalize. It was a trait unusual in a policeman, even more so given the horrors he had witnessed over the years. But Mike felt that was how he stayed sane. He had to be able to distance himself. It wasn't that he didn't care. He did, deeply, but he always felt that this ability to switch off and enjoy life made him even more effective when he returned to his job.

Despite his success and his many promotions, he never, as they said in his homeland, 'lost the run of himself'. He always kept his feet on the ground and always saw himself as simply a policeman. He had never wanted to be anything else for as long as he could remember. Even as a boy growing up, he was always the one who intervened in disputes, often preventing the bullies from getting their way or calming disputes between rivals. His great gift was that he always seemed to be able to do it without resorting to violence himself. Apart from the fact that he was always big and strong, he seemed to radiate a presence, a calmness that said "I'll respect your views and I'll tolerate you as long as you behave but if you don't or if you mess with me, you'll suffer the consequences." Most didn't chance it and the few who did regretted not taking the implied advice. He had continued in this vein all his working life and was widely respected for it.

He was also a deep thinker about police work and had a finely honed detective's sense of how to solve even the most complicated or devious crime. He had superb listening skills, vitally important in his trade and the ability to absorb, assimilate and analyse vast amounts of information, yet grasp the one key piece of evidence which may have been overlooked and come up with an alternative approach to solving a particularly difficult crime. On many occasions when colleagues were at a dead end with a case, they might be recommended to "ask the big Irishman to take a look at it." They often did and he never refused a request for help. While he couldn't and didn't solve them all, his insight was often invaluable in making that vital breakthrough.

His wine arrived with his meal and both were excellent. He'd have to do more of this type of flying! After lunch, he tried the in-flight entertainment and watched the latest Hollywood blockbuster before briefly nodding off to sleep. These business class seats were the real deal. He awoke just as the aircraft began its descent to Reagan International.

Chapter 7 – The Request

Around the same time, Carl Walker was firing up his Harley-Davidson to return to his Orlando home. He had had an interesting morning but was looking forward to the trip back. He loved to take his motor cycle along the seemingly endless back and side roads that crossed the wild marshlands west of Orlando. The area was vast and contained millions of acres of preserved and protected areas either side of I95 and out as far as Cape Canaveral. This area was his refuge, his space to think, where he could clear his head. Whether along the shores of Lake Poinsett or all the way out past Cocoa Beach or any of the millions of deserted spots in between, this was a place you could breathe, relax and think. A man could disappear and not be troubled or disturbed. In fact he believed that many had done just that although none had been by his hand.

He had collected the letter from the old, unused mailbox that he had instructed the man from Charleston to deliver to. He assumed that the man had made the delivery the night before, and was sure he was long gone from the scene. Nonetheless he had approached the area with caution, checking and rechecking that he was alone. He knew these roads like the back of his hand and after a thorough check, he reckoned there wasn't another human being for fifty square miles. The old homestead that was serviced by the unused mailbox had been abandoned in the 1950's but the box was sturdy and intact. Walker had chosen it for that, and of course its remoteness, but also the fact that it blended into its surroundings. He had carefully installed his own locking system on the box, just as an added precaution, although he was sure the only ones who ever even saw the box were the protected wild animals and birds that heavily populated the area.

Still wearing his biker's gloves, he used his key to open the box and retrieved the envelope. He then drove the 40 or so miles to another, even more remote area where he had acquired a piece of real estate over fifteen years before. It wasn't much to look at to the casual passer-by, of which there would have been very few, if any. It was situated on a dirt track, off the paved road and wasn't accessible by an automobile. It was no trouble to the Harley, though. He checked the road in both directions, satisfied himself that it was clear for miles and turned left into the forest.

After about three miles on the dirt track, the forest closed in on him and he had to duck frequently to avoid overhanging tree branches and overgrown foliage. After a further two miles, the forest gave way to a clearing that contained a single cabin that sat at the far side, just before the tree line. He put the Harley on its stand, stood, inhaled the thick scented air, and stretched.

Everything seemed in order but he still went through his routines, checking and rechecking that nothing had been disturbed since his last visit. Again satisfied, he used another key to gain entrance to the cabin. He had a small gas-powered stove upon which he now placed a small kettle, filled with water from a bottle he had brought with him. He fired up the stove and decided he'd brew some coffee. He took the cup he had made and strolled out to sit on the ancient weather-beaten sun-darkened porch.

When he was seated and had had several sips of coffee, he extracted a packet of cigarettes and lit one. He had few vices but this was one. He allowed himself an occasional cigarette. Only then did he open the letter he had collected, which had brought him here this morning.

The system had worked smoothly again. His courier had alerted him by text at precisely 08.30 as agreed. The wording of the text merely offered him a discount on some obscure beauty product if he became a valued customer of some retail outlet. It was similar to tens of thousands of other promotional texts sent every day and had merely been forwarded from his courier's phone as an alert mechanism.

He took his time perusing the letter. He was a wealthy man with investments in both high-performing equities and solid blue-chip stocks. He also had numerous offshore bank accounts, which could be emptied at short notice. He used these to pay off his intermediaries and for expenses associated with his "business trips." All had very healthy balances and he had been asking himself recently if he needed to work again. Still, he did have heavy expenses, and while his retainers could be discontinued at any time, they were small potatoes compared to the cost of his and Cindy's lifestyle.

He was almost 58, but that in itself didn't worry him. He was still the best, a legend in his business, and he could operate successfully for a while yet. Perhaps he should consider increasing what he charged for his services? If you wanted the best, you should be prepared to pay for it. Did he need the buzz of it, the adrenalin rush? He had asked himself that question over the years and he had convinced himself that he did not. He was a professional; it was a job; that was all. Yes; there was a huge thrill from planning an operation meticulously from start to finish and then concluding it successfully. Then there was the tension, which actually helped his concentration when he was close to the denouement; and, of course, the rush of the kill itself. But he was confident he could leave it behind him. Everyone had to retire sometime. He had done a hell of a job of reinventing himself before and he could do so again. But not quite yet – he had a few more jobs in him, possibly starting with the letter he now held in his hand. Happy that he was now fully relaxed but focused, he slid open the letter.

The envelope contained one double spaced typed sheet. The paper was plain white vellum, the letters Arial Black script.

Dear Sir –

We have reason to believe that you provide services that might be of use to us. If you agree to deal with us, please be so kind as to let us know by replying to the e-mail address at the bottom of this letter. Let us assure you that the amount of your fee is of no consequence. We would, however, insist on a face-to-face meeting to discuss our proposal.

The letter was unsigned. All of the wording was in the plural. Definitely the sign of an organisation he felt, and given the

78

repeated use of the plural, probably a big one. He thought about the proposal in detail. Money was of no consequence? Come to me, he thought. But that could also be a trap, a come-on designed to lure him into the open. But he doubted it. Very few people even knew he existed and as far as he was aware, those that did bore him no grudge. He was not the type of person you would want to take a pot shot at unless you were absolutely certain of hitting your target. There would be no second chances. Anyway, the people who knew of his existence would have no reason to want to eliminate him, as he did provide a useful service that they might need at some point. No one had ever come after him or try to take him out or even try to track him down, as far as he was aware. If they had tried, they had obviously failed.

He didn't always agree to face-to-face meetings, but he couldn't trust an intermediary to conduct the delicate business of negotiation or discussion of the potential target. So, if the proposal was complex, there was no option but to have one. He had plans for handling that too. He had met many of his clients, but always in different locations far removed from his home, and usually far away from the location of the proposed hit. He had a list of up to twenty locations in his head where he knew he could meet a client and feel totally safe. After all, he had been doing this for years, whereas most of his clients might only hire his services once. He decided to take a long slow drive back to Orlando and think it over.

He re-read the letter in his mind as he eased the Harley up and down the back roads through the Canaveral Marshes and up towards St Johns. "Fee of no consequence, huh?" Maybe he could retire after this one but he immediately banished the thought. Not for him the mind of the gambler, dreaming of the one big win that would help him quit and set him up for life. The problem with dreams is that they were just that – they rarely came true and they distorted reality. It was dangerous to think like that, because if you were in that frame of mind, it would tempt you and even allow you to take unnecessary risks. He had always been content to work from job to job. His fee was always substantial anyway but he never pushed it. He knew what he was worth and charged accordingly. He had turned down some jobs over the years, because in some instances he felt they carried an unacceptable level of risk; others, where the idea just did not make sense or sit right with him.

He thought back over the years to the jobs he had done and wondered how he had got into the business. Was it just chance? Had it to do with his upbringing, his social background, his life experience? But deep down he knew it was none of those things – it was quite simply because he was good at it and people tend to do what they are talented at. In his case, this just happened to be killing people. He never thought of himself as a bad guy, though; he was just a professional doing a job. He didn't take any undue pleasure from it, nor he did he feel displeasure. It was a job; he was good at it. End of story.

Everyone has to live with themselves, and Walker did this quite comfortably. He never had a problem looking at himself in the mirror, never had any doubts. In his own mind, Carl Walker was a nice guy. People went through life doing different jobs, but what they did didn't make them good guys or bad guys. Who knew who the bad guys were anyway? He reckoned that most of the guys he had disposed of, if not all, had deserved it. Most were involved in violent death in some way, and some had murdered and tortured brutally. So he could argue he did the world a service by getting rid of them. There had been the odd political leader but who knew what sort of underhand dealings they had been involved with, either, particularly in some of the tin-pot countries where he had eliminated them.

He thought of the bombs and the gun attacks in the earlier part of his career. Well, that was all for the cause, wasn't it? And sure, look where it led; they didn't get a United Ireland, but the whole place had changed, and lots of the guys he had operated with were now elected representatives in both the North and South of the country. There was what they now politely called collateral damage, but they all had it. All conflicts did, and everyone justified it the same way, so why should he be any different? No, he slept soundly at night and was quite happy with his lot, thank you very much!

But there was another valid reason why he slept well at night. It was because he was comfortable in the notion that he would never be caught, because he would never leave evidence behind linking him to any crime. He only took on jobs that afforded him the opportunity to get cleanly in and out without detection. Even then, his research and planning were meticulous, often taking months until the time was right – never rushing a job, always waiting for the opportune, the optimum time to strike. Apart from never having left any evidence behind, there were no official photographs of him anywhere. For sure there were lots of family photos but without something to compare them with, investigators were powerless.

Of course he also had a passport and a driving licence – in fact he had many of each, interchanging with ease. He was a master of disguise and he was content – and rather proud, actually – that the likenesses in each passport photograph were almost totally different from each other. He had rarely been stopped or queried, always choosing the correct disguise and clothing to fit the situation.

He remembered once, in the Caribbean, a too-fussy immigration official had detained him for a short while, even though his passport was genuine, if issued to a non-existent personage. The official was sure he was on to something, so a medium-sized bribe was offered, which solved the immediate problem. But he couldn't take chances on the immigration man doing a solo run later and rechecking the data, so unfortunately the man met with a tragic accident that very night. Walker later departed the island on a different passport from a different nation, looking altogether transformed from the person as whom he entered the country, and no one was any the wiser. Needless to say, that passport was burned and the disguise was never used again.

Passports and driving licenses – in fact, all types of genuine documentation – were ridiculously easy to obtain if you were willing to pay for them. He also held numerous credit cards in the names of each of his personas, all genuinely applied-for and granted, all used regularly and paid promptly.

For these and numerous other reasons, he had never been caught, and he firmly believed that he never would be. Not only had he not been caught, he hadn't even been suspected. In fact, in many of his jobs, he was already back at base sipping a beer before the crime was even discovered. Some might have said he was cowardly for not taking on some of the big risk jobs – others knew better, particularly the ones who eventually took on the job and were now incarcerated or worse! He was a professional; he abhorred people who did not do their jobs well in any walk of life. He led a comfortable life, spending his time with his family and managing his investments.

The more he thought about it now, he realised that having a family was absolutely necessary, and probably something he should have done earlier. For too long he had been the relatively reclusive loner who lived in the shadows. That was fine then, but nowadays he felt it would be far too risky; too likely that, at some stage, he would draw attention to himself, or that someone with nothing to do would become suspicious. His business trips a few times a year were easily explained away, and he was always careful to return when he had said he would so as to establish a pattern of complete reliability, to the point where some who knew him would have said he was predictable to the point of being boringly conservative. The impression suited him just fine!

Apart from in his 'professional activities', he never broke the law. He hadn't ever even gotten a parking ticket so there was no record of him anywhere on any police files. He actually had no problem with police at all, and was a vociferous supporter of the "get tough on crime" brigade. There were far too many thugs mugging old ladies and young girls for his liking. He would lock them all up and throw away the key. He actually had huge respect for the police and the work they did – he just didn't see his line of work as in any way impinging on *real* police work. No, he was just a professional doing a job and doing it excellently. The police would never have the resources to solve all crime anyway, and even if they had more personnel, as in many of the old Soviet bloc countries, he doubted they would be any more efficient. In any event, he felt they would never catch *him*.

People had visions of hit men as brooding sinister loners. Most weren't; in this case, Walker was the complete opposite! Also, he was neat. Clean kills were his specialty; he could kill with his bare hands, with a knife, or any implement in an emergency, but he rarely had to. Most of his victims never saw him or it coming; just a quiet double tap with a silenced Glock put them to sleep, and he was on his way. Torture or information extraction was not his thing and he turned such offers down flat. On one rare occasion when the price was very high, he had agreed to a kidnapping of a certain person who knew too much but he had insisted on following his usual pattern: rendering the victim unconscious before they even saw him, then quickly removing them for hand over to his paymaster at an agreed rendezvous. Total time involved: probably less than twenty minutes. Neat, quick, clean and gone. Whatever ransom had been demanded or paid was not his problem.

He nearly always used the same M.O. His Principal would be informed of the date of the hit and was requested to provide a driver at a specific time and location. He was not given any other information. The driver collected him and he gave him instructions on where to take him. He always made it clear that he would need drivers who were skilled at their trade and who knew how to keep their mouths shut. A back-up driver was often also requested to wait at a specific location. Both drivers were to be given one-use cell phones, and both numbers were to be provided to him in advance. He always arrived on schedule and never spoke to the drivers, other than to give them a location or to ask them to wait or circle. The drivers never had any idea what they were party to until afterwards. At that stage, Walker was long gone, and given the stealth and efficiency with which he carried out his task, they knew better than to ever speak about the matter.

When the driver collected him after he had carried out his work, he always insisted on being driven to a different location than the pick-up, often an airport, train station, or underground; not that he always exited through these facilities. The cars used were always to be legitimate taxis, because taxis were invisible in every town or city. On rare occasions he drove himself but he preferred the standard M.O. Automobile hire left a trail and was always one of the first things police checked. Even though he always used one of his false identities, it was one more potential risk that he could eliminate. He had always disappeared without trace. Really, he couldn't understand why guys got caught – in his view, if you planned something well enough with great attention to detail and left no evidence, it was impossible to be detected.

He was still wondering what this group wanted him to do and whether he was interested. Although in his mind he was still undecided, he realized that he had come back on Route 408 heading into Orlando but had subconsciously diverted on to 417, the Central Florida Greeneway, heading southeast. He then switched to the Reagan Turnpike which brought him due south. He indicated right and took the exit for Kissimmee.

Chapter 8 – The Cut-Outs

Every year, Walker changed at least one of his cut-outs, sometimes two. He had never had any trouble – the network had never been broken, but he thought it prudent to keep the system fluid anyway. He had used the Dutchman from the start, although he was neither the first nor the only one to use him. Although he often worried about him, he had decided not to try to fix what wasn't broken. The man had served him well and had never attracted the slightest suspicion. He knew about the rumours of Van Henkel's involvement in the narcotics business, but he knew it was nonsense. In fact, it may have served to divert attention from the man's real purpose.

None of his cut-outs knew what any of the others looked like. Most of them never met each other; except when it was absolutely necessary, only briefly, and without any direct communication and always late at night at a remote location. He varied the pattern constantly; probably needlessly, but it kept people alert and ensured that no one he didn't want to had ever located him. None of the cut-outs knew the identity of the next link in the chain, or how long the chain actually was. None of them knew who was ultimately at the end of the chain or what part of the country he was in or what business he operated in, although he felt most would have had strong suspicions about the latter. But when he chose, he chose wisely and only made the briefest direct contact himself.

When he was dropping a contact, they were advised by mail that the business had changed and that their services were no longer required. They were thanked sincerely for their services. No one had ever complained or tried to make contact. This was possibly to do with the fact that when he dropped or replaced someone, a large bonus was always paid. Also, there was never any violence; the guy or girl just got their thank you bonus and never heard from anyone again. All were sensible enough to know that they had outlived their usefulness and that it was probably best to keep their mouths shut.

Choosing a cut-out or messenger was relatively easy. All one needed was time and patience, and he had plenty of both. With today's technology, it was becoming even easier. With his computer skills, hacking into credit card companies and credit rating agencies was child's play. You could see at a glance who was solvent and who needed cash.

He always picked people who were vulnerable, but not too much so. People who were out of work or in debt or even both were ideal. He had never had a refusal as he chose carefully and after due consideration. He usually plumped for people who lived alone and were single but not always. He usually chose men; but, again, not always. One of his most reliable couriers had been a housewife from Atlanta with a gambling problem. She had grasped the opportunity with open arms, and he reckoned he had saved her marriage more than once! He wondered where she was now. Had she shaken the habit or had the gambling consumed her? In fact, gamblers were an easy mark and with the growth in online betting in recent years, there was almost an embarrassment of riches to choose from.

He usually picked his people in another State and always in another city. The way it worked was like this: after personal observation of a number of "possibles" over some days, he made his choice. He then hand-delivered an envelope addressed to the person, having ascertained in advance that this was possible. The envelope always contained one sheet of notepaper with the following message:

Dear Mr /Ms. X
I have a business proposal to put to you. I need a package delivered to (stating a nearby city). I am unable to deliver this myself, but I would be prepared to pay you the sum of $1,000 for your inconvenience. Let me assure you that the package does not contain narcotics or any form of contraband whatsoever and that

there is nothing illegal about the transaction. I also guarantee that there is absolutely no risk to you personally. If you complete the delivery successfully, I may well have other deliveries that I would wish you to undertake for a similar fee; again, under the exact same conditions. If you are interested, please meet me tomorrow evening at (nominated bar) at seven. Please keep this confidential and come alone.

The letter was always unsigned. He never mentioned that he was aware that they needed the cash. It was as if they had been chosen in a lottery. He always chose a bar that was convenient for the subject, was very public, and that was capable of being observed. And almost all of them fell for it – all the time. It was amazing what people would do for a few bucks, and here was someone willing to pay them a thousand to make a delivery! It was a no-brainer! They were always a bit wary and slightly suspicious but hell, what was wrong with meeting some guy in a bar to discuss it? Anyway, when you were six months overdue on your rent or had credit card bills or gambling debts, could you afford to be choosy?

He would always arrive well ahead of his quarry and take a seat where he could observe the bar opposite. He was always disguised but never noticeably so. He had become a master at it over the years and could make himself up to look like almost anyone without detection. He was medium height and was slim and fit so he could pass for a man or a woman. He particularly liked being disguised as a woman; not that he had a fetish about it, but he got a huge thrill from being able to act out different personas without detection. He had studied styling and colour matching and was an expert in make-up application; he had learned from observation over the years that many women were not!

He usually reserved his female disguises for assignments where it might be difficult obtaining access and egress as the same person. The last time, he had dressed in a dark brown suit, white button down shirt with a brown tie that matched his eyes and hair colour. He looked, and sounded, to all intents and purposes, like a college professor. At precisely seven o'clock, his chosen one, an eager-looking man in his mid thirties, arrived, sat at the bar, looked around eagerly, and ordered a beer. Happy hour was just finishing and the bar was still quite busy. At precisely 7.10, after having carefully checked his surroundings, he nonchalantly crossed the road and entered the bar. He took a seat directly beside his subject but did not make eye contact or conversation. He withdrew a large manila envelope from his inside pocket and placed it in front of the man, to whom it was already addressed. Inside the envelope were two smaller envelopes; one addressed to him, and one to a fictitious person at a mailbox number in a nearby city. This was what he was expected to deliver. There was also a note:

Dear Mr X –

Thank you for meeting me. In the envelope addressed to you is $500. Write your bank account number on the back of this note and hand it back to me. When you deliver the other letter in the next few days, a further $500 will be wired to your bank account. You should not attempt to open the other letter at any time, nor should you ever attempt to open any packages I might entrust to you. My affairs must be conducted in absolute privacy. Should you successfully carry out this task, I will consider asking you to undertake further courier assignments, for which you will be rewarded. If you agree with my proposition and with my conditions, either nod or answer yes.

Of course, once they came to the bar, he had them in the palm of his hand. They never refused at this stage. The sight of the five hundred bucks was enough to wash away any lingering doubts. They were tripping over themselves nodding and blurting out, yes, yes, of course and scrambling to write down their bank account details. He already knew these, of course but was not going to make his couriers aware.

The "test" letter with which he entrusted them always contained three folded pages of blank paper and always went to a mail box number that had been rented remotely. The letter was usually delivered the following day and they never interfered with it. If they had, he would have known, and ceased all contact with the person. The money was duly deposited in the bank accounts from an untraceable offshore account. Then he had another link in his chain.

It was simple, really. When they were established, he eventually paid all of his cut-outs three thousand dollars per month, whether they were used or not. Expensive, but it was important to keep people happy, and distant. All payments were handled through a bewildering series of offshore accounts with locations as diverse as Liechtenstein, the Bahamas, the Cayman Islands and Andorra. As well as being an effective assassin, he was also a master at managing his finances, and there had never been a breach. When he carried out an assignment, he was always paid into a one-time only account, and as soon as he was paid, the money was dispersed in a number of directions, barely resting before it was moved on again. Without Walker's codes, not even the most diligent auditor would ever untangle his finances, as he only operated in countries or territories where absolute discretion was assured.

All of this cost money, and he didn't come cheap. Mind you, this never seemed to be a problem with the clients who approached him. He was always paid on time and he rarely had to haggle. He charged according to three relatively simple criteria: the difficulty and scale of the job; the type of people, if any, that were likely to come after him; and how long and how far they were prepared to look. He only rarely met his clients in person, but he always demanded to know who they were or who they represented. On this occasion, his potential employers had insisted on a face-to-face meeting, so he would give them one; but he would make certain he could not be either identified or attacked or traced.

He arrived in the centre of the small city of Kissimmee. He parked the Harley in a lot and walked a couple of blocks to an internet café. He made a mental note that he would have to consider an alternative method of communication, as with the advent of iPhones and 3G technology, internet cafes were becoming rarer. He paid a dollar to a bored-looking attendant who barely looked up from the magazine she was reading. "Number 15, right side at the end and you've got fifteen minutes." He nodded his thanks and made his way to the pre-assigned computer. It was mid-afternoon on a hot summer day and the place was practically deserted.

He created a one-time email address that would be untraceable. He assumed the author of the letter had done the same as the address he had been given seemed particularly obtuse. He typed: Pier Chic Restaurant in Madinat Jumeirah Dubai, 8.30 pm, Monday. Book a table for two people only, in the name of Mr Abboud.

Chapter 9 - The Meeting

Abdullah was initially somewhat shocked when the man had agreed to a meeting and stunned to find that he had proposed to hold it in neighbouring Dubai, only an hour's flight away. Had he done this deliberately? Was he that good? Did he already know who wanted to hire him? Abdullah was wise beyond his years, but he had never done anything like this before and he was nervous. What had sounded perfectly logical and straightforward in theory was an altogether different prospect when you had to put it into practice – and nothing had even happened yet.

He became, probably for the first time, aware of his own mortality and the awful consequences that might befall him if he failed. He needed to remain strong. He passionately believed in the cause, but it was one thing planning from the comfort of your country estate, contemplating the deaths of the enemy and the sacrifices of your own people. It was quite another when you had to go into the field yourself.

He needed to calm down. He was only going to a meeting. He relaxed momentarily; then he realised the importance of the meeting and the great weight he was carrying on his shoulders. He rarely indulged, but he reckoned a stiff Johnny Walker was called for. It helped steady his nerves. The phone in his hotel suite rang and he was told his car and driver had arrived at the door of the hotel. He said a quick prayer and hurried downstairs.

Walker did not know who was trying to hire him, nor did he waste time speculating. He would know soon enough. He did suspect that his potential employer might be located in the Middle East, as the first link in the chain, the Dutchman, had placed the letter inside another envelope and had added a post-it note containing one word – Bahraini. A nice touch, that, and one for which he had already rewarded the Dutchman by transferring a bonus of $10,000 in addition to the usual payment of $25,000 to his bank account. That didn't necessarily mean that his potential employer was from Bahrain, but the Dutchman was helpful when he could be with bits and pieces of information.

He had noticed the meeting venue some years earlier and had identified it as perfect for his purpose. The restaurant was actually located over the water, well out from shore on raised pylons sunk into the soft sand of the gulf. An ornate wooden bridge traversed the 100 or so metres from the shore. It was fully outdoors, and had a 360-degree view of the surrounding area. It could be approached by boat and was small enough to ensure that there could be no hidden surprises. In any event he didn't expect any. He was just another Arab businessman meeting a potential client for dinner to discuss a business proposition.

He had identified numerous similar locations around the world over the years where he could meet a client if it was required. He always chose locations he had already been to and checked out. He also always made sure they were secure and that they allowed him to enter and exit more or less without detection if he required to do so. Waterfront locations were his favourite but he did not choose them exclusively. He had met people in Acapulco, Havana, Barbados and once on Long Beach in L.A.

The Pier Chic restaurant was part of the huge Jumeirah Complex, which had been built from scratch over the previous ten years along the beautiful white sandy shores of the Emirate. It was a vast resort that featured four hotels, including the now-famous Burj-Al-Arab, reputed to be the world's most exclusive establishment, and purportedly the world's only seven-star hotel. There were also dozens of villas, private cottages and conference centres, numerous swimming pools and spa centres, a large shopping centre, and an artificial lake and waterways linking each sector of the complex. It was an ideal location in which to meet someone and then disappear. Abdullah had assumed this was why his man had chosen it, but when he saw the location of the restaurant offshore, he was unsure.

Walker hadn't the slightest intention of disappearing in the complex. In fact, he did not even intend to visit it. He had arrived the day before and had spent the intervening time resting and reconnoitring the meeting location, ensuring that everything was just as he had remembered it. He stayed at the equally comfortable but less opulent Dubai Marine Beach Resort, which was located about five miles further up the coast, also on Jumeirah road. He was registered in the hotel as a Mr Thomas Clarke, the same man who had arrived at Dubai International the previous day on a U.S. passport. The real Thomas Clarke was long since dead, but Walker had had nothing to do with it. He had merely assumed the man's identity, as he had done with several dozen others over the years.

He paid 100 Dirhams for his Dubai Visa on arrival. The hotel could have arranged it, had he booked in advance, but as the trip was arranged at short notice, he merely availed of the facility extended to all U.S. citizens. Abdullah stayed in the Burj, of course, as he felt befitted a man of his fine tastes. He too had come the day before the meeting and checked out the location.

It was a stunningly beautiful evening on the Gulf Shore when Walker eased the speedboat up to the small dock at the sea-facing side of the restaurant. The heat of the day had abated somewhat although it was still quite warm. It was only 7.30 so he had plenty of time to tie up his craft and admire the magnificent sunset. Many people described Dubai as a tourist paradise, and on evenings like this one, you could believe it. Unfortunately, his business tonight was connected with darker matters; but never mind.

An attendant rushed down to see if he required any assistance and was told that he was just fine. He was dressed in Arabic clothing, with a Bahraini Thawb covered by a loose Bisht. He also wore full headdress, and he had somehow acquired a deep mahogany suntan and a generous dark moustache. Facially he was almost unrecognizable from the man who had been riding his Harley in Florida just a few days before, or indeed the man who was staying in the Marine Hotel. His face was much fuller. His eye colour was now a deep brown, almost black. He had acquired deep furrows in his brows and he had an overall weather-beaten look. To any observer, even a forensic examination would reveal an Arab businessman. He could not speak Arabic, but that was not a problem, and was also one of his reasons for choosing Dubai. Only 17% of the population of the Emirate was Arabic, with the majority of the rest made up of migrant workers from India, Pakistan, Bangladesh, the Philippines and other parts of Asia. English was the common language, and it was rare to hear Arabic spoken anywhere apart from between locals.

He walked up the polished wooden steps to the restaurant and announced himself as Mr Abboud. He said he was a little early and wondered would his table be ready yet?

The charming Filipino girl assured him that it was and that he could go to it if he wished; or would he care to use the Shisha, the traditional Arab smoking pipe, in the smoking area?

He thanked her politely and declined the offer of a smoke and said he would relax while he awaited his guest. She seated him at the table, which was located in the middle of the restaurant. To her offer of a drink, he said he would have only still water for now.

He sat and relaxed. The table was almost perfect, situated midway between the seaward and landward sides, affording him a full view of everyone who came and went from both directions. The restaurant was beautifully laid out, with each table just far enough away from the next to allow a degree of privacy. The tables were set over fine starched white linen tablecloths and each place setting contained an expensive bone-china designer plate. The cutlery was fine silverware. It was a balmy evening but not too hot. The air was perfectly still. The only sounds were the polite chatter of the few diners and the slap of the warm waters of the Gulf as they washed against the pylons underneath the wooden construction.

Even though it was summer, by now, it was already quite dark. As Dubai is located close to the equator, it has almost the same amount of daylight and darkness year round. This often confuses western tourists who cannot grasp the concept of twelve-hour days and nights in summer time. The tables were lit with candles, and even though he was heavily disguised, this gave him even more anonymity and suited his purpose completely.

At about eight o'clock, he thought he spied his man. It was Monday evening and the restaurant was only about one-third full so his view was unimpeded. Three men were walking briskly across the bridge, having alighted from one of the many golf carts used to transport patrons around the resort. One man was in heavy formal robes with two outriders in traditional white thawbs and headdresses. The man was tall and well-built and his two companions looked like they could handle themselves.

He had felt sure that his man would not come alone, and that he would also come ahead of schedule. The two acolytes would occupy a nearby table, ready to pounce if their master was threatened. A reasonable enough plan, he thought, and given his reputation, he didn't blame the man for being cautious. Still, he could have relaxed. It was only an exploratory meeting and he had never harmed a hair on the head of any of his employers. To be fair, the man would not have known this; and after all, Walker had been meeting clients and staking out locations for most of his life, so he was bound to anticipate the man's moves.

He now heard him proclaim to the waitress, a different Filipino girl, that he was having dinner with Mr Abboud but that he was a little early. He stated that his two colleagues had a separate reservation. She gave him a charming smile and told him that he was in luck as Mr Abboud had already arrived. From the corner of his eye, Walker noticed the man's momentary hesitation and possible embarrassment but he affected to take no notice and continued working on his iPhone.

The man was shown to the table and the smiling Filipino girl announced to Mr Abboud that his guest had arrived early also. She seated the man, placed menus and a wine list on the table, and left. Both men briefly nodded a greeting to each other. Thankfully, the waitress had seated his guest's two friends out of earshot, although he felt that there wouldn't be much conversation to be heard anyway. He was neither surprised nor annoyed that the man had brought along two bodyguards. He was unarmed but was well capable of handling them. In any event, there would be no trouble.

The Bahraini fidgeted with his napkin, examined his menu in great detail, and generally seemed to be nervous. Perhaps he had been thrown by Walker's appearance, although he surely would have anticipated it. He was hardly likely to turn up dressed in a pair of jeans and a t-shirt.

He assumed at this stage that the man was from Bahrain, although he had no way of knowing if he had been the one who had delivered the message. Probably not, he thought, although the man was relatively young. Was this the man who had written to him, or was it an intermediary? Would the man have a free hand or would he have to call someone else for authorization? Walker had sat there since the man's arrival, observing him silently.

The waitress returned and enquired if they had made their choice? The Bahraini chose the lamb, rare, and Walker decided on the Hammour, a local fish delicacy. Neither man wanted a starter. At the girl's suggestion, both agreed to share a large house salad. From the wine list, she recommended an Amarone with the lamb and a Puligny Montrachet with the fish. Both men nodded their agreement. When the waitress had cleared the menus and left them a basket of assorted breads, the Bahraini began.

"Forgive me, my friend; I am not familiar with such situations. I am not aware of, how would you say, the protocol." He paused. Walker was silent and the man continued.

"We need, ah, we need some work done, and an associate told me you are the best in the business." He paused again but still Walker said nothing. "As I said in my letter, we are prepared to reward you handsomely should you be successful."

Walker wondered if the man knew what he charged, and what his concept of a handsome reward was. He knew that many of these people were ultra-rich, but they didn't have a reputation for paying their servants particularly well. In fact, earlier in the year the entire Middle Eastern region had been beset by protests from poor, disenfranchised people. Rulers had been forced into exile in Egypt and Tunisia and the conflict was continuing in Libya and Syria. There had been a backlash and the place where the rulers had reacted most harshly had been, surprisingly enough, the small island Kingdom of Bahrain.

The sommelier, a small pleasant faced man from Nepal, arrived with their wines and made a little ceremony out of opening the bottles, checking the vintage and requesting both men to sample their chosen wine. Walker's Montrachet was chilled to perfection and he nodded and smiled as the man waited eagerly. Abdullah did likewise and they spent a few moments savouring the drinks.

"As I was saying," the Bahraini recommenced, seemingly more relaxed and confident now, "we need some tasks undertaken, but we need to be sure who we are dealing with. How do I know that you are who you purport to be?"

Walker knew what the man meant but he smiled briefly. The question was ridiculous in the circumstances as he had not as yet said one word. He made direct eye contact with Abdullah for the first time and said his first words. "Because I'm here."

The Bahraini seemed to recoil slightly, then recovered his composure and nodded. "OK my friend, let me get, as you Americans say, straight to the point. I represent an organisation whose aims are to, shall we say, cause some disruption. If you agree to work for us, I am prepared to wire the sum of five million dollars to your nominated bank account tomorrow morning."

It was Walker's turn to be taken aback. Christ, this guy was bloody serious. Perhaps he could retire after all. He took a sip of his wine.

"This is to be an advance payment, of course," the Bahraini continued. "I have with me a list which, if you agree to my proposal, I will entrust to you. I would expect you to commit it to memory and then destroy it. No one but you and me must ever see it or even know of its existence. This is of the utmost importance." He paused for breath and took a large sip of red wine. Walker nodded to him to continue. "After each task on the list is accomplished, I will lodge a further five million dollars to your account. When the final task is completed, provided all other work has been done to our satisfaction, I will be prepared to pay you a bonus of fifty million dollars."

Walker now spoke at length for the first time. "How do you know I won't abscond when you pay me the first $5m, or the second, or the third? What if I cannot undertake all your tasks?"

Abdullah paused before he replied. "The first is a risk I will have to take, but I have, as you people say, done my homework on you. You come very well recommended, my friend, and you have a reputation for delivering and always keeping your side of the bargain. I feel sure you would do the same for us. If you do abscond, it is not of any great consequence. I do not wish to boast but let me assure you that $5m or even $50m is of little consequence to my partners and I. There are many more people involved in your trade whom we could then turn to, but for now, we wish to deal with you. Finally, if you cannot undertake some of the tasks due to unforeseen circumstances, you will obviously not be paid for them, but your final bonus will be paid provided you complete the last task on the list."

"So what exactly is it you wish me to do?"

With that, he withdrew a single sheet of type written paper from the pocket of his robe and placed it in front of Walker. Carl tried to hide his initial shock and surprise when he perused the list but the Bahraini was watching him intently. Momentarily, he thought, is this a joke, a wind-up? But he saw that his fellow diner was deadly serious and dismissed the thought.

He read the sheet a few times, storing the information, thinking names, places, dates, security systems, exploring possibilities, assessing risks. His usual strategy was to request some time to think over the offer. He would then conduct a more thorough analysis and give an answer within a few days. He might not be afforded that luxury with this one. Nevertheless, he couldn't agree straight off. He sipped more wine and considered.

Their food arrived and they paused to allow the charming Filipino to serve them. They ate in silence apart from agreeing that the food was really excellent. Walker had more time to think as he chewed his food. This was the big one, the one he never believed would come his way, and his natural pride was forcing him to say yes. But he was a cautious man. That was why he had lasted so long, and he sure intended to be around for a lot longer. If he decided to agree to the work, the tasks the Bahraini had presented him would probably represent his greatest challenge but, at first glance, none of them appeared to be impossible. All had been done before. Still, there would be great risks involved. Then again, he had encountered risk before and defeated it.

When he had eaten enough of his fish, he put down his knife and fork and returned the list to the Bahraini, who looked slightly alarmed. He began. "Your proposal is an interesting one but I cannot commit myself to your employment tonight. I will need to undertake much research. If you wish to go ahead and wire the money to my account, that is fine. If I decide not to accept your offer, I will guarantee you that it will be returned to you if you tell me the details of where to send it. If I decide to accept your offer, I trust you will keep to your part of our agreement. You can destroy the list yourself. I have already memorized it." He didn't mention that he had also used his napkin to wipe it clean of prints while Abdullah was helping himself from the salad bowl.

"But how will I know if you accept my offer? How do I contact you again?"

"You don't, other than through the same process that you contacted me the first time. When the first task on your list is completed, you will know that I have accepted. We will exchange bank account details before we part so that you can send the money and I can return it if I decide to decline your offer of employment." With this, he extracted a card from his robe and handed it to Abdullah. It contained the number of the new bank account he had opened that morning. He had, as a precaution, left instructions that all receipts were to be divided and forwarded to alternative accounts. The Bahraini scribbled a set of numbers on a separate card and reciprocated.

Walker had a final question. "There is much preparatory work to be undertaken if these tasks are to be accomplished. Do you have a timescale for their completion?"

"A perfectly understandable question. No, we have no timescale, but knowing what we do about your, as you say, 'track record', we trust that you will do your research thoroughly but will expedite the matter as quickly as possible."

He then called for the tab and paid with a credit card, leaving a generous tip. Both men declined dessert and coffee. Abdullah then got up to leave and they shook hands.

Walker stood and said, "Thank you for a pleasant evening and goodbye. I don't think we will meet again." The Bahraini nodded to the other table and walked back towards the wooden bridge, followed hurriedly by one of his associates, whose dessert had been unfortunately interrupted. The other man left a large wad of cash on the table and rushed after him.

Carl Walker waited and watched the three men board another golf buggy which then turned round and headed back along the small private roadway which paralleled the Jumeirah complex. The buggy passed most of the main buildings and seemed to be headed to the Burj Al Arab, which was where he had assumed the men would be staying. The Burj was now resplendent with its constantly changing light displays that ran up and down its frontage projecting kaleidoscopes of colour towards the night-time sky. He waited until the buggy was out of sight. Then he walked down to the little wharf, retrieved his boat, started the motor, and sped away into the night.

When he got back to his hotel room, Abdullah was elated and decided to treat himself to a nightcap. He felt sure the American was tempted by his offer and it would only be a matter of time before he convinced himself he could complete the tasks. These men were professionals, but they loved a challenge. He could sit back and watch as the American created chaos at his behest. And it had been his idea; his alone. Not the Afghan's, not that slimy Iraqi's – no, only his. And he would be rewarded!

He felt a cold shiver as he realized the enormity of what he had set in motion. He also recoiled as he remembered the moment the American's eyes had locked on to his and what he had seen there – or, more correctly, what he hadn't seen. It had been like looking into a bottomless pit, because there had been nothing there – nothing at all. He fell to his knees and faced Mecca. It was time for the night prayer.

Chapter 10 – The Visit

Seven thousand miles and nine time zones to the west, Mike Lyons was in a taxi on his way to Reagan International to catch the early evening flight back to London. He had had a very enjoyable weekend and was looking forward to working with the Americans.

As he had thought, he established an instant rapport with Paul Lincoln and they had got on famously. Paul insisted that Mike come home to join him and his wife Barbara for dinner on his first evening. They had connected immediately. Barbara and Paul had thought Mike was British, but once he spoke a few words, Barbara detected a definite trace of Irish in there. Both her parents were first generation Irish who had left the old country in the previous wave of emigration in the 1950's. Barbara had been indoctrinated in all things Irish when she was growing up, so she could talk to Mike for hours about everything from music to literature to sport. After a while trying to keep up, Paul had left them to it and went to check that the children were heading to bed.

Mike spent the first day and a half in intensive discussions with Paul and his deputy, Robert Weitz, before Paul took off with his family on a long-planned holiday to Disney World. There had been a very frank exchange of information and intelligence. Paul and Mike respected each other as seasoned professionals with the same ultimate purpose and neither man held back on the latest advances in anti-terrorism techniques.

While the D.H.S. had initially been set up as an umbrella body and a coordinator between the U.S.'s many existing agencies in order to streamline terrorist prevention and preparedness, it had evolved and effectively held the same remit as MI5 – the maintenance of internal security. Much of the work was desk bound and involved technology-based research and coordination, and analysis of intelligence collected by other agencies.

With more than 200,000 employees and a budget of almost $100 billion, D.H.S. was the third largest Cabinet Department. Mike had known it was big but even he was taken aback at the extent of its operations and sphere of influence. D.H.S. was responsible for determining the level of terrorist threat on a daily basis and it raised the threat level, which ran from green – low – to red – severe. It had subsumed a number of existing Government agencies, including Immigration and Border Protection, Customs, Transportation Security – responsible for aviation, land and water based security – the Coast Guard and the Secret Service. There were countless other components and one of their in-house jokes was that it was just as well they had high-powered computers to keep track of the numbers of sub-agencies and advisory groups.

It was in one of these sub-groups, The Office of Intelligence and Analysis, that Paul and Robert worked. They received masses of information from all of the various agencies and it was their job to ensure it was constantly updated, to analyse it and to identify and assess any threats. When they identified a threat, any other agency that needed to know was advised. If action was required in the field, this might be carried out by local police, state police or even F.B.I.

Paul and Robert's role was to identify, advise and observe, but they were also policemen and often took an active part in the operations mounted to neutralize the threats they had identified. The main aims of the office were all about improving, integrating and sharing intelligence so they were delighted to cooperate with an ally who had similar goals. Mike wondered if some of the mandarins back in London would have been as open and sharing with their information. To be fair, over the years, the British had probably been better at sharing and co-ordinating information amongst themselves, as he remembered from his constant liaison with the Secret Intelligence Service (SIS), Government Communications Headquarters (GCHQ) and the many other security and intelligence organisations in the UK.

After his first day of discussions, he was 100% certain that it would be useful, if this was a two-way exchange process. There were things he could advise D.H.S. on but there were also huge advances that they had made that would be useful to the British. There was always a certain amount of cooperation and information sharing between the transatlantic agencies, but this varied depending on the colour of the Government in power in either country, although he had to admit that that had changed greatly over the previous fifteen years, despite the leaders of both nations sometimes holding different philosophies.

But it would be good to advance it to a structured level. It would be as important for some of the Americans to visit the UK as it was for him to visit the States. He had proposed this to Paul, who had readily agreed, and he had called the Director General of MI5 that evening from his hotel to obtain clearance. While he had technically left MI5, he was still on assignment on a consultancy basis but when he spoke to Sir Marcus Evans by phone, he was greeted as warmly as if he was still part of the service.

"Why my dear chap, I think that is a splendid idea, we should have done it years ago. I'll trust you to organise it with your opposite number over there and you can give me all the details when you get back."

Mike's finely-tuned ear and his highly-developed listening and analytical skills kicked in, and for a moment he wondered if he was being played. They hadn't wanted him to leave but they knew he had wanted to travel, initially and especially to the U.S. Had the old codger come up with the assignment to keep him on board? He wouldn't be surprised! Still, if he was being played, he was not unhappy – in fact it was quite flattering in a way. Mike had never lost the modesty and self-effacing traits that are a mark of his countrymen and while he was as confident as the next man in most of his dealings, he still needed the approval and validation that most people ultimately need. So, it was nice to be appreciated and to feel wanted.

With this thought fresh in his mind, he had decided he would go and see some of D.C's nightlife. It was only eight pm. He was a free man and he had two more nights in this town. He loved to sight see, but there would not be time for any of that on this trip.

He had an early morning session with Robert who was bringing some guys from Secret Service. But that was not for another thirteen hours and he always liked to see how a city looked at night. You got a totally different perspective on things when it was dark. There were many things that you could not see because of the absence of light, but there were many others that only came properly into focus at night. Some cities he had visited looked marvellous at night but could look like slums in day time. Yet, some cities that were magnificent during the day could look boring and uninteresting when the sun went down. It possibly depended too on what the observer was looking for or what they wanted to see.

People were different in the evening too. Rushing around during the day completing whatever tasks they had set themselves, putting pressure on themselves, getting stressed. But for the majority, the night melted all that away. People relaxed, ate dinner, watched TV, had a beer, went to a club, whatever.

And then there were the night people, those that only seemed to come out when the sun went down. Mike recalled when he first became a policeman, realising that there was an entire subspecies out there that only appeared when it was dark. There were the obvious categories like pimps, hookers, thieves, burglars, drug pushers and countless other smaller groups. Then there were the addicts themselves, often far more dangerous, completely without scruples as they scrambled for their next fix. But there was also a whole raft of other groups doing legitimate tasks, from waiters, waitresses, bartenders, night-desk employees, security guards and the people who worked the night shifts of regular day jobs. This included the cops like himself, taxi drivers, ambulance crews, health service employees, and a whole range of other people.

It was now almost mid summer in Washington so it wouldn't be dark for hours yet but that didn't worry him. He decided to shower, grab a bite to eat and look at the town. Mike was a free spirit and loved to roam but he was not foolish. He could take care of himself but he was aware that D.C could be a dangerous place at night, particularly if you didn't know your way round.

He was staying in the Washington Plaza in Thomas Circle and decided to take the advice of the concierge. He was dressed in blue jeans and a pale blue polo shirt. He carried his light jacket as the evening was warm. All he wanted was a burger and a few beers so the man recommended Stetson's Bar and Grill, on – he thought he said U Street. He ordered Mike a taxi, even though it was a relatively short walk and a nice evening for it.

Mike arrived in the bar just after nine and it was crammed. He immediately liked the look and feel of the place. There was a beat-up black and white tile floor, large wooden tables seating groups of all shapes and sizes. The TV was showing a baseball game and everyone seemed to be talking at once so the din was incredible. There was a long polished wooden bar with numerous high stools and he spied one that had just become free at the far end. The bar itself was impressive and well stocked.

"My, you sure arrived at the right time," said the lady seated on the adjacent stool as he seated himself.

"Looks like it," he said. "Perhaps it's beginner's luck?"

"Ah, first time in town, huh?"

The girl was tall with dark hair, brown eyes, with a clear olive skinned complexion and she looked good enough to eat. She was dressed in blue jeans and a cowboy shirt, like about 90% of the bar's patrons.

"Yes, it's my first visit to Washington, although I have been to the States before."

'You're, let me guess, English; no, Irish, right?"

"Guilty as charged," he said with a smile.

The bartender arrived. "So what's it gonna be, Long Neck, Pint or Pitcher? Or maybe you fancy a shot?"

Her name badge said Jan and he had a recollection of American bartenders introducing themselves before they served a customer; as in, "Hi, I'm Jan, I'm your bartender for this evening. So, what's it gonna be?"

"Ah, have you made your mind up sir?" Jan said.

He suddenly realised he was staring at her and immediately apologized. "Sorry ma'am, I was distracted; the atmosphere in here is really good. I'll have a Miller Long Neck please."

"Why, thanks for the compliment; coming right up, sir."

She went to get the beer and placed in front of him. He thanked her and took a long sip. The lady beside him excused herself to slip out to go to the ladies' room and he sipped his beer and drank in the atmosphere. Apart from the bar, he told himself, hey, he liked Washington. He had only been in the bar two minutes and he had met two stunning women.

Well, OK, Jan was not stunning, but she had that easy captivating smile that made the hairs stand up on the back of your neck when she flashed it; which, in her line of work, she did frequently, he was sure. He imagined she could pull you into her cocoon and make you totally subservient within a short space of time. She was not classically beautiful, with a small heart-shaped face, smallish nose, blue eyes and brown hair - but she was extremely attractive and then there was that smile. Oh, if women only knew the power they possessed. For sure, many did, but for him a nice warm smile could transform an ordinary girl into a queen. She looked to be in her late 20's. Yeah, dream on he thought.

The lady with the dark hair and the cowboy shirt returned and resumed her seat. "So, you spending long in town?" she resumed, propping her right elbow on the bar and giving him a sideways look.

"Four days," he replied. "It's business, but I'm managing to get a lot done."

"Good for you," she said. He always loved the positive attitude Americans showed in almost any situation. He smiled.

"Ya mind if I ask what business you're in?" she asked.

"Not at all," said Mike. "I'm in law enforcement." He never thought there was any point in trying to pretend otherwise as friends had told him from his earliest days on the force that he looked every inch a cop.

"Hey, that's cool. An Irish cop. Good to meet you, I'm Wendy," she said, and offered her hand. Mike reciprocated and didn't bother to complicate things by telling her he was really a British policeman even though he was Irish. He rarely did unless asked.

"Good to meet you," he said. "Name's Mike. I'm spending a few days with some of your fellow countrymen, exchanging a few ideas. What business are you in yourself?"

"Ah, I'm in real estate. It's real tough right now. You know we had the crash in '08 with the sub-prime crisis?" Mike nodded. "Well, things have picked up a little, but it's still a jungle out there. Ah, I did OK in the boom, so I can't complain really."

"Good for you," he said, and she smiled, realizing he had repeated what she had said; so perhaps there was some chemistry? She was older than Jan, but not by much, maybe 35? Ah, hell, it was impossible to tell these days. He himself was nearly 49 but probably looked a few years younger. So he was told, anyway. Why was he comparing her to Jan?

He had finished his beer and noticed that Wendy had drained hers also, so he asked politely, "May I buy you another beer?"

"Why, sure," she said, balancing on her right elbow again, which caused her hair to slip down over her face. She brushed it back and he signalled Jan for two more beers. Did he detect an ever-so-slight cooling in her attitude as she placed the two long necks on the bar? No, it was probably nothing, because then she smiled that smile again. Christ! He turned back to Wendy and resumed their conversation.

"Is right now a good time to buy a property in D.C.?"

"Well, maybe. It depends on what area you'd wanna buy in, though. You thinking of investing?"

"Uh, no, I was just wondering. The property market back home went through the floor when the recession hit and has continued to go down. I was just wondering if the same thing happened here?'

"Ah, sure; well, maybe not to the same extent."

They spent the next two hours lost in conversation about property, traffic, the armed forces, life in D.C., family, the U.S. federal debt, and God knew what else. Time seemed to fly and Wendy was brilliant company. He completely forgot about his plans to visit a number of other bars. He also forgot to have his burger, but not to worry; he had had a good lunch and the breakfast in the Washington Plaza was excellent. Mike was in no way cocky or over confident by nature, but he had a hunch that he might be sharing it. He didn't want to push his luck, but sure; what was there to lose? The bar didn't seem to be closing any time soon so at around 02.00, after, was it seven or eight beers?

He'd lost count; he took advantage of a break in the conversation to say: "Ya know Wendy, I've gotta look and sound half intelligent to some of Washington's finest cops in the morning so I should really head back to my hotel. Can I drop you somewhere? Or maybe you'd like a nightcap, or do Americans use that term?" he added as an afterthought. She laughed, showing perfect, glistening white teeth.

"Why, yes we do, and that would be lovely, thank you very much Mike."

Ah yes, his first night alone in Washington had been a great one, and he was looking forward to returning. To the best of his recollection, he couldn't remember having a nightcap of any sort, but he did remember a night of sheer passion and he felt a warm glow as the memory came back to him. Wendy had been loving, caring and completely uninhibited, comfortable and at ease with herself and with him. He asked her if she could meet him again the following night but although she said she genuinely would have loved to, it was the weekend and she had promised to drive down to Baltimore to have dinner with her Mum. She kept her promises and although he would have liked to have seen her again, he was impressed that she had; he liked that in people. Anyway, he had her number and he would be back. And then there was Jan – why did she keep intruding on his thoughts?

He never thought of himself as promiscuous. He was single, and he thought that meeting girls was the most natural thing in the world. He didn't subscribe to the largely western notion of faithfulness to one woman only. Now, if a guy got married, that was a different thing but he never had. He fell in love often, and could never remember falling out. He remained on good terms with anyone with whom he had ever had a relationship. At one point, he had loved someone very deeply, but that had ended sadly so he didn't dwell on it. No; life was good, the world was his oyster, and he was about to see a lot more of it.

However, first he would return to London, brief the DG, then bury himself in his P.C. for about two weeks, working out the joint programme with the Americans. The taxi pulled to the sidewalk and he got out, took his bag and paid the driver. The weather had become slightly overcast, and there was a threat of rain. He checked his watch and found he had two hours before his flight was due to take off. As he was in Business Class again, he decided to use the rapid check-in counter and priority security and immigration channels, and enjoy the charms of the Business Lounge. He cleared everything within fifteen minutes and settled down in the lounge. He took a glass of Chablis and opened the latest Michael Connelly blockbuster while he waited for his flight to be called.

Chapter 11 – The Planning

The Bahraini had not said whom he was representing, but Walker had no doubt. He was sure the man had resources and operatives everywhere, but could he rely on them? Fanatics had their uses, but professionalism wasn't their strong suit. Also, he was fairly certain that 90% of these guys might have been under surveillance.

He thought long and hard. He would need complex arrangements on this one, but the slightest slip or the wrong word could derail him. He decided the only really safe way was to make his own arrangements. He would avoid all communication and speak to no one unless it was crucial to his mission. It would be difficult, but he had done it before.

Then there were the contacts he had in many of the locations the Bahraini wanted him to operate in. He was owed favours in most of them. Perhaps it was time to call them in? But would people cooperate if they knew what he was undertaking? Initially, no one would be aware, of course, but they would eventually realize it, and that might compromise his own personal security. It was a poser. He knew he had perfected his routine of disappearing, and was confident he could repeat it, but there was a direct relationship between his ability to continually repeat the act and the amount of resources deployed to try to apprehend him. He did have contingency plans worked out for most situations. If the worst came to the worst, palms could be greased and accommodations arrived at – but that too would only stretch so far.

He even had a contingency plan in place to vacate his Lake Mary home if it came to that. If truth be known, he had two, one which included his wife and children and one for him alone. He tried to put that to the back of his mind as he felt it would not come to that. He may have been a ruthless, cold-blooded killer with few scruples when it came to his profession, but he still loved his wife and kids and didn't wish to spend the rest of his days drinking tequila in some little taverna in Mexico or South America. No, he would research, check, double check and research again and he would plan and then disassemble the complete plan into its component parts, reassemble it and back up each section. Then he would construct and deconstruct alternative plans. He would read everything he could find on all of his potential targets. He would learn everything there was to learn. He would have to get to know them as much as it was possible to; their routines; their lifestyles; their strengths and, more importantly, their weaknesses. There was no margin for error on this one. It might be easier at the beginning but if anyone discerned the pattern, it would make it progressively more difficult.

After careful consideration and reconsideration, he decided not to involve anyone else at all. It would mean contacting known associates and if people started asking enough questions and offered enough incentives, someone might talk. One thing would lead to another and he might be tracked down. No, better to trust to his own resources, plan and act on his own – tell no one. He had done it before on dangerous jobs in the early days when he hadn't been sure where loyalties lay, and when he couldn't afford to be as choosy about the jobs he took on as he was now.

Why was he doing this? What drove him on? Did he need the buzz after all? Would he still need it when he was finished, if he managed to finish? Would he be able to retire? The thought unnerved him and he needed a coffee and a cigarette to calm himself. He strove to re-concentrate and returned to his planning and research.

He mentally went over the list again. He was happy enough with half of the targets. More work was required on the other half. He just had to find the openings, then decide the specifics and the back-up plans. Everyone was vulnerable; there was no such thing as total security. Everyone had their weak spots or even blind spots. You just had to search for them and use them. Some people made it easy, some difficult, but he'd get there in the end. If he found someone with no weaknesses, he'd have to create some – create a diversion of some kind to flush them out.

He'd never failed to complete an assignment when he'd agreed to undertake it and he'd operated in lots of places where people had felt they had tight security. He doubted he'd have gotten to Saddam Hussein in the man's heyday in Baghdad; but then again, he'd never tried – no one had asked him. He had taken out dictators on more than one continent, all of whom were heavily guarded.

One of his greatest strengths was his invisibility. He never exposed himself, so police never knew who they were looking for. If people didn't know who they were looking for, and they were under enormous pressure from their bosses or political leaders to come up with a suspect, they often invented one. Over the years, many innocent men had served long jail sentences because of huge political and populist pressure to "get" the people who had planted a particular bomb or carried out some atrocity. The history of British-Irish relations was littered with such cases. In some of the jobs he had carried out, it might be said that police were looking for a tall Englishman or a small French man or a German of medium height or whatever. It didn't necessarily mean that they were, but it told him that they were unlikely to be looking for him. He would then slip out of the country or the region in the guise of someone who didn't remotely fit the description of the suspect, if he hadn't already gone.

He remembered once in Central America being somewhat worried. He had liquidated a senior member of the cabinet, apparently on the instructions of the Prime Minister, although he had dealt with an intermediary. He had decided against an immediate exit, just in case of a trap. He had thought his cover had been blown when, lying low in his hotel room a few days after the shooting, he heard in the bar that police were looking for an American of medium height and build. He had shrugged and affected disinterest.

However, the following day he had checked out and taken a taxi to the airport. But no American flew out that day. No one attracted the police's attention at all, least of all a hunched weather-beaten man who constantly chewed on tobacco and smelt like he hadn't washed in weeks. The man had flown to Guadalajara where he had morphed into a British tourist. He flew onwards to Mexico City and from there to Los Angeles, where he spent a couple of leisurely days. Later that week, a Mr Thomas Clarke had flown from L.A. to Orlando.

It never failed to amuse him that whenever he affected the guise of someone whose personal hygiene habits were questionable, he was waved through without question. Whether it was people's wish to avoid contact with someone who smelt foul, or whether security forces imagined that no self-respecting criminal would look or smell like that, he wasn't sure. Whatever it was, the guise had served him well. He kept most of his wardrobe in a concealed room in his cabin outside Orlando, where he had also concealed a large cache of weapons and ammunition. He also had several "drops" in various parts of the country where he kept back-ups. He thought he would be accessing most of his resources on this one, and he thought he might even have to introduce one or two more personalities, but that wouldn't cause a problem.

He stopped his musing and returned to his research. The internet, he thought, was the greatest tool ever invented. He accepted that a lot of the information on it was far from reliable, but if one double-checked and cross-checked the information, he was happy with the degree of accuracy, at least for research purposes. It would only be used as an aid to his plans. Everything would be double-checked on site.

The other great advantage of the internet was hacking. He wasn't what hackers would call a legend, but he was more than competent enough for his purpose. He could not penetrate the complex firewalls of government agencies, but commercial set ups were usually child's play. Corporations chasing dollars didn't want to spend millions on security systems when they couldn't imagine people wanting to break in to their systems anyway.

Basically, if your computer was in any way connected to a phone or data line or a Wi-Fi link, it was vulnerable.

Take hotels – obtaining guest lists was a stroll. Room numbers – no problem. Pattern of use – whether the guest usually ate out or took room service; whether they used the mini bar. All seemingly innocuous information, but very useful if you wanted to gain access to a room or someone in it. You could compile quite a dossier in a very short time. To gain access to a lot of information nowadays, you didn't even have to hack. Social networking was the latest craze, and people were tripping over themselves to tell people where they were going or what they were doing at a certain time on their Facebook page or on Twitter. The people he was interested in this time didn't all subscribe to social network sites, but nonetheless, any of them in the public eye usually announced well in advance where they would be on any particular day, or had well-established patterns. People didn't think about this when they released information, because nobody wanted to think they were vulnerable, and most would be shocked if they heard they were a target.

His extensive trawls through the internet and his protracted hacking for information could not be traced back to him. He was adept at hiding his IP address and routing his searches through a multitude of other servers and addresses. If someone tried to track what he was accessing at the moment, seated in his comfortable Orlando Mansion, they would end up in an internet café in Johannesburg.

Yes, he was happy that all precautions were in place and he hummed to himself as he discovered another interesting connection to one of his research subjects. This offered yet another alternative. He decided to treat himself to another coffee and a cigarette. Like everyone else, he needed to reinforce his own belief in himself to gain self-confidence. He constantly told himself he was the best; and he was, wasn't he?

He began to feel a few qualms as he scanned the list. He only took out people who deserved it, right? He could argue that all his previous hits did or was that just his own self-justification? He scanned the list again. There might be some collateral damage on this one. Pity, but he had had collateral damage before; went with

114

the territory. He poured the coffee and lit his cigarette. It would work out fine.

He took a break and went to pick up his wife and children at the mall. Cindy had wanted to get some clothes for the girls, and he had promised to meet them and bring them to McDonalds for a treat afterwards. He parked in the underground lot and took the escalator up to the food hall.

He saw Cindy and waved as Abigail and Paige rushed to meet him, almost tripping over each other in the process. "Hey Daddy, Daddy, look what we bought," they squealed, competing to open the packages and show off their new summer outfits.

"Hey, these are so cute," he said. "Is your Mommy good to you or what?"

They ordered their food and found a table overlooking one of the retail floors. The girls tucked into their burgers and fries. Carl had got some chicken but Cindy was just having a salad.

"You are so disciplined, babe," he said. "That's how you stay so slim and beautiful." She smiled and their hands touched.

Over to the right sat another family, a Mom and Dad with a little boy and an older girl. "Hey, ain't they cute?" said Cindy, and Carl briefly looked in their direction.

"Sure, but so are we, honey," he laughed. Hmmm, he thought, guy looks like a cop.

Chapter 12 – The Senator

Senator Dan Carter was the coming thing, the new-kid-in-town, the flavour-of-the-month, the darling of the society matrons of Atlanta and almost everybody else in the Deep South. He was now making a serious impact on national politics as well. He had come to prominence with the rise of the self-styled Tea Party, composed mainly of Republicans and those to their right.

Starting as a populist movement as lately as 2009, they were conservative and libertarian, with basically twin aims of reducing Government spending and opposition to taxation. They also had an adherence to an old-fashioned interpretation of the Constitution. They saw themselves as representing old style free enterprise America, the "I worked damn hard for what I've got and I don't see why I should pay taxes to support layabouts" type of approach. The actual origin of the name was clouded in mystery; some said it stood for Taxed Enough Already, but most agreed that it was a reference to the Boston Tea Party in 1773 when colonists objected to a British tax on tea by dumping it in the harbour.

The Tea Party was not an organised political party, but more of a movement. They would have seen their natural home as the Republican Party, even though they were strongly critical of many in that party. Likewise, some prominent Republicans had severely criticized them as a disruptive influence. They had groupings in both houses of Congress and sponsored candidates sympathetic to their twin causes.

In the summer of 2011, they had reached the zenith of their power and were blocking the President's bill to raise the federal debt ceiling. For the first time in its history, the biggest economy on earth was close to default on its debt and would not be able to pay its bills. Commentators hyped up the possible consequences of a failure to agree the budget. Employees might not get paid, such as the troops on the ground in Iraq and Afghanistan. It was likely that a deal would be done, but with a third political grouping in the mix, severe compromises would have to be made to push through the legislation.

To be fair, the Tea Party's simple message was that the Government should not spend any more than it took in and that borrowing had reached frightening levels. At the same time, they were unwilling to support higher taxation. The fact that they had strong support in both houses and that the polls showed significant populist support suggested that mainstream politicians had not been listening to all their people. Having achieved a strong platform, it was likely that the group was here to stay. Georgia, with its strong history of fiscal conservatism, was home to many of the group's members including its most prominent spokesman.

Dan Carter was a two-term Senator who had already had a lot of influence in Congress and he caught the Tea Party wave in late 2009. He was a shrewd, savvy politician and, in many people's opinion, he was destined for power broking at a higher and maybe the ultimate level. He was being strongly spoken about as a candidate in the following year's Presidential election and many believed that if he kept riding the wave, it would become overpowering and sweep him all the way to the White House. In terms of campaign funding, he had already been promised millions of dollars and a lot more would be forthcoming when he started to gather momentum.

He was in many ways the ideal candidate for the top job. He was tall, well built, with dark hair cut short. He was heavily tanned and extremely fit. At 52, he was young and energetic. He looked the part and said all the right things. He was married to the beautiful Cheryl and they had two boys aged twenty and eighteen. He was highly intelligent, graduating Georgia Tech at the very top of his class in I.T. studies. He had served in the military, most notably with distinction during the first Gulf War in 1991 as the commander of a unit that had infiltrated behind enemy lines and successfully reconnoitred targets for the smart bombs of the air force.

He had seen action when their unit was discovered and pinned down inside occupied Kuwait. Thankfully by that stage, the Iraqi forces morale had been seriously dented and once the Americans showed they were prepared to stand and fight, the Iraqis had disappeared. Still, it had been a highly dangerous situation and Dan had been awarded the Army Distinguished Service Cross.

He was highly communicative, having majored in I.T. and was constantly issuing statements on Facebook and Twitter giving his views on the issues of the day. He used every media outlet available and knew *how* to use them. There was no doubt that as well as appealing to conservative Middle America, he would command the attention of younger voters. When he met them he spoke their language and seemed to understand their problems.

He was from old Georgia moneyed stock; in fact, very old. His family had been among the settlers during the gold rush of 1829 in the north Georgia Mountains. They had been one of the successful ones and had invested their wealth wisely in great tracts of rich farmland, particularly when the Cherokee Nation were moved west in 1838. The family had taken the wrong side in the Civil War but although the war was lost, they won the peace and became one of the richest farmers producing pecans and peanuts as well as livestock including cattle and hogs. The family became heavily involved in State politics from around the 1880's and Dan's great-great Grandfather, old Cletus Carter, had been Governor of Georgia in the 1890's.

Other members of the family had continued to serve but Dan was the first to make it on to the national stage. He had won a close contest in 2002 and having consolidated his position and largely delivered on his promises, had been re-elected easily in 2008. He had been a very successful public representative and had been a close ally of the military and big business in his home state, campaigning for tax breaks and working in a highly effective way in Washington's powerful committees. He had always been nationalist-minded and had been a strong supporter of the set up of Homeland Security after 9/11, a stance that did him no harm in his election campaign. Georgia probably has more military bases than any other State and the military is a huge employer. But big business is also present and the State is strong in automobile and aircraft manufacturing, food and chemical processing, printing and publishing. Dan tended carefully to the lobbying needs of each sector.

He had huge energy and was a tireless worker for his interests and supporters. He was also particularly politically astute and could see opportunities faster than others. This was probably why his forebears had only made it as far as domestic politics whereas Dan was going to go all the way, or he sure as hell was going to try.

He hadn't yet indicated his interest in obtaining the nomination as things were complicated. The atmosphere in Washington was toxic and in the current upheaval, it was difficult to know who would support you or who your friends really were. There were talks of splits on both sides and disillusionment with the President. But he supposed politics was always like that. It was knowing how to play the game and he felt he knew just how to play it. While he had made no formal announcement, it was an open secret that he was going to run next year. It was just a question of timing his entry to the optimum advantage.

He had already discussed it openly with his closest supporters and had the bones of a campaign strategy and key staff on board. He had also, perhaps more importantly, discussed it with his wife, who was also 100% supportive and enthusiastic.

She stopped him in his tracks, however, when she said, "You're gonna have to clean up your act though Dan; you go running for that job, those vultures are gonna dig deep to get stuff on you so you need to be squeaky clean."

He was slow to reply. "But honey, I mean, I've got a perfect military record, exemplary academic and political C.V. I mean, what's the problem?"

"Shit Dan, you think I'm totally stupid? Those two bitches have gotta go. You really think I don't know? Yes, Dan, both, the one here and the one in Washington. I might be your wife, but I'm also your strongest political ally, and don't you forget it. I know what gives, Dan, and if we are going on this journey, it's gotta be just us, or we will fail. I know it."

Shoot; man's oldest failing had been his undoing, he thought. He managed a sheepish, "OK honey, I guess you're right. I'd better speak to them."

"I think we need to do a bit more than that – *honey*," she stressed. "It might be better for everyone if you just didn't see them again. Leave the details to me and don't worry about it. Just behave; keep your head down and your zipper up!"

He knew Cheryl was very bright and fiercely ambitious in her own right. She was a trained lawyer and a very senior executive in Coca Cola, whose headquarters were in Atlanta; and she was nobody's fool. How did she know? Did she have him followed? Had he been careless? Mind you, they say women always know, and Dan was no different from most other men; naïve in such matters. He was a lucky man, he thought, as she was prepared to stand by him and their life continued as normal.

Quietly and without fuss, Cheryl paid unannounced visits to both of Dan's mistresses in their apartments when they least expected it. She was calm and business-like, almost as if she was wrapping up a deal for her employer. She didn't play the injured or hurt wife role in the slightest. There were no hysterics, no tears – at least not from her – and no violence. She presented each woman with an ultimatum: they were to cease all contact with her husband right now and into the future. They were not to call him, text him, e-mail him or see him in person. They were furthermore not to speak to anyone about the affair now or in the future.

They were both presented with an agreement to sign to indicate their assent. They could have a day or two to think it over if they wished or they could run it by their lawyers. If they signed the agreements, Cheryl would:

1.   Not make their lives a misery. She assured them she could and they seemed to believe her.

2.   Wire the sum of $250,000 to their nominated bank accounts on receipt of the signed agreement.

If they broke the agreements in any way, the money would have to be returned and enough dirt would be shovelled in their personal direction to bury them. If they were ever questioned about the Senator by anyone, including but not limited to members of the media, they were to say that yes, they knew the Senator, they had met him many times in the course of their work or at political gatherings. The Senator was a fine man and no, of course there was no question of them having had a relationship. The Senator, as far as they knew, was devoted to his wife and family.

Both women had signed up, banked the cash and moved on with their lives. Neither had been in love with Dan, but he was a very attractive and charming man and they had loved the feel of involvement in powerful Washington politics. But the money provided more than adequate compensation.

It was a beautiful sunny July afternoon but almost too hot and stifling in the city when Dan emerged from the committee meeting and hurried down the steps of the Capitol Building. He had just had another victory. Having been thwarting the White House for months, they had now managed to block proposed legislation from their own party because they were still unhappy with the level of cuts in public spending. The whole thing had become a circus, but he was happy to be a player as he was attracting more and more publicity. He was accompanied by his Press Secretary, Mel Thomas, and his Personal Secretary, Shirley Roberts. As usual, he was approached by a phalanx of reporters. He feigned hurry and his face took on a very grave expression.

"Senator, is it true you are gonna continue to block this bill until you get everything you are demanding?"

"Senator, surely your group are playing games and this is not good for the image of the United States abroad?"

"Senator, isn't it true that you are using this issue to further your own personal profile with a view to seeking a nomination for the Presidency?"

He paused as he reached the sidewalk. He looked carefully at the cameras and put on his best "someone has to care about America" face.

"Ladies and Gentlemen," he began. "Look, we've been through all this already. As y'all know, it is simply the case that America is living beyond its means. We cannot keep raising the borrowing limit indefinitely. I mean, come on, the figures are alarming. Do you want your children and your children's children paying for the waste of today? Well, I sure as hell don't. Someone has to shout stop. There have got to be budget cuts. This administration has borrowed recklessly and has brought our great country practically to its knees financially."

"But Senator, what about healthcare? What about the people who cannot afford it? Surely there can be balance, and aren't higher taxes the answer?"

He paused again, for effect. "Look, most of you folks are no different to me. We've all worked damn hard for what we've got and we've earned it. Why should we pay higher taxes to fund crazy federal schemes? I believe in taking care of the poor and disadvantaged as much as the next man, but what I'm talking about here is the sheer size of the Federal Government. You wouldn't believe the amount of money that's wasted in there."

"Senator, Senator, is there any room for compromise?"

"For sure there is. We Americans will always work out our problems, but we've got to have realism and I'm afraid that's lacking right now. Look, folks, I really gotta go. Thank y'all for your time."

"Senator, a final question: Have you decided to seek a nomination for the Presidency?"

He smiled that brilliant white-toothed golden smile:

"Look folks, we've got a President and a damn fine one. There isn't a vacancy right now and that's all I'll say on the subject. Thank y'all again."

He rushed to the air-conditioned comfort of the chauffeur driven town car. "Hey, that was just great, Dan," said Mel Thomas when the car had pulled away from the curb and they were secure behind the smoked glass. "Keep them guessing but don't commit till the time is right." All three did a high five and Shirley positively beamed.

As clever as she was, Cheryl had missed out on Shirley. She was 27 years old and had been his personal secretary for the past four years. She had a prodigious work output and was totally devoted and committed to Dan. She was highly professional but as they had spent so many long hours together, and as the Senator was a highly attractive man who had a problem with his zipper, the inevitable had happened. He wasn't worried about it, though, as he had no doubt that Shirley was stone mad crazy in love with him and would never betray their trust.

The thought briefly occurred to him that perhaps Cheryl had known that too but had left well enough alone, lest he stray on to more dangerous territory. Whatever, he mused. He had been in Atlanta for the weekend and was looking forward to checking into his suite at the Fairmont. He was also looking forward to seeing more of Shirley, a lot more! She was small and slim and curvy and dynamite in the sack. Mel and Shirley were also staying at the hotel and as they each headed for their rooms, they all agreed to meet for dinner at 8.30.

Dan used his key card to enter the opulent suite and threw his briefcase and jacket on to the couch. He went to the bedroom and used the adjoining bathroom. He ran the shower and came back to the main room to head for the liquor cabinet. He poured himself two fingers of bourbon and downed the drink in one. He was on a high. Everything was working to his advantage. He was orchestrating this campaign perfectly. He went back to the bedroom and stripped off the rest of his clothes to shower. As he was purposefully striding towards the bathroom, he momentarily thought he detected a shadow in his peripheral vision and he turned to check. He never completed the movement and never felt the double tap of the silenced Glock.

Shirley had a card key for the Senator's suite as she needed to move back and forth for work so it never raised any eyebrows. She had gone back to her own room, showered and then dressed in underwear and a bathrobe. They had almost two hours before dinner and she was going to make the most of it. She padded down the soft, carpeted corridor, and used her key card to enter the suite silently. The connecting door between the main living room and the bedroom was open and she could hear the shower running.

"Hey honey," she called. "Don't be too long in there; somebody's bought something new in Victoria's Secret!" She crossed the room and entered the bedroom.

She gasped in horror as she took in the sight of the Senator's prone body on the carpet. Then she saw the bullet wounds and she screamed and screamed and screamed.

Part Two
July

Chapter 13

Mike knew Paul would not be waiting for him, as they had agreed when he arrived back in Washington to put the Anglo-American anti-terrorist cooperation programme in place. He had landed at 7.30 pm, switched on his cell phone and seen the message, "Sorry, can't meet you this time Mike, something really heavy has come up; will catch up with you later." He thought no more of it, as he could easily get a taxi, until he noticed the heavy security presence throughout the airport. The queues at Immigration control were longer than usual and he noticed the officers were taking a little extra time to process each arriving passenger.

Something heavy must have happened for sure, he thought. He approached a slightly nervous-looking heavily armed policeman and queried, "Sorry to bother you, but is there a major alert in place?"

"I'm sorry sir; I'm not at liberty to disclose that information." Then, as an afterthought, "Say, buddy, are you a cop?"

Recognised again, Mike thought, with a wry smile.

"Yes" he said, offering his police ID. "I'm working with some of your guys on some mutual cooperation."

The cop briefly scanned the ID and said, "Follow me sir." Mike was brought directly to the Diplomatic entrance where there was no queue and rushed through.

He profusely thanked the policeman, who dismissed this with a wave and replied, "Sir, this evening a senior elected representative has been shot dead. There's a major alert out there for his killer, so expect to encounter delays. Enjoy your trip to Washington, sir."

Mike again thanked the man and rushed to the luggage belt to retrieve his bag. As he stood waiting, he hit "reply" to Paul's message and typed, "Heard the bad news. I'll proceed to my hotel. You need any help?" He offered this last as a natural policeman's inbuilt instinct to help another if he could but he didn't expect a reply. He was surprised when, two minutes later, just as he had collected his bag, his phone rang.

"Hey Mike, welcome back buddy. Sorry for the inconvenience."

"Not at all Paul, I understand completely. So what's happening?"

"Ah shit, Mike, we've got a major one. Everyone's favourite Senator's been shot dead. I've got everyone including the Police Chief, the F.B.I. and even the frickin Speaker of the House on my tail. I've got a press conference in half an hour. The press and everyone else are screaming for information, and I've got zilch!"

"You want me to come down there to offer some support?"

"Why sure, why not? Join the party. Everyone else is here. Drop your bag at the Plaza and I'll get you cleared through the cordon. Oh, it's at the Fairmont. See you soon, man."

Mike was struck at how calm Paul sounded. It must have been mayhem down there, and yet he had the good sense to remain focused and even invited Mike to join him. Well, no one ever solved a crime by getting highly stressed and ranting. At times like this, you needed to keep calm and think. Mike as yet knew nothing about the crime but as he jumped in the taxi and asked the driver to take him to the Plaza, he decided to use the transit time to do some thinking himself.

He had been involved in many high profile cases over the years but he had never seen anything like this before; not even close. Television station vans and trucks stretched for over two full city blocks. Reporters with cameramen and sound engineers in tow were everywhere, waiting like vultures to swoop down on anyone who might have had the tiniest scrap of information. Had anyone seen something? Did anyone have information on the crime? Had anyone seen or thought they had seen the perp? Nature abhors a vacuum and in the absence of any official announcement, people were busy speculating and manufacturing their own stories. There was no shortage of passers-by and fascinated onlookers willing to offer an opinion or to say what a dreadful crime it had been, and how the city wasn't safe, and what were the authorities doing about it? Some were even bolder and speculated that they had seen something relevant to the case. As time went on, the stories got wilder and even more far-fetched. Conspiracy theories were thrown around. Were we entering a new era in politics in this country where political opponents with strongly held diametrically opposed views were willing to kill each other? Surely not?

It was pushing 9 pm when Mike approached the barrier that had been erected about half a block away from the hotel, and was stopped by a uniformed policeman. He explained who he was and that Paul had agreed to allow him access. Having validated that by radio, the man waved him through.

As he got closer to the hotel, he got an even greater sense of the drama that was unfolding. There were two ambulances, numerous police cars all parked at crazy angles, and several limousines, which all seemed to be abandoned. Uniformed police were everywhere. There were serious-looking men in suits and fit-looking guys in flak jackets with the letters FBI stencilled on the back.

He found Paul in a corner of the front lobby, in conversation with three men that he introduced as Lieutenant La Vonn Thomas and Sergeant Chico Perez from Homicide Division, Washington P.D. and Special Agent Pete Stewart from the F.B.I. All the men seemed easily familiar with each other. Each stood and shook hands with firm grips, warmly welcoming Mike as a fellow police officer.

"Excuse me, guys," Mike started, "but if this is a bad time?"

"Not at all," said La Vonn, "sit right down and join us. This is just the calm before the storm," he said wistfully.

"No one's quite sure about jurisdiction on this one," Paul began, "so for now, we are all just cooperating. The Senator returned to the hotel after committee, got here at approximately 6.30 with two aides, including his secretary. He apparently went straight to his room. The secretary went to her own room, showered, then she went to the Senator's room to do some work before dinner." Mike caught the slightly-elevated eyebrows, which suggested there was more that was not being said.

"She found the Senator shot dead on the floor of his bedroom at 6.40 approximately. A passer-by heard her screams and alerted hotel security, who rushed to the room and then called 911. The secretary, Ms Shirley Roberts, is heavily traumatized and is not a suspect at this time. We do, however, hope to speak to her as soon as we can. It's highly likely the perp entered the room using a master key card, source of which is unknown but we have checked the in-house room key control and it doesn't seem to have been issued from here. All key cards issued are coded and assigned to individuals. The one used to gain entry was a rogue card, possibly duplicated by hacking into the hotel's computer. The master computer that records all door movements shows an entry to the Senator's suite at 6.05 using the rogue card. There's an entry with the Senator's own card at 6.32 and one using the secretary's card at 6.40. The door was also exited at 6.34. There were no signs of any forced entry through doors or windows so we have to assume the 6.05 and the 6.34 are our perp. Hotel confirmed the suite was fully cleaned and serviced this morning. Entry and exit times of 11.45 and 12.05 tally."

"The Senator was shot twice with a pistol, presumably silenced, at close range. Make and model of the pistol yet to be established. Both bullets to the head. Death would have been instantaneous. The ME has had the body removed for immediate post mortem examination. We're waiting on the SOCO boys to finish up but we don't really expect them to find anything. Looks like a professional hit, and as of now, we have got zero to go on. The Senator's wife and family are at home in Atlanta. They've been informed by the Governor, I believe, and are being comforted by friends. Did I leave anything out, La Vonn?"

"No, I guess that about covers it, Paul. Clear, Pete? Chico?" The others nodded.

"I gotta go talk to the ladies and gentleman of the press. You guys coming?"

Mike could sense the weariness in Paul and Pete Stewart as they rose to join La Vonn for the press briefing. "Hey Mike, you ever seen a feeding frenzy?" said Pete.

"Yeah right," said La Vonn, "except that in this case we don't have anything to feed these piranhas so I guess they'll just eat us instead."

"Best of luck guys," Mike said, "I think I'll sit this one out."

An impromptu press centre had been set up in the hotel's ballroom. Paul, La Vonn and Pete sat at a hastily arranged plinth that had been erected at the far end. La Vonn introduced himself and his two colleagues and started.

"Ladies and gentlemen, this evening, Senator Dan Carter was brutally murdered in his suite here in this hotel by a person or persons unknown. The full and complete resources of the City, State and Federal law enforcement agencies have been assigned to the investigation of this crime. We are at a very early stage of our investigation right now, and we are following up on all possible leads. We would appeal to any members of the public who may have seen something, no matter how seemingly insignificant, or who may have reason to suspect something or somebody, to come forward and contact the police at the special number I will give out at the end of this news conference. We are making no further comment at this time."

There was an immediate uproar with everyone trying to ask questions at once. Was this a politically motivated crime? Was it a terrorist act? Was it a burglary that went wrong? Did the police have any suspects? Who were they? What leads were they following?

La Vonn reiterated, "Ladies and gentlemen, as I said, I have no further comment at this time. We will hold a further briefing tomorrow at a time to be advised to you. Thank you for your patience and may I remind you that an elected member of Congress was murdered here this evening, one of our key legislators; and we will leave no stone unturned to bring the perpetrators of this crime to justice."

Mike had watched the show from the back of the room and felt empathy with his colleagues. Strange how he was already thinking of them as colleagues. He supposed, after all, they were in the same business. He felt for them, too – the request to the public to come forward had to be done. It would bring out the crazies, but what could you do? You could not take the risk of overlooking a major piece of evidence, so every statement would have to be painstakingly checked out and validated. Somewhere in the mass of information might lie the nugget that would give them the breakthrough, but the difficulty was often in identifying it.

Paul rejoined him. "So what you think, man? They as bad as this back home?"

"Perhaps not quite yet, but they're getting there."

"Ah, you wanna see the crime scene? I mean, it's getting on for 10.30, but if you ain't got plans this evening?"

"Absolutely, if that's ok?"

Paul spoke as they walked. "For sure; Look, Mike, we've got everything covered on this one. As we speak, every employee of the hotel either has been or is being interviewed. We've got another team calling every employee who is off duty. We're searching for someone who didn't turn in or left abruptly, but no dice. We're checking out all ex-employees. We're checking every firm in the city that delivers to, collects from, or supplies the hotel. We've got a bunch of the I.T. guys going over every frame of CCTV footage for the past 24 hours, and we may extend that later. We're using staff to identify a lot of people in those videos. We've spoken to every guest who was in the hotel when the shooting happened. We also spoke with casual visitors to the hotel. We're trying to track down all the other guests to interview them also. We've searched every inch of the suite and the adjoining ones. SOCO guys are just finished now, but we won't know until tomorrow what we've actually got, if anything. We are also looking into any enemies the man may have made in either his personal or political life, but that will take more time."

They had arrived in the Senator's sixth floor suite at this stage. The crime scene officers were packing up.

"Ok with you guys if we take a look now, Andy?" said Paul.

"Go right ahead, my man, but try not to fall over anything. Given the size of this one, I wouldn't be surprised if the feebies wanted to take another look tomorrow. They won't find anything, though."

"Cheers, Andy. By the way, this is Mike Lyons from MI5. Mike, Andy Hill, Chief of Crime Scene Investigation, D.C.P.D."

"Pleased to meet ya," said Andy, removing a plastic glove and extending his hand. "Jesus Paul, you really got the cavalry on this one, ain't you? I mean, now you've even got the Brits involved." All three men laughed and Andy departed with his team.

Mike surveyed the suite and took his time. It certainly merited the term "luxury". Everything seemed to be where it was supposed to be. It was almost like the photographs they showed on the websites. Nothing was out of place. A solid oak door gave into a small hallway-cum-reception area with a closet for coats, etc. This led to a large living area. Thick beige carpeting covered the entire suite. On the left side there was a solid oak table with twelve chairs that could be used for either meetings or private dining. A matching unit stood against the back wall, which contained a well-stocked bar. The front of the unit was opened and a bottle of bourbon had been taken from the bar. The bottle was open and about half full. A single crystal whiskey tumbler sat beside the bottle. To the right of the room was a large seating area with deep dark brown leather couches, which would seat perhaps 20 people. Obviously, the place was used for entertaining as well as living, he thought. Velvet drapes over net curtains covered the floor to ceiling windows. Occasional tables were placed at strategic locations throughout the room and contained ornate lamp stands with primrose coloured shades to provide subdued lighting.

The living room gave on to an extra large bedroom with a king size bed to the right. Again, huge floor to ceiling tinted windows allowed a panoramic view of down town D.C. Large walk-in closets were located either side of the bed. To the left was an extra large bathroom with a Jacuzzi, shower unit, toilet, bidet, and double washstand. Everything seemed pristine and undisturbed, apart from the dark brown stain on the carpet midway between the bed and the bathroom. The space where the Senator's body had lain had been outlined.

"So what do you think?" said Paul.

Mike surveyed the scene. "Looks like it's as you said, mate. Subject was shot here, presumably on his way to the bathroom. Eerily tidy scene. No blood spray, so presumably bullets didn't exit the body. If, as you say, the dead man suffered two rapid-fire rounds to the back or side of the head, and fell here, the murderer presumably hid in the closet. Nowhere to hide over there in front of the picture windows, so he must have concealed himself in the area to the left of the bed, then emerged as the Senator turned his back. You did say the man had undressed, yeah, presumably headed for a shower?"

Paul nodded. "Yeah, clothes have been removed for examination but nothing else was found. Our guys have been through that closet with a microscope but found no traces of anything. Guy had to be in there, though." Mike agreed.

"We have to see what the forensic boys turn up tomorrow, and hopefully we'll get a lead on something or someone on the CCTV tapes. Trouble is, it has all the hallmarks of a professional hit, so… what do you think?"

Mike walked the suite again for a moment, careful not to touch or disturb anything. "If you want my honest opinion, and that's what I'm in the habit of giving, I'd say you're wasting your time."

Paul smiled briefly.

"You know, those are my thoughts precisely. Let's go get a beer."

In the Gulf, the Bahraini had just finished his dawn prayers. He switched his TV to Al Jazeera as he started his breakfast. The news was all about the previous night's murder. He quickly switched to CNN for more comprehensive coverage. He allowed himself a small smile of congratulation and gave a deep sigh of satisfaction – it's started, he thought.

Chapter 14

Mike was awoken by a loud banging on his hotel room door. He struggled to wake up. He glanced at his watch and saw that it was – what? 12.30? He must have overslept.

"OK, OK, I'll be right with you," he shouted as the knocking continued. He was dressed only in his boxer shorts, so he struggled to shrug on a robe and checked the spy hole. It was Paul. He opened the door where Paul stood with two tall mugs of coffee and a big grin on his face.

"You plan on sleeping all day, or you plan to help us on this case?" he joked.

"Jesus, Paul, sorry, I couldn't get to sleep last night and it also looks like I forgot to change my watch."

"Not a problem, bud, and no need to hurry. We've got a situation meeting at 09.30 and I thought you might like to sit in. We're gonna need all the help we can get on this, so how about we turn theoretical cooperation into practical, eh? Oh, lots of milk, no sugar, right?" as he handed Mike a coffee.

"You got it right on both counts mate," he said as he took a long sip of coffee. "Give me ten minutes to shower and shave and we'll go get breakfast."

"Sounds like a plan."

The U.S. and Britain may have different traditions in many areas but breakfast isn't one of them. A famous author had said one time that if a man wanted to eat well in England, then he should have breakfast three times a day! The Americans had taken it to another level, Mike thought, as they surveyed the menu in the hotel dining room. Neither man had had dinner the night before, so when the waitress arrived, they both went for the full works.

"Could be a long day, bud, so best to get fuelled up early."

"Right on, I love your breakfasts here."

The waitress returned with juice and a container of coffee that seemed to hold about a gallon. Both men thanked her but seemed reluctant to start a conversation. It was as if both knew what was on the other's mind and didn't want to be the one to state the obvious. Their giant breakfasts arrived and both got stuck in.

Mike eventually broke the silence. "I guess this is the one nobody wants, huh?"

Paul chewed on a mouthful of bacon and egg and contemplated, eventually putting down his knife and fork and pushing his plate aside.

"You got that right, for sure. Nobody wants to say the words "hit man", but that's what we've got here. Almost impossible to catch if he's planned well enough, and these guys do. I mean, when did you ever hear of a hit man on trial? You didn't. When did we ever catch one? We didn't. End of story."

Mike mused, "Yeah, realistically neither did we. When terrorism was at its worst in the UK back in the '70s and '80s, the heavy hitters in the IRA and UVF were never caught – only the small fry or the stupid ones served time. Then there were the dozen or so guys who served fifteen years because they happened to be in the wrong place at the wrong time and the police were under pressure to apprehend someone to calm the public mood. If they're intelligent and plan well, you won't catch them."

"Yeah," Paul continued, "most murders are solved – know why? Because a huge number of them are domestic. When a woman is murdered, first guy the police look at is the husband; horrible for the poor guy at times but that's the way it is. If it don't turn out to be the husband, chances are it's someone else in the family. The number of complete stranger murders or stranger rapes is rare. Other murders are drug or gang-related, and also often committed by idiots; relatively easy to solve. Then there are the real idiots who just leave clues all over the place. And forget all the novels you read where someone connected to the investigation, a police officer or your police analyst connected to the crime, is involved or guilty – that's bullshit and is only used to sell books or movie seats. It doesn't happen in real life. No, if someone wants to commit the perfect untraceable crime, I won't say it's relatively easy to do, but it's not difficult. The biggest problem an assassin has is the security surrounding his target – once he figures out a way to get past that, he's in. In this case, it was negligible. He will have already planned his exit, and believe me, we won't come dashing over the horizon to cut him off at the pass. If there had been heavy security around, he wouldn't have acted. He's got plenty of time and can try again."

"Indeed, awful for the public to contemplate but that's the way it is. We feed the masses the myth that things are relatively safe out there and, that's what they want to hear, but realistically they aren't. Our only chance with this guy is if he makes a mistake, and he doesn't appear to have on this one. I've seen this in Britain. These guys are in, out, and in the wind before we even know a crime has been committed. All we can be thankful for is that we aren't important enough to be targets, because if we were, they'd take us out too."

"I'm afraid you're right, man. If the guy has no connection to the Senator and if he planned well enough, we're not gonna catch him. Forget CSI – if the guy hasn't left trace, and my guess is he hasn't, then forget it. You know, most contract killers are never caught. The police and politicians don't like people to think about it so they don't talk about it. Check the crime statistics and you'll find most murders are solved and this allows people to sleep soundly in their beds at night. Our guys work hard and do an excellent job but realistically, there's a lot of crime that they simply do not have the resources to fight. There's just too much of it. Then, of course, we have political priorities – some crimes naturally get more attention than others, and hence get more resources allocated to them. We've got huge resources on this one but will it help us? Who knows? On the other hand, I'm sure there were other people who bought it in D.C. last night. They'll get the minimum of police time, but the ironic thing is that many of those crimes may well be solved. Crimes of passion, committed without forethought or planning – relatively easy. Drug or gang wars – again, easily solved, as there is usually a limited range of suspects, so, process of elimination; but even if you don't solve it, who gives a shit? One less druggie on the street. May not even make the papers. Then there are the cases where we know who the killer is but can't prove it through lack of evidence. But when a high profile guy is killed, everyone gets scared, and it gets worse if we don't come up with a whodunit!"

"Yeah, I don't want to sound negative, as I know your guys have a lot of analysis to do yet, but it looks to me like the killer was meticulous and left no trace. It's frightening to think of. I mean, take serials. How many did Bundy kill before he was caught? How many other guys are out there? We had a Russian police officer over with us a few years ago and he reckoned they had a guy who had done over 150, and he was never caught. Now, if you acknowledge that most of these sickos are psychopaths or sociopaths, then mental instability should create a greater risk of getting caught, right? But psychos are usually cleverly devious and adept at planning and covering their tracks. Many are only caught through a simple mistake or slip up. Then there are the guys who want to boast of their deeds and want to get caught. Now, think of a serial killer who isn't mentally unstable in any way, doesn't kill to satisfy a need, but merely to order. It's a frightening scenario. You know, you're right in what you said. I can't remember a single case of a hit man being arrested or tried and convicted – I doubt they rarely, if ever, are. It's an uncomfortable fact of life that we don't widely advertise but you know, even if we did, I think most people would get on with their lives and comfort themselves that *they* would never be the target for a hit man. You never know but everyone likes to think they're immortal."

"So do you think this guy is in the wind or will we get a shot at him? Do you think he'll try again?"

"Why do you say that?"

"Ah, I don't know, just a hunch. Something tells me this might be the start of something. I mean, why take the Senator out? Okay, nationally known political figure, but what threat did he really pose? You could argue that he was taking this country in a particular economic direction, but I don't see anyone willing to off him for that, do you?"

"Well I'm not as familiar with your politics, but no, not really. So, what do you reckon?"

"I think he's long gone and unless he shows his hand again, we're not gonna get him."

"You're probably right, Paul, but if we ever do get another shot at him, we'd need to make it stick. I mean, these guys just don't leave evidence. If we catch a break that leads to him, we'd need to cover all the angles. There's no margin for error on this one."

Paul checked his watch. "You got that right. OK, so are we gonna sit round here all day feeling sorry for ourselves or are we gonna see what the guys have turned up?"

They left the hotel restaurant and headed for Paul's car, which was parked at the curb. It was another glorious day in the capital. It was a short drive to Police Headquarters.

"I spoke to my boss about this last night and we both agree that most of our guys are gonna be tied up on this one for a while, unless we catch a break, that is. She's willing to co-opt you to assist and provide your expertise, if that's OK with you?"

Mike smiled. "Well, you've got a beautiful city here, but to be honest, I can't see what else I'd want to be doing right now."

"OK, deal. Now let's see what Andy Hill's guys have dug up."

It was a relatively short drive from the hotel in Thomas Circle to Metro Police HQ on Indiana, where the agencies had agreed to meet. Both were in North West D.C. Mike sat back and stretched. "Sorry, with all that's been happening, I never asked you about Disney World. How was it?"

"Ah, man, it was great but it's a never-ending fantasy world down there, at least for us visitors. You've got seven separate parks in Disney, then you've got Universal, Wet & Wild, Busch Gardens; it's a kid's dream world, except you'd need a few months to see it all. But we did a lot, and Dad's credit has been fully restored for now," he laughed. "Oh, and pardon my manners too; Barbara sends her love, plus an invitation for dinner if we manage to get home in time to have it some evening."

"I'm sure we will, Paul, don't worry."

They caught a red traffic light on Massachusetts Avenue. A silver car at the front of the line on the cross street slowly accelerated across their path. It was driven by a man wearing dark shades. Mike thought he caught a momentary flash of recognition, but it was only for a microsecond, then it was gone. He then remembered where he was. Hell, he thought, I don't know anyone in this town. The thought stayed with him though.

"Here we are," said Paul as he parked outside Metro H.Q.

Chapter 15

Walker was on his way out of D.C, heading at a sedate pace, enjoying the morning sunshine. He was taking care; no point risking being pulled over for speeding and anyway, he had plenty of time. He had driven to Washington two days before; 12 hours at a steady 65. He had changed cars in Atlanta, where he always kept an anonymous-looking Toyota Camry in a private lock-up garage. He had parked his Orlando car, a Cadillac Escalade, and driven north on I95 in the Camry. It was registered to a Mr John Robinson at an address in Atlanta owned by Walker.

Mr Carl Walker, if anyone had asked his wife, was on business in Atlanta, and a hotel record would show that he had spent four nights there at a relatively small but comfortable hotel. He had made sure to choose one that did not have security cameras or electronic door locks. Too easy to leave a record. He would eventually return to the lock-up garage, collect the Escalade, then drive to the hotel and check out, thanking the receptionist for an enjoyable stay. During planning, he had briefly thought about reactivating his Atlanta contact and have her "use" a room with an electronic record, but he considered it too risky. This thing was gonna get nationwide publicity, and she just might put it together. Better to act alone.

He hit the on ramp of the 495, part of the Washington Beltway, and accelerated. He took the exit to Route 66 and headed west. The Senator had been child's play. Of course, there had been security at the hotel, but it was minimal – the man wasn't seen as a target. Walker had hacked into the hotel's computer system and obtained his suite number. He had also hacked into the Senator's office computer and obtained the cell phone numbers of the Senator, his secretary, and a number of his aides. He had done enough listening and cross-checking to establish a pattern. Most days when the house was sitting, he would return to his hotel in the evening unless there was a late session. He would work for another two hours and then either go to dinner or a function if there was one.

Ah, but there was time for pleasure too – not all the time spent with his pretty little secretary was for work alone. He had discovered this in both phone conversations and texts they had sent to each other. He knew they tended to get together when the Senator returned from the house, or else late at night, and he had hoped that, on the evening he chose to surreptitiously enter the Senator's suite, the secretary would not be with him. If she was, well, tough – he would have no choice. It would have been a great waste, but he was being paid to do a job.

Thankfully, Carter had been alone. The man was a bundle of energy, so he had to wait until he stopped moving round the suite and was ready for his shower. Then he calmly emerged from the closet and shot him. He had entered and exited the hotel through the service entrance dressed as an employee of the hotel's laundry service. There were no security cameras on the service entrance. If anyone stopped him, he was collecting laundry. No one did. No one even noticed him.

The only small weakness in his cover was that he could not acquire a van with the laundry company's logo, but that was a minor issue. He had arrived in an old Toyota pick-up, which he had parked near the rear entrance of the hotel. He had stolen the vehicle that morning from the long-term lot of Dulles Airport. It had been a relatively simple task to park his own vehicle in the lot and then wait until someone left a suitable vehicle. He was looking for something that was fairly common and that did not have an in-built alarm system.

If a person uses a long-term facility, they are not going to be back for at least twelve hours, and usually a lot longer. After he identified the vehicle he wanted, he waited a full hour. People often forgot things in cars and rushed back for them. After the hour, he locked the Camry and walked calmly to the pick-up. It took him about a minute to gain entry, start the engine and drive to the pay machine. The car park contained thousands of vehicles and was totally automated. As he knew the van would not be missed, and therefore not reported stolen, he didn't even bother to change the plates. He had placed a number of "repair work in progress" signs in the space the pick-up had been parked in. They were still there untouched when he had returned the Toyota later that night. He had replaced the vehicle, collected his own car, paid and drove away. He had already removed the overall with the logo of the laundry firm. He dropped that in a dumpster on his way back to his hotel.

He turned off the 66 at Strasburg on to the 81 heading southwest. He drove south and took the Harrisonburg exit. He had reconnoitred the area on his way to Washington and he drove easily now, effortlessly negotiating the turnings he wanted until he found the secluded spot on the back road. He parked the Camry under some trees and popped the trunk. He did a slow, full 360 and checked that he was alone. One of the things he loved about the U.S. was that despite the population of over 300 million, there was more than enough room for everyone, and lots of places to hide or to be alone. It was so unlike the old country, but no matter – there were always deserted places where no one would disturb you. People loved their cars and drove everywhere but if you went anywhere in the countryside, particularly on a weekday, you were assured of solitude.

He rolled back the rear seats and clicked open the hidden compartment he had installed beneath them. He extracted a heavy leather pouch from there and put it over his shoulder. He locked the car and walked towards the trees. After a few minutes, he came to the slightly elevated spot that he had previously reconnoitred. He checked the surrounding area again – he was alone. He opened a bottle of water he had brought with him and drank deeply. He then checked his watch. He had lots of time, so he found a comfortable shaded spot and settled down to wait.

The meeting was chaired by the head of D.H.S., Maria Gonzalez. Apart from La Vonn, Chico, Pete, Paul and Mike, there were representatives from all the law enforcement and advisory agencies. The atmosphere was business-like, although the mood was sombre and energy levels seemed low. The tensions of the old rivalry were parked; for now, at least. People seemed to realise that this was 2011, and if America was threatened, America was sure as hell going to stand together. Mike scanned the room. He reckoned there must have been twenty-five people present. He had already met Paul's boss and she now introduced him to the rest of the group.

Maria was mid-fifties, slightly plump with dark hair swept back from her face. She had a friendly, down-home Mom look, which belied a razor-sharp brain and astute political know-how. She was known to be tough but immensely loyal to her people. She would brook no silly inter-agency competition, and her focus was on solving crime, detecting threats and neutralizing them. She was Paul's direct boss and he had briefed Mike on her style on the way in – he had been impressed.

"OK, good morning, people," she began. "Let's cut to the chase here. From everything I've heard so far, this looks like a terrorist hit, and that's the way it is being classified. That is why I am your Chairman here this morning. Why Senator Carter would be the target for this type of act is as yet unclear. For now, we do not intend to raise the level of threat, but as usual, it is being kept under review. Thank you all for coming. I realize many of you people have been working most of the night and I appreciate your efforts. Now, let's see what we got. As this is a briefing meeting, can I ask all of you to be succinct and to the point. We can go through the detailed reports later if we need to. Jose, you wanna go first?"

Jose Aguero, the smiling, dapper-looking Latino Medical Examiner, nodded. "Sure, Maria; not much to report, really. Post-Mortem was completed overnight. Subject died from massive brain trauma caused by penetration of the skull. In a word, he was shot in the head. Two entry wounds in the right upper cranium; no exit wounds, suggesting the use of soft nose bullets. Subsequent examination of the brain confirmed – you don't need the graphics, but this guy wanted to do as much possible damage in the shortest period of time. He succeeded; in my view, death was instantaneous. The angle of entry of the bullets suggests that the killer was slightly below the victim when the bullets were fired. The Senator was six two, so we could be looking for a killer who's, say, five ten, but don't hold me to that – he may have been crouching slightly to avoid detection. No other marks on the body. Nothing out of the ordinary; body did not contain alcohol or narcotics of any kind, and apart from the head wound, was in superb physical condition; an advert for good southern living, I'd say." There were some brief smiles around the table. Jose was known for his ability to cut to the chase, and for his humour, despite the morbid nature of his profession.

"Thanks, Jose. OK, La Vonn, you wanna take it?"

The broad-shouldered, normally bright-eyed African American sighed deeply. Despite the amicable atmosphere of this meeting, he had the look of a guy who had been getting some serious heat from his own bosses. He and Chico looked like they'd been up all night and were decidedly downbeat. They were both red-eyed, with shirtsleeves rolled up and ties undone.

"Sure Maria, thank you," he began. "We've put every available man we've got on this. We've called in guys off leave. We've been over every frame of CCTV. We've spoken to the staff. We've spoken to the guests. We've checked every street and alleyway and outlet for four city blocks in every direction. We've got several officers still checking on possible leads, but I gotta tell ya folks, it don't look good. We spoke to the Senator's secretary, Ms Roberts, early this morning. The lady was initially traumatized but she's better now. She readily admitted to a 'relationship' with the Senator over and above being his secretary, which probably explains why she was in his suite in just her underwear, but I'll ask you to respect her confidentiality on that one. She has no idea why someone would want to target her boss and I have to say I believe her. We guessed something wasn't right about the relationship so we checked out the jealous boyfriend angle etc. and it doesn't go anywhere. Ms Roberts is 27 years old and has no other romantic relationships. Neither, in my opinion, has she anything whatsoever to do with what happened to her boss. We've looked at the political angle, and while the man was involved in high stakes poker, our view is that it surely wasn't worth killing him for. Some of you other folks might like to comment on that later. Chico, you wanna take it?"

"We've hit the streets on this one big time," Chico began. "We've shaken down every snitch, every grass, every contact who owes us a favour throughout the city, and we've come up with nothing, a big fat zero! Nobody knows nothing. Nobody's heard nothing."

Mike found himself tuning out. He understood they had to do this, but his mind was elsewhere. He was sure the killer was long gone – it just had the smell of assassination about it, and the combined efforts of every policeman in D.C. probably wouldn't make any difference. He felt for them. The reports went on and the conversation went round the table; then he heard Andy Hill start to give his report.

"If you ask me, this guy must have been wearing a rubber suit; or else he's an alien who beamed himself in and out of there. There's just no trace evidence; not a hair, not a nail, not the most microscopic fragment. Nothing! Guy sure as hell must have been in the closet, but he left nothing. I mean, Carter's clothes were in there and we vacuumed the lot. Nothing there that didn't belong to the Senator. The only bodily fluids we got were from the bloodstains on the carpet. Apart from that, the room was clean, and I mean, spotless. It's also likely, judging from the angle from which the Senator was shot, and the remarkably small amount of blood, that the perp's clothing wasn't marked at all – I mean, there was no blood spray. As the man said, he may have got clean away! We've recovered the bullets from Jose's guys and although they are badly damaged, we are looking at your standard 9 by 19mm parabellum round, suggesting the bullets were fired from a Glock pistol; exact type not determined as yet. Forensics may have more later, but I'm not sure where that leads us. I mean, there must be over a million of these things in this country alone."

Maria turned to her immediate right. "So what do you think, Paul?"

"Ah, look," Paul began. "Let's be straight about this. Can I say what everyone in the room is probably thinking? This was a hired killing. A paid hit, presumably from out of town. If it was, gun is gonna be untraceable. D.H.S. has checked all known and suspected terrorists and we've come up flat. We are not saying it isn't a terrorist hit because it looks like it is but right now we have no idea who might be behind it or why. We are gonna continue checking and cross checking our databases. We've looked for possible enemies or people who may have had a grudge against the Senator and we can't find any. Believe it or not folks, despite playing serious hardball politics, this man seemed to be universally popular. Even his strongest opponents can't think of anyone who would have wanted to off him. I don't know; Pete, anything you wanna add?"

Pete Stewart more or less nodded in agreement. "I agree we've caught a tough one here. We haven't had time to do a complete profile, but our perp is obviously very clever and planned his entry and exit well. He managed to access the Senator's room with a key card he created by hacking the hotel's database. So he, or his accomplices, if there are any, have obviously got strong computer skills. The fact that he chose the moment when the Senator was alone but wouldn't have wanted to be disturbed, as he was going to meet a lover, tells us he may have known about this liaison. It may have been pure chance but it's not a big leap to think that if he hacked into the hotel system, he may have hacked the Senator's office or phones also. If he did and chose his moment, he's even better than you think. No trace evidence, no trail so I'd say we are looking at a specialist, someone brought in from out of town specially for the hit; but as you say, by whom and for what – well, who knows? All I will tell you is, if our profile is correct, we are gonna have the devil's own job to nail him."

Mike sat quietly throughout, listening and absorbing the information. Maria now turned to him. "Mike, welcome to D.C. I understand you arrived last night and you're up to speed. Anything you'd like to add or any angles on this thing?"

Mike realized the eyes of the room were on him.

"Thanks for the opportunity, Maria," he acknowledged. "I'd have to say that I'm in complete agreement with all you guys on this. This is the case we all dread and unless we get a break soon, it's gonna be a difficult one. Just one thought occurred to me when I was listening to the reports. It's probably nothing, but in relation to the motive; I must admit I know little about American politics but I think I read in Newsweek magazine on the flight over that the Senator was likely to be a front runner in the Presidential race next year?"

No one spoke but you could hear a pin drop in the room. La Vonn broke the silence, "Ah shit man, does this mean what I think it means? Hell, Chico, who else has declared an interest or who's looking like they might? I think Secret Service is gonna be telling lots of guys to watch their backs?"

Everyone started talking at once and Maria had to call them to order. Just as they were settling back, the door burst open and a red faced young uniformed officer burst in.

"I'm sorry Mrs Gonzalez," he began, "but I think you might want to hear this. We've had reports of a multiple shooting at a golf course in Harrisonburg. There's confusion down there but it appears that the Mayor, the Vice Mayor and a member of the City Council have been shot by a sniper during a round of golf. That's all we have right now, ma'am."

The meeting turned into uproar. Who? What? When? Why? How? All the usual questions reverberated around the room.

Paul looked at Mike. "That's only a bit more than 100 miles from here. Coincidence?"

"Doubt it."

"I think we got a terrorist on the loose here. We need to get down there, rapidly."

Maria signalled for quiet. "Guys, this might be nothing and it might be connected. I'm sure the local police will do a fine job down there, but I suggest we give them a little neighbourly assistance. I mean, this is a small town, right? Who knows how well equipped they are down there? Paul, Mike, Andy and maybe Jose, can you get down there and take a look?" All nodded agreement.

Paul grabbed his briefcase and rushed toward the exit. "Can someone get us a phone number for whoever's in charge down there and pass it on to my cell phone? And Maria, can someone get on to those guys and tell them not to touch anything – I mean anything! Oh, and give the press guys our very best regards," he winked. She gave him a withering smile and then they were gone.

Chapter 16

Paul's Honda was parked at the curb but they waited until Andy brought his Chevy Suburban round, as he had it pre-loaded with all the gear he would need and besides, it was far more comfortable for four. Andy had already switched on his integrated flashing blue light and now switched on his siren as they screeched away from the curb. It was just touching the lunch hour but traffic was light. They zoomed through the city streets and were on 495 in ten minutes.

Paul's cell phone rang. The guy in charge was Sheriff Donald P Westwood or D.P. for short. It was he who called Paul and assured him that the crime scene had been sealed tight. Nothing would be touched until the group arrived. The press was being kept back and was not even allowed access to the golf course. He couldn't legislate for helicopters if they had a mind to use them but the story had been kept pretty quiet as yet. They had erected a temporary cover over the crime scene so he was confident they could keep it under wraps. He added that road blocks had been set up on all roads in the county and that any suspect vehicles were being searched but nothing as yet had been found.

Paul thanked the man, assured him they'd be there in about an hour and closed the phone. Andy was already on Route 66 and still had his lights going at close to 90 mph.

"You know," Paul said, "I think I'm gonna like this guy." The satnav on Andy's dash announced that it was just less than 100 miles to Harrisonburg and Mike reckoned that at their current speed, they'd arrive in just over an hour.

The scene at Heritage Oaks Golf Club was as serene as the one at the Fairmont had been chaotic. As yet, only one or two local reporters were present, and even they seemed willing to wait for the official statement. Sheriff D.P. Westwood stood respectfully, hat in hand, awaiting the group from D.C, and introduced his two deputies, Arthur Wilson and Doug Scott.

"Your boss, Ms Gonzalez," he began, "said we were to preserve the crime scene till you folks got here so as not to contaminate anything and I think you'll find everything is as it happened. We're not used to anything this heavy in these parts but we sure do know how to protect a crime scene, particularly when it's on the 14th hole of a golf course."

"Thanks a lot D.P. We really appreciate it. This may be connected to something bigger or it may not but we can't take the risk."

"Ah shucks, crime this big, I reckon it's gotta be connected to something."

"I think we ain't ever had a triple murder here, least not in my twenty three years so we can sure use the help from you big city folks." This was from Doug Scott.

"It's sure the worst one I can remember," added D.P.

They rode in silence, in the golf buggies that had been provided, to the 14th hole, which, although none of the course was too remote, was probably the farthest from the club house. All was quiet in the sylvan scene. Giant oak trees overshadowed the beautifully-trimmed fairways and manicured greens. An odd stray leaf fluttered in what little breeze there was, but, almost as a mark of respect, it became totally still as the buggies slowed at the 14th green. The hole was probably one of the longest on the course, Mike thought. Looking back up the fairway, it seemed to dogleg to the right and then come in over a water hazard to the green, which was only visible from the latter part of the fairway. Two small white tents had been erected; one towards the centre of the green and one just off the green to the right.

"OK guys," D.P. began, "as you've probably already heard on the way down here, what we got is this: today is the Mayor's Open Day, and the highlight is the Golf Tournament he hosts and sponsors. Mayor Edward Barrett teed off first this morning at 08.30 in a three-ball with Deputy Mayor Dennis King and Councilman Mitch Foden. We can't be absolutely precise on timings but we reckon they reached the 14th hole around 11.15. The next threesome was two of the older Councillors and a local businessman, and they had fallen some way behind the Mayor's party. When this group came to the dogleg, right up there, they saw the bodies but I reckon it took a moment or two before they figured out what had gone down. None of them were carrying cell phones so one of them had to dash to the clubhouse to raise the alarm."

"We logged the 911 call at 11.36 and I got here at 11.45. I can't for the life of me imagine why anyone would want to take out the Mayor. I mean, he's not exactly controversial. I figured we're looking at real heavy stuff here, and y'all up in D.C are gonna want to take a look, so I put it on the wires straight away. We've spoken to all the other players and golf club staff: no one heard nothing, no one saw nothing. You'll appreciate we got limited personnel, but we put out a major alert and got the State Police involved soon as we could. We got roadblocks operating for a radius of fifty miles but I wouldn't be hopeful – too many escape routes outta here and too many cars. Our man could have gone anywhere."

Paul, Mike and Andy seemed to simultaneously check their watches. It was now 1.30, over two hours since the shooting. All shook their head in empathy with the Sheriff.

D.P. introduced his forensics chief, Josh O'Neill, who seemed anxious to get on with the investigation. He was a small, neat man, and was already suited up and prepared to survey the scene. Andy had brought his own gear from the Suburban and was also anxious to get started. Josh offered white plastic suits to the others but they declined, only taking the bootees to avoid contaminating the site, but leaving the forensic examination to Andy and Josh.

The group proceeded to the first tent, set up on the green. The scene was not pretty; two middle-aged men, both shot twice in the head. The exit wounds had done severe damage, spreading blood and brain matter over the pristine green.

"The M.E. will sure have his work cut out for him to restore these guys to a presentable state for identification," said Andy.

"Way I figure it," Josh began, "Mayor and Councilman Foden were on the green putting out. Dennis King had presumably putted earlier as there are only two balls on the green. All three men were shot twice in the head and seemed to fall where they stood. There's no evidence of any reaction – Jesus, it's almost like these guys took a sort of collective triple heart attack and just dropped. There's no evidence of anyone else being on the course so I reckoned we're looking at a high powered rifle from distance."

He pointed towards a small hillock located on the edge of the course midway up the fifteenth fairway. "Y'all see that crest up there? Well, that's where I figure our boy fired his shots from. It's the only elevated area and it's got road access."

Something about the whole scene was bothering Mike – it was too predictable, too easy; or was it?

"So, you reckon the shooter was lying in wait for our three golfers? But how would he know when they were going to arrive, and would the previous threesome not have seen him? It looks pretty open to me."

"Ah, shucks, no," said Josh, "guy must have had it all figured. Mayor's group was the first threesome of the day. What's more, the playing order was published on the city website and even on his personal one. This whole thing's for charity, so the more publicity they got, the better for them."

Paul and Mike exchanged glances and nodded – another well-planned hit. After a brief look in the second tent, which contained the unfortunate Deputy Mayor, who was sadly in a similar condition to his erstwhile colleagues, the group walked the hundred yards or so to the small crest where Josh figured the perp had lain in wait. They were careful not to disturb or contaminate the scene, although the knowing looks which the D.C. visitors had exchanged suggested they wouldn't find anything anyway. Josh's assistant, Mel Hanson, awaited them under a magnificent oak, calmly smoking a cigarette. He directed the group via a circuitous route whereby they bypassed the crest, exited the golf course and came around the full 180 to face back towards the 14th green. The guys could just about see the course from where they stood.

"You wanna take this, Mel?" said Josh.

"Yeah, guy was good – made his way from the road, about two hundred yards back there. I reckon he tried to cover his tracks, but there are indications someone was through here this morning. We're gonna go over it with a fine tooth comb soon as we get the go-ahead from you folks. Grass near the boundary fence is slightly disturbed but other than that no indication. Angles of the bullets would suggest they might have been fired from hereabouts so I reckon he just rested his rifle on that old boundary fence and let rip. Air is pretty still here today and when we got here, there was a faint smell of something that might have been cordite but we can't be sure. No evidence though – guy obviously collected his brass. Whaddya think? Any questions?"

Paul queried, "Any tire tracks back towards the road you can identify?"

"Not as yet, but we've got that area sealed off and soon as we get clearance from Andy here, we'll start a full examination."

"OK, you got it. Let's start there on the roadway and work our way back towards the bodies," said Andy.

Josh, Mel and Andy took off in the direction that led away from the course. Jose had stayed with the bodies and was conversing with his opposite number, who also doubled as the coroner. Mike, Paul and D.P. strolled back towards the green.

"I know this must be difficult for you, D.P." said Mike. "I assumed you knew all these gentlemen personally?"

D.P. nodded and shrugged. "Sure, but I'm at a total loss as to why anyone would target them. I mean, we're talking small town politics here. These guys, I mean, hell, everyone knew them – not everyone agreed with their politics but they were decent folks and well-liked. I mean, it's gotta be something else. You guys are investigating the Senator's killing last night so ya figure there might be a connection?"

Paul shrugged. "Ah, look, if there is I can't see it in terms of motive, but we've already got our people checking any possible link. There may not be any, but I mean, we seem to be looking at a professional hit here and two in the same State in 24 hours seems a hell of a coincidence to me. You and your people have done a fine job here, Sheriff, in difficult circumstances and we're very grateful to you all, but I think this is gonna be another tough one."

Mike nodded apologetically. "Seems like I've arrived at just the wrong time for you guys."

"Ah, don't sweat it man, looks like we're gonna need your help; and that of a hell of a lot of other people as well."

"Can you think of any connection between your elected officials and the Senator? I mean, anything at all?" Mike enquired of D.P.

"Well, they're all very wealthy men and all were members of the same party, and I do believe our officials would've been staunch supporters of the Senator for sure, but so would a lot of other folks."

"Would anyone have good reason to seriously damage the campaign even before it gets started? I mean, we know who would gain immediate benefit, but it's very early days; would taking out these guys do irreparable damage at this stage?"

"Search me!" said the Sheriff.

Paul shrugged. "Me too; we'll just have to get the analysts back at base working on it to see if they can pinpoint anything."

Mike surveyed the sad little scene again. The tranquillity of a beautiful, peaceful little town had been broken. Something like this might be a blip in a big city, but it would leave deep scars in a small community such as this. Even though it was likely that the perpetrator was from out of State and was long gone, never to threaten the community again, that would not change people's attitudes. Doors that had previously lain ajar would be locked. Windows would be shut. Children would be shepherded indoors before nightfall. Burglar alarms would be purchased. Rifles would be taken down, oiled and checked and placed at the ready. Gun sales would increase. Tension would grip the community and people wouldn't walk the streets alone at night. The irony was that it was likely that the townspeople were never safer than now, but folks didn't think like that – and he understood. He had seen it before, not just in the UK, but in his own country. Suddenly the sureness, the certainty that country life in the small town was and would be safe and secure – the illusion of being untouchable – had been shattered. For some, for a brief period, for others far longer and then for other people, things would just never ever be the same.

Why, he thought? What caused an assassin to wreak havoc in a serene golf club in a small country town on a beautiful July morning? It was connected to the other hit – had to be; but how? And where would the next hit be? Would there be another one or was this it? He felt certain that something was afoot and that they hadn't seen the end of this, not by a long shot.

The Sheriff disturbed his thoughts: "The forensic boys are gonna be some time yet, so it will be a while before we can remove the bodies. Whaddya say we leave them to it and grab us some lunch?"

Paul and Mike both agreed and D.P. drove them quietly back to the clubhouse.

The Sheriff had indeed been correct when he said the shooter could have been anywhere. Right then, he was proceeding cautiously south. Timings had been perfect. He had figured the Mayor's party would hit the 14th green around 11.30, but they were obviously fast players. He was in position by 11.00 so he was more than ready. It was kind of them to take their time over the putts, too.

He had put the automatic rifle on two-round bursts and had taken out the man off the green first. The rifle was silenced, and the two on the green didn't even see their colleague fall. After that, it was simple. Two more double taps and he was gone.

He wasn't aware, but he was already back on the I81 before the bodies were discovered. He had hit the I64 south of Stanton before the 911 call, and a few minutes later he joined the I95 at Glen Allen, just north of Richmond. Before any roadblocks had been erected, he was already in North Carolina. They could put up barriers on county roads and some interstate two lanes but provided he kept to the speed limit, no one was going to stop him on I95.

He was pleased with his little trip north. Two tasks completed; Christ, including his advance, that was fifteen million bucks! He could stop now and retire; the Bahraini would never find him, even if he tried, which he doubted. But wait, fifteen mil was big bucks, but he intended to live a long time and damn it, he always followed through when he agreed to take on a job. It was a matter of pride.

Anyway, he had nothing to worry about. The police did not have clue one about who had carried out the hits; he had left no trace and no trail. There were no photographs of him, no fingerprints in AFIS, no DNA samples, nothing. Yes, he could relax.

It would be dark when he reached Atlanta. He'd change cars, have a good night's sleep, check out of his hotel in the morning and hit Orlando some time after lunch. He realised that it was only now that his adrenalin had stopped pumping and he could totally relax. He hit the button on the car radio and found the local country station. Alan Jackson was singing about his Mercury and Walker found himself singing along.

Chapter 17

There is nothing more frustrating for a police officer than a search with nothing to go on, nowhere to start, no leads, no tips and no breaks. It's not that the police resent the work; quite the opposite – the vast majority of police work bears no resemblance to the way it is presented in TV dramas. It takes a lot longer than a few hours to resolve most crimes. In particular, when they are what are termed "stranger crimes", breakthroughs usually only come after painstaking searches and minute attention to detail; and even then, there can often be a large amount of luck or chance involved. Something doesn't gel, something seems out of place, the policeman digs deeper, doesn't let go, often thinks it over for days, until the pieces fall into place or the vital clue that will piece everything together reveals itself.

But all this assumes that one knows roughly where to look, or at least gets a decent indication of where to start the search. If it's a sex-related crime, it doesn't mean you look exclusively in the sex offenders register, but it's a hell of a good place to start. If it's a simple burglary and you assume it isn't a first timer, the field can still be wide, but it is finite. Drug-related crime is more complicated but also relatively straight forward. The police in every city in the world know virtually everyone who is involved in the drugs trade at a serious level. The trick here is not to detect but to find enough evidence to arrest and convict.

Murders tend to be different. It is said that if police don't solve a murder case during the first 48 hours or thereabouts, their chances of ever finding the perpetrator diminish exponentially; and it is true. Serial killers or planned homicides are some of the most difficult crimes to detect. You can have all the trace evidence you want – if it doesn't match anyone on the crime index, you are back to square one. If you have no trace evidence and no leads, you don't even know where square one is located.

The F.B.I.'s Integrated Automated Fingerprint Identification System, or IAFIS, has, since it was computerized, revolutionized crime investigation techniques in the U.S. While the system has been in existence since 1924, the fact that it is now available online to all law enforcement agencies makes it the most frequently-used resource in criminal investigation. Until 1999, the processing of fingerprint submissions was largely a manual, labour-intensive process, often taking weeks or months to process a single submission, during which time suspects could be out on bail or have absconded completely.

The first use of computers to search fingerprint files took place in 1980, but it was the introduction of the online version that made the quantum leap. IAFIS is the largest biometric database in the world, housing the fingerprints and criminal histories for more than 66 million subjects in the criminal master file, along with more than 25 million civil prints. Included in the database are fingerprints from 73,000 known and suspected terrorists processed by the U.S. or by other international law enforcement agencies including from the UK's MI5 and other allies.

It contains not only fingerprints, but corresponding criminal histories; mug shots; scars and tattoo photos; physical characteristics like height, weight, and hair and eye colour and aliases. The fingerprints and criminal history information are submitted voluntarily by state, local, and federal law enforcement agencies. IAFIS responds to requests 24 hours a day, 365 days a year. It provides automated fingerprint search capabilities, latent search capability, electronic image storage, and electronic exchange of fingerprints and responses. The average response time for an electronic criminal fingerprint submission is about 10 minutes, while electronic civil submissions are processed within an hour and 12 minutes. IAFIS processes an average of approximately 162,000 ten-print submissions per day.

But all this information is useless unless you fulfil certain criteria. To access the database, first you need evidence to compare it with – fingerprints, DNA, etc. Alternatively, you need a suspect whom you can check out on it. If you get a match on the first, you try to find the criminal. On the second, you presumably already have them under surveillance or arrest. If the criminal isn't in the database, no amount of evidence will further progress your case but at least you still have your evidence which might be used on another day. On the other hand, if you have *no* evidence and *no* suspect, then you are really back at first base.

Mike, Andy and Paul discussed this over a beer several days after the hits in D.C. and Virginia State. They and the collected brains trust of most of the law enforcement agencies on the east coast had explored every database, gone down every possible line of enquiry, and literally left no stone unturned in their quest for the killer or killers of the Senator and the three Councilmen; and had gotten absolutely nowhere.

"So, where do we go from here, guys?" said Paul Lincoln, taking a deep draught from his longneck Miller. "I mean, we've run checks on every known or suspected hit man or contract killer in the country and drawn a blank. We've run all known aliases, even those used up to twenty years ago, through every database that might pick up the use of a name, and it led nowhere. We've looked at miles of video and digital audio tape and seen nothing of value. We've been through every database in every agency and we've come up with zero. The slugs we took out of the victims lead nowhere."

It was true. They had viewed video recordings from street cameras in D.C. situated in the vicinity of the hotel and come up with several possibles for a vehicle which might have brought the perp to the rear entrance, but none offered any leads. The quality and clarity of the recordings was sometimes poor, and it wasn't always possible to read a licence plate or distinguish the driver. Where it was, they had investigated but the drivers had all checked out clean. They had checked the hotel's computer systems for traces of a hacker and while they ascertained that the systems might have been infiltrated, the trail led nowhere.

"I don't know," said Mike. "I have to say I'm impressed with your systems guys – I mean, if the perp had stayed anywhere on the east coast on any night two weeks prior to the killings, if he ate, flew, rented a car, bought gas or did anything with plastic and used any of the names in the base, we'd have identified him – not necessarily apprehended him but we'd be somewhere, we'd have some idea. Right now, even with the tools at our disposal, we're nowhere and I'm sorry if I'm not being encouraging."

"Ah, forget it, man," Andy responded. "You're just saying what we all feel. I don't think I've ever worked one this hard before. I mean – the Senator's bedroom was antiseptic! There was nothing on the golf course – not a hair, not a fingernail, nothing. Ballistics tells us the bullets were 7.62mm, which could have been fired from a whole range of high-powered rifles, although most probably an old fashioned Kalashnikov. But without the weapon or a suspicion of its whereabouts?" He spread his arms wide. "The vague tire treads we got from the earth near the site of the Heritage Oaks shooting were standard Bridgestone 215-60's, which are usually used on a whole range of Japanese imports, but will fit a zillion cars in this country; so another dead end!"

"Yeah," Paul added. "The only relief we've had in the past week is that at least the press have moved on to the next story, although they really gave poor Maria a hard time for a few days. NTAS is still maintaining an Elevated Threat level on terrorism. The worry is that there are guys operating out there that we don't know of – could be Al Qaeda, could be some group we've never heard of, or it might be something else entirely."

"What happened with all the searches on possible linkages between the victims?" asked Mike.

"Nothing – same party, same backgrounds, but light years apart in terms of the levels they operated at. No known personal links – it's not even certain that any of the three Harrisonburg victims ever met the Senator. Jesus, this is depressing." He flagged down the bartender and ordered three more long ones. Out of the corner of his eye he saw Pete Stewart had just come in so when the bartender arrived, he ordered another one. "Anything new on the profile, Pete?"

"Naw, man, I mean, we've got a killer whom no one has ever seen, who may or may not be of medium height, and who doesn't like right wing politicians and that's assuming we are only looking for one guy."

161

Mike attempted to raise their spirits. "Look, I know we've been over this a thousand times, but let's do it once more. What have we done? We've looked for something that doesn't fit or a connection or a name, some chink of light, anything; but we've come up flat. What does that mean? We're looking in the wrong place? We're looking for the wrong type of person? Bear with me for a minute – we looked for 'known' hit men or 'known aliases' of hit men. Surely the word 'known' hit men is an oxymoron? As in, if they were known, would they not have already been apprehended? OK, perhaps not, but can you see where I'm going with this?"

The others nodded assent. Andy took it up. "Right, let's take it a step further. There can't be too many guns for hire out there, not to our man's standards. So is our man a terrorist, trained by a terror group? Where does he live? Where does he store his guns and ammunition? Where does he practice? Does he work? Where? Where does he get his instructions from? Where does he get his funding? Fuck it – the guy has to be somewhere; he can't disappear into thin air. He has to sleep somewhere, eat somewhere, be seen by someone, somewhere – yeah, but I suppose that applies to millions of people in this city every day! Sorry guys, if I'm not making sense, it's just a combination of frustration and beer getting to me."

"OK, again, I appreciate NSA has spent a lot of time monitoring and analysing this but again to no avail. So maybe we've got a terrorist who's already been given his instructions? Pete, I take it we've shaken down every known terror group or terrorist cell?"

Pete confirmed that they had. "Look, we've turned over every suspected cell on the east coast and a hell of a lot elsewhere. We've pulled in everyone who even looks like a terrorist! No one knows diddly – not a thing. We've put thousands of hours and millions of dollars into this thing and splat! Whoever's operating out there is on his own, is my guess. Sorry guys, but I'm exhausted and I sure as hell haven't a clue what we do or where we go from here."

There were murmurs of empathy as everyone returned to their beers. Mike sipped thoughtfully, fixed his colleagues with a deep stare and offered: "Guys, I don't really want to be the one but can I put into words what I think everyone else is thinking? Where we go from here is nowhere. There's no point. I know, I know – heresy, but I mean, I don't want to offend anyone, but who killed J.F.K.? We know it sure as hell wasn't Oswald, but almost 50 years later, are we any closer to finding out?" He could see Paul, Pete and Andy sobering before his eyes. "We can continue to monitor but Paul's guys do that all the time anyway. No, all we can do is to wait. I mean we wait until this guy tries again and we can only hope that next time we get some warning or catch a break somewhere that allows us to get to him before he strikes. I'm no pessimist but I wouldn't be hopeful of that either. Guys, I've a hunch this could be a long one. Perhaps it's best for us all if it ends now but if it doesn't, the more this guy tries, the greater the likelihood is that he'll make a mistake. With the technology you guys have over here, he's gonna have to be one ultra-careful dude to avoid getting caught eventually. One other thing – I know we've considered that these could be paid hits, but we can't figure out who might benefit. Have we considered that it isn't terrorists as in paid-up members, but that a terrorist group might be footing the bill? There are probably lots of mercenaries out there who would be glad of the bucks."

"It's a hell of a point," Paul responded, "but I don't know where we can take it? We could check out all known mercenaries – maybe, – let's give it some thought in the morning. You know, a few months ago, I wouldn't have agreed with you on the detection point. I thought we had this whole deal sussed. We hadn't had a successful attack in years, and we'd been catching these guys wholesale. Most would-be terrorists couldn't sneeze or fart without us knowing. Now, I'm not so sure. Even if this guy strikes again, I've no confidence that we can apprehend him, or even get close. Gee, sorry if I'm sounding negative now too – I guess it's affecting us all. Ah listen, I'm beat and I promised Barbara I'd be home for dinner. Mind if I run out on you?"

"Naw, I gotta run too" said Pete, "I've got a flight to Chicago at 08.00 in the morning."

"Me too," said Andy. "Gee, don't think we're deserting you Mike."

"Not at all, guys, I've got some things to do myself, and the thinking time might be useful also. Paul, give my best to Barbara. See most of you guys tomorrow."

They were in Grand Central Bar on 18th St, yet another bar that Mike was impressed with. In fact, he had yet to visit a bar in D.C. that he didn't like. The guys excusing themselves actually fitted his plans perfectly as he had arranged to take Wendy to dinner at nine and it was still only 7.45.

He decided to call her to see if she could meet him at the bar for drinks first. She readily agreed and said she might even make it by 8.30. Wow, this girl was eager to please, wasn't she? He had met her now – what was it; this would be the third time since he had returned to D.C. and he felt himself getting closer to her, thinking about her at odd times and needing her at the end of the day. Christ, very romantic, he thought! But no, Wendy was a special, wonderful girl and he was a – a what? A middle aged Irishman who had never got married and never tired of playing the field? Ah, so what, he mused; it takes all sorts, and after all, Wendy was a happy-go-lucky girl-about-town too, wasn't she?

When he had first returned to the city, he found himself thinking about Jan and threatened several times to go back to that bar, what was it called, the hat place – yeah, Stetsons, to see if she might be working. He thought there may have been chemistry there, but he eventually dismissed the notion as fantasy. Perhaps it was his subconscious mind sounding a warning that he was getting hooked? But what if he was? Why should he go back there and possibly make a fool of himself when he had one of the most gorgeous girls in the city to go out with? They had similar tastes, really enjoyed each other's company, could talk for hours, and as for the rest, ah, he smiled.

Then he saw her come bouncing through the door, smiling that beaming, welcoming, and massively sexy smile and he felt something catch somewhere inside, which surprised him. Mind you, she had dispensed with the blue jeans and the cowboy shirt and she *was* wearing a stunning black dress that ended some way above her knees. She had a simple gold chain around her neck with matching earrings. She kissed him, first on the cheek, then softly on the lips, and then looked so deeply into his eyes that it was almost as if she was absorbing his every thought and taking over his being. He stared her back and went with it and something passed between them – he couldn't say what, but it was like an understanding, or that they had reached a point in their relationship where they were soul mates, totally at ease, completely comfortable with each other.

She spoke and broke the spell. "So how's my Irish copper this evening?"

"Well, he was very pissed off and very tired but he just got a whole lot better. How's the sexiest girl in real estate, or is that a very politically incorrect thing to say?"

"Yeah it is, totally, and I love it. Go right ahead!" Even though Wendy was dressed for dinner and they had intended visiting a restaurant, she was totally at ease in the bar and insisted they stay if Mike was happy.

"You're asking an Irishman if he wants to go to dinner or if he's happy to stay in a bar? Are you serious?"

"Oh yes, very," she said, and she gave him that smile again which caused the twinge he had had earlier to return. He picked up the double meaning in her reply, but was comfortable with it, again surprising himself.

When he recovered his composure, he said, "Wendy, I'm not great at compliments but you've got to be the nicest, most easy-going girl I've ever met and I can't think of anywhere I'd wanna be than right here with you."

Had he really said that? Yes he had, he thought, and he had really meant it. She didn't speak for a moment and he thought he saw just the slightest mistiness in those huge brown eyes. She started to reply, then kissed him, soft and tenderly, her tongue probing gently as she wrapped her arms round him and stroked his hair, eventually resting her head on his chest.

When she eventually settled back on her stool and resumed drinking her beer, he noticed that her eyes had indeed misted over. With typical male tact or lack of it, he said, "Sorry, did I say the wrong thing just now, or have I upset you?"

"No, you idiot, you just said one of the nicest things anyone's ever said to me and you really meant it, because I'd know, I always know. This is a tough town for a single girl, Mike, and no, no, don't say I have natural advantages. Well, perhaps I have, but that often just means that I attract the wrong type. This town is full of movers and shakers and high rollers and it can sometimes have an air of fantasy, of unreality about it. Most of the guys are married and a lot have a mistress, sometimes several. It can be really hard to make out the genuine ones, so you sort of develop a sixth sense for it, know what I mean?"

"Yes I do," he said, "but hey, that's just my luck because if the place was full of genuine guys, you'd have been snapped up a long time ago."

"Thank you but Jeez, what must you think of me? I tried to pick you up the first night we met, and I jumped right into bed with you. Christ, you must have thought I was a real one-night-stander?"

He gripped her tightly. "Now it's you who's behaving like an idiot! I can't even remember who picked up whom, but I do remember a beautiful, warm, caring lady, who behaved not the slightest bit inappropriately."

"Ok, fair enough, touché; now can we stop all this lubby-dubby crap and get some dinner? I'm starved and I'd murder a burger!"

They both ordered the House Specialty Burger with everything and washed it down with more beers. Mike couldn't understand why some people criticized American beers – to him, they were all magic, brewed to perfection, and always served ice cold; the way beer should be. Perhaps they were not as strong as European beers, but that didn't bother him – in fact, it was a positive, as he got the taste of the beer he liked and didn't wake with a hangover or that dehydrated feeling the following morning.

They talked all evening, totally at ease in each other's company. Wendy was bright and could speak on almost any subject and usually had an opinion on it, but she was also open and broad-minded and willing to accept different viewpoints as well. Some time around midnight, they managed to draw breath long enough to order a taxi, pay their tab and head away into the night – to Wendy's place this time.

She had a super apartment in the Waterfront Centre, near Washington Harbour Plaza, overlooking the river. Floor-to-ceiling windows gave a spectacular view over D.C. by night. She handed him a glass of chilled Sauvignon and went to the bathroom.

Mike said, "Wow, this place is really something – the view is just spectacular. One of the benefits of working in real estate, huh?"

"Ah, yeah, maybe something like that," she said coyly. He was still admiring the view as he glanced over his shoulder to notice that she had shed her black dress and almost everything else she had been wearing. He almost dropped the glass of wine.

He felt his voice going hoarse as he stuttered, "Just when I thought the view couldn't get any better."

He took her in his arms and carried her to the bedroom where she proceeded to do with his clothes what she had just done to her own. They took their time, kissing and touching everywhere, in total unison, gently bringing each other to places neither had ever been to before but yet seemed totally familiar and at ease with. When they had finished they replenished the wine, and after discussing and analysing some other topic, they started again, each time seemingly reaching even greater peaks of ecstasy. At one point, he had looked into those deep brown eyes and thought for a moment he saw hurt there – but it was only for an instant and then he saw her kindness and openness and deep love and he thought his heart had swollen in his chest.

When they were eventually spent, light was peeping through the hastily drawn drapes. Mike lay back against the pillows, his arm around Wendy, her head resting on his chest, listening to her soft breathing. His ability to switch off and put away the cares of the day had long since kicked in and he was totally and completely relaxed. The only thoughts in his head were about Wendy. He had uncovered a gem here, but he knew what he was like and where his lifestyle took him, and he found himself having brief doubts. Not about Wendy, but about himself. This lady was special and he would have to be careful never to hurt her.

He banished the thought immediately as ridiculous. He had told her he loved her tonight and he had meant it. She had responded in kind. Anyway, when had he ever hurt anyone?

When had he been in a position to? Again, he shook his head – no worries, man. He looked down at the gorgeous, gentle creature that was draped across his chest; oh yes, this girl was a keeper!

Although it was after 05.00am when his cell phone rang, he was still wide-awake. He eased out of bed to retrieve the phone from his jacket, which had been hurriedly draped over a chair earlier. Who was calling him at five in the morning? He was still using his British cell phone as he hadn't bothered to get a local number.

"Hello."

"Is that you, Mike? It's Alan Williams here. Sorry to bother you so early over there mate, but it's tragic news. The Prime Minister's just been shot!"

Chapter 18

Heathrow Airport was literally crawling with police and troops, most heavily armed. The biggest security alert in modern times was in full swing. Another case of closing the stable doors after the horse has bolted, Mike thought. He had come through the diplomatic channel having caught the first available flight back from D.C. and had been met by his old pal. Alan Williams had joined both the Met and MI5 around the same time as Mike, and they had soldiered through many a campaign together. Alan was still visibly shocked, as were the majority of people he noticed as they passed through the arrivals hall.

The press and the public were outraged. This was a direct attack on Britain at the highest level; a violation of everything British people held dear. The only thing that might have caused a greater reaction and outcry would have been an attack on the Monarchy itself. Democratic politicians, particularly those in the West, have to be seen to be visible. After all, they have to stand for election, and even when elected and in Government, are still subject to intense scrutiny, public criticism, and constant media polling. In order to maintain any reasonable level of popularity, they have to run the country in a decisive manner, but must take cognizance of a huge variety of different interest groups and walk a fine line if they are to retain the confidence of the electorate. While both of the two previous Prime Ministers served with distinction and were fine leaders and astute politicians, both had fallen foul of the media and eventually became so unpopular that they had had no option but to resign. While American politics was also cut-throat and the President was constantly criticized, it often appeared as if there was even more pressure on his European counterparts. This may have had something to do with the relative size of the countries or possibly the fact that in many European countries, democracies had been longer-established and people took a greater interest in politics.

This was particularly so in Britain and was possibly the reason why the incumbent P.M. had been so readily available and visible. One of his favourite routines was to go for an early morning run in one of the beautiful parks that were a feature of central London. It was good for both his health and his ratings, and was widely publicized. Unfortunately for him, it was also highly dangerous.

It was now approaching early evening as the police car carried Mike & Alan towards the city and MI5 HQ at Thames House. Mike hadn't hesitated for a moment when Alan had called him. He'd had to wake Wendy, make his apologies and head for the airport. Metro Police had provided an escort so he had managed to exit D.C. and get back to the UK in time to witness the massive manhunt that was underway.

"So what have we got, mate?" he asked Alan as they sped along the M4.

"Well, you know the Prime Minister likes to go running in the early morning a few times a week, sometimes in Hyde Park. He varies it – he has been known to run in other parks. He's always accompanied by at least five very fit personal bodyguards, but let's face it, a public park is about as open as you can get. It's a chance, of course, but really all the assassin had to do was turn up every morning and wait. Chances are, the P.M. would eventually show. If not, he could always try one of the other parks at another time."

"But where was the guy situated? I mean, he didn't just walk up to him, did he?"

"No, as you might expect, there was huge initial confusion. The P.M. was shot twice; headshots, presumably a high velocity rifle from a distance. The security detail heard nothing – the poor man just dropped like a stone beside them. The weapon was obviously silenced. So no one knew where to look or where the attack had come from. The security detail initially took cover and tried to render assistance to the P.M. but to no avail. Death was instant, apparently.

"And any update yet on where the attack took place from?"

"Yep, I'm coming to that. The guys called for back up and a major alert was put in place almost immediately, well within ten minutes. Most of Central London was shut down. The Tube and the buses stopped running. Roadblocks were erected on all streets. In fact, much of the city is still closed off, but I'm afraid we've got nothing as of yet." He sighed deeply. "Look, Mike, you know the way these things work. Realistically, a good marksman with a telescopic sight could have fired those bloody bullets from anywhere within half a mile. It's impossible to get a proper trajectory as when you are running, your head is going from side to side so no one can say what angle the man was at when he was shot." Alan's voice caught and he was clearly distressed.

"It's OK, mate, I know how you feel." Mike threw an arm round his shoulder.

"Sorry, it's just – anyway, we feel pretty sure though that the attack was either from the roof or from inside one of the buildings on Park Lane or Bayswater Road. The Met and Special Forces are currently systematically searching every room in every building, but we are talking seriously heavy real estate along there and it is taking some time."

Mike's cell phone rang. It was Paul.

"Sorry for running out on you bud but I thought I might be of better use here than I've been to your investigation."

"Hey, hey, no need for that, none of us have exactly got gold stars on that one. What's happening over there, man? It must be awful."

"To be straight, Paul, you'll probably get more on CNN right now. I'm just heading to HQ for a full briefing. I'll get back to you soon as I have some news."

"Sure thing – hey, just a parting shot. I know we're talking thousands of miles apart, but are you thinking what I'm thinking?"

Mike frowned deeply and looked at Alan. "Yeah," he said. "Unfortunately I think so."

Sir Marcus Evans greeted Mike & Alan warmly when they arrived at Thames House but the man was clearly under severe stress and seemed to have aged ten years in the few weeks since Mike had last seen him.

"Good to have you back, old chap. Dreadful business, absolutely dreadful. Really appreciate you coming to help straight away." Mike smiled inwardly. No matter how grave the circumstances, the English never forgot their manners.

"We have a meeting here with the Home Secretary at 17.00," Sir Marcus continued, "then I go on to the Joint Intelligence Chiefs meeting at 19.00. It's being chaired by the Deputy P.M. so I hope we bloody well have something concrete to report by then."

They filed hurriedly into the oak lined meeting room. Mike greeted many former colleagues and some of the military men that he had worked with. Hasty introductions were made to others. There was an air of frustration, tension, and barely controlled anger in the room. People took this personally. This was no ordinary act of terrorism. Several conversations were taking place at once and nervous glances were being cast at the door in anticipation of the arrival of the Home Secretary.

Mike found himself lost in thought. Although the institution of Parliament in England had existed since 1241, it was only after the overthrow of King Charles the first in 1649 and the subsequent Act of Union in 1707 that a real parliamentary democracy commenced. In over 300 years since, only one previous Prime Minister, Spencer Perceval, had been assassinated, in 1812, if his schoolboy history studies served him correctly. He scanned many of his former colleagues and knew how they must be feeling – awful to have a tragedy like this happen on their watch.

There was a hush as the Home Secretary was ushered into the room. His countenance appeared grave and he seemed to reflect the public mood. Nonetheless, he remained stoic – none better than the British to maintain the stiff upper lip, thought Mike.

He immediately dispensed with all formalities and waved everyone to be seated so he could get straight down to business. "Thank you for coming, Ladies and Gents," he began. "I don't need to tell you that this is the most serious terrorist attack we have ever experienced in peacetime. There is a great fear, almost a panic, out there amongst the British public. I can't say our press is helping either with their claims that this will rock Britain to its foundations, et cetera. What I can tell you is that we are putting absolutely everything at your disposal on this. Whatever you want, name it. But I must stress to all of you, it is absolutely imperative that this assassin is apprehended, and quickly. Apart from easing public disquiet, we owe it to our Prime Minister, to our Government and to our democracy; indeed we are talking about the preservation of our British way of life to bring this person to justice. I trust we are all in agreement."

There were murmurs of assent and nodding heads around the table.

"Now, the Deputy P.M. has recorded a statement appealing to the public to remain calm. This will be broadcast at 19.00 and Her Majesty is going to make a statement at 21.00. We are hopeful that this will allay fears somewhat, but what we really need is some hard information. Sir Marcus, can you or any of your people give us anything new?"

"With your permission sir, if I may bring everyone up to speed on the events of the past nine hours or thereabouts?"

"Of course, of course, man, go ahead."

Sir Marcus very briefly updated the gathering on what had transpired and their efforts to date to track down the culprit. "Home Secretary," he continued, "before I ask each section head to report on the various measures we are undertaking, I think you may want to hear from Senior Investigative Officer, Anne Parker."

"Of course, go ahead, Ms Parker."

"Well, sir, we think we may have a definite location on where the shots were fired from. We have conducted a thorough search of all buildings within range of the shooting and, well sir; we think the gunman operated from a suite in the Dorchester Hotel on Park Lane."

There was a collective gasp in the room. There goes their reputation, thought Mike.

"Please continue, Ms Parker," said the Home Secretary.

"Sir, we found minute traces of gunpowder in one of the Park Suites in the Dorchester. The suite was rented by a Sheikh Rashid Al Faroukh, a gentleman of Saudi Arabian origin. It was booked and paid for online. The reservation was for fourteen nights, and the bill was paid in advance by credit card. Hotel reception says the Sheikh collected the keys seven days ago but they have not seen him since. Our forensic people are currently examining the suite but it looks like it is unoccupied. I mean sir, that it looks like it was never used. There were no room service orders. The mini bar was untouched, and nothing was charged to the room from any of the bars or restaurants. We checked with the hotel cleaning services and they confirmed that the suite was vacuumed daily, but beds did not appear to have been slept in and the entire suite appeared to have been unoccupied."

"Just a minute; was the room vacuumed this morning?" asked Alan.

"Yes, at around 10.30. We are inspecting the vacuum cleaner for any traces but the machine was used in other rooms and suites so it may be difficult. By the way, the staff say vacant suites rented by wealthy clients are not exactly unusual so they wouldn't have attracted attention – just one less room to clean. We have been conducting interviews with as many residents as possible, but to date none of them saw a gunman, or our Saudi gentleman; but we will continue our enquiries."

Mike had been concentrating hard. "Anne, may I? – Can you get your team to search for another resident who's been in the hotel for the same length of time or longer than the Saudi, and who now appears to have vacated the hotel? I mean, if the guy rented a suite for a week and didn't use it, he hardly hid in the broom cupboard. He had to live somewhere. I know it's a long shot and that room may have been cleaned also but it's worth a try."

"Good idea, that, and excellent work, Ms Parker. Well done," said the Home Secretary. The remainder of the meeting consisted mainly of briefings on the lock-down of the city, the country's ports, airports and other transport systems. The group was impressed and felt sure that no matter how clever the assassin was, he was still inside British territory and would no doubt be found, given time and the expected cooperation of the British public. Mike wasn't so sure.

"Didn't they install a Digital based Security System at the Dorchester some time ago that's absolutely the last word in video surveillance?" he asked Alan.

"Think you're right, mate. You reckon we should get down there?"

"Well, we have to start somewhere and it beats hanging round here."

The Head of Security at the hotel was Arthur Ward, who was a very affable, dapper English gent, who, apart from being highly embarrassed at what had happened in his hotel, was delighted to show off his state-of-the-art IP Video Surveillance system. Arthur explained that all the data was digitized so he could access a video recording of any part of the hotel at any given time of the day or night for the previous three years.

Mike said, "OK, so let's call up the corridor where the Saudi's suite was located at, what time did the P.M. go running, eight am? So, say from 07.15." Arthur pressed a series of buttons and an image of a corridor came into view.

"Can you fast forward, I mean, play it at say, times 20?"

"Absolutely." He pressed another button and the frame flickered ever so slightly but remained blank. All watched as the digital clock crept onwards towards eight o'clock and beyond. "The man was shot at approximately 08.15, right," said Mike, "so if we missed the guy going in, he's gotta be coming out soon." But he didn't. They continued watching as the clock zipped through the minutes until it was after 09.00 am.

"Bloody hell, this can't be right," said Alan. "Is there another exit from the suite?"

"No sir, only this door."

"Well then, either our man is invisible, or he stayed there all morning, or he didn't use this suite at all. I guess we continue watching. Can you call up another date and time simultaneously on this system?"

"Absolutely sir, when would you like to see?"

"Reception said Mr Saudi checked in last Saturday morning at the centre desk at around 12.15. Start me at say 12.00 and run through to 12.30. Mike, can you staying watching that one and I'll see if we can we get him here?"

Arthur pressed more buttons and the hotel lobby came into clear view. A receptionist could be seen greeting guests and assisting them with reservations. They ran the tape at rapid speed, then again at a reduced level but there was no Saudi to be seen, no gentleman in Arabic attire came near the reception desk. Mike began to have that sinking feeling again.

"Ah Arthur, this system, it is top of the range, right? So, it's got to be connected to the internet, yeah?"

Arthur nodded. He seemed offended. "Are you suggesting it may have been interfered with in some way or images erased sir? Surely not, I can't imagine..."

"Arthur", Mike began, "can you run the receptionist section again and actually count the precise number of minutes and seconds in the slot?"

"Why, certainly, sir."

It only took a few minutes. Arthur's eyes widened as he checked and rechecked and then his face fell. "I'm really so dreadfully sorry gentlemen, it appears as if, dear oh dear..." The digital read-out said 28.04. There were two missing minutes.

Mike's cell phone buzzed. It was Anne. "I think we may have something here. All hotel guests are contacted and accounted for, with some still being questioned, but there's a double room on the fourth floor that was supposedly booked for meetings by a group called Intrepid Offshore Enterprises. The room was booked around the same time as the Park Suite and was also paid for in advance by credit card, and an advance of £1,000 was also paid for extras. We are trying to run a trace on the card right now. No one at reception can remember who collected the room card or when but we will keep checking. Someone sure did, because there were a large number of room service meals and drinks delivered to the room, and extensive use was also made of the mini-bar. We've called the room continuously, but no one is answering – I think this could be it. The duty manager has offered to let us in quietly. You wanna join us?"

"We're on our way. We'll meet you in the lobby in two."

It was a standard hotel room; that is, if anything in the Dorchester could be called standard. It was a beautifully appointed room, with precise attention to guest requirements in the design and placement of everything it contained. It had more extras than Mike had ever encountered in a hotel room, but for all that, it was as empty as the Park Suite. The Forensic squad was on the way so all wore white zip-up coveralls, plastic gloves and bootees to prevent contamination of the area. They needn't have bothered, thought Mike.

He enquired of the duty manager, who had waited in the hallway, "Presumably this room was also thoroughly cleaned and vacuumed today?"

"Oh yes indeed sir, all rooms are thoroughly serviced daily, regardless of whether they have been in use."

It was what they hadn't wanted to hear. Alan tried a long shot. "Would the linen that was removed have already been laundered?"

"I will double check for you, sir, but I'm afraid it probably has."

Mike looked around the room again, trying to think, trying to visualize, and trying to concentrate. You were in here, you bastard, he thought. But who are you? What are you doing? Why are you doing this? Is someone paying you? Who? Most importantly, where the hell are you now?

Although he was three and a half thousand miles from D.C., something told him, made him almost certain they were looking for the same killer. Too many similarities; two gunshots to the head, silenced weapon, no trace of the killer, hotel computer systems hacked expertly. No, it had to be. Although the room was precisely air conditioned, he felt a cold shiver run through him and a sense of weariness seemed to descend on his spirit. He had fought and won against many foes and faced down many attacks from every quarter. He had seen it all, but this was new; this was sinister; this guy was pristine; this was terrorism meets organised crime.

He shrugged off his lethargy as the forensic boys arrived with their cases of equipment. "Best of luck, boys," he said. "Take the place apart – everything; floorboards, carpets, AC ducts, light fittings – I want everything, every microbe in there analysed!" The duty manager watched and recoiled in quiet alarm. Mike clapped him on the shoulder. "Don't worry, mate, they'll put it all back together."

The head of Forensics gathered his team to allocate responsibilities and confirmed that they had already taken the Park Suite apart and had bags of microscopic particles – but very little else – on the way to the lab. Even though it was probably futile, Mike, Alan and Anne wanted to visit the Suite; to walk the ground, as it were. The assassin had chosen well. It was about ten paces to the elevator, then up two floors and another ten paces to the door of the suite.

"It's amazing," Anne mentioned, "hundreds of people walk around hotels every day, but can you remember anyone you ever saw in a hotel? It's the ideal place to get lost or hide in plain sight. No one we've spoken to remembers seeing anyone going into or coming out of either room."

"Yeah," said Alan, "we'll check the digital recordings of this room also, but if he's as good as we think he is, they'll be erased also."

"He was careful with the room service people as well," said Anne. "Bob McDonald's team are talking to them right now and trying to track any who are off duty but those they've spoken to so far never had sight of the occupant of the fourth floor room. He either asked them to leave the food outside or he was in the shower and asked them to leave it on the table. They say he had left generous tips for the guys who came into the room, so no one paid any heed. We're speaking to the guys who service the mini-bar also but up to now, they confirm that as far as they can remember, neither the room nor the suite was ever occupied when they came."

"Do you not have to sign a tab when you order from room service?" Mike said.

Anne smiled. "Not if you are paying £700 a night in the Dorchester, old boy, or certainly not if you are paying £2,600 per night for one of the Park Suites, with a, and I quote – 'magnificent view of Hyde Park'."

Mike sighed deeply again; perhaps it was jetlag beginning to take hold. "Well, I suppose that gives us one piece of information – this is obviously a seriously funded operation. For fourteen nights for a suite and a room in this place, then we must be talking over fifty grand; that's eighty thousand dollars. Jesus, whoever's funding this has got serious dosh."

Anne's phone went again and she moved away to take it. She was tall, about five seven, long limbed, athletic, very slim but supremely fit. She was blonde, blue eyed and attractive, if not classically beautiful. She had dimples around her mouth, which became more prominent when she smiled. She was forty-three years old, divorced, had two children in private school and she was also Alan Williams' partner. It was unusual in the service, but it had never been a problem for them.

Anne had joined MI5 straight from university as an analyst, but had quickly realised she had a talent for investigation and had been promoted rapidly. Alan had travelled the same route as Mike, starting with the Met. They were thoroughly professional colleagues, and if Mike hadn't known they had lived together for over ten years, he would not have guessed.

Anne thanked the caller and turned back to the guys. They knew from her demeanour that it was not exactly good news.

"Right, the bad news first. We've been in touch with the Saudi Embassy; interesting – they believe that the passport is genuine although it's difficult to tell from a photocopy. The Saudi gentleman exists but there is a problem with that – they absolutely assure us this man has never been further than Mecca; so, presumably, it's identity theft. The credit cards used to make both reservations were both genuine Visa Cards, but were registered to an offshore agency. Bills are paid through a web of bank accounts and are untraceable."

"Damn it," said Alan. "I wish they'd clean up those off shore banking havens. They make things impossible for us. Oh, sorry, you said you have good news?"

"Oh yes, we have indeed," she smiled. "Police boarded the 17.30 Eurostar train from St Pancras to Paris Gare du Nord and have apprehended a gentleman who was travelling alone. He was apparently carrying a number of passports including both British and French and refused to disclose why or where he was going or what his business was. But wait, Transport Police, using their powers of search, examined his luggage and it contained a disassembled high-powered Steyr rifle with a telescopic sight! He is refusing to speak to anyone until he is provided with legal advice. He is being transported back to London as we speak and should be at Scotland Yard in about half an hour."

"I think we'll leave here to the forensic boys. Let's get over there," said Mike.

Chapter 19

Although it was still high summer, the sun had hidden behind dark clouds and it was threatening rain. The atmosphere seemed bleak, almost as if the weather had chosen to match the public mood. They drove through practically deserted streets, unknown for central London at this time of day. Transport systems were operating again, albeit heavily policed, but there were few takers. Mike had witnessed the city in the immediate aftermath of the 7/7 bombings, but this was even worse. It was like wartime, or what he imagined wartime would have been like. It seemed that almost everyone had fled to the countryside and those few who hadn't were staying safely indoors. There appeared to be a collective sense of shock at what was being perceived and portrayed as a blatant attack on the institution of British democracy.

"It doesn't take much, does it?" he commented.

"Nope," said Alan, "this generation scares easily, but it's hard to blame them. They have been brought up in an era of relative peace and plenty. Something like this leaves them lost and confused, and moreover, scares the bloody hell out of them."

"Let's hope this guy they're bringing to the yard leads us somewhere; but I have my doubts. What do you think Anne?"

"Have to agree. It sounds unlike our man. I mean, why go to the trouble of making such painstaking plans that allow him to remain undetected for a week and then get clean away if he's going to board a train with his rifle slung over his shoulder? On the other hand, perhaps he's just an incredibly cool customer, who likes to hide in plain sight?"

"Or perhaps he's a patsy, a plant, a dupe," added Alan. "I mean, this guy is clever so he's probably got contingency plans. All our people are still on full alert anyway."

"You know," Mike said, "Society is a strange thing. It can go along from day to day through months and even years, then something like this happens and it is shaken to its foundations – confidence can disappear in an instant. Later on, it will gather itself together again and, as they say, life will go on, but you'd wonder will it be the same and for how long?"

"True," Alan responded. "You know, every time we have a terrorist attack, we get repeated political pledges and promises that we will retain and even strengthen our culture and way of life, but if you ask me, they have been seriously eroded in recent years by global terrorism. We no longer have the freedoms of heretofore to go about our daily lives. People expect *us* to hold the line, to catch the bad guys and make them feel safe again, but there is a limit to what we can do."

Anne added, "If the public lose confidence in us or if we are made to look incompetent, then our leaders look incompetent. People lose confidence and pretty soon, darker elements emerge; right wing reactionaries, advocates of a police state – it can happen quite easily you know. There are umpteen examples in Africa, Asia, and South America. Democracy is a very fragile flower and unless it is carefully nurtured, it can wither away quite easily."

"Agreed," said Mike. "What has taken 350 years to achieve could be lost very quickly. I suppose we are all asking ourselves who would want this sort of situation or who would benefit? There are a number of possibilities but one obvious answer. Somewhat strange that no one has been claiming responsibility. You would have thought that they'd be positively gloating; or perhaps the silence is part of the plan – to keep people confused and fearful. Anyway, let's see what this guy looks like."

Guns - any amount of them, or any type – can be obtained in any city in the world, if you know where to look. Walker had known where in London and had acquired what he needed easily enough.

He was an excellent marksman and wasn't fussy about the type of rifle he used, having practiced with nearly all of them over the years. In London he had acquired an Austrian Steyr Mannlicher Aug 223 which would literally stop an elephant in its tracks. He initially had not intended to use it again, but after quickly disassembling it and making good his getaway from the Dorchester, he had the problem of how to dispose of it. Had he left it at the hotel, there was a possibility, however slight, that it might be traced to the person who had supplied him. Given the magnitude of the crime and the public outrage, severe pressure would be placed on the supplier to reveal whom he had sold the rifle to. The possibility of tracking him was still remote but no point leaving any loose ends, no matter how small. The second problem was that the police dragnet had swung into action more quickly than he had envisaged and he had been forced to change his persona sooner than he had planned.

He had dressed as an Arab each morning when entering and leaving the Park Suite, but he had encountered no one at any stage – he entered each morning at 07.00 and left at 09.00, except on that morning when he left at 08.17. He knew it was a gamble; the man he wanted could have decided not to run that week, or he could have used one of the other parks. Staying in the hotel wasn't a problem, but he couldn't do it indefinitely. The fall-back plan was to hit his man at a constituency function that was to take place the following week. It was slightly riskier, as he would have had to get much closer, so he was glad his favoured plan had worked out.

The morning had been clear and bright and he'd had sight of the party from quite a way off. He had no idea which way they would go, and as they could have turned behind a group of trees at any moment, disrupting his aim, he fired at the first opportunity. Then he had calmly disassembled the rifle, gathered up his brass, and briefly wiped down anything he had touched.

He exited the room and walked to the lift where he went to the room on the fourth floor where he had effectively lived for the previous week, only leaving the hotel on a few occasions to acquire items he needed and once to visit Paris for the day on the Eurostar. He had always been careful to access the hotel's computerized security system on his return and quickly delete any images of himself that appeared on the system. It was easy to erase a few minutes or 30 seconds from the security system; child's play when you knew how.

He had envisaged a massive police manhunt so his initial idea had been to leave the hotel dressed as an Australian tourist, then to change into his favourite "smelly old man" routine which would allow him to negotiate London's streets with total impunity. No one stopped a homeless person, particularly one smelling strongly of alcohol and various other noxious odours. Still, he did have quite a bit of luggage and while it could be carefully disguised as the poor man effectively carrying his life on his back, he didn't want to risk it. The police were likely to stop everyone when something of this magnitude occurred. No, better to change more quickly into the persona that would get him out of the country – that of a charming and attractive middle-aged lady.

It was disarmingly simple, really; he had perfected the accent years ago and worked on it constantly when alone in his cabin in the wilderness in Florida. He had never been detected. When police hunted a gunman, they automatically thought *man* – women don't do assassination, right? To make it better, no one ever questioned a woman with lots of luggage; it was almost another validation in itself.

The doorman at the Dorchester had been very helpful when the "lady" had indicated that she wished to travel to Heathrow, and had whistled a taxi from the line almost instantly. The black cab driver had cautioned that they might well be delayed as "there seemed to be some major police incident or operation underway." She was perfectly charming and said she had plenty of time and she was sure he would get her there on time. As it happened, Central London was almost totally locked down, much to the chagrin of the cabbie. London taxi drivers are probably the most knowledgeable in the world, and this one tried numerous alternative routes, but to no avail.

As his passenger had indicated that 'her' flight was due to depart at two o'clock and as it was now 10.30 and he was making very little progress, he suggested, reluctantly, that she consider the Heathrow Express Train Service from Paddington. She readily agreed and he managed to get her there by 11.15, apologizing profusely throughout the journey. She dismissed the delay as beyond his control and in addition to the fare, added a generous tip. In fact, the delay and diversion to Paddington served his purpose perfectly. The plan had been to travel to Heathrow, spend an hour or two and then get a taxi back to the city – a Mrs Catherine Ramsey had a reservation on the half five Eurostar to Paris and that was the name on the passport he was currently using.

Now, all he had to do was drink coffee and read a newspaper in Paddington for an hour or two, then get the tube over to St Pancras. He was sure the service would be disrupted and probably quite slow but he had plenty of time. He still had the disassembled rifle but the problem was where to dispose of it. He could leave it in a rest room or try to find a bin large enough but the difficulty was that if it was discovered, he was sure that the entire transport system would be shut down in the search. This would have thrown his plans awry and might even lead to greater problems. It was highly unlikely that anyone would dare to search a middle aged lady's baggage so he decided to keep it for now.

He was delayed transferring to St Pancras station by underground but he had lots of time so there was no panic. Mrs Catherine Ramsey collected her pre-booked ticket for the Eurostar without incident. He knew it was a risk taking the rifle case on board the train, and it was something he wouldn't have normally attempted. However, the rifle broke down beautifully and was carried in a bag indistinguishable from a normal gym hold-all. At the station, there were security checks but no scanners.

Mike had never seen Scotland Yard like this before. Heavily-armed police backed up by troops were guarding all key installations, and getting into Police HQ required scrutiny of a type they had never experienced. The general mood of alarm and disquiet seemed to have spread to the troops, who were nervous and edgy. Mike supposed that, regardless of political preference, everyone abhorred the idea of assassination, and when it was the leader of the country, it provoked a sense of outrage as if each individual felt that he or she was being attacked. He felt sure the Prime Minister would now be far more popular in death than he was when he was alive.

The prisoner had been placed in one of the usual questioning rooms and was under constant observation. The room in question had three separate CCTV cameras so the man could be viewed from a variety of angles. He was alone in the room and was seated at a table. He was not handcuffed and had been given a cup of tea. He was of medium height and looked like he spent lots of time in the gym. He had broad shoulders, a strong chest and narrow hips. He had neat dark hair cut short, a square jaw, a face that was set firm and difficult to read and dullish blue eyes that stared straight ahead. Age was difficult to determine although both his passports stated that he was 48. Three heavily armed policemen stood guard outside the door but the man was going nowhere. He appeared remarkably calm and unconcerned despite being at the sharp focus of one of the biggest manhunts in history.

Detective Chief Superintendent Bob McDonald was watching him intently through the CCTV monitor. He stood up to greet Anne, Alan and Mike as they entered. "Good to have you back, old son," he said warmly. "Don't know what we have here, he's a strange one for sure."

Bob was a very sharp and wily Scotsman who had grown up in the tougher parts of Dundee. He was thirty years out of Scotland, but the casual observer wouldn't know it. He had the reputation of being able to spot a criminal from about a mile away and his instincts rarely if ever failed him.

"So what do you think, Bob?" said Mike. "Is he our boy? I presume you haven't questioned him yet?"

"No, we haven't. I'm gonna go in there soon and have a chat with the wee man. Oh, I reckon he's a bad boy alright, but whether he's the bad boy we want, I'm not sure. We've sent the rifle to ballistics for checking and they should be back shortly. I believe the bastard used soft nose bullets that more or less disintegrated on impact but they should be able to tell us something. OK, let's see if we can get him to say anything. He's asked for a brief but we'll tell him it'll take time. It is Friday evening after all. You want to sit in, Alan?"

"Absolutely, do you want to take him yourself or will I pitch in?"

"Hmmm, not sure, let's see how things develop – that's if we can get anything out of him at all."

They entered the interrogation room and took seats at the table, Bob facing the man and Alan to his left. Mike and Anne and their colleagues kept watch by CCTV. One of the cameras was strategically placed so that the prisoner would know he was being taped. The other two were surreptitious and designed to try to gauge the man's mood although they were of limited value. The prisoner did not make eye contact with either man and stared straight ahead. Bob noticed that the man had drunk his tea.

"So, how was your tea?"

"It was fine, thank you."

Hmm, he speaks, Bob thought. Accent difficult to place – polite English but not an Englishman he felt. "Would you care for another one?"

"Not just now, thank you."

"Right, old son," Bob began, "so let's try to get this over with quickly so we can all get some rest. Who are you, where do you come from, and who are you working for?"

"I'm sorry; I told the arresting officer when he read me my rights that I wished to remain silent. I have nothing to say until I am given access to legal counsel."

"Yes, but you haven't named your legal adviser, old son, and as it's Friday evening, we may not be able to get you one until Monday. Now, do you want to sit here all weekend pussyfooting around? I mean, suit yourself, but Alan and myself here, we can go home at any stage and someone can take over from us."

"But you cannot question me indefinitely. I am entitled to some rest."

"Aye, perhaps legally you are, me old mate," said Bob, leaning in close to the man, "but right now, given the feeling in this country, I doubt anyone would mind if we questioned you till next March."

The man gave no reply but appeared momentarily to be unsure.

"Fine, suit yourself; I'm away for mah supper. If ya feel like talking when I'm gone, give Alan here a shout." Bob noisily withdrew his chair, got up and left the room. Alan made to go with him, then hesitated.

"Look," he said, "my colleague is just going through the motions here. Now I'm not playing good cop with you because I think you're far too bright to fall for that, but to be honest, I don't think he cares whether you talk or not. I certainly don't. I mean, we'd like to know who you're working for and why you did it but it doesn't really matter either way. You are in deep, deep shit, my friend – you are going down for a long time, possibly forever. There are gonna be no deals for the likes of you."

Again, the man said nothing, but that flicker of uncertainty or perhaps confusion passed across his eyes again.

"OK, if you don't want to talk, I'm not hanging round wasting my time."

"Are you just going to leave me here?"

Ah ha, he scares just like the rest of them, Alan thought. He decided to try something – maybe a long shot.

"Well no, I mean, we'll leave you here for a while just in case you change your mind. Then we'll send you down to the cells. Now, a guy like you, as important as you, should really get their own cell, top security and all that; but, as I say, given the public mood and all that, I think we might just throw you in with the riff raff. We've got some choice cookies in tonight – you know; you could be someone's new girlfriend before morning!"

The man remained impassive and Alan felt maybe he had pushed a bit too far. He was just closing the door when the man said, barely audibly, "Wait."

"OK, but make it quick. I've wasted enough time on you already."

"Look," the man began, "I've done nothing; you cannot prove I have committed any crime."

Strange choice of words, Alan thought. "Don't make me laugh," he retorted, "we have your bag and we found you travelling on a false passport making your getaway. What more do we need?"

"But the bag is not mine. I was, ah, only delivering it for someone, ah, to someone."

"Oh I see, only delivering it – but to whom?"

"I'm sorry, that I cannot say. It would make my life worthless"

"Well then we're back to square one, mate," Alan said as he slammed the door. He returned to the observation room. "What do you think, folks?" he enquired.

"He's guilty as sin," Anne felt, "but of what I'm not sure."

Mike was confused. "I agree he's sure as hell guilty but it doesn't make sense that an assassin would shoot someone, keep the rifle, and then pay someone to deliver it to Paris for him, or would it? Perhaps he has more business in Paris; or perhaps he's sitting in front of us in there?"

Alan said, "Anne, do the voice analysts have any idea where he's from? I mean, did they come up with a read from the tape?"

"Well they say the base is English, as in, he is a native English speaker; but they can't place it. It could be someone born in Ireland or the North of England but who has spent a lot of time out of the country, but that's as close as they can get."

"So what do we do, wait around and hope he changes his mind?"

"You can if you want, but I'm gonna go get a coffee and see if I can make any more sense of this thing. Anyone want to join me?" said Mike.

"Yeah, why not," said Bob. "The coffee here isn't the best but at least it'll keep us alert."

Just as he was about to board the train, he had seen the solution standing a few paces away from him. A dark-haired intense-looking man stood in line with a suitcase and a bag remarkably similar to his own. He manoeuvred himself discreetly into the line and just as they were about to board, politely asked the man if he could be of assistance in loading the luggage. The man looked nervous but chivalrously agreed to help a lady and it was incredibly simple to switch bags. Now, if the man was stopped and searched, it would create a nice diversion. If not, he could switch the bags later – or maybe not.

He didn't see and wasn't aware that the man had been arrested as they were seated in separate carriages. However, he was aware that the train had made an unscheduled stop before it reached the Channel Tunnel and he noticed that the both the man and the bag had disappeared when he visited the carriage to use the bathroom. There had been police on the train earlier and they had checked all passengers' passports. His had been in good order. It had been examined and returned to him without even a hint of suspicion. As he had thought, no one suspected middle aged women; no one was going to search a refined looking glamorous woman on a train to Paris, especially when all her papers were in order and when she was charming and not unattractive.

When they reached the Gare Du Nord, he collected all his bags, including the substituted one. He then paid a visit to the invalid rest room and emerged ten minutes later as Mark Denby, just arrived from Melbourne. He took a taxi to the Royal Monceau Hotel, just off Charles De Gaulle Etoile at the top of the Champs Elysses, where he checked in and told the pretty receptionist that he was looking forward to his first visit to Paris. It was getting late but this was Paris and he still had plenty of time to have dinner in his favourite restaurant in Montmartre.

He had always known, or thought he had known, what the aims of his Principals were. But it was deeper than that. Now, he realized what these guys were at; by striking at will at specific strategic targets, they spread terror on a much greater scale and on a different level than they had previously achieved with random attacks on the public. People might criticize their leaders but they also looked up to them and expected to be protected by them. If they couldn't even protect themselves, where did that leave the public? Bloody scared, that's where.

In London, Anne, Bob, Alan and Mike were deep in conversation when Alan's cell phone rang. He was in animated conversation for several minutes and his demeanour went from pleased to hopeful to apprehensive. The others looked on expectantly.

"That was Trevor Diamond, ballistics. Listen to this – the bullets were soft nose, Remington 223's. They say they cannot be 100% sure but it is very likely that the bullets which killed the P.M. were fired from the rifle in our suspect's bag."

The others rose as one. "Let's have another go at him," said Bob.

Alan cautioned, "Wait, hold it, there's more. We got a match on his fingerprints. He's been arrested before but got off on some technicality; the charge – narcotics smuggling or trafficking."

"Has he graduated to higher things?" mused Anne. "Unlikely, I'd say."

Once again, Bob sat opposite the suspect, only this time Alan took the right flank. The cameras were switched on. The suspect had been fetched up from the cells where he had after all been given a cubicle to himself. They couldn't afford to take chances with this one so the guy had been placed in an isolation unit and was being monitored on CCTV.

"Ok, old son," Bob began, "now it's close to midnight and I'm tired and cranky so don't give me that old shite about wanting a lawyer. I'm sure they're all tucked up in their beds at this stage anyway. We've got the match from ballistics so you're a goner either way. Now, I can't promise a thing on this one but look, make it easy on yourself and tell us who you work for and where your accomplices are and we just might go easy on you."

The man now looked utterly confused and worried. He was silent for a time, seeming to think hard, and then he ventured, "Excuse me, but I am not sure I understand. What is this ballistics report? I do not use weapons. I am a simple courier, but perhaps I can help you?"

Bob glanced at Alan and they both subconsciously glanced towards the viewing area where the others would have been watching intently. Bob caught Alan's eye and nodded almost imperceptibly.

Alan began. "You were arrested in possession of a false passport and you were carrying a grey hold-all bag which contained a rifle that we are certain was used in the commission of a major crime earlier today."

The man seemed thoughtful. "And that is the only bag you seized from me, is this correct? I am not being charged with any other crime?"

"We are going to charge you with capital murder if you don't come up with a bloody good reason why we shouldn't and bloody quickly!"

"OK, if I help you, can you guarantee that the charge of possession of the passport will be forgotten about?"

"We can't guarantee anything at this time of night son, but I wouldn't worry about it if I were you," this from Bob.

"O.K., I have been thinking about the situation all evening and I was prepared to wait it out but I think we can resolve this fairly quickly. I boarded the half five Eurostar to Paris this evening. I had one bag, a grey hold-all containing my clothes and personal effects and a small parcel I was bringing to a friend in Paris. My bag did not contain any firearms or any weapons of any sort." He paused. "But I think I know what happened."

"Go ahead," said Bob. The atmosphere reeked of tension.

"Well, I'm fairly sure; no, almost certain that my bag was switched, and I think I know now when it happened."

"Yeah, right; well, did you get a look at the guy who switched it or do you know who it was?" said Alan, expectantly.

"Oh indeed I did, in fact I can provide you with a full description, but I would need a guarantee of immunity from prosecution."

Alan and Bob exchanged looks. "Give us five minutes," said Bob.

They left the interrogation room again. Bob raised his eyebrows.

"Well, what do you think? Is he on the level or is this a cock and bull story?

"Hard to call it, but if I was pushed, I'd say the man is telling the truth, or at least a part of the truth. I doubt he's our man, Bob, sorry."

"Get me the D.P.P. soon as you can," Bob said to Anne.

"Holding on line three for you, sir," she replied. "We thought you might need him. Everyone's available on this one."

It took Bob about two minutes to explain the position to the Director of Public Prosecutions and another two minutes to have the document typed up, signed and faxed through to Scotland Yard. Alan and Bob were back with the suspect within the five minutes they had asked for.

"Right," Alan said, "give - full description of the man who changed bags."

The man smiled, "Of course, he said, but it wasn't a man, it was a woman!"

Both dashed back to the observation room. Mike offered, "We need to get the French on this straight away. I have an old friend in the Surete I can call who'll get on it immediately. It shouldn't be too difficult to match the names of passengers with hotel reservations, or will it? We do have the names of all passengers, don't we?" He thought again how the assassin in the U.S. had managed to disappear without trace, presumably using aliases. It would probably be another fruitless search – but they had to try. Mike squeezed the paper coffee cup, crushed it and kicked it into the corner. "Fuck it," he said. "How many hours have we wasted? I was always a bit doubtful of the guy but damn it, we had the bloody rifle, so the guy was on that train – well, he must have been, and must have switched bags; clever bastard. Damn it, we were so close."

"Not close enough, old son," said Bob. "I'm afraid this bastard won't be caught easily. We've already alerted the French and asked them to follow up on all passengers who were on that train, particularly the ones in the carriage where our suspect was arrested."

"Yeah, pity we didn't do it earlier, though," Mike retorted, "when he was on the train. At least now we know what we're up against. I think he must be using disguises. I don't buy the idea for one moment of a woman assassin, certainly not one who's five feet nine and wears a round neck top, but I don't think our friend in there is lying either; at least, not about the description."

"There's a late night service on the Eurostar, guys," said Anne. "Who wants to go home to bed, or who wants to go to Paris?

"I suppose it's our only lead, so put me on it," said Mike, wearily. Bob & Alan agreed.

"You know," Mike said to the others, "the guy could still be in the UK, but I wouldn't be surprised if he's somewhere in Paris right now, relaxing with a drink. Then again, I wouldn't be surprised either if he was already half way to Bordeaux or, come to think of it, anywhere on the entire continent."

The deep resigned sighs of his colleagues echoed his thoughts.

In Bahrain, it was quite late but Abdullah could not sleep. He was ecstatic. He kept changing from one channel to the next and all told the same story. The world was changing; people were terrified. Leaders were paralyzed and helpless, and this was only the beginning! The thin false veneer that covered western society would soon be shredded into tiny pieces. And when it did, they would be ready, and would achieve a glorious triumph. This evening, the unprecedented had happened – several members of the Council had broken their self-imposed silence to send him coded messages of congratulation. All traces of his previous nervousness and apprehension had gone. Nothing would stop him now – he was sure victory would be his.

Chapter 20

The Head of the Sous Directorate Anti-Terroriste, or Anti-Terrorist Sub-Directorate, Chief Inspector Jean-Pierre Chretien, was working late at Surete Headquarters. For a Frenchman, he enjoyed an excellent relationship with MI5, and they had cooperated in numerous Anglo-French crimes in recent years, particularly since the advent of the Channel Tunnel and the ease of travel it had brought between both countries. The Tunnel had greatly improved transport links, but as with any service, it created lots of opportunities for criminals.

He had been having a late supper with Marie when the call had come for assistance and without hesitating he returned to his office and set to work. He had called his closest colleagues from the car and all had also readily agreed to help with the manhunt. There had been almost 500 people on the Eurostar train, but he had deployed his entire department and had already tracked down and eliminated over 300 of them, even though it was only just after 04.00 am.

The British were particularly interested in a middle-aged lady with three pieces of luggage, including a silver grey holdall. While he would eventually check all the passengers, the search for now was focused on a Mrs Catherine Ramsey. The waiter on the train had confirmed that a woman answering her description had definitely travelled on the train and that he had served her coffee and a baguette. A porter had confirmed that he had helped this lady off the train.

But there the trail had ended; for now, anyway. A citywide alert to every taxi company had drawn a blank. Several taxi drivers had confirmed collecting passengers at the Gare du Nord who had presumably travelled on the Eurostar, but none had carried a middle-aged lady. This did not necessarily mean that the woman hadn't exited, but it did complicate the search. If they had only known beforehand, they could have cordoned off the entire station and searched everyone on the train. Now, the woman could have caught another train to any one of hundreds of destinations. Over thirty trains had left Gare du Nord since the Eurostar had arrived, mainly provincial services, some of which stopped literally everywhere. A TGV had also left for Brussels but it had already arrived there. The person could have been met at Gare du Nord. He or she could have been picked up by a taxi that was not registered with any of the major Paris taxi companies.

But Jean-Pierre was not beaten yet. He was an old style, attention-to-detail, check-out-every-possible-lead policeman. As the Eurostar had arrived relatively late, and as the assassin had been trying to escape the UK, it was unlikely that he would have undertaken another journey. His old friend Mike had told him that their suspect was in fact probably male and travelling in disguise so it was a natural step to assume he had again changed identity on arrival. That would account for the fact that no one remembered carrying a middle-aged English woman. He now broadened the alert to the taxi companies to include all men of medium height with luggage collected at Gare du Nord – yes, a long shot, he felt, but it had to be pursued. Something told him that the man was still in Paris.

The door burst open and a rather haggard-looking Mike, Anne, Bob and Alan trooped in. Handshakes and embraces were exchanged and Jean-Pierre offered his heartfelt sympathy to his British colleagues on the death of their Prime Minister.

"Rest assured, my dear friends," he told them, "if this man is in Paris, we will find him." Mike thanked him sincerely but wasn't so sure.

Jean-Pierre was the exact opposite of what was often described as an archetypal French man. He was tall and fair-haired, and almost Germanic in bearing. He was barrel-chested and had a slight paunch, but he was as fit as his younger colleagues, with whom he still played five-a-side football every week. He had a permanently pleasant face, which often lulled people into a false sense of security and belied the steel behind the mask. He also had smiling twinkling eyes and an easy manner that made him extremely popular. He was rumoured to be pushing 50 but no one was really sure and he wasn't saying.

"So, I hear you have sold out and are now helping the Americans, my dear friend," he joked.

"I'm not so sure help is what you'd call it Jean," Mike replied, stifling a yawn. "It is ironic though. I was over there for the attacks on Senator Carter and the three local politicians and I worked with Homeland Security but I'm afraid we hit a brick wall."

"And now you think the assassination of your Prime Minister is connected, yes?"

Mike raised his eyebrows. "It's really impossible to say Jean, but the M.O. is so similar – silenced weapon, guy gets in and out before we are even aware there's been an attack. He leaves no trace evidence, obviously plans well, and covers his tracks."

"And you think it is what? Al Qaeda? Another terrorist group? A right-wing reactionary, like that lunatic in Oslo? Or someone else?"

"You know, it could be any of the above, or even a combination but I doubt it. Realistically, this is one guy – one who has definitely killed before, probably many times. He's working for someone or some organisation, but up to now, they seem to be shy about claiming responsibility for the killings."

"Hmmm, perhaps this is part of the strategy, eh? Look at the impact the killings have had. Every politician, and particularly would-be Presidential candidates in the U.S, are looking over their shoulders. I have heard there are rumours that one or two that were expected to run are having second thoughts. Security details have been doubled, I hear. The British nation is, I understand, in deep shock and who knows what the response will be?"

"You know Jean, I think you're right, and the fact that the assassin hasn't been apprehended and is obviously adept at avoiding capture could well be a key factor. Nothing worries people more than when there's a bogeyman out there; a hidden threat, who can strike at any time. Never mind the general public; it sure keeps the politicians, and if we are honest, the police, awake in their beds at night."

"It's true. A serial killer who preys on the vulnerable is bad enough, but can be distanced; one who operates on this level cannot."

Jean-Pierre's desk phone rang and he immediately picked up. "Oui, Chretien."

He had a long and detailed conversation, asking several questions, eventually hanging up the receiver, "Oui Michel, merci, c'est bon."

He turned to the group, suddenly serious. "Now my friends, we have what you would call, a 'situation'. When we could not trace your mystery woman Mrs Ramsey this evening, I worked on the assumption that 'she' had changed identity again, and asked the cab companies if any of their drivers had collected a man of between 1.7 to 1.8 metres with three pieces of luggage from the Gare du Nord around the time the Eurostar arrived. A long shot, of course, but we may have gotten a, what would you call it, a slice of luck." His cell phone buzzed. "Oui, oui Michel. Sorry, my friends, but we must leave now. I will explain. You may come along but merely to observe, you do understand."

They agreed and all dashed downstairs. A number of police people carriers were being readied outside and they saw heavily armed police officers with helmets and flak jackets going through final checks of their equipment before leaping on board. A dapper, dark haired man signalled to them and they all climbed aboard a Renault Espace SUV. Jean-Pierre climbed in the front beside the driver and introduced Michel Blanc. He invited him to brief the group as he had calls to make.

"So," Michel began, "we have a report from a taxi driver who says he picked up an Australian tourist from Gare du Nord at around 9.30 this evening. He says the man was about 1.7 metres tall. He brought the man to his hotel, but the key point is this – the man had three pieces of luggage, including – the driver says he's certain – a silver grey training or gym bag answering the description of the one you asked us to be on the look out for."

"And he's still at his hotel?" Mike asked.

"Oui, the receptionist has been on duty all evening. She says she remembers the Australian because he said it was his first visit and she was recommending some places he should visit. She says he went to his room and she has not seen him since. The only other way he could have exited was through the kitchens and the staff are adamant that he didn't." He held up a hand, "I know, I know, there is also the fire escape, but we have reason to believe he is still there. The lights and the TV are on in the room and the drapes have been drawn. It appears that he is staying in for the night."

"OK, maybe we'll get a result here," said Bob.

"Our SWAT team will secure all exits first and then approach the room. We would ask you to stay clear of the target area, although you may come to the third floor landing if you wish."

"For sure, good luck to you," agreed Alan.

The hotel was one of Paris' most well-known places to stay. It enjoyed a superb location just off the city's main thoroughfare, the Champs-Élyssées, and was extremely popular. The police cars arrived silently; there would be time for lights and sirens later when they apprehended the culprit.

When the group arrived, the lobby had been cleared. The few residents and other patrons who had been awake had been quietly shepherded to a nearby bistro where they were being treated to breakfast and assured that they would be allowed to return to the hotel quite soon. The leader of the police assault unit was giving his team last minute instructions. All exits had been sealed. The lift had been deactivated and all stairwells secured. Mike felt a surge of adrenalin even though he wasn't directly involved in the assault. Would they finally get their man? He could only wait and hope.

The team silently made their way along the carpeted corridor, all linked but maintaining radio silence. All were armed with Heckler & Koch MP5 sub-machine guns. They had decided against a forced entry; they had a key card from the hotel reception. The corridor was narrow so they had to line up three to each side in a delta-type movement. The team leader and one other police officer led the way. They listened for a moment in the doorway – the TV was still playing, tuned, it seemed, to CNN. One of the other officers leaned across and in one clean movement he swiped the card while his colleague kicked in the door.

The team leader dived low into the room, submachine gun cocked. The second man in raced to the bathroom and kicked in the door. It was a standard hotel room with en-suite bathroom – and it was completely empty.

The team checked the closet, the windows, under the bed, even the drop-down ceiling, but there was no one there. Neither was there luggage nor personal effects. Everything was as it would be in a vacant hotel room. Jean-Pierre, Michel, Mike, and his colleagues rushed down the corridor – the disappointed looks on the faces of the assault team told their own story. Mike punched the partitioned wall in frustration – he had eluded them again.

When he had checked in, earlier in the evening, he had initially felt secure in the hotel. But he had had one small problem – he still had the bag that he had swapped with the man on the train. There was no real hurry as he was almost certain that no one had suspected him of anything. Nevertheless, he lived and survived through caution so he would handle it now. He decided to empty the bag and redistribute the contents, bringing them with him covertly, and then disposing of them on the way to dinner. There were numerous refuse containers on the long hill up to Sacré-Cœur and the walk would sharpen his appetite for dinner.

He took another pair of plastic gloves from the packet he carried, put them on, unzipped the bag and emptied the contents on to the bed. The holdall contained the usual array of clothing; jeans, a sweater, socks, underwear, and a toilet bag. There was too much to dispose of all at once so he would have to vary his route and use a number of different drops. But then he was also conscious that the police would follow the trail when they discovered that they had been duped into arresting the wrong man. The trail would certainly lead to Paris and although he had changed his persona, the substituted bag could be the giveaway. He decided to forego Montmartre, at least for this evening.

Lifting the carrier bag to repack it, he noticed it was too heavy for an empty bag. A quick check of the lining revealed what was a poorly-concealed package. He took nail scissors from the man's toiletries and slit open the lining. It contained a heavily-sealed plastic wrapper, which he also cut open. A sniff and a quick taste confirmed his suspicions – about two kilos of pure cocaine! No wonder the dark haired man was nervous. Value? He could only guess, but he was sure it ran to hundreds of thousands of dollars – pity, but not his game. He realized that more people than the police would be looking for the bag so further evasive action was required.

He rearranged his luggage, placing the bag he had stolen inside one of his own suitcases. He then spent ten minutes transforming himself into Madame Frederique Laclaviere, essentially using the same clothes he had worn as Catherine Ramsey but with a dark wig instead of a blonde one. His French was not fluent, but it was more than enough to communicate in a provincial accent with a doorman and a cab driver. He wiped down the room even though he had barely touched anything, left the television on, and departed.

He again used the elevator to the lobby and took a taxi from the rank to the Gare du Lyon, telling the driver he was catching the overnight TGV to Marseilles. He got a coffee at the station and took out his laptop computer to access the free Wi-Fi provided. He used another IP address and a separate credit card to reserve a suite in the Hilton Arc de Triomphe under the name of Madame Laclaviere for three nights. He then took another taxi from the station rank. He was just a middle-aged, slightly stooped French lady taking a cab to her hotel. Neither the driver nor the hotel receptionist gave "her" a second glance.

He was too late for dinner but it wasn't a problem. He realised that he was high on adrenalin; probably had been all day without realizing it. He treated himself to a large Jameson from the mini-bar and allowed himself a toast, feeling the tension drain away with the glow of the distilled liquor. He also smoked a cigarette, even though the room was non-smoking.

Eventually, he relaxed and congratulated himself. He had done it again – he had succeeded in the U.S. and he had now created terror in Europe. The effects were spreading throughout the world. It was the number one story on every network. There was talk of a fearsome population – newscasters and chat show hosts were postulating that no one was safe, and unless leaders stayed in bunkers, all were fair game. And it was he who had done it all.

He was somewhat surprised by the unprecedented reaction, so he changed the channel a few times, tuning into Sky News, BBC, and CNN – the story was the same. BBC had a story that police may have apprehended a suspect but it was an unconfirmed report as yet.

The whiskey relaxed him and he suddenly realized that he was very tired. It was one am French time and he realized that he had been awake for almost twenty hours. Finally happy that he could not be traced, he settled down to sleep, speculating that by morning the reports of the police arrest would have been confirmed and then probably denied again.

Mike and the team were tired, pissed off and angry. Their French colleagues were apologetic but they had done all they could and the British team were gracious about it. Their ire was directed elsewhere. No one was in any doubt but that their man had been in room 309. The question was why he had left it – surely he didn't have an informant? Both teams dismissed the thought out of hand, but why did he bother to check in, exposing himself, using one of his aliases, only to leave again?

A sudden, sickening thought hit Mike – what if he had suspected the approach of the police and was still in the hotel, hiding out, possibly holding another guest as a hostage? He dared to venture the thought to Jean-Pierre.

"It is OK, my friend, we anticipated that. All exits have been secured. No one gets in or out without my agreement. We've decided not to wake the guests for another hour so we can deal with everyone quietly and without fuss or panic."

"Sorry Jean, I should have realized. Stupid. I guess I'm tired."

It only then occurred to him that it was six o'clock on a Saturday morning, and the last time he had slept was on Wednesday night in Washington D.C. Christ, he needed to call

Wendy. She'd understand. If he didn't get some rest soon, he'd be of no use to the investigation.

They were seated in the hotel lobby watching the morning sunshine peep over the rooftops of Paris. The energy level was low and no one seemed to know what to do next. Their man had definitely been in the hotel but by now could be anywhere – he was in the wind.

A waiter brought them coffee and croissants and all tucked in hungrily. An elderly gentleman with a slight stoop, dressed in hotel livery, approached them tentatively.

"Excusez-moi, Madame et Messieurs; can I inform you of something that has been playing on my mind? Oh, it's probably nothing but I overheard from the receptionist that you were looking for someone with quite a bit of luggage."

All immediately perked up. "S'il vous plaît," said Michel. "We can do with all the help we can get here."

"Well, sir, I work as a doorman here at the hotel and I start my shift at ten. When I came on duty tonight I'm sure I saw the gentleman you were seeking enter the hotel. I haven't seen him since, but at around ten thirty I did notice an elderly – well, perhaps middle-aged – lady leave the hotel and take a taxi from the rank. She had two large suitcases and a smaller bag. It's not unusual for guests to leave at odd times of the day to catch flights or trains but I did take the liberty of checking with reception to see if there had been a late checkout. You see, I had not seen this lady before; but then again, I work nights, so it would not be unusual. Well, no one had booked a late checkout and we checked the list of guests. Sir, you see, there was no one who checked out of the hotel who would answer the description of the lady I saw, if you understand what I mean?"

The mood was suddenly upbeat again and all attention was now focused on the doorman.

"We most certainly do understand, sir, and thank you so much for the information and for being so observant," said Michel. "Did you by any chance hear where the woman asked the taxi to bring her?"

"Well, no, sir, I didn't, but the driver who took her works the rank all the time, and I took the liberty of enquiring from him."

They waited expectantly, almost afraid to draw breath. "Sir, he drove her to the Gare du Lyon and she said something about a train to Marseilles."

There was a collective exhalation. He was gone – again. It was now almost six in the morning. God knew how many trains had left the station since 11.00 the previous evening. The man could be anywhere in Europe by now.

"Thank you indeed, sir," said Jean-Pierre. "Ms Parker, gentlemen, perhaps it is best at this stage if we all try to get some sleep. My assistant has managed to get you all rooms at the Hilton. We will take you there now. Our people will wrap things up here and you will be informed immediately of any developments." They rose heavily and trooped out of the lobby.

Chapter 21

It was past midday when Mike awakened slowly. There was a persistent noise in his ear, which he couldn't quite place. In fact, he had difficulty ascertaining where he was. As the fog of sleep cleared, he realised it was his cell phone and dived to answer it.

"Hello," he croaked.

"Hey there!" It was Wendy. The sound of her voice immediately brightened his mood.

"Hello you," he said. "Ah, sorry, it's been crazy over here and I didn't get a chance to call – but I miss you."

"Me too," she said. "Look, I've been following things from here and I realize you must be under, like, serious pressure, but if you need a shoulder, I'm not working until next Wednesday."

The invitation was like an infusion of energy. "You know, that's just about the best idea I've heard in the past 48 hours. But hey, wait, I'm not in London, I'm in Paris, so if you can get here, it'd be great."

"Paris – wow, even better. Let me check what's available but I can probably be there by tonight. Hang tough Mike, I'll be right there. Oh, and I love you."

"You too, Wendy. Let me know your flight and I'll try to meet you if I can. If not, I'm staying at the Hilton at the Arc De Triomphe."

"OK, hon, see you soon."

The six hours of deep sleep had certainly refreshed him. The shower had helped wake him up, and he found his mood was more upbeat than earlier. But it was really Wendy's call that had given him his biggest boost. The thought of spending a few days in Paris with this gorgeous woman made him so giddy with excitement that he momentarily forgot what had brought him there.

Reality soon intruded, though, and he felt the weight of responsibility press down on him. They had failed to catch their man, again; damn it, they had been in three hotel rooms where he had been only hours earlier, but he continued to elude them.

Still, Mike thought, we got a lot closer than we did in the States; that is, if they were dealing with the same person; but he was convinced they were. He was also convinced that there was even more to come, and he felt that the man might make another mistake. Trying to bring the rifle to Paris seemed most unlike him, unless – he felt himself breaking out in a cold sweat even though he had just showered. He called Alan, Bob and Anne and suggested they meet for coffee.

"Sorry guys," Mike began, "but I've been so fatigued and jetlagged I haven't been thinking straight. I've been thinking - our man must have brought the rifle to Paris for a reason. He may have had difficulty disposing of it, but something tells me this guy is not finished."

"Yeah; it's cool, though, the same thought occurred to the French," said Anne. "They're actually shit-scared, because there's a top level meeting here today between the French President and the German Chancellor to discuss the escalating financial crisis. I wouldn't be overly concerned, though. They've moved the meeting from the Élyssées out to Versailles, and security is so tight out there that you would have difficulty getting within a mile of them."

"Yeah, perhaps," said Alan, "but there was security with our P.M. too and he got through."

"No," Mike replied. "I tend to agree with Anne. We shouldn't underestimate him because he's very clever, but so far, he's only hit vulnerable, exposed targets. Sorry, I'm operating here on the assumption that the same man is responsible for all five political assassinations to date."

They all nodded in agreement. He continued, "Look, the Senator was alone and effectively unguarded; the three councilmen were like shooting fish in a barrel; and the P.M. was, well, running in a public park is pretty exposed in my view. I don't think he'll try to hit somewhere that there's heavy security. Too difficult to get in, and twice as difficult to get out again. He's good but surely not that good?"

Bob added, "Oh, by the way, your friend M. Chretien is nothing if not thorough. He's had every ticket clerk and train porter who was on duty at Gare du Lyon last night thoroughly questioned, but no one remembers a dark-haired French woman with luggage booking a ticket or catching a train, so I guess that's another dead end. What do we do now? Go back to London or see if we can catch a break here?"

There was silence and a few shrugs, then Mike offered, "I'm afraid there's really no other option; we wait and hope the French come up with something."

He hadn't operated in Paris before, so he did not know how to acquire a weapon or ammunition there. He had business to complete in the city but it could wait. There was no hurry – better to regroup and lie low until the massive manhunt, which he knew was underway on both sides of the English Channel, had abated. The fact that it was underway in France was entirely down to him, and he was annoyed with himself about it. Perhaps he had gotten cocky; over confident.

Whatever the reason, it had been stupid to attempt to bring the weapon across the channel. He could have dumped it in Paddington before he left; but no, there was a downside to that. The more he thought about it, the more he forgave himself. It would have been even more difficult to dispose of it – but that assumption was predicated on his plan to head to Paris immediately. He might have been better advised to stay in the UK for a while. But there was a risk in that also, and his style had always been to get clean away, as far as possible from the hit and as soon as possible. Besides, he had business in Paris.

Overall, it was an error of judgment, but he had gotten away with it and he would not repeat it. He had committed no crime in Paris, but when he had woken that morning, he decided not to take any chances. He rose early and left the hotel at 06.30, now dressed as Patrick Houlihan, an Irish businessman; fair hair cut short, business suit, dark glasses; a bit early, but the sun had risen and after all, it was July.

It was a beautiful morning and the city streets were all but deserted. He still had the luggage but the gym bag had been carefully stored inside his large suitcase along with his other personas. The cocaine had, sadly, long since been disposed of in the washbasin in his bathroom. Too risky to use the toilet as some may have become lodged in the bend. He found it was much easier to dispose of it slowly, pouring it under the hot water tap. He placed the plastic wrapping in his briefcase. He decided not to risk a taxi, but to walk to the Metro, which was only a few hundred metres away. On his way, he deftly dropped the plastic wrapping in a refuse bin.

As he walked, he noticed that every café, restaurant, shop or other commercial premises had left at least one – sometimes several – large disposal bins on wheels on the sidewalk for collection. He spied a refuse disposal truck about five hundred metres away, slowly making its way towards him.

He saw the opportunity immediately. He did a 360 quickly, but no one was taking the slightest interest in him. He ducked into an alley, removed the gym bag from his suitcase, quickly lifted the heavy lid of the nearest bin, and dropped the bag inside. The smell was foul, but he didn't care; it lessened the chances that anyone would look.

There was a small coffee shop on the opposite side of the road so he strolled over and ordered a coffee and some filled croissants for breakfast. The attendant, an African immigrant, barely noticed him as she served the coffee. He took a window seat and settled down to watch the progress of the refuse truck. When he started to eat, he realized that he had missed dinner the previous evening and was ravenous. The truck slowly meandered its way up the street. There was a driver and two loaders, all of whom also looked like recent immigrants from the African continent. As he had suspected, the loaders had no contact with the refuse. They merely wheeled the bins to the rear of the truck, two at a time, and placed them on a lifting mechanism. This then raised the bin upwards, flicking back the lid as it turned the bin on its side, dumping the contents into the rear of the truck. The refuse was then crushed and compacted and they moved on to the next pair. He saw the bin he had used emptied without any of the workers even suspecting or caring about what was inside.

Now he had only one large suitcase, a smaller bag attached to it, and his briefcase. The case was on wheels so he was good to go. Finally free of the incident that had led to him deciding to leave Paris in the first place, he took a deep breath, stretched, finished his coffee and strode towards the Metro at Charles De Gaulle Étoile. In his original plan, he would have had to leave Paris anyway as he had no idea how to acquire any 'equipment' there. He knew where he could get it, though. He toyed with the idea of a slow-moving train, but trains to where he wanted to go to departed from Gare du Nord, and he didn't wish to revisit there right now. Perhaps a flight from Charles De Gaulle? Why not? But they would be watching the airports, wouldn't they? No one knew him, but if he was subjected to a random search, which all airport security forces are empowered to do, he might have a difficulty explaining how he was carrying a number of women's outfits and a full selection of cosmetics. He could say he was meeting his wife, but it might complicate things. Then there were the many passports and credit cards he had inserted beneath the lining in the false bottom of his briefcase, although it was so slim that it had never caused a problem. All he had done was to take out one strip of leather and replace it with thin hard plastic. This created a small cavity, which provided ample storage space for his numerous documents. It was unlikely that it would be discovered but there was a major alert on so caution was best. He decided he would take advantage of the beautiful summer's day to see some of the French countryside. After all, he was in no hurry.

Wendy managed to catch an Air France day flight, and even with the time difference, arrived at Charles De Gaulle at nine in the evening. As it seemed the case had hit another buffer, Mike went to the airport to meet his new-found love.

Despite exhaustive checks all day by the French Authorities, there had been no developments. Personnel at every destination served from Gare du Lyon were questioned for signs of the 'woman' who had presumably departed the previous evening, using the detailed description provided by the doorman at the Royal Monceau. No one could remember seeing her. Mike appreciated their efforts but felt the search was probably futile, as, given their previous experience, it was likely the man had changed again en route.

No one actually thought to check to see if the man had had the nerve to turn round again and stay at another hotel in Paris, which of course was exactly what he had done. However, even if they had tried and managed to trace Madame Laclaviere to the Hilton, they would have found another empty room with the occupant long since departed.

Wendy had travelled in jeans and another cowboy shirt, but she still looked good enough to eat as he saw her come through Customs into the Arrivals Hall.

"Hey," she said.

"Hey yourself, Miss," he replied.

They just looked at each other longingly and instantly reconnected. Now he knew why he had been tired and irritable. He had been missing a part of himself. He was amazed that it was happening, but it was true; she had that effect on him.

"You must be tired. Let's get you home to bed," he smirked.

"Ah, hey, it's only mid afternoon with me. I wanna go to dinner in Paris with my man!"

"Only kidding, babe. I'm gonna take you to the top restaurant in Paris."

"Fantastic Mike, but are you sure you have time? I mean, with this situation and all?"

"To be honest, there's very little I can do here apart from advise and observe. I don't speak French, so even my options there are limited. No, seriously, the guys here are top notch, and if there are any developments, they'll let me know."

They dropped Wendy's bags at the Hilton and then literally went to the top restaurant in Paris – the Jules Verne situated on the second level of the Eiffel Tower. It was almost impossible to get a reservation, but when Jean-Pierre heard that Mike had a new girlfriend and that she was visiting from Washington, he reckoned this must be something special, so despite being under enormous pressure, he took a minute and managed to reserve a table for them.

It was a magnificent evening in the old romantic city. The heat of the day had abated and it was just touching 20C as they re-emerged from the Hilton. The taxi wound its way through the back streets between Champs-Élyssées and Tour D'Eiffel. There wasn't a cloud in the sky and the quality of light was astoundingly clear for a big city. This must be the ideal night to view Paris, Mike thought, as they were ushered into the private restaurant elevator at the southern pillar.

They were brought straight to the Champagne Bar at the summit. It was Wendy's first visit to Paris, and she was starry-eyed as she viewed the magnificent panorama over the city. The shadows had just begun to darken and were ushering in the twilight. The vista seemed endless and it almost seemed as if they could see all of France. For a long time they just held each other and drank in the magnificence of the view. Then he gently suggested they descend to the restaurant for some dinner.

"Thought you'd never ask," she said. "All this romance gives you a hell of an appetite – I'm starving!"

The waiter ushered them to their seats in the corner – specially requested by Jean-Pierre – delivered menus and the wine list with a flourish, and departed silently.

"You know," she began, "if Paris is the most romantic city on earth, then this has got to be the most romantic part of it. I mean - what a place to start! It's like being transported to another world."

Even the normally difficult-to-impress Mike had been taken in. "Yeah, it is really something, isn't it?" he responded.

"You know," she said, "forgive me if I'm interfering, but apart from wanting to spend time with you, I've been really worried about you. I know you believe that one guy has carried out all the killings and you've been chasing him now for almost a month."

Mike sighed deeply; he was suddenly torn from the magic image he had been savouring and jolted back to reality. "Yeah; not very good, then, am I?"

"No, please, don't say that – I think, no, I know you are very good, but this is excruciatingly difficult for you. I mean, it must be so frustrating for you, and I can tell you are obsessed with catching this guy."

Mike had never been one to bring his work home with him, partially because there was rarely anyone to bring it home to! He had had his share of relationships over the years, but had never felt comfortable discussing his work with anyone. But Wendy was different – she brought a different perspective to everything. She didn't interfere in any way or ask him to breach any confidences, but she had a way of making helpful comments, which he found useful, and also helped to reduce his stress levels.

"Look Wendy, you know I really appreciate you coming over here. In fact, I can't think how bad a place I'd be in if you hadn't." He closed his hand over hers as he said this and she responded gently. "But look, it's not just me. Paul wants this guy badly as well. Alan and Bob feel personally affronted that the guy would attack their leader in their own country. They are as obsessed as I am and I don't blame them. I mean, none of us will be able to rest until this guy is either dead or behind bars and right now, I'm not sure I care which it is."

"Look, Mike, that's partially why I worry. You told me back in D.C. how difficult it is to catch a professional hired killer if he plans well. I think you even used the word impossible if the guy is clever enough. I know all the other guys are obsessed too but you are trying to handle things on both continents. You can't go on like this indefinitely. You need to take a break."

"But that isn't particularly stressful. I mean, the fact that I flew over here keeps me involved, keeps me close to the guy; I mean, Wendy, this guy is close. I know it; I can feel it. Believe me, I don't wish any harm to befall anyone, but this guy is going to kill again. There's still no real pattern to what he's doing other than to spread terror, and by Jesus, he's succeeding there. But he's not finished. He has more to do, and to do it, he is going to have to keep exposing himself. He plans well and doesn't sweat it because he thinks he's invincible, but sooner or later he will make a mistake and bang, we'll be there. I mean, he already made a big mistake trying to transport a rifle on the Eurostar, or at least it seems so, unless it was part of a plan to throw us off the scent but I don't think so. What does that tell you?"

"That he was either trying to fool you or that he plans to kill someone in Paris – or, of course, anywhere on the European continent."

"Yep, correct – that's why Jean-Pierre and his guys have got every French politician wrapped up in cotton wool or shipped away to private country retreats right now."

"Is there any possible way you could set a trap for this guy? I mean, there must be some pattern to his attacks."

"There isn't any that we can discern. Well, they're all right-wing politicians; maybe he's a mad left winger who wants to weaken the resolve of the right, but I very much doubt it. In terms of a trap, what do we do? Wrap up all right-wingers but put one on parade somewhere and announce it? Sorry, I don't mean to be cynical, it's just frustration."

"No, no, you're fine – I mean, maybe it's an assault on democracy or democratic systems, or perhaps it something to do with attacking governments with troops in Afghanistan or Iraq or wherever? Maybe it's connected to the Israeli-Palestinian conflict – all those scenarios fit."

"Jesus, if it's connected with Afghanistan, he's got a long ways to go – there must be twenty other countries in NATO with forces over there! I dunno, I mean, why just hit right-wing people? All parties support the war over there, and all parties to both left and right in the U.S. and the UK support the war on terror."

"Maybe there's no pattern. Maybe he just hits the most vulnerable ones?"

"Yeah, we have thought of that – you know, it's an awful scenario, and I hate to admit it, but we are almost handing the initiative to him; show us your next move, mate, because right now, we haven't got a clue."

"Ok I see what you mean, but what if he doesn't strike again? What if this was the end of it? And if he does strike again, have you considered that he might not make a mistake? That you'll never get him? I mean, you told me yourself – these guys are the ultimate killers. If there's no record of them anywhere and they leave no trace, then normal police work won't catch them."

"Perhaps; no, you're right – you're absolutely right, and I don't want to sound pompous but maybe I'm not a normal policeman. I don't mean I'm better than the rest, but; ah, look, it's hard to explain. When you've been in the business as long as I have, you develop a nose for this; call it a sort of sixth sense. I've caught more than a few guys in unorthodox ways over the years."

"I know you have, but have you considered for a moment what happens if you don't get the guy; if he just disappears into – what do you call it? The wind? I mean, I don't want to be selfish, but I'm gonna be selfish about you. I've just met you, Mike, and I don't want to lose you because you want to spend the rest of your life being obsessed with something that's just out of your reach."

He noticed that her eyes had moistened and that, at the same time, the waiter approaching with their starters had done a discreet U-turn.

"Ok," he began, taking both her hands into his. He smiled. "Wendy, you're not going to lose me to anyone, least of all some cold-blooded bastard who wants to create mayhem. Look, please trust me. I know I've spoken about this case non-stop and I apologise." She made to wave away the apology but he stopped her with a finger to her lips. "No," he said. "You're right. I can normally completely switch off and unwind. On this one I haven't been able to. Maybe that's why I haven't been as fresh as I should have been. But from right now, you've got the old me back – I am switching off right now. I'm in Paris with a beautiful woman whom I love very much and I am going to have a romantic evening. The cares of police work can wait until tomorrow. I do not want to hear one more word about this case tonight!" He noticed that the waiter had returned and he motioned him to set down their plates. "Now, how does that sound, Mademoiselle?"

"It sounds wonderful, Monsieur – now shut up and eat your foie gras!"

Chapter 22

France has always invested heavily in the train, and probably has the best high-speed train network in Europe, if not the world. It is also highly democratic in the traditional French way – high speed doesn't necessarily mean high price and the network is available to all. Railways have always been seen as a key part of the transport infrastructure, and unlike many other European countries, were never allowed to decline or, as happened elsewhere, be taken up completely. They were maintained by heavy state investment throughout the car boom of the 1960's onwards. The railways were always popular but really came back into fashion when, despite an excellent road and autoroute or motorway network, the system just became blocked with too many cars, particularly at holiday time.

The high-speed network or TGV was a huge success when first launched on the Paris-Lyon route and has been so popular that the network now reaches all parts of the country. Eager to emulate the success of the French network, neighbouring countries such as Belgium, Italy, Spain, and Germany built their own high-speed lines. France is now also linked by high-speed trains to the Netherlands and Switzerland, and of course the latest link in the chain is the Eurostar to London, which Walker had already experienced.

He had thought about slower provincial trains as a more anonymous way to travel but he eventually decided TGV's were as anonymous as any other. If there was space on the train, advance reservations were not necessary. This suited him fine as he had time to kill and could wait until he found a train that did have seats available. His initial provisional plan for Paris would have to be delayed and modified, if not totally replaced. He did have a back-up plan, although security was now likely to be even tighter. But he wasn't apprehensive – there was always a way if you were patient and prepared to wait long enough.

He took the Metro to the Gare Montparnasse and made his way to the main line concourse. He bought a copy of the London Times at a kiosk and settled down in the coffee shop to read. He was still hungry so he bought a brioche and a cappuccino. There was a large electronic arrivals and departures board in full view out in the concourse. He sipped his coffee and read the Times.

Almost half of the newspaper was given over to the events of the previous day. The tributes were long and fulsome. The British people were shocked and angry at the attack. But, he noted, they were also totally in the dark as to who would do such a thing. There were still-unconfirmed reports that police had detained a man trying to flee the country. Ah, but this paper would have been printed early the previous evening in order to hit the news stands in Paris this morning. He needed to find a more up-to-date news source.

There was a large flat-screen TV in another corner of the coffee shop so he gathered his things and ambled over. The TV was tuned to a French 24 hour news channel and it was just coming up to 08.00 am.

"British Police think murderer of their Prime Minister is here," was the opening headline. His French was average but he managed to discern that the British strongly suspected that despite tight security, the assassin of their P.M. had managed to escape to France on the previous evening.

"You would like me to change to the English version, Monsieur?" said the coffee bar attendant.

He was momentarily taken aback. He briefly toyed with the idea of pretending confusion but realized that the guy had caught him seriously concentrating on the French announcer and trying to interpret the headlines. The fact that he had been reading the Times and his Irish accent when he had ordered his coffee in French would do it too. In the rush of the previous 24 hours and his euphoria, he had, just for a split second, forgotten that he was Patrick Houlihan. He regained his composure instantly.

"That would be very kind of you, my friend, thanks."

The attendant took the remote control and found Euronews. Another few flicks of a button and he had the English version. At this stage they were featuring a brief statement by the French President assuring their allies and good friends the British that the full resources of French law enforcement would be deployed in order to bring this brutal killer to justice. They cut back to a statement the previous evening by the Queen, urging the British people to remain calm during this difficult time and to cooperate in any way they could with the police.

Euronews operated on a fifteen-minute loop so he decided to wait for the full version. It started with the news that the British were strongly of the opinion that the killer had fled to France. It was believed that he had set a trap for police the previous evening, deliberately incriminating a passenger on the Eurostar, while travelling in disguise. It had been initially thought that the man had stayed in Paris but French police now believed he had left the city. It was believed the man was 1.7 to 1.8 metres or five feet eight to five feet nine inches tall, but apart from that, the description was sketchy. Checks were being set up at all airports, ports and key pieces of transport infrastructure.

Set them up fellas, he thought, but what or who are you looking for? Still, the full resources of French law enforcement were looking for a guy of his height. He quickly scanned the concourse; more than half the people he viewed answered to the same description. He felt he was no closer to being apprehended now than he ever had been. He was totally relaxed and confident again as he pondered the list of departures from Gare Montparnasse. Perhaps Bordeaux would be nice to start with. He thanked the young man who had helped him with the TV, left a generous tip, and strolled off in the direction of the automatic ticket machines.

The first train to Bordeaux with seats available didn't leave until 11.30. He contemplated an alternative but eventually decided to wait. After all, the French thought he had already left

Paris. He found another coffee shop in a different part of the station and began reading his paper.

He made a mental note to call his wife later that day using one of the pre-paid SIM cards that he carried. He still had several British ones, and had purchased French SIMS the week before. It was quite simple to carry a standard Nokia and insert a once-off card. Cindy and the girls were in Nebraska, holidaying with a friend of Cindy's who had married a farmer. They were about as close to unreachable as you could get, as the nearest town was seventy miles from the ranch and there was no cell coverage. He had suggested to Cindy that she might like to catch up with Sue and Todd, as he would be away for a few weeks in Switzerland, setting up a portfolio for a new client as well as checking up on his own investments. He had in fact, entered Europe via Switzerland, but not as Carl Walker.

Fooling his wife was one thing, but the forces of law enforcement might look a little closer. Carl Walker was, as far as anyone knew, back in his house in Orlando. He had called Cindy a few days previously and she had told him that she was going to have a hell of a job getting the girls back home as they had fallen in love with the ranch and had bonded again quickly with Chad and Ricky, Sue & Todd's two boys, not to speak of their two dogs, Clyde and Chloe. He told her to relax as he might be delayed for a few days. Anyway, it was summer break so there was no need to hurry back.

This suited his purpose perfectly. He wondered again if Cindy ever suspected that he wasn't quite what he said he was. Deep down, he often got an inkling that she did; but hell, this was not the time to worry about that. Even if she did, it was extremely long odds that she would ever betray him. He dismissed the thought. No, all was fine in his domestic world. It would still be the middle of the night in Nebraska, so there was plenty of time to call later in the day.

While perusing the Times, he spotted a story on page six. It was quite interesting and might well serve his purpose even better than the plans he already had rehearsed in his mind and on which he had more or less settled. It would be a new theatre of operation for him, so his lack of experience there and the absence of

218

contacts, fall-backs, bolt-holes or exit strategies would have to be factored into the equation. Not to worry, though – he had his laptop and a large loose-leaf pad in his bag and he would have lots of time to assess different scenarios on his journey to Bordeaux.

Later that day, Patrick Houlihan, sadly, disappeared. He was close to certain that the coffee shop employee had no suspicions whatsoever, but the guy would remember him if he was questioned and the police would check late bookings from the station if they got that far, so Patrick had to go, for now anyway.

He watched the beautiful sun-splashed countryside whiz by and he was in Bordeaux by three in the afternoon. He would have liked to have stayed but decided to keep moving. Italy was probably a little too far for the day so he decided to stay in Toulouse. He took a slow regional train that wound its way into the Gare de Toulouse Matabiau just after six in the evening. He took a taxi to the city centre and sought lodgings in a small pension. He then decided to take a walk to the Place du Capitol. He was now Piet Viljoen, a South African tourist. He was aware of the French requirement for each guest to fill in a registration card, but as he was using multiple identities and passports, he had no worries on that score. He ate a quiet dinner at a little restaurant overlooking the Garonne and retired early.

Next morning, he decided the TGV was in order again, so Mr Viljoen travelled via Nimes to Avignon and then south to Nice. From there, he took the train along the beautifully scenic French Riviera coast, past Monaco and into the Italian Riviera. He thought of alighting in Genoa but decided to continue north to Milan. There, he exited the train and, on a blistering afternoon, asked a taxi driver to take him to the Four Seasons. He had made his reservation en route and had decided Patrick Houlihan was safe to use again as he was now in Italy and it was extremely unlikely that the names would be matched.

He was assigned a luxury room on the third floor. He dumped his bags, placed his valuables in the room safe, changed into shorts and a T-shirt, and went back downstairs. The hotel was conveniently located in the city centre so he walked to see the

Duomo, the city's landmark Cathedral. He decided afterwards that a cold beer was in order.

Now he was just another tourist. In two days of travel, he had not been stopped or searched. In fact, he couldn't even remember whether he had seen a policeman. He certainly hadn't aroused the slightest suspicion.

In Paris, passenger manifests had been obtained, where possible, for every train that had departed the Gare du Lyon the previous evening. Attempts were made to match a name against police files in France, Britain, Ireland, the United States and anywhere else that was willing to release the data to the Surete. All known aliases were scanned. The search was later extended to all the other train stations in Paris, airline flights, car hire agencies and anywhere plastic left a trail. The time frame was also considerably widened.

Numerous potential leads were discovered and dutifully followed up but led nowhere. The public were very helpful and reported sightings of the suspect in every city, town and village from Calais to the Pyrenees. Any sighting that could be pursued was; quite a few tourists had been surprised, upset, or downright indignant to be stopped, searched or suspected. All were quickly verified as having nothing whatsoever to do with the London killing through the simple fact that they could prove they were a long way away when the crime was committed.

Jean-Pierre didn't like to admit it, nor did not want to dismay his guests, but he felt the task was, quite literally, of the needle-in-a-haystack variety. France had a population of over sixty million. Add to that an annual influx of eighty million foreign tourists. Paris itself was the world's busiest tourist destination with an estimated seventy million visitors annually. Asking people to be on the lookout for someone who spoke English and was of average height would be excruciatingly difficult at any time of year, but surely next to impossible in late July.

The summit meeting out at Versailles had been conducted entirely indoors. The leaders' cars hadn't even drawn up to the entrance for the usual press wave. Armoured limousines had been driven into a narrow, partially-covered courtyard, and the Chancellor and President ushered in through a side door. The press conference had been strictly by select invitation only and was conducted in a room where even a Government Minister couldn't gain entry without accreditation. Was this the way business was to be conducted in the future, he wondered?

"A centime for your thoughts, Jean," Mike said.

"Ah, we don't use those any more; it is all euro and cent now."

"Ah well; a penny then?"

"I was just thinking about the summit meeting yesterday. Our orders are to maintain this level of security until this scare is over or this person has been captured. I mean, I understand, but it is going to place an enormous strain on our resources."

"Yes, and I presume the politicos don't like it either. This bloody scenario of meeting in virtual secrecy is what they do in dictatorships in Africa or South America where El Presidente thinks every second person wants to shoot him, and given the records of some of these guys, is probably right."

"Yes, I agree Mike, mon ami, and although it might ultimately provide us with fewer headaches, we surely cannot continue it indefinitely in a parliamentary democracy?"

"Of course not, but perhaps that is what our man is waiting for – us to let our guard down thinking the danger has passed and then he strikes again?"

"Possibly, but why are you so convinced that he will try to kill again?"

"Because there is no pattern to it, Jean; well, none that we can discern. I believe it will emerge eventually; or alternatively, his aim is to target democracy or western society. If it is, God knows when or where he'll stop. Sorry, I know we aren't even sure it's one guy, but if there's more than one, they have a remarkable similarity."

Apart from air travel, the only way to get from Milan directly to Amsterdam was by regular train. Walker could have ducked back into France and taken another TGV, but he preferred the longer route through Switzerland and Germany. He considered an overnight but decided the journey through the Alps in high

221

summer was just too good to miss. Given the nature of his profession, he always tried to enjoy his downtime as he was never sure when or even if he would pass this way again. If it went bad and he had to leave the U.S., it might be years before he could return.

There was a train leaving the next morning at 09.25 which would give him a magnificent day passing through some of Europe's finest scenery and would get him into Amsterdam's Central Station at 21.56. Plenty of time in a city where the places he remembered didn't really get going until after midnight.

After a relaxing stroll through the city, he ate a delicious meal in a little side street close to the magnificent cathedral. He washed it down with a good Amarone and returned to his hotel by foot. He booted up his laptop computer and accessed the hotel's Wi-Fi service, engaging the filter he had had installed. He decided that Donald Clarke definitely needed a holiday. He dug out the passport and booked the American on the train for the following morning – expensive, at $927 for first class, but where he was going, it was the only way to travel, and he could certainly afford it.

It was Mike, Alan, Bob and Anne's third day in Paris and their spirits were beginning to wane. The latter three were returning to the UK that evening, but as Mike was technically an independent consultant – although still attached to his former employers – he decided he would give it another few days. He had shown Wendy around some of the sights but she had managed most of them on her own, which actually suited him just fine. They had had a magnificent night-time cruise on the Seine the previous evening on a glass-roofed boat. No wonder Paris got so many visitors. It was just his luck that the one he wanted had slipped through unnoticed.

Still, when the French did romance, they did it in style. Tonight he was treating Jean-Pierre and his wife Marie to dinner in Montmartre, both as a thank you for arranging his reservation for the Jules Verne in Tour D'Eiffel and also because he wanted to introduce and show off his new love.

All of them had been allotted desks in the National Police Headquarters. It was getting on for five o'clock and as they were booked on the Eurostar at six, they were finishing up some final checks and tidying away the detritus of the previous few chaotic days.

Mike's phone buzzed. "Hey man, how're y'all doing over there?"

"Personally, I'm ecstatic; but no, seriously, don't ask, Paul."

"I might have something for you here. Not sure if there's anything in it, but since you don't seem to have much else to go on, well…"

"OK, Paul, give."

"Well, we've been taking feeds from the computers over there and trying to match them with what we got here. We didn't find anything to go on, so we took all the data from over there and started to mix and match it randomly to see if we'd get anything to match at all. I mean, we know this guy is using aliases and disguises like crazy, but we figure he's gotta leave some sort of a pattern eventually."

"True. That's what we are counting on too, but the difficulty is finding where it starts."

"Right; well, these super computers over here can do some seriously sophisticated tracking, so if there is anything to match, they'll find it. Try this; it might be nothing but it's all we've got. Someone called Patrick Houlihan, an Irish citizen apparently, travelled from Paris to Bordeaux on the TGV two days ago. We have no description, because the ticket was bought at a machine, but the name was used as the passenger. Now, if you book a ticket by machine, you could technically use any name you like, but then what do you do if a policeman or ticket checker asks to see your passport or ID and it doesn't match?"

"Where are you going with this, Paul?"

"Bear with me. Now, this guy gets the TGV to Bordeaux, but then he disappears – I mean completely. There's no record of him staying at a hotel or pension in Bordeaux, or anywhere else in France. There's no record of another train reservation, no use of plastic anywhere – nothing. He just disappears off the system."

"OK, I'm listening. He could have used cash and stayed at a pension that didn't record him as a guest or at any of the small hotels who haven't lodged their registration cards yet."

"True, true, of course, and we think that is more than likely what he did, unless he slept on the street or stayed in a private house. But that's not the point; listen, last night he shows up at the Four Seasons in Milan. Reservation was made by internet a few hours before. Internet address untraceable. Debit card used also untraceable."

Mike could feel his excitement building. He gestured silently to his colleagues who gathered closely. Anne picked up an extension and listened with Alan.

"Now," Paul continued, "another interesting thing: we contacted the Gardai in Ireland. They tell us that as far as they know, there are fifty-seven people in Ireland with the name Patrick Houlihan. They cannot be absolutely sure about that but the Irish Department of Foreign Affairs have confirmed that they have only issued passports to twenty-three individuals with that name; but here's the clincher. The Gardai say they've checked, and they are virtually certain that none of those guys was anywhere near Paris this week!"

"Jesus Christ!" Mike could feel his heart pounding and sweat begin to break out on his forehead. "Is he still there? Tell me the fucker is still there."

"Nope, sorry to disappoint you bud, but according to the hotel, he checked out this morning."

"Shit," he said, squeezing the phone until it almost broke. "Did the hotel take a photocopy of his passport? Do they have his description?

"Negative on the passport copy, but you might get a description if you contact the hotel directly. I'll "business card" the numbers to you."

"No, no, it's ok, no need; Jean-Pierre will have them. Paul, I owe you big time – this is our boy, I can sense it. Got to go man, see you back there."

He dashed into Jean-Pierre's office and related what Paul had told him. Jean hit a speed dial button and asked someone to get him Alfonso Baretti at Polizia di Stato HQ in Milan. The line buzzed almost immediately and Jean-Pierre spoke rapidly in English to Alfonso, relating the problem.

"OK, Alfonso, mila grazie. He says he'll put every man he can on it right away. He's going to isolate the room and will give priority to tracking down anyone who might have encountered this Monsieur Houlihan in the hotel or in the city."

"Thanks, Jean-Pierre, but I've got to get down there. Can you assist me?"

"I will do better than that, mon ami, I will go with you."

Mike suddenly realised he had promised to take Jean-Pierre and his wife to dinner. "But what about the girls, the dinner?" he said.

"Why, we will bring them with us," Jean-Pierre smiled.

He hit another button on his desk and asked, "Elodie, can you please get me four tickets to Milano immediately? Either by plane or TGV, whichever is the fastest."

Meanwhile, Mike called Wendy, hoping she would have left the Louvre, where she had planned to spend the day.

"Babe, something urgent has come up, where are you?"

"Back at the hotel, why?"

"We have to go to Milan straight away. Can you throw a few things into a bag and do the same for me? Oh, Jean-Pierre and Marie are coming with us."

"Sure thing, where are we meeting?"

"Not sure, hold on a second." Just then, Jean's secretary came back to confirm that they were booked on the 18.30 from CDG to Malpensa. Mike checked his watch – it was just gone 17.30. "Okay, we'll pick you up at the hotel in, what?" He glanced at Jean-Pierre. "Say ten minutes, OK? We'll be in a police car."

"I'll be ready and waiting at the door, master," she joked.

Christ, he thought, a woman who can be ready and waiting in ten minutes! She was definitely a keeper!

The plane touched down at 20.15, ahead of schedule, and they were rushed to the city centre where Alfonso was waiting. Introductions were made and hands shaken and the head of the anti-terrorist division of the State Police made everyone comfortable in the spacious lobby of the Four Seasons where he ordered coffee and refreshments. Rooms had been arranged in the hotel and the ladies had gone to check in.

"OK, gentlemen," Alfonso began. He was a broad-shouldered round-faced man with a seemingly permanent beaming smile. He was 43, had jet-black hair, thinning slightly at the temples, and skin that was almost mahogany in colour. He was of average height and, like all of the men and women of his division, was superbly fit. He was wearing a fitted Armani jacket and slacks, white shirt but no tie and looked good enough for Milan Fashion week. Mike had only dealt with him briefly in the past, but he knew of his reputation as a skilled policeman who had a knack for getting results.

"We have identified the receptionist who checked in Signor Houlihan, and a waiter who thinks he served him at breakfast. I have already spoken to both and I have obtained a good description of the gentleman you appear to be seeking. However, you are more than welcome to speak to them if you wish. They are willing to talk to you and both speak excellent English."

"Excellent, Alfonso, mila grazie," said Jean-Pierre.

"I have already sent scanned copies of the description to every police station in Italy and through the cooperation of Interpol, we should have it all across Europe by morning."

"Great stuff, Alfonso; and the room where he stayed, can we see it?" asked Mike.

Alfonso threw up his arms. "But of course; at the moment, though, our forensic people are going through the room with, what do you guys call it? Yes, "a fine tooth comb"; so if you can give them a little time – ah, here's the coffee. No hurry, gentlemen; first have a cup of the best espresso in Milano!"

The coffee was so strong that Mike thought he was being administered with it intravenously. No doubt about it, Italians knew how to brew coffee. Alfonso wanted full details of all developments in the case to date, which Mike gladly provided.

"Unfortunately, the developments have been mostly one way up to now," Mike reported. "This guy is clever beyond belief. We have tried every possible angle. Paul Lincoln's computers have run hot in D.C. trying to track him down, but we've come up short or just missed him every time. Of course, we don't know that the guy who stayed here is our man, but we have strong suspicions. I mean, whoever he is, he seems to be going to great lengths to hide his identity. Hopefully this could be the break we need."

Alfonso's cell phone buzzed. "Ah, si, grazie Mario. Let's go see the room gentlemen; our people have concluded their examination." Mike checked his watch. It was just before ten o'clock in the evening.

At precisely that moment, the train slid to a stop at the Amsterdam Centraal Station. Donald Clarke alighted and strode towards the Park Plaza Victoria Hotel, where he had reserved a room for two nights. He had chosen a hotel close to the station as he could walk there directly from the train, and it was close to the bars he intended to visit later in the evening. It wasn't a particularly seedy part of the city, but it wasn't for the faint-hearted either. He wondered if things had changed much, but he was confident he could find his way without too much difficulty.

He checked into the hotel and headed for the fourth floor. He had had a wonderful relaxing day, had been pampered in first class and had dined in great style on the Dutch train. As a result, he wouldn't require dinner, but would have a quick nap before changing and heading for the city's nightlife after midnight. As he passed the hotel bar, something caught his eye and he hesitated. He took a quick look into the bar and froze.

The T.V. was showing a photofit picture of – him; but no, wait; it was Patrick Houlihan. He quickly regained his composure and caught the elevator to his room. There, he switched on the in-room television and went through the channels until he found one of the 24-hour news ones. There it was again – quite a good likeness too. He did a quick scan of himself in the mirror and sighed with relief. Realistically, he looked nothing like the man in the photofit picture. For a start, his hair was now black instead of fair. His skin was lighter as he had dispensed with the fake tan. He hadn't shaved since Paris, and although he had always had a light beard, which greatly facilitated his female personas, it was now well on the way to a goatee, if not a full beard.

He decided to let it grow. He donned a pair of dark glasses to complete the picture. There, he was finally satisfied. But how? As always, he had left no trail. Was it the waiter in Paris? Christ, these guys were good. They obviously had records, and computers to analyse them. On reflection, it was his own fault again – he shouldn't have used the Irish passport a second time in such a short period. Was he slipping? Losing his edge? Or worse, was he getting careless?

He dismissed the thought but vowed to himself that this would be his last error. He didn't have an endless supply of documents, but he had more than enough for this trip, so he should use them. He could obtain more when he got back to the States.

He decided to forego the nap and hit town. He wouldn't sleep now anyway. He took one last quick look in the mirror and decided a pair of plain clear glasses would look less noticeable than the dark ones until he got to the clubs. He donned them and headed downstairs.

As they had expected, the cleaning staff in the Four Seasons in Milan were as efficient as their counterparts in Paris and London, and the room had been thoroughly valeted. They hadn't held out much hope for it anyway. The main thing was that they had the description, and by morning, everyone in Europe would have it. They walked into the room just as the forensic team was wrapping up. Mike felt a sense of deja-vu.

"All done, boss," said a small, balding man whom Alfonso introduced as Mario Bianchi. "Clean as a whistle, I'm afraid."

"Thanks Mario, ciao."

"I guess we're not gonna get much out of here," Mike said. "If it's our guy, he usually does a good job of cleaning up."

"Well," Alfonso said, with his smile beaming even more broadly than usual, "we have to wait until the guys do the analysis tomorrow, but until then, we're gonna have to be satisfied with this."

"With what?" said Jean-Pierre.

The beaming smile again. "With this," he said, and raised a sealed plastic bag containing a small toothbrush. "We found this wedged between the fascia and the wash basin. There was a slight gap and it seemed to slip down there. Now, there is no guarantee that it belongs to our friend, but it was wet when we found it, which suggests it was used recently. We've gotta test it also but my money says we get DNA from this."

Mike punched the air with delight. They were getting closer and closer. "Hey Jean, let's go talk to these two helpful people downstairs and then, jeez, we'd better take those two ladies to a late dinner!"

Chapter 23

He decided to start where he had left off. He had known everywhere in the city twenty-five years ago, but cities change rapidly with bars, clubs, restaurants and all manner of retail outlets all springing up and closing again incredibly fast. There are always places that stand the test of time but if you want to get an idea of how quickly a city changes shape, go away for a year or two and see what you recognise when you come back. Oh, all the regular landmarks will be there, but the chances are that most of the premises that were rented will have changed either their names or even their mode of business.

He wasn't surprised, therefore, to discover that the club/bar/late-night drinking den called, ironically enough, 'The Alamo', which he had frequented when he was an occasional visitor to the city twenty-five years previously, had long since gone the way of progress. The building was still there, but now, it housed a retail outlet selling second-hand ladies fashions. Probably in keeping with the tone of the area, he felt. Frequenters of late-night bars in questionable areas of a city never tend to stray far from their home base, so he felt sure he could make contact with someone if he tried nearby. In fact, just down the road was "The Casbah Club" so he decided it would be his first port of call.

As with most bars and clubs in this part of town after midnight, the door was guarded by two mean-looking individuals, both of whom seemed to have tattoos on every part of their anatomy apart from their faces, but even this lack was amply compensated for by the numerous rings in their ears, noses, eyebrows and lips. Dangerous things to have inserted into you if you happened to get involved in a fight, he thought, but by the look of these two, their sheer size alone would have avoided that. They were both at least six inches taller than him, and probably twice as heavy. There was lots of muscle in there too, indicating much work with gym weights. But there were also serious rolls of fat, suggesting that these guys had been living high on the hog for some time. Good, he thought, there should be no trouble. If there was, he was certain he could take out one of them, hopefully while he distracted the other. If it came to it, he could probably manage both. He was completely unarmed and didn't even carry a pocket-knife.

"Evening, guys," he said. "How's business tonight?"

"Terrible," said the guy on the left in the leather vest. "This fucking recession is a disaster."

"You'll be letting me in, then." They frisked him briefly but it was half-hearted and they stood aside to allow him enter the club.

The place was shabby and dimly-lit, and looked like the last time it had been renovated was probably in the 1970's. The floor was sticky underfoot from too much spilled beer or other liquors that had never been properly cleaned. It had a relatively large dance floor directly inside the entrance door. Behind this, facing him, was a substantial bar counter with access on all four sides, which provided lots of bar stools and places to view the punters on the dance floor. Behind the bar were doors leading to ladies and gents toilets, and in between, a spiral staircase leading to the second floor, which looked to all intents and purposes like a balcony where you could view the customers downstairs or have a quiet drink away from the main bar. A few scantily-clad attractive girls sat to the left and right sides of the bar. All looked up and smiled as he entered. He politely smiled back but did not maintain eye contact. He had occasionally used call girls in the past, but he had far too much on his mind right now to distract himself.

He walked right round the bar and took a seat at the far end, towards the left corner. This was the best he could manage in terms of covering his back, as there were no seats at the wall. The barman smiled and was friendly and attentive. He caught a trace of Southern Hemisphere in the accent; Australia, New Zealand, he could never distinguish. Probably some guy working his way around Europe, or funding his studies. He ordered an Amstel on draught, drank deeply and savoured the cool beer. If you wanted good beer, come to Holland or Belgium. In fact, most of Europe was pretty good. Having had no option in his youth except bottles of lukewarm ale or stout, he always appreciated a cold beer.

One of the girls seated on the left wing of the bar, to his right, climbed down off her bar stool and ambled slowly across.

"How you doing tonight? I'm Katya, that's with a 'y'. Would you like to buy me a drink?"

She was probably the prettiest girl in the bar. She was literally glued into a little skirt that seemed about two sizes too small for her, and a top that just about covered the essentials. She was sheathed in multiple necklaces and bracelets, and while she was pretty and not heavily made up, she was wearing bright red lipstick that clashed with the rest of her outfit. Age was always difficult to determine, but if he'd had to guess, he wouldn't have given her more than her early 20's. She still had a freshness about her; not quite innocence, but she lacked that cynical, hard-bitten look that comes with experience, which he had seen in girls of her trade many times.

"You know Katya, I'd love to because you're a really pretty girl but I can't spend time with you tonight because I have to meet some people." He signalled to the barman to give Katya and her two friends whatever they were drinking.

"Ah gee, that's a pity but perhaps later, or another night?" She deftly extracted a business card from her purse and pressed it into his hand. "Or if you're feeling lonely during the day, give me a call, any time. Hey, and thanks for the drinks – you didn't have to do that."

"It's cool, no worries."

He found himself actually feeling sorry for the girl as she returned to her seat. What sort of life could she look forward to? Turning tricks till she was what? Perhaps thirty, then getting passed down the food chain to even lower lowlifes? Or maybe she would be lucky and meet some John who took her out of the life – unlikely, though, even for a pretty little thing like her. Still, that was the way of the world and there was nothing he could do about it.

Judging by the lack of punters in the bar, he wondered if the recession really *had* bitten here, or if he had chosen the wrong club. Alternatively, he might just be too early. As if to answer him, the door burst open and a group of revellers entered – about ten guys, all with a fair share of liquor on board and seemingly looking for fun. They were too young for a stag party, or were they? Who knew any more? He caught the English accents and assumed they were just a group of young guys letting off steam. They all ordered beers and took seats opposite him at the bar.

There was a flurry of activity behind him to his left and he turned to see two even more scantily dressed girls literally totter down the stairs in their huge platform heels. The music, which had been relatively low, was cranked up several notches and changed to upbeat rock and roll. The girls each took a corner of the bar and climbed on the counter, dancing and swaying to the music. Although they were attractive, striptease of any sort was not his thing so he took only a vague interest. Not so the English guys at the front, who very quickly whooped it up. The girls responded in kind, squatting in various provocative poses until money was placed either in the tops of their stockings, or if the guy was more generous, in the top of their thongs.

The girls were down to the bare essentials and had almost finished their act when a dark-haired man in a leather jacket and jeans with a white t-shirt took the bar stool beside Walker. Despite the loud music and the distraction of the show, he had noticed the man approaching from over his right shoulder. However, he had not seen him enter the club and he certainly had not been there when Walker had come in. The man seemed to have a friendly face although it was difficult to fully ascertain this in the dim light. He ordered a bottle of beer and drank deeply. The girls finished their act to loud applause from the young partygoers and the music reverted to normal decibel level again.

"Quiet tonight," said the man in the leather jacket.

"Is it?" replied Walker. "Sorry, I wouldn't know. I'm not a regular."

"Yes, we have established that," he said with a grin.

Walker didn't reply. We? Who were we, he pondered? He thought the man's accent was more South African than Dutch, but then again he couldn't be sure. The fact that the man spoke to him in English was no surprise. Practically all Dutch people could speak English and it was joked that there is often more English spoken in Amsterdam than their native tongue.

"So, what can we do for you?"

Walker raised an eyebrow. The guy was totally relaxed, with a slight grin on his face, seemingly very sure of his ground. No doubt he was, as it appeared that it was either his club or he had at least an interest in it. He decided to play dumb. Amsterdam is one of the world's great trading cities – for anything. Soft drugs are legal in Holland but the country is also used as a hub to distribute huge quantities of illegal hard drugs throughout Europe. A lot of this came through the port in Rotterdam but it was also a factor of life in Amsterdam.

"Who said I needed anything?"

The man smiled. "*You* did my friend. No one of your age comes into a club like this alone late at night to drink beer; unless, of course, he is interested in the ladies, and it would seem that you are not."

Now it was Walker's turn to smile. By way of response, he signalled to the barman for another beer for him and his companion. "It depends on what you have for sale," he responded.

"Well, you tell me what you need and I will see if we have it. If we don't, I'm fairly sure it can be obtained."

"Perhaps; have you ever heard of The Alamo?"

The man smiled again. "The battle or the club which used to be located up the street?"

"As you say, I didn't come here to discuss the Old West. I used to drink in The Alamo Club many years ago."

"Did you now? Well, it was before my time; but yeah, I've heard of it. Ah, so this is your way of telling me what type of business you wish to transact, yeah?"

Again, Walker did not respond, but merely shrugged his shoulders. The man was obviously keen to do business so he'd let him fill the silence.

"OK, so what'll it be? A pistol? A shotgun, full barrel or sawn-off, a rifle, ammunition, ground to air missile, Inter

Continental Ballistic Missile?" He laughed uproariously. "Sorry, only joking about the ICBM, although there was so much Russian stuff floating around until fairly recently that I'd swear that if you looked hard enough."

"I need a name."

"What you mean a name?"

"And a number; can you provide them both?"

"I'm sorry, my friend, but I don't follow."

"Yeah you do. Now, can you provide them or not?"

"Depends on where you want them but probably."

Walker selected a beer mat from the stack at his elbow, took a pen from his jacket pocket and wrote the name of a European city. He passed it to the man who, when he read it, laughed uproariously again.

"Jesus, are you joking? Over there we might even be able to get you an ICBM."

"As I say, I don't need one – just the name and number and of course a guarantee that the person is ultra discreet and trustworthy."

"That's the business we are in, my friend. This will be a sort of, how you say, a referral, yes?" He paused, seemingly thinking. "But of course referrals cost money too although I feel this will not be a problem for you, eh?"

Walker nodded briefly.

"OK, it's late now so it will have to be tomorrow. We can do this the old fashioned way or the modern one. You can come here tomorrow night with $5,000 in cash and I will give you the details or you can wire the money to a nominated account in the morning and then I will give you the name."

"I'd prefer the speedier version."

The man extracted a card from a zipped pocket of his jacket and wrote a ten digit number and a bank address on the back. He then flicked the card over.

"Wire the money to that account and give it a couple of hours to clear. Then call the number on the back. I will answer and give you the details of where to meet me. It's best not to do our business by phone."

Walker nodded in agreement. The man raised his beer in a toast and they clicked glasses.

"It has been a pleasure doing business with you, sir. Keith, two more beers over here mate."

The problem with putting out a description of a suspect, or even, as in this case, a photofit likeness, is not the lack of a response from the general public. More often, the opposite is the case.

Alfonso had been as good as his word, and through Interpol, the photofit picture compiled from the recollections of the receptionist and the waiter in the Milan Four Seasons was all over Europe by the following morning. The police in any country cannot do their work without the cooperation of the public, and in the vast majority of parliamentary democracies, the public are more than willing to help. Sometimes this works like a dream and you get a quick result. Other times, it just creates work and ultimate frustration. This is not just because of the 'crazies' who will call police regularly anyway and admit to everything including having committed horrendous crimes, seen aliens and suspects and maybe even Elvis himself! They were relatively easily dealt with; it was the genuine ones which often necessitated more leg work.

Because many people looked alike or often had similar features, the number of sightings was always likely to be high. Also, the higher the profile of a case, the greater the publicity; the bigger the crime, the greater the number of sightings. When you factored in ethnicity, the issue became even more clouded. People often have a difficulty distinguishing features of people who do not belong to their own ethnic group or are of a different skin colour. In this instance the suspect was a white male, and as most of Europe is populated by Caucasoid people, it might be less complicated.

Nevertheless, Mike was in no doubt that by lunchtime of the following day, their suspect would have been spotted in locations as far apart as the North of Scotland to as far south as Gibraltar and from Lisbon in the west to Moscow in the east. Most sightings would be too late to follow up on but where they could, local police would diligently pursue the lead. Obviously, most were dead ends, but it had to be done. This crime was going to continue to undermine law enforcement for as long as the killer went free, so police in every country would be giving it high priority.

Part of the problem, Mike knew, was that the killer himself was likely to see the photofit picture and take evasive action. He might lie low or change his appearance or have another alias on stand by. Or he might do all three. He was assured that if the killer had seen the photofit, he certainly wouldn't use the Patrick Houlihan alias again, if he could avoid it. They had checked airline flight bookings for three months either side and any bookings in that name checked out as genuine so if the man was using air travel, he was not travelling as Mr Houlihan.

Mike was having coffee and rolls for breakfast with Wendy, Marie and Jean-Pierre. They had had a delightful evening in a little fish restaurant recommended by Alfonso. The breakfast room in the Four Seasons was spacious and airy and caught the warm morning sunshine just perfectly. All were in good spirits after their breakthrough the night before. They were still not even halfway there and not even close to catching their man but they were closer than they had been and they knew more than they had previously.

"So what do you think?" Jean started. "Is he trying to escape in a convoluted fashion, or does he have unfinished business in France or somewhere else in Europe?

Mike rubbed his temples. "I think he's definitely operating to a plan. There's still no real pattern to it; or if there is, we can't see it; but I still think it will emerge eventually. All we can hope for is that if he does strike again that we can thwart him or if we get really lucky, apprehend him. Alfonso is convinced he can get DNA from the toothbrush but if he does, it's going to take a few days even giving it top priority. Then we have to try to match it to our data banks and you know my opinion of our chances there."

"Oh come on guys, don't be despondent," retorted Wendy. "You got within a few hours of him here. He's human – he's fallible. I mean, he's made mistakes at least twice now. He has to make more. He can't have aliases for every day of the week. Paul's guys are still running the data, right?"

"Sure honey, but he needs somewhere to start. I mean, yeah I know – Milan but then he needs to match that with somewhere else. The numbers of people who leave Milan every day runs into hundreds of thousands and they leave on planes, trains, buses and in cars. No way to track them all even if there were complete records and there aren't. This isn't the States but it's still one hell of a big place for a guy to hide in."

"I know, but those computers are good and they already got you a match, so if he's running details of every guy travelling alone and matching that with hotel reservations and credit cards, he may well come up with something."

The same thought had occurred to Walker who was examining his options for the next part of his odyssey. He had already changed his well-made plans in Paris and was now on his laptop in his hotel room, working furiously on his alternative idea.

Getting into the country wasn't a problem per se. Getting access to the building he needed to get into might be. Still, he had options. That was the beauty of the Bahraini's plan – it always gave him options. He decided to err on the side of caution on every phase of this plan. Even the easier parts might become complicated now that most of the police forces of Europe were looking for him – well, looking for Signor Houlihan. Sadly for them, the remains of Houlihan's persona were resting at the bottom of one of Amsterdam's multitude of canals where he had dumped them the previous evening on his way to the club.

That was the thing – they weren't looking for him as he was now Donald Clarke. But they knew by now that he changed identities frequently. They had tracked him to Milan, albeit through his dual use of an Irish passport, which would not be used again. They would be looking – if they were looking at all where he was going, he thought – for a man travelling alone. He searched his jacket pocket and found the two cards he had been given the night before. He had already transferred the cash electronically four hours ago so it should have hit the account of the man from the Casbah Club by now. He dialled the number using one of his pre-paid throwaway SIM cards. The man answered on the second ring.

"You should have received delivery by now."

"Yeah, the goods were delivered a couple of hours ago. I wondered where you'd got to. Can you meet me at the club again tonight?"

"No, sorry mate, meet me in the coffee shop in Centraal Station in twenty minutes."

"But, ah, twenty minutes." He could almost hear the man thinking. "Hmmm, OK, why not – makes no difference, deal."

His hotel was about three minutes walk from the station so he was in no hurry. He thought again about his next move and thumbed the other card. He pondered calling Katya. Would he be safer with a complete stranger? Probably, as her friends had seen him in the club. Still, what had they seen? A man in dark clothing with dark glasses who had business with the owner that no one got involved with; and hers was a transient business – girls came and went all the time without anyone batting an eyelid. She could probably disappear and he would be thousands of miles away before she was missed. He checked his watch – just after five in the evening; even someone who worked all night would be awake by this time. He dialled the number.

She answered on the first ring.

"Hi Katya, we met last night – I decided to take you up on your invitation."

There was a slight hesitation in the voice as she tried to place him but failed. "Ah sure; am, you wanna come to my place, or you want me to go to your hotel?"

"Neither, can you drive?"

"Yes, of course."

"Do you own a car?"

"Ah, umm, no, why?"

"Not a problem. Do you have a driving licence, and are you over 21?"

She laughed but it was hesitant.

"Yes, of course, but why?"

"I'll tell you why, Katya. My regular driver is not available so I need someone to drive me round for a few days, with a few optional extras thrown in of course! Can you meet me in the coffee shop in Centraal Station in an hour? Bring your driving licence and enough clothes for a few days. How would you like to take a trip home?"

"But how do you – I mean, yeah, that would be great, but I've never done this before so it would be expensive."

"That isn't a problem. Name your price and I'll pay you in the coffee shop in advance; like, before we go anywhere, deal? And Katya, I presume you own a credit card?"

"Wow, yeah, for sure – deal, and yeah, I have a Visa, I'll bring it. One hour – gee, I better run."

"One final thing – this is between us, OK? There'll be no funny or kinky stuff, but I want you to tell no one about our trip, OK? If you have to leave word, just say you have to leave town for a few days to see a friend who's ill or something."

"Oh gee, absolutely, sure. I won't say a word."

The innocence of youth, he thought, as he packed his remaining clothes and dwindling number of personas into his suitcase and went downstairs to check out.

He met the man from the nightclub briefly and got a card with a name and a number. Katya arrived bang on time with a small suitcase on wheels. She looked even better than the previous night, now that she was in natural light and dressed in casual clothes. She hesitated briefly and he nodded in her direction. She approached tentatively and sat down on the edge of the chair opposite him.

"OK, Katya, here's the deal. I need you for a few days, say a maximum of ten." He passed her over a slim envelope. "In there you will find twenty 'five hundred' euro notes. Don't bother trying to add it up; it's ten thousand euros. It's yours." He immediately noticed her eyes widen but detected wariness behind the beaming smile.

"Now, here's another envelope which contains two thousand euro. I want you to go to any one of the car rental desks and hire a car for the next ten days. Get something you are comfortable with, but not too small; we are travelling a considerable distance. Use your credit card to reserve it, and pay it off with the cash whenever you want. Use the rest for whatever other expenses you have. Now, you could walk out the door of the station and disappear, but I don't think you will; but just to give you an incentive to come back, I will give you a bonus of another ten thousand if you get me back to Amsterdam. How does that sound?"

The girl almost tripped over her own feet in her rush to put the money in her purse, get up from the table and rush to the car rental booths.

"When you get the keys, come back here and we will leave together."

"OK, I'm on it," she said.

She rented a Citroen C5, which was ideal. It was fast, comfortable and unobtrusive, and there were probably about another five million of them on Europe's roads. While in some ways they may have seemed an odd couple – she 25 and he in his late 50's – really, they were no different from thousands of others. To the casual observer, they could be father and daughter, or a young girl on the make with a sugar daddy. The latter might attract some disapproving shaking of heads, or even mild jealousy, but the main thing was that no one would remember them. While he may have initially had reservations about the plan, he had warmed to it and felt it would work just fine.

"Ok boss, where to?" Katya enquired as they belted themselves in.

"East," he said. "Try the German frontier first."

"Right, but can you be a little more specific, you know? How far do you want to go tonight, and do you have any preference for a route?"

"As far as possible, and no; just use your satellite navigation to set the route. I couldn't care less what way you go. As regards the ultimate destination, I told you; you're taking a trip home."

"Whatever you say, man," she said. "You're the one who's paying."

He would have been more than willing to share the driving but she didn't ask and as she was an excellent driver, he left her to it. She managed to get close to Hamburg by midnight and he suggested they stop at a motel off the autobahn. Motels were great because she could go to check in and he could access the room directly from the car without being seen by any of the staff

241

or customers. She handled the room reservation and picked up sandwiches and cokes from a vending machine in the motel lobby. There were two double beds in the spacious motel room and while she looked at him, expectantly, he suggested sleep was the better option.

"You've done enough work for one day, my dear, so try to get a good night's rest. We have lots to do tomorrow again."

She shrugged. "Whatever you say, man," she said.

Walker was asleep about a minute after hitting the pillow.

Next morning she bought more sandwiches and coffee, this time from the motel buffet, and they were on the road by 08.00 am. If she thought his behaviour was strange, she didn't show it and she said nothing about it. But she was an intelligent girl and a lively conversationalist. They found they enjoyed each other's company greatly and the miles flew by. He found himself thinking of his ultimate plans for her; he put the thought out of his mind.

They stopped for lunch at 12.30 in a large autobahn stop. After they ate, he used his laptop to access the internet and told her to go look at the outlet mall which was attached to the service centre. She gleefully headed off and he spent the next two hours researching and planning potential strategies for his next assignment. When he had finished, he had the outline of a plan, but he needed some serious thinking time to put flesh on the bones and assess the risks of each element. That he would do during the next driving stint.

She was waiting for him when he finished, laden down with bags from seemingly every boutique in the outlet. She raved about the fantastic value she had obtained and told him in detail about all the outfits she had just purchased. He found himself feeling happy for her. They had definitely established a rapport, but he needed to distance himself, as he needed to be clinical again very soon.

"Katya," he said, when they were back on the autobahn, "I'm sorry about this, but I need some peace and quiet on this leg of the journey as I need to work on the information I've just downloaded."

"Peace and quiet I can do," she smiled back. "You know something? You are a real gentleman."

He didn't reply but just smiled. He took out his loose-leaf writing pad and powered up his laptop again, using the cigar lighter adaptor to keep it charged. He began to plan out the possible what ifs. He knew he had to try to conceptualize them all and then run through them for possible flaws or downsides. He knew he could not accomplish this on his own. He would need Katya for more than driving; and he wasn't thinking of sex, either.

No, where he was going, he was definitely going to be a foreigner so he needed to attract as little attention as possible – he would try for none at all and work back from there. He would have to make contact with the man whose name he had purchased in Amsterdam, but that wouldn't necessarily be a problem; not beforehand, anyway, and afterwards – well, was the guy suddenly going to admit that he was an arms dealer? OK, that was that area taken care of. Hotels, food, drinks, in fact, any of the ways in which a person has to make contact with others; these could be handled by Katya who had showed herself more than capable so far. He had not spoken to another soul since he had left Amsterdam.

He possessed not one word of the language of his destination. This wasn't necessarily dangerous, or even inconvenient, as English was commonly spoken, but it would make him stand out, and possibly be remembered. He could pass for a native in the U.S., UK and in Ireland; even in France, he could make a fair stab at it; but here he was most definitely a foreigner. Local support? A lot of it was available, and he understood from the man in Amsterdam that it was not expensive; but was it reliable? He decided he'd pass.

Another thought struck him. His contact in Amsterdam had given him a name and a number, but the man was wily – would he put it together? Would he twig to what Walker was up to? Had been up to? Ah, no; relax. The man had no idea who he was or what he was at. No doubt he handled queries like this all the time – and if he did suspect, was he suddenly going to become patriotic and risk his business? No, this guy could ill afford to put his head above the parapet at all. OK, so it was fine.

But all of this was peripheral. If he couldn't get into where he wanted, the plan was a non-runner. He could only do so much on the internet. The rest would have to be done on the ground when they got there.

He was deep in thought and barely noticed as she pulled into yet another motel, but this time it was at their destination. "Well done, young lady," he said. Katya had been as good as her word. They had driven the entire final leg in almost total silence.

There was total silence in Milan also, as Mike was having a late drink with Wendy and trying to figure where to go from here. Alfonso had come back with confirmation that a full DNA sample had been obtained from the toothbrush found in the suspect's room. It had been run through every known database on two continents, and it had shown no relationship whatsoever to any existing records. The painstaking checking and rechecking and matching of other data had also come up empty. The trail had gone stone cold again.

Chapter 24

The Wilanow Palace dated from the late 17th Century and was a reminder of the nation's past glories. It had originally been built as the residence of the King and had had many owners over the years. It had survived numerous wars, been extended, redesigned and changed a number of times but was still regarded as a unique building, combining local architectural style with a French influence.

Even during the communist Warsaw Pact era, when all were supposedly equal, the ruling elite had spent serious money on its refurbishment and restoration to its former splendour. Now that Democracy had returned and particularly following accession to the E.U., money had started to flow again and the Government used the building as a showcase when hosting foreign dignitaries. The President had already met the German Chancellor and the French President here in talks to plan the upcoming Presidency of the E.U.

The outer walls of the palace were said to be over six feet thick and virtually impenetrable. But there were more ways of entering than through the walls. In fact, Walker had no intention of storming the castle, or even damaging the tiniest part of the structure. No, the way he planned on getting in and back out again would be through the front gates.

It would the first time that Poland would hold the E.U. Presidency. The leaders of the country were anxious to show both the splendour of their past and the great strides that the country had made since the Warsaw Pact days. Warsaw was now a modern thriving city, if not yet up to the levels of its new-found western partners. Yes, Poland had lots of migrant workers in the rest of the E.U.; some, like Katya, engaged in questionable professions. It might be one of the largest beneficiaries from the E.U. budget these days but it needed to catch up. Its people were hardworking and willing to travel to support their loved ones and repatriate their earnings to support their economy. The country and its people had always been imaginative and dynamic. For nearly fifty years, they had been held back by communism, but now they were free to trade and to take their rightful place in Europe's pantheon of great nations.

Their first time holding the E.U. Presidency, which rotated every six months, was a huge honour and they would want nothing to go wrong. Security would be tight; it would have been tight anyway, but the events of a few days previously would now lead to efforts being redoubled. But there was always a way. One of the ways to defeat any system was first to ascertain what the other side was thinking and then what they were not thinking. Now that a description had been distributed around Europe of a suspect, police and security would be on the lookout for a man answering this description or even a person of similar size. The last person they would even begin to suspect would be a young native Polish girl.

When he had read the newspaper in the Paris train station the morning after his brief stay in the city, he immediately saw the possibilities the Presidency offered. He had originally intended to take his next victim in Paris, and had already pre-selected a number of dates and places where his quarry was due to appear. He had checked each one out but had been undecided on the optimum. His potential apprehension in Paris forced him to rethink and eventually abandon that plan. But when he read the details of the meeting, he thought it ironic that perhaps the quarry would come to him rather than the other way round. He thought the situation ironic, given the persuasion of his employer.

The great thing about magnificent palaces, he thought, was that countries always wanted to show them off, particularly to tourists. There was good money to be made by turning them into museums and charging the punters $20 a pop or thereabouts. Almost the entire Russian tourist industry was based on visits to palaces that showed the former splendour, not of Communism, but of the Tsarist era. Versailles received millions of visitors annually. In recent years, even the Windsors had got in on the act and had opened Buckingham Palace to the public.

The morning after their arrival in Warsaw, he and Katya had breakfast in an anonymous roadside café, drove to the palace, parked, and strolled up arm in arm just like hundreds of other tourists on day trips. The castle was indeed magnificently appointed and featured priceless works of art from the 17th and 18th centuries. They visited every room that was open to the public and studied the audio commentary in great detail. They saw the Crimson Room, the King's Library, The Palace Chapel, the Lapidarium or Cabinet of Antiquities, and numerous other side rooms and ante rooms. Walker affected interest in every exhibit but paid particular attention to the Royal Apartments, including the Queen's Antechamber, The King's Antechamber, the Queen's Bedroom and The King's Bedroom. He took great care in examining each and every exhibit but took particular care to note the positioning of any security sensors or detection devices.

They took lunch in the museum's restaurant and in the afternoon, they explored the 45-hectare grounds, comprised of a two-level Baroque garden, a neo-Renaissance rose garden, an English landscape park and an English-Chinese park. So much space to lose oneself in, he thought. The park could be entered through a gate from the Palace courtyard, which was adorned with beautiful magnolias and roses.

In the afternoon, he called the number he had gotten in Amsterdam and arranged a meeting in a bar in the city later that evening. The man he called spoke perfect English but he still needed Katya to locate the bar for him. All he had told her about the day was that he had business to do here, and she seemed to fully accept his explanation.

He knew he was still taking a big chance but he felt confident that she had no idea who he was or what he was about. She was, however, an intelligent girl, and despite her seemingly total lack of interest in anything connected with politics or current affairs, he was confident she would put it together soon enough. What he had on his side was her seemingly total devotion and commitment to him. Perhaps she was just doing a job that she had been well paid to do but he felt there was something more there. The way she smiled at him and checked that he was OK with the route and that he had enough food and drink. She could be playing him but he had been in this game long enough to know it from a mile off. No; if he was reading the situation correctly, this girl had half fallen for him. Not surprising, really – wealthy man comes along offering more money than she had possibly ever seen and offers her a chance of a break from a tough lifestyle for a few days – or who knew, if she played her cards right, maybe even longer. The lady may have liked him, but she hadn't fallen for him – she was basically enjoying herself while looking after her future. Well, that was fine with him; for now, anyway. He needed her a lot more than she needed him right now, although he was sure she hadn't realized that yet.

Despite all this and his innate cynicism, he found himself thinking about her and even, heaven forbid, caring about her. They had spent two nights and two days in each other's company and had yet to sleep together; well, yet to have sex anyway. She hadn't queried it and apart from holding hands and a brief kiss on the cheek at the palace visit, they had had very little physical contact. Maybe that was why, he thought. She had called him a gentleman. He could have taken advantage of the situation.

He burst out laughing. She was a hooker he had paid for; what advantage would he be taking? And yet, he felt it would be wrong; this girl was worth a hell of a lot more than that. Careful, he thought; don't get distracted. Eyes on the prize!

She found the bar without any great problem. He told her he wouldn't be too long and asked her to wait for him in the car. Whenever he set up meets like the one he was headed to, he never had a problem identifying the man or men he was due to meet. There was always something; an aura, a look, a set to the person that identified them or set them apart from the rest of the clientele. And it wasn't just he who was able to identify it. Other punters usually gave these people a wide berth.

He was early. He was sitting in a booth at the back when his mark entered the bar. He nodded briefly when the man scanned the place. He bought a beer and took a seat beside Walker.

"I believe we have a mutual friend," he began.

"You could call him that."

Walker wasted no time on small talk but placed a printout from an arms website in front of the man and enquired if it was available, and for how much. He looked deep into the man's eyes as he said it, so he would catch the slightest pause or hesitation or perhaps an effort to overcharge him.

The man never blinked as he said, "For sure, two thousand euro for the piece. Back here in one hour. How much ammo you want?"

"Two clips should be fine. See you in an hour."

The man rose and left. Walker waited a few minutes, ordered another beer and told the bar girl he'd be right back. He headed out to the car, opened the trunk and took some money from his briefcase. He told Katya she was free, provided she returned within the hour.

The transaction was completed without incident and they returned to their motel for a second night. Walker had formulated a plan for the next few days, but he lay awake for some time trying to figure out how best to implement it. It was a simple idea really but what he agonized about was as to how much to involve Katya. For a start, he could not tell her what he was here for. Loyalty and devotion, albeit after three days, was one thing but there was no way he was risking anyone else's direct involvement on this one.

Yet he needed her assistance. She wasn't central to the plan, and if all went well, she would only have a minor role; but he had to consider the possibility of a snag, and have a contingency in place. That was why he abandoned his original idea, to tell her she was free to drive to her home in Katowice for a few days. Too risky if something went wrong.

At about two in the morning it came to him.

Over breakfast, he decided to reveal his plan.

"Katya, we have been together now three days and you know I know that you are an intelligent girl." She nodded. "So, with my shyness about being seen, etc, you have probably guessed that not all of my business activities are legitimate."

"Look, Don," she smiled. "I've known that since I first saw you in the club. Don't worry about it; goes with the territory, as they say. I mean, hey, no sweat, ok?"

He placed his hand on hers and she responded with a gentle squeeze.

"Thanks, that's cool, but I've gotta do a job here and I need your help again."

She sighed. "Hey, name it Don. You've paid me already. Just say what you need. Hey, I hope it's not too scary, is it?" He felt a strange sensation – maybe even close to amusement – when she called him Don; but that was the name on the passport he was using.

"Don't worry, you won't get arrested, I promise, but *I* might if I'm not careful. What I'm going to do is this. Now I need total and complete secrecy, understand?" he said, looking her straight in the eyes and giving her the stare.

She touched his arm and looked slightly hurt. "Look, I said it's OK."

"Right, sorry. Now, sometime over the next few days, I'm going to steal one of those Rembrandts we saw in the palace."

She giggled. "Wow, that must be worth, like, millions."

"Well, not quite so much on the black market, but it will pay for our trip."

They both laughed and headed for the car.

At a large hypermarket he gave her a shopping list. Included were a black rucksack, several litres of water, and some high-energy candy bars. He entered a large department store himself and tried on a series of jackets and trousers until he got what he required. He then gave the items to Katya to proceed to the pay point. The final purchase was two pre-paid cheap cell phones, one of which he gave her; he placed the other in his newly purchased rucksack. They were back at the hotel in just over an hour.

In the afternoon, they set off for the palace again, waiting until a large queue formed to tag along behind a German coach party.

Visitors were ordinarily requested to leave rucksacks in the cloakroom but they were allowed to bring them in if they contained video cameras, on payment of a fee.

Walker had spent hours studying the plans and layout of the palace on the web, and he had already identified numerous places to hide. During a quiet moment, he and Katya ducked into one of the restrooms and she passed him the dark jacket and pants they had purchased that morning, which were almost an exact match for the clothes worn by the room guides.

The palace was closing early today and would not re-open to the public until the following Monday, after the summit meeting. When Katya left, later that afternoon, she left alone. Security staff carried out a cursory check to ensure all visitors had left, but by this stage, Walker was well-secreted in a void located over janitor's closets and an adjoining staff restroom. He had a comfortable space and access to all the facilities he required. He settled down to wait.

It always fascinated him that security services were almost entirely focused on keeping people out or restricting access – i.e. stopping people from getting in. They rarely, if ever, focused on people who were already there, and never stopped people from getting out! He had accomplished what was potentially the most difficult part of his task with ease. He was in! He had memorized the layout of the palace and had several exit routes worked out.

It was, perhaps, his luck that the Foreign Ministers of the E.U. were meeting here over the weekend. But it was an immense stroke of good fortune that they had all decided to use the full facilities of the palace and stay overnight. Of course, he had no idea what the sleeping arrangements were, but that was the only element of the plan that bothered him. He had a pre-arranged meeting point with Katya. All that he was required to do was to text her with a time.

Almost sixty hours after they had parted, he was ready. He sent her a two-word text, which read 'one hour'. It was 01.00 am on Saturday morning.

He left his hiding place, where he had stayed totally undisturbed for over two days. He placed the candy bar wrappers in the empty rucksack and disposed of the empty water bottles in a trashcan containing more of the same. The flattened rucksack went underneath his dark sweater, and over that he pulled on the dark jacket.

He emerged silently into the vast hallway and moved swiftly and silently towards his targets. He had had plenty of time to think over the previous two days and he had mentally travelled the route hundreds of times. He felt he could almost do it blindfolded. He had also had time to think through the sleeping arrangements. He guessed that the French Minister would be allocated the Queen's Bedroom. Other than that, he couldn't say, and even this was a guess; but he thought again of the flexibility of the Bahraini's plan and smiled to himself. This was working like a dream, he thought, adrenalin flowing freely.

Suddenly he froze. Shit. There was a guy outside the bedroom door. Damn it; he should have known. The guy stood easily, seemingly relaxed. He obviously hadn't seen Walker, as he was dressed from head to toe in black and the light was poor. Now, what to do? The security man would almost certainly be a highly-trained Special Forces type. Not the sort of guy you wanted to take on in hand-to-hand combat; certainly not after lying inert for sixty hours. Furthermore, the guy would have a radio, and even if he put him down, someone would check with him every few hours – or would they? Perhaps this was a token presence? Perhaps he was just the personal bodyguard of the Minister and had no contact with the locals? After all, the exterior was enclosed in a ring of steel, or so the Poles had said.

He had to think fast. Either he was going to do it now or slip back and hope tomorrow night was more lax. No; some of them might leave the next day, so that was not an option. It had to be tonight. Sorry mate, he thought. He had no qualms offing politicians but he disliked putting down the foot soldiers; he could identify far more with them. Still, it was them or him.

The guy outside the door made the decision for him. He twisted to his right towards where Walker was hiding and, pretending he had not seen him, tried to covertly reach inside his jacket for his weapon. Walker's newly-acquired silenced Glock coughed twice and the man fell silently. The only sound was the radio clattering to the floor. He closed the distance to the man in four strides and grabbed the radio with his gloved hand. He waited, listening intently, but there was no sound, no call, no check, and no alarm given. He stuck the set into his pocket.

He opened the door silently and stepped into the darkened bedroom. The gun coughed twice again and he was gone. He paused outside the door and decided it was better to drag the security guard's body inside the bedroom. Twelve quick strides along his pre-planned route, but more cautiously this time, scanning for more security personnel – he saw none. He arrived at the second bedroom, The King's Bedroom. Again, he entered noiselessly.

He jumped briefly and his adrenalin spiked as he realized the Minister was awake, reading by a bedside lamp. The man went to cry out a warning but the words froze in his throat as Walker's Glock coughed again.

From there it was easy – to the end of the long corridor, down the servant's stairs to the kitchens, moving quietly, cautiously, gun at the ready, scanning left and right for security personnel. It was deathly quiet in the kitchens and he soon relaxed somewhat as he realized that the whole house was sleeping and the guards had more or less gone into shutdown mode to allow their masters and mistresses to rest. All doors to the outside were sure to be locked and probably alarmed, if the entry detectors he had seen a few days ago were operative, and he had to assume they were. But he was confident that no one ever put alarms on kitchen windows and he was right.

He slipped through easily and departed across the manicured lawns and gardens, not even casting a shadow as he manoeuvred his way around trees and hedges, avoiding the few spotlights that were still operating. He did spot perimeter guards, but they appeared to be in pairs, and merely patrolling the perimeter in a relaxed fashion. He waited until they were well out of range and slipped away into the trees. From there, he crossed through the woods and outer parts of the property to where Katya should be waiting. And she was.

He dumped the rucksack into the back seat, sat in the passenger's seat and released a long slow breath.

"Good evening, kind sir," she said, smiling. "And where would you like me to take you this evening?"

"How about the German border?" he said. "And did you bring the food? I'm starving."

"It's all in the picnic basket, my darling," she said, as she quietly started the engine and turned towards the motorway.

Walker wolfed down the delicious sandwiches and coffee she had prepared for him. Nothing had tasted as good in a long time. He felt totally at ease with Katya, and slowly felt his adrenalin level subside and his body return to normal. The Friday night weekend rush had long since ended, leaving the roads free for them to cruise at will.

He asked her to briefly detour to the east to cross the Wisla River. There, he dumped the Glock, the remaining ammunition, the rucksack, the black clothing and the guard's radio deep into the black swirling waters. Then they headed west and he became Donald Clarke again, American businessman travelling late to avoid traffic.

He felt himself relax as Katya drove and hummed along to the all-night radio show. R.E.M. were singing about losing their religion. When had he lost his? A long time ago, probably. He knew he would not fully relax until they were back in Germany; if the bodies were found, the entire country might shut down. Katya would help him, but how far could he push her, particularly if she realized what he had done?

He noticed that she had not asked about the painting. He decided she was like many women he had encountered over the years. They hadn't asked questions that did not concern them directly, or when they were unsure whether they would like the answers.

Despite his anxiety, he did take time out to congratulate himself again. He had accomplished the first five tasks on the list and he was still a free man. That was twenty-five million bucks, plus his retainer! From now on, though, it would get more difficult and he would have to plan harder and be even cleverer. Mistakes like the ones he had made in Europe were not an option; they would be fatal. Why? Because he knew the outcry after what he had done tonight would be deafening, and would probably dwarf that which had succeeded his hit on the British Prime Minister. Tonight he had crossed a line; one he had not even contemplated before.

He argued with himself that he had had no choice. While the Bahraini's list had been flexible, it had stipulated certain criteria which, given the circumstances, necessitated that he cross that line. Tonight he had assassinated the Foreign Ministers of France and Denmark, two of the NATO powers with troops in Afghanistan. The Dane had been optional, but not the French or the British, according to his employer's list. But the line he had crossed, and which he was certain would cause outrage across the globe, was the fact that the French Foreign Minister was a woman.

Chapter 25

On the banks of the Elbe River, 70 miles inland from Travemünde, lies the city of Hamburg. This city, although lying inland, has been a major shipping centre for over 1,000 years, and was even at one-time a Hanseatic League port. Hamburg was one of the first German cities to emerge from the shambles at the end of the Second World War, and after post-war restoration it became a prosperous and confident city featuring striking architecture, both modern and ancient with an epic history and splendid art galleries, cosmopolitan shopping, dining and nightlife. It was a major hub for all sorts of commercial goods and was second only to Rotterdam as Europe's busiest port. But what was of particular interest to Carl Walker was that it offered cruises to almost every part of the world.

He sat with Katya sipping beers in the sunshine on a Saturday afternoon. His worries of the previous night had been unnecessary. They had been safely across the German border and asleep in their motel bedroom before the bodies had been discovered in the palace. Of course, he wasn't to know this. What did seem strange was that there appeared to be a news blackout in operation. TV reported that the Foreign Ministers had met but that there had been no press conference afterwards or no group photograph. Ministers had been rushed away in dark tinted Mercedes and flown home in private jets. Speculation was rife among the media that there had been a major disagreement, and even though they were the Foreign Ministers, it was assumed to have been about the future of the Euro single currency. The markets were forecast to drop severely at the start of trading on Monday morning.

Amazingly, the real story had not leaked out. Why, he thought? But he knew; leaders were obviously deeply shocked and fearful of the panicked reaction that might ensue. They obviously realized by now that the same killer had struck again. He had visions of them all hiding under their beds and he smiled and almost laughed out loud.

"What's so funny my dear?" she said.

"Ah, nothing, Katya; well, just a private joke - it's too complicated to explain. Hey, let's get another beer and take a look at that brochure – see where you'd like to take a cruise to." He had already given her the $10,000 bonus and she was on top of the world.

"Wow baby, this is really living. Oh but, I forgot, it's got to be somewhere I'm allowed to go. I've got an E.U. passport but I think it's restricted. I mean, I can't go to the U.S."

"Ah, don't worry, my dear, we'll find somewhere. Let's go and get some dinner."

Back in Paris, a crisis meeting of the Heads of Europe's Police Forces and their top investigators was underway. The politicians were still dithering and had, incredibly, managed to suppress the story so far. Mike and Jean-Pierre felt the strategy was unwise as the outcry was likely to be far worse if people felt that their leaders were trying to hide the truth from them. He could see the headlines – what else is being suppressed? What are our politicians hiding from us? Is there another wave of terrorism that we are not being kept informed about?

They were in Surete HQ awaiting the arrival of Alan and Bob from London, Alfonso from Milan and their counterparts from all over Europe and beyond. This crisis was going global. Their colleagues in Warsaw had come up with the same story as before; no one had seen anything; no one had heard anything; there were no clues; there was no trace evidence. The killer had obviously lain in wait, but where? Police were searching the palace inch by inch but hadn't found a trace. It appeared that the killer had come in and presumably escaped again through a window in the kitchen area but there had been no prints – no trace at all actually – no clue even as to what direction he had gone in after that. At this stage, no one had any doubt about Mike's theory that the same killer was responsible for the assassinations on both sides of the Atlantic.

"Worst we've ever encountered," said Bob as he came in and took a seat.

"I'm not so sure he'd see it that way," Jean-Pierre intoned. "He'd probably consider himself the best we've ever had to deal with, and even though he's a cold blooded murdering bastard, he's probably right."

Mike nodded vigorously. "Guys, Jean is right, we've never dealt with anything like this before. For all we know, this guy may have been killing for years; probably has. The sooner we start thinking like he does, the quicker we'll catch him."

"He's right," said Alfonso, "and you know, when this news breaks, this is gonna spread real terror amongst people, the likes of which we haven't seen before."

Alan joined in. "The only thing that's gonna catch someone like this is to shut the whole bloody continent down or compulsorily gather DNA from everyone – even then we might not be sure we'd get him. But one thing for sure, it will definitely strengthen our hand with the politicos for tougher legislation. People's memories are short, but this one will run and run and will fester until we apprehend a suspect."

"OK guys," from Mike. "This story is gonna break real quickly because when people start to realize the exhaustive checks we've put in place on all transport movements, they're gonna realize very quickly it isn't due to the health or otherwise of the euro."

"Aye," said Bob. "Full body and baggage searches on everyone, and extra special attention for anyone, male or female, in the five-foot-seven to five-foot-ten range. Christ, this is gonna cause uproar."

Jean-Pierre's phone buzzed.

"Oui, merci – guys, TV - Canal 1 – right now."

The President, clearly visibly upset, announced to the nation the tragic death of their Foreign Minister and that of the Danish Foreign Minister at the hands of an assassin who had attacked them while they slept after their meeting in Warsaw. He stated

258

that it was a tragedy for France, for Denmark, and for Europe. The murder of the French Foreign Minister was an assault on the French nation and an affront to the freedom and dignity of all French people. He appealed to the nation to maintain a dignified calm and promised that the full resources of law enforcement would be deployed around the clock, not just in Poland but throughout Europe until the killer or killers were captured and brought to justice.

"Dignified calm? Was that what he said?" Bob McDonald quipped. "Great chance of that. Our place has gone crazy since the P.M. was hit and shows no sign of cooling down. Bloody thing could spread right across Europe."

"OK, my friends, let's calm down and examine what we have here," said Jean. "The Poles are saying the whole place was locked up tight. They cannot figure how he can have gained access. They say the palace was surrounded by a ring of steel."

"Ring of steel, my arse," said Bob. "They'd obviously shut down for the night thinking their charges were away to bed."

"Perhaps you're right but I'm not so sure," Mike mused. "Their focus would have been on keeping people out, but what if our man was already in there? That place is huge, by all accounts, and it's open to the public most of the time. Can we find out how long it was closed before the Ministers arrived?"

"Excellent point, mon ami," Jean responded. "It would be a lot easier for him to lie in wait and then exit at his leisure. The bodies weren't discovered until morning. This guy is smart and the only way we will find him is to start being smarter and to try to think ahead, anticipate his next move, if there is one. Mike, you've been on this from the beginning. What do you think?"

"I'm afraid it's the same pattern as before, guys. He hits vulnerable targets, so we've got to appeal to our politicians to eliminate anything at all that might be potentially insecure. It's the only way. I'm going out on a limb here, but I'm gonna suggest that we now have time. Look, this guy is working to a plan – no question. He left London for Paris. He had to have been targeting the French Foreign Minister here but got scared away. Now, look at Warsaw – Jesus, there were 26 of the 27 E.U. Foreign Ministers present. He potentially had all night. Why didn't he kill more of them?" There was a collective gasp. "I know, I know," he continued, "an appalling scenario, but quite achievable, unless he was disturbed by someone, and we have no reason to believe that happened, apart from the French Special Forces Sergeant who was guarding his Minister. No, this guy is American, has to be – why else would he start his killing spree over there and then move to Europe? He could have killed more here, but chose not to do so. We therefore have to assume he's finished here – hence my theory that we have time. I believe though that he is still somewhere in Europe, although probably not Poland, and he will try to re-enter the U.S. at some stage. That is, unless he has plans elsewhere, but I don't think this thing plays like that – call it instinct or whatever, but I'm gonna suggest that we try to lock down all exit points from Europe to the U.S.A. Now, he could take an alternative route, so I'm gonna be asking Paul Lincoln and his people to try to put as many people as they can on all entry points to the States. I don't know what they'll use; hell, there's lots of options – Customs Service, Immigration, the Coast Guard, whatever. We can't ask them to collect DNA from thousands of people but we've got to do something. I mean, this guy's in the wind, whether we like it or not, so we're gonna have to use methods we've never employed before. Can I suggest we discuss this again and come up with an agreed position to put to the politicos?"

There was general agreement. They thrashed it around for another hour, and variations were tabled and discussed. They eventually agreed that although business would hate it, both politicians and public would co-operate fully in an almost total slow down of all passenger movements between the suspected areas. They nominated Mike and Jean-Pierre to meet with the Police Chiefs, Prime Minister's and Presidents to seek their approval.

Following consultations with their superiors, a late night private meeting was arranged with a visibly shocked French President, who was linked by teleconference to the Deputy British Prime Minister. Full assent and support was confirmed for whatever measures they wished to put in place to attempt to apprehend the killer or at least make it more difficult for him to operate. A quiet call from the President to his counterpart in Washington D.C. confirmed the same would apply in the U.S. They returned to Surete H.Q. to meet with the rest of their colleagues and formulate their plans.

He had known Katya was Polish from their first meeting in the nightclub. He had already formed the bones of a plan in his mind to head to Warsaw, provided he could get a name from his contacts in Amsterdam. The lack of language skills and resultant visibility was an issue, but he was aware that there were hundreds of thousands of Polish people living and working in the EU since the country had acceded to membership. Poles revelled in their new-found freedom of movement. They were excellent workers and would demand lower salaries than employees from longer established E.U. member states. He had toyed with the idea of how to use this to his advantage. He was vaguely aware that some of these migrants were involved in the sex industry so when he encountered Katya he had guessed straight away that she was Polish. The fact that she seemed pleasant, open, trusting and could help him with the language made him warm more and more to the idea.

The original plan had been to eliminate her when the job was completed. In her profession, girls moved on all the time, so her non-return to Amsterdam wouldn't raise an eyebrow. It would just be assumed she had found a better life or indeed business elsewhere. But things had moved on considerably from there. Apart from the fact that he liked her and that she was good company, he felt he might need the cover for some time yet. There was no doubt they would look for a man travelling alone if they ever released the true story, although he felt it would have to get out – no way could they keep a lid on something this big.

He thought of paying her a large bonus and ultimately sending her back with the car, but that was really unnecessary. The vehicle was hired from Sixt and could be dropped off anywhere for a fee. Also, she could betray him when she discovered what he had really been up to in Poland. They were bound to offer a substantial reward. OK, but what could she tell them? That he had forced her to help him? That she had played no part except as his driver? Both were more or less true, but in a case this big, the clever thing would have been to keep her head down and do nothing. Anyone remotely connected with this case in a culpable way was likely to end up in a prison cell somewhere, if only to appease public disquiet. And Katya was a clever girl, so he felt sure she would keep her mouth shut. Anyway, she knew very little yet, so he would definitely hold on to her for another while. Getting papers for her to enter the U.S. might be a problem now, but he could wait until things cooled; well, theoretically, anyway.

People had seen them together, but that was hardly a big issue – a few shops, diners and motels; largely forgettable places where thousands of people moved through every day, all marked by anonymity. When the police in Warsaw figured out that he had actually gotten out on the night of the assassination rather than gotten in, they'd scan the videos from the previous week or so for suspicious visitors. They'd be wasting their time as he had already accessed the palace's security system and wiped the relevant sections. Much more difficult than when he had scrubbed brief sections of the hotel's digital records, as they had spent a considerable amount of time in the palace, but it was doable. He had substituted sections from thirty days previously so there would be no gap in the recordings. He figured they'd only check back a week at most – how long could someone lie in wait? Anyway, if they had already figured out they were dealing with the same guy, and he was sure they had, then six days earlier they knew he had been in Milan.

He felt sure Katya would want to quit her previous life now that she had had a taste of freedom. Perhaps get a real job; she was bright, and she had also said that her original plan was to go home after she had made some money. But first he'd ask her to take another little trip; a very pleasant one, in fact. Apart from liking her company, he found that he actually trusted her – he knew she wouldn't betray him. Not in the same way that he knew that Cindy would never betray him, even if she found out his real profession – she was more into self-protection. Katya was different. He had not had sex with her and he had almost acted like a guardian. She had already told him that he was the first man she had ever met who had respected her for what she was, not for her body or what he or she could do with it. She had gotten quite tearful when she had confided in him and he had placed an arm around her and held her gently.

That had been last night. This morning he had sent her shopping again. This time she was to buy large suitcases for him and for her; clothing for him and for herself if she wanted more, although she had previously bought almost an entire wardrobe in the outlet. When he told her, she shrieked with delight and asked how much time they had. More shrieks and giggles followed the revelation that she had all day as they were not leaving until that evening and she had as long as she wished.

When she returned to the motel at 5.30 pm, she initially thought she had inadvertently stepped into the wrong room. She was startled as the man who stood before her had aged at least thirty years. His hair had thinned and was now totally white. His arms, which showed beneath his short-sleeved shirt, had acquired a yellowish hue, and there were large liver spots on the backs of both of his hands.

"Sorry if I frightened you, my dear," he said, "I'm just taking precautions ahead of our trip."

She regained her composure and nodded uncertainly. "Ok, ah, I've got the large suitcases and the clothes in the car."

"So what are we waiting for? Let's go," he said.

That evening, the P&O cruise ship Ventura departed for Barbados, scheduled to call briefly at Southampton, Madeira, Antigua and St Lucia. Among its 2,700 passengers and crew of 1,226 was one Herr Fredrik Schoenbaum, a frail elderly gentleman of German descent but a U.S. citizen. He was accompanied and assisted by his young grand niece, for whom he had booked a mini suite. Herr Schoenbaum had reserved a full suite for the voyage. He was unsteady on his feet and had requested a wheelchair for boarding, which the cruise firm was more than pleased to provide.

After they had settled into their suites and had assured the attendants that they were more than comfortable, Katya assisted her "grand-uncle" to dinner in the Marco Pierre White Silver Service Restaurant. He could walk with the assistance of a cane.

There was such a gap in their ages that Walker was sure they had been accepted for what they purported to be and not a young girl on the make with a sugar daddy.

They made quite an impression on the polite staff and fitted in with the ambience to perfection. Even if paratroopers were to storm the ship, Walker mused, he was probably the last person on board that they would suspect of any wrongdoing! He smiled at Katya and they drank champagne and dined on foie gras, fillet of Dover Sole and veal. He then suggested to his 'niece' that it was time he got to bed, and she assisted him again.

When they got back to his suite, he locked the door, threw away the walking cane and stripped off his disguise. He couldn't do much about his hair but he was himself again and they exchanged a look. He took her in his arms then and they attacked each other with a passion approaching desperation. They somehow transported themselves as far as the king-size bed in his suite and eagerly explored each other. The tension of the previous days was still with him; he was like a coil spring, and climaxed too quickly. But no words were spoken – she held on to him for dear life and they both knew the next time would be slower and fulfilling for both. Why had he waited for so long, he thought, as he finally allowed himself to come down and to relax.

Later, as she lay sleeping peacefully, he poured himself a cognac from the container of X.O. on the credenza in the living room. Sleep would still be some time in coming. He allowed himself another small stroke of congratulation. He was the man again! No mistakes on this run. He had had to change plans but he would always find a way. If you waited long enough and planned well enough, you'd get there.

He found himself mentally reviewing the Bahraini's list. When he had first seen it, he had felt somewhat daunted at the enormity of what the man was asking him to attempt. But when he had reviewed it a few times, what struck him was the flexibility it contained.

The first name on the list had said 'A prominent U.S. Presidential candidate'. Sorry, Dan, but you were the only real contestant, even if undeclared; but such was life.

Then, a strange one – "any three elected U.S. officials." That gave him plenty of scope and was the easiest task on the list. He wasn't at all sure that the man wanted him to take out all three at once, and in a minor town, but he had fulfilled the instruction and he could have no quibble. In any event, he assumed the man's intention was to create terror at a number of levels – the 'no one is safe' strategy.

The next said "senior ministers of the Governments of three European powers who have troops in Arab countries; must include Britain, France and one other." Again, there was lots of flexibility here. The Bahraini had gotten a bonus with the British P.M. and he felt sure he would acknowledge this in his next payment. He had only specified a senior minister, but as Walker's research found that the P.M. was the most exposed, it had to be him.

His mistake in trying to hit targets in London and Paris within days could have led to him being apprehended and he made a mental note to himself to be more careful and not to get over confident. Yes, he was the man, but even the man wasn't invisible or bullet proof. In fact, without Katya, his task in Poland would have been immeasurably more difficult and dangerous. She still seemed to have no suspicion of what he had been up to. The news had broken on TV, but she didn't speak German and appeared not to have taken any notice of the stringent security searches when boarding that evening. Why would she, he supposed – after all, she had never been on a cruise ship before, and they were going to spend the next two weeks on board, so the cruise line would be sure to carry out a thorough security check on everyone.

He had been very aware of what had caused the comprehensive checks of both persons and personal effects, and although confident that he was extremely unlikely to be detected, he had still been tense as they had edged their way to the top of the queue. He had spent the day when Katya had been out shopping disposing of any traces of his previous personas. All documents, other than those of Herr Schoenbaum and one other U.S. passport, had been burned and the ashes flushed. Clothes, hair and make-up had been disposed of in a number of garbage containers. But he was still tense, and Katya's presence and assistance had been invaluable as she had smoothed a path through each of the searches in good humour and total innocence. It had served to mask and deflect his own apprehension. Only now, as the Ventura powered her way through the cold dark waters of the North Sea en route to their first port of call at Southampton, which they would reach in the morning, did he allow himself to fully relax.

He poured himself another cognac and savoured the slow burn of the smooth amber liquid. He had tested himself and had come through. He had accomplished an enormous amount in a relatively short period, but while they still had no idea who he was, he was certain he was the most wanted man on the planet. From now on, things would get even more difficult; but he would be ready.

Part 3
August

Chapter 26

Paul Lincoln was about to take his first full weekend off in over a month; his first real break since they had come back from Disney World, in fact. The pressure from government, press and public to find the killer or killers had been unceasing. The phenomenon that Paul referred to as the five P's, which was encountered constantly in anti-terrorism policing, was firmly in play here. The press and the public put pressure on politicians, and they in turn put pressure on the police. He noted that the chain always ended with the police, so that was naturally where the greatest amount of pressure was focused.

Often, when a massive amount of law enforcement's resources were thrown at a crime – such as the murder of someone with a high profile – or a criminal trend –such as a spate of gangland or drug-related killings – when allied to public disquiet and therefore complete cooperation, a breakthrough is achieved. But past experience had shown that it wasn't always the correct breakthrough. The pressure to apprehend suspects was often so great that the wrong people were arrested, tried and sentenced – to the death penalty, in some cases – and the perpetrators got off scot-free.

But with modern advanced crime detection methods and increasing use of forensics and DNA evidence, the likelihood of a wrongful conviction had greatly diminished. In fact, the availability of technologies that hadn't been around when a serious crime was first investigated had led to the formation of "cold case" units in practically every major police force throughout the world, and significant success had been achieved in bringing criminals to book who had escaped detection first time round. Even if perpetrators could not be apprehended because they had already themselves died or been sentenced to long prison terms for other crimes, the resolution of a long-outstanding case gave closure and peace of mind to relatives and friends of the victim.

Conversely, and cynical as it might sound, this put even more pressure on police officers to apprehend the 'real' perpetrators and to gather enough evidence to prove guilt beyond a reasonable doubt and ultimately achieve a conviction. There had been a number of high-profile cases where the 'obviously' guilty parties had escaped censure through the use of legal loopholes or the strategies of highly paid defence counsel.

On the other hand, serial killers often operated below the public radar, as most of their victims were classed as missing persons until bodies were found. Police were sometimes aware that a serial was operating in a particular area but did not put the word out for fear of causing public alarm or putting themselves under even more pressure to find the killer.

Political killings or assassinations were rare and given that law enforcement ultimately reported to political masters, vast resources were usually deployed, sometimes successfully. But not in this case; it just would not go away. Conspiracy theories abounded. Every weekend, another Sunday newspaper or magazine came up with a new one. Paul listened to the latest advertisement on his car radio as he fought traffic on the beltway –

"This Sunday, we reveal who killed the Senator and why. And is there a so-called transatlantic killer about? We reveal all, including what the police didn't tell you. Read all about it etc."

Well, if you know that much about it, I wish to hell you'd tell *us*, he thought. He had been in constant touch with Mike Lyons and the guys in London, Paris and Milan, but the trail had gone quiet after that; until the events in Poland a few days later. This had driven politicians in Europe apoplectic with fear and rage. That democratically elected people could be slaughtered as they lay in their beds had created a level of terror not experienced before; all the more so because the killer had, once again, seemingly vanished into thin air. It was pointless blaming the

Polish police as their counterparts elsewhere had also come up empty handed.

There was growing support for the populist theory that there was more than one killer operating. People couldn't conceptualize how one person could seemingly travel around Europe (and the U.S.?) with impunity, constantly avoiding detection or even sighting. There was talk of Arabic, extreme right wing, and all sorts of other terror groups operating sleeper cells who had faded back into oblivion, only to strike again when people least expected it. This speculation only added to the sense of public fear and apprehension.

But the police – or at least the ones that mattered, he thought – didn't buy in to the theory. Mike Lyons was still convinced of his one killer theory, and Paul agreed with him. As to where their man was right then, both knew as much as they had a month previously, which was very little. However, Mike was convinced that the killer was American and that he had probably returned to the U.S. at this stage.

Paul had worked long days and every weekend since the first murder and the lack of progress was beginning to frustrate him. They also needed to be careful not to over-commit resources at the cost of ignoring or neglecting other terrorist threats. If only they could catch a break, he thought. They had DNA from the hotel room in Milan, but without a match from a database, it was useless. He had run his powerful D.H.S. computers twenty-four hours a day, seven days a week, but nothing else showed. Still, he thought, computers are fantastic machines; but no matter how sophisticated, they are after all only processors of information, and if the correct information is not in there, it doesn't matter how much money you spend or how sophisticated it becomes; it is not going to give you the answer you seek.

They had had another team meeting this morning. Despite the frustrations of the previous weeks, or perhaps because of them, the group was working stronger than ever together. There had been no inter-agency rivalry, no mavericks, and no solo-runs; at least none he knew of. Everyone had worked flat out, and to be honest, they were all beat.

"Don't lose sight of the main objective," Maria Gonzalez had told them this morning. She absolutely insisted they all take some time out with their families or partners this weekend. Every political figure that might be a target was either away on vacation in a secret location, lying low at home, or under round-the-clock protection. It was August anyway, the silly season, so there was very little political activity. Maria was right, he knew. Anyway, Mike was due back in the U.S. on Monday and they'd take another cut at it together.

Herr Schoenbaum was due to arrive back a day beforehand. He had had a marvellous cruise with Katya. He felt that she must have learned about the killings in the Wilanow Palace but she gave him no indication that she was aware. Neither did she demonstrate the slightest nervousness when around him. She was perfectly charming and loving for the entire voyage. His need to put on complicated make-up when going out in public meant he spent long periods in his room 'resting'. He used the time well, though, spending countless hours on the web researching his next tasks and drawing up plans on his laptop.

He scanned the crystalline waters of Long Bay as the American Airlines flight banked after take-off from Grantley Adams Airport. They had spent almost two weeks cruising before they reached Barbados, their final port of call on the Saturday. They then spent a night in the luxurious Sandy Lane Hotel and Resort. He would have to leave Katya here for at least a week, or maybe longer, so he had prepaid for her stay and left a large deposit so she could enjoy the facilities of the resort to the full.

They had had long conversations throughout the voyage, and Katya was now convinced that she wanted to go to the U.S. There was, of course, the small matter of obtaining a visa, but he assured her that it could be arranged without too much difficulty. In fact, what he intended to do was to obtain a U.S. passport for her, but that might take a little longer. Why not, he thought? She's completely loyal, seems totally devoted, and could be very useful to him back in the States. In fact, if truth be told, he had grown rather fond of her; maybe he even loved her a little. Did he love Cindy? Yes, he did, but in a different way. But Cindy would be horrified if she found out about his activities. Katya didn't seem to bat an eyelid.

Arranging documents in Miami would be child's play. If he wished, he could go the legal route, picking up birth certificates and applying officially, but it took longer; and until everyone was required to carry a fully biometric passport, the documents he could buy in Miami would do fine. In fact, he was sure there were already ways of forging the biometric ones as well, or of bypassing the information contained in the chip.

But that was for later. The hostess offered him a snack and a glass of wine and he dismissed the thought for now. His next focus was to re-enter the U.S. himself. He did have one other authentic U.S. passport, but he was loath to use it just yet. It would have required purchasing materials to affect the disguise, and he did not want to do this in a relatively small place like Barbados. Anyway, he might need that identity later.

He always liked to pick a large airport for re-entry on his forays outside the U.S. That was, of course, when he was not entering as Carl Walker. Some might favour a smaller, quieter place; he preferred to lose himself in the crowds. Besides, in a large airport that doesn't have a grouped queuing system, you might have a choice of up to thirty different Immigration Officers. He was nearly always adept at picking the guy (always a guy) who was close to the end of his shift, tired, or pissed off. He avoided women if he could help it – they tended to be far more perceptive. He also liked to pick an airport where his persona at the time was least likely to attract attention. Miami is the largest gateway from Latin America to the U.S.A. Officers would be looking for drug mules, illegal immigrants, and people wanted for questioning related to the narcotics industry. An old man of German descent would hardly raise an eyebrow.

AA arrived right on time on a glorious evening, and he made his way through the concourse to the Immigration Hall. He was mildly shocked when he saw the queues. Miami was always busy but never this much so, particularly on a Sunday evening, also a favourite time of his to fly. He was so far back in the queue that he could not make out the features of the officers manning the Immigration Desks. It seemed as if half of Latin America had decided to emigrate to the U.S. all at once. But he had checked the flight schedule; there weren't that many flights due this evening and after all, this was the line for U.S. citizens!

And then he knew. This was his doing. As he inched his way through the long, snaking queue, he noticed that each individual was being questioned at length by individual Immigration Officers. Each 'interview' seemed to be taking between three to four minutes. Well, there was nothing for it but to brave it out. He had gotten this far. But what if they searched him? Should he duck into a rest room and dump his one other remaining passport? No, wait, Immigration did not conduct searches; that was Customs and they'd be looking for contraband, which he did not have. Still, it was a risk. He could easily say he needed the bathroom and re-join the queue – after all, he was an old man so people would be sympathetic. He decided to stay put for now.

Eventually, he got close enough to scan the Immigration Officers. He was in a one-line queue so he wouldn't have his choice of desks to approach. Still, if several came free at once, he knew which one he'd head for. That too was unlikely, given the amount of time that was being taken with each person. After a long wait, his turn came. The Officer was male, African American, pleasant, early thirties but very alert. Schoenbaum proffered his passport.

"Good evening sir, I'm sorry to have kept you waiting. I suppose you understand it is due to the major security alert." Should he say yes or no?

"Ah, ja, of course, I heard. Terrible thing, but I've been travelling and have been away from the States so it hasn't impacted much on me."

"I see sir, you are an American citizen. Can you tell me your background, please?"

Shit, this was getting complicated; he kept his cool.

"Ja, Officer. I was born in Berlin in 1930 but my father didn't like the Nazi Regime so he left for the United States in 1935. I have spent all of my life here."

"Whereabouts exactly, sir?"

"Ah, San Antonio, that was where my parents settled."

"Very good sir, but why have you chosen to enter the U.S. through Miami?"

He could feel the perspiration on his neck and hoped it hadn't spread anywhere visible, or that his complexion hadn't coloured.

"Ah, you see, I was on a cruise which terminated in Miami; I mean, sorry, in Barbados, so this was the best way to come back; and you see, I have some family, a grand-niece in Miami, and I thought I'd spend a few days with her before returning to Texas."

"I see, and where did you first board this cruise sir?"

"In Germany, of course. I was visiting with my remaining relatives there."

"OK, sir, I think that's fine; and you boarded the cruise ship where, exactly, did you say?

"Ah nein, I didn't, but it was in Hamburg."

"Fine, and what route did you take when you travelled from San Antonio to Europe on your departure from the U.S.?"

"I took Delta Airlines, Officer, from Atlanta, departing for Switzerland and on to Berlin."

The man nodded and put his passport through the electronic scanner. He was still staring at him intently and Walker was using every ounce of self-control to remain calm. Perhaps it was the fact that he had come from Europe? But he was 81 years old, for Christ's sake; how could he be suspect?

If the man suspected him of being twenty-five years younger, that was how. Calm down, we'll be through this in a minute. He silently thanked the U.S. practice of not always checking citizens' passports on departure from the country. If it had, he would have required an exit stamp from Atlanta.

"Right, sir, passport seems to be in order," the immigration officer said as he placed an entry stamp on a blank page and returned it. Walker accepted the passport gratefully and moved to enter through the small metal gate.

"Oh, just one final thing, sir." The man paused, and then looked up. "Do you have an address for your grand-niece that we can verify?"

He was prepared for this. "Yes, of course I do, Officer, and a telephone number."

275

The man fell for the bait – Walker had him now. He gave the man the number and he used the Immigration phone to dial the local Miami number. Walker had, of course, electronically diverted it earlier.

"And your grand-niece's name sir?"

"Sure, Katya Flederstein."

The call was answered on the second ring: "Hallo?"

"Hallo, I'm looking for a Miss Katya Flederstein?"

"Speaking, who is this?"

"Sorry, this is the United States Immigration and Customs Service, ma'am. Sorry to bother you, but are you expecting your Uncle Fredrik this evening?"

"Yes, I am. Why, is he alright? Has something happened to him?"

"No, no, ma'am; sorry if we alarmed you, he's fine. He's right here with us, but can you describe him to me?"

"Well, he's just over 80 years old, he's got sort of sallow complexion, white hair, blue eyes I think, and, well, he's about medium height."

"That'll be fine, ma'am. Thank you for your assistance." He replaced the receiver.

"Everything is fine, sir. Welcome home to the U.S.A, and sorry for the delay. Have to check everyone out these days."

"Not at all, Officer, and thank you."

He tottered off towards the baggage hall to retrieve his bag. He waited until he was well out of sight of the Immigration area, and then ducked into the first rest room he saw, hit a cubicle and emptied the entire contents of his stomach in about ten seconds. Sweat was pouring off of him freely now, but he wasn't worried. He had made it through, but by Jesus, it had been close. He was sure the Immigration Officer had suspected something, but what?

He retrieved his bag and strolled through arrivals. He had left the Escalade here and had flown to Atlanta on his outward journey. He caught the bus to the long-term park and paid at the automatic booth. He threw his bag in the back seat and sat in. Despite being left idle for almost a month, the vehicle started immediately. He slowly left the car park, checking all the while to ensure he was not being followed. He joined the 836

Expressway and took it direct to I95 where he turned north. He had decided not to hang around Miami. He could buy documents elsewhere.

About an hour into the journey, he stopped at a huge mall-outlet complex and used the rest room. Here, he stripped himself of the last of Fredrik Schoenbaum and finally became Carl Walker again. He flushed the special effects and the clothes went in a dumpster. He grabbed a quick coffee and a donut and found he had calmed down enough to congratulate himself again.

He headed back to the car and hit I95. This time he hit the country station on the dial and completely relaxed. He was Carl Walker, the man again, and he'd be home in less than three hours.

The following afternoon, Paul met Mike at Ronald Reagan again and they decided to head straight to Paul's place, where Barbara was preparing dinner for the four of them, Wendy now being fully accepted as part of their group. The children were still at summer camp so they would have the place to themselves. They made small talk on the short trip from the airport, neither man wanting to be the one to bring up the only topic of conversation that was likely to dominate the rest of the evening. When they got home, Wendy had already arrived and was deep in conversation with Barbara. They had also opened a bottle of wine and Barbara handed glasses to the two men after greetings had been exchanged.

"OK, dinner is in about an hour and is out on the deck, so if you two guys wanna talk shop, go right ahead. We have lots to catch up on in here."

They shrugged and looked at each other and headed out on to the patio. It was early evening and the sun was still high in the sky. It was warm but not high summer hot – just perfect for a relaxing evening outdoors. They sat in silence for a few moments, each man gathering his thoughts.

Paul eventually ventured, "So how was it over there? I mean, I know we were in touch but, you know, not the same is it?"

"No; it's difficult to describe, really. I mean, have you ever had total mayhem going on all around you, and yet you are powerless to do anything about it?"

277

"Yeah, frequently, you should see our office! No, I know what you mean, man; I mean it's been frustrating as hell here also. You know, we gave it top priority here but we couldn't very well say to folks, well, we can't catch the guy because right now he's on holiday in Europe doing some more killings."

Despite himself, Mike laughed. "Yeah, and you could say, well folks, as soon as our colleagues over there tell us he's done killing for now, we'll assume he's come home so we'll get right on it."

It was Paul's turn to laugh and the humour eased the tension. They clinked glasses and drank, and Paul went for a refill. He brought out a fresh bottle of Californian and refreshed both of their glasses.

"I'm pretty certain I go with that theory of yours but just run it by me again, will you?" he said when they were comfortable.

"OK, sure. Well, first we must accept the theory that it is one guy, right?

"Yep, got that one."

"Right, if you accept that, then he's got to be American, or at least based here. Why? Well, killers like this operate logically, so his first killings were on his home turf. I'm not saying he hasn't operated overseas before – the likelihood is that he has, but on this one, we have to assume he started at home. He acts quickly and decisively; his two hits here were within 24 hours of each other, and both showed planning and research. In Europe, due to geographical distance – and the fact that half of Europe's police were chasing him – there was, what, eight days between his kills? Because he hit the EU Foreign Minister's summit, he had to wait anyway. He may have planned to take out the French Foreign Minister at an earlier stage, but the fact that his daring attempt to take the rifle on board the London Paris train was thwarted possibly slowed him down."

"But why do you think he was going to operate in Paris?"

"Well if he wanted to head directly to Poland, he could have laid low in the UK for a few days and then flown there. I mean, he appears to have been equipped to assume multiple identities, so why not?"

"Well, he would have had to assume your people would saturate the airports, so what if his dodgy identities didn't have fool-proof passports?"

"Yeah, good point, but he managed to get away with it on the Eurostar to Paris. If he had been heading for Poland, he could have got the Eurostar to Brussels. We've looked at the itineraries for the French and Danish Foreign Ministers and if our man had been targeting them from the start, he would have definitely had an opportunity to hit the French Minister in Paris the day after he hit the British P.M."

"Yeah, and I suppose the Danish Foreign Minister appeared in public shortly afterwards."

"Indeed, the poor man did, on three of the following five days, so it is possible that our killer planned to take them separately. But I think he erred. In retrospect, it wasn't really daring to take the rifle on the Eurostar train; it was dangerous. He must have known it would be crawling with police. OK, he switched bags cleverly, but there was still a good chance of him getting caught. You know what I think, Paul? I think the guy gets cocky. He took out the P.M. at his ease and strolled out of the hotel, safe in the knowledge that it would be hours before police even nailed down his firing position, let alone find which way he was headed. He got away so easily that he felt he was on a roll."

"And let me guess, you think this trait might help us catch him?"

"Yes I do, the only problem is he's gonna have to either kill or attempt to kill again to allow us to even get a shot at it."

"You may be right, but I hope not. We're gonna take a look at everything we got all over again, starting tomorrow morning with a meeting chaired by Maria at 09.00."

"Sounds good to me Paul, I'd like to go through it with the guys again, but..."

The sliding patio door burst open and Barbara stuck her head out. Both noticed that she had gone very pale.

"You guys better come in here and take a look at this."

The TV was on in the kitchen and Barbara had it on live pause. Wendy was seated on a stool and seemed spellbound.

"This thing is on a loop, guys, so go right ahead, just press play," she said.

They caught the announcer in mid sentence: "following the brutal murders committed during the past month which have left police baffled on both sides of the Atlantic. Well tonight, this statement delivered to the Arabic TV Channel, Al Jazeera, seems to finally throw some light on the killings, or rather who is behind them." The camera panned to another TV monitor, which showed a man dressed in Arabic clothing. His face was almost completely covered by a heavy headdress and he wore very dark wrap-around sunglasses. He spoke slowly in Arabic and the TV Channel gave a simultaneous translation into English.

The man began: "We have now proved that our operatives can assassinate your leaders at will. Two weeks ago, you are aware that we could have wiped out all of the Foreign Ministers of the European Union. Let the fact that we only killed two serve as your warning! We have operatives in every country, men and women willing to martyr themselves for our cause. You will have no advance warning. We can strike when and where we wish. We will continue our campaign unless you agree to our demands. All of your armed forces are to leave Afghanistan, Iraq and any other sacred soil immediately. For this process, we will allow you two weeks. Furthermore, you will dismantle all of your military bases situated on any other holy soil. You will then withdraw all of your people from these bases and from the countries where they are situated. For this process, we will allow you three months. We assure you, if any further assurance is necessary, that we will not hesitate to eliminate all of you and any foolish enough to succeed you without mercy unless our demands are met. The deadlines we set will be respected provided that you immediately show good faith and intent to withdraw as instructed."

The man did not identify himself or say what organisation he spoke for but it didn't matter. Everyone knew who and what he represented. All four looked at each other in virtual shock.

"What do we do now?" said Barbara.

"I know what I'm gonna do," said Paul. "I'm gonna enjoy my dinner. Let's all get out there. If the phones ring, we'll answer, but I doubt it. I think tonight's demands will worry higher-paid people than us, eh?"

"Absolutely, we've got it all to do tomorrow morning anyway," Mike agreed.

"Yeah," Wendy joined in, "this bastard has ruined your lives, all our lives for the past month so he sure as hell ain't ruining tonight."

"I'll drink to that," said Barbara, who had emerged with a large casserole dish. And they all did.

Chapter 27

"Who's a clever boy then?" said Walker aloud as he watched the re-run of the ultimatum played on Al Jazeera while having breakfast alone in his Lake Mary home. Cindy and the girls were still in Nebraska and wouldn't return for at least another week.

"But does this mean, my friend, that your employee has gotten a surprise two week holiday?" Like fuck it does, he thought. Clever bugger gives them an ultimatum that he knows they cannot agree to. He knows I'll continue, he thought, so he decides to make political capital out of it. But there was no time limit on his list so if Walker wanted to take a two week holiday, he bloody well would and to hell with your man and his ultimatums. Calm down, he thought, I've just had a two week holiday! Aye, he thought, and smiled, and with a fabulous bird in tow too.

That reminded him; he needed to do something about papers for Katya. He hadn't wanted to dwell in Miami and he absolutely never did 'business' in Orlando. It just meant she'd have to wait a while – no better girl, he thought. Jesus, she might even pick herself up a millionaire in Sandy Lane if he left her there long enough. Longer term, that wouldn't be a problem, but right now, no, he had decided he would need her to assist him with some of the complex tasks which awaited him.

Speaking of which, he had done some serious planning on the voyage across the Atlantic. Up to now, he had carried out the tasks on the list in chronological order. He now thought seriously of changing that. He never thought for an instant that his employer would betray him but it was always good to have an edge. He knew it was an extremely long shot, but just in case someone else had seen the list. The tasks up to this had been very flexible but now some of them became a little more specific. Having said that, no one had any idea when or where he would strike – in fact, he wasn't sure himself. There were numerous possibilities. He again thanked the openness of western society and the willingness of its leaders to advertise their programmes well in advance.

He checked his i-Phone. It was Monday morning. Cindy would be back on Sunday next, or maybe she would stay another week? Either way, he'd have enough time to get there and back by then. Or he could go north and acquire some documents for Katya – or perhaps do both? A plan started to form in his mind. He got up from his breakfast table on the patio, took the dishes through to the kitchen and stacked them in the dishwasher. He then headed for his den and powered up his mainframe computer.

Maria Gonzalez had been under severe pressure to use the vast array of law enforcement personnel and machinery at her disposal to come up with something, somebody, anything, on the political assassinations. All such appointments in the U.S. are political, but she was the fourth head of the D.H.S., although the organisation had only been founded after the 9/11 atrocities in 2001, and there had only been one change of President. She did not want to go the way of some of her predecessors, but she was an honest and straight administrator and although subject to the whims of politicians herself, would not descend to petty politics when dealing with her own people. She believed she had some of the best people in law enforcement on the planet reporting to her and the way to keep them focused and producing results was to treat them with respect and not to second guess them or demotivate them by using them as political pawns.

It was a hugely difficult job but Maria had earned enormous respect from her colleagues and subordinates by her astute methods of assigning just the right people to each particular threat. She seemed to have an innate ability to judge how people would perform in any given situation, and to date no one could say that she had ever got it wrong. The result was a safer America; as she saw it, the very reason why she had been appointed in the first place.

Because she was straight and treated people with respect, she commanded huge loyalty. Her people would go to extreme lengths to defend her and would work tirelessly to produce results. She was thinking about this ahead of the morning strategy meeting, which had now taken on added significance after the previous evening's broadcast. Had she assigned the right people this time? Despite the lack of results, she was sure she had and she was also sure that each agency had pulled out all the stops but had just failed to catch a break.

It was strange, she thought. Even though last night's broadcast had upped the ante several notches, conversely, it had removed some of the pressure on her and her people. Results would still be demanded, but people now realized what they were up against (or thought they did) and the pressure had now shifted squarely on to the shoulders of the politicians. She knew, though, that the respite, if it could even be called that, would be short lived. As soon as the politicians realized that there was very little they could do, the pressure would return to apprehend the perpetrator or perpetrators.

Everyone filed in, bang on time, some clutching take-out coffees and small bags containing donuts or breakfast sandwiches or whatever. The meeting today was back in D.H.S. headquarters, in the Nebraska Avenue Complex. Although it was 09.00, she knew that they were not having breakfast, as most would have been at their desks since before 07.00. It was more likely to be a mid-morning snack. Greetings were exchanged and more coffee poured from the large jugs that had been left on a side table. There was a warm welcome back for Mike from many of the attendees and several enquiries about the killings in Europe.

"Good morning, people," Maria began. "Unless something has come up which will bring us further along the road with the investigation than we were yesterday, I propose that we change the agenda for our meeting to discuss the fall-out from last night's broadcast?"

There were noises of agreement and nods throughout the room.

"OK, well, now at least we know who is behind the killings, or at least the motivation for them. Our faceless man from last night or his organization is being both clever and stupid at the same time, in my view anyway."

There was a pause. "Go ahead, Maria," said Pete Stewart.

"Well, from the very start, politicians have been the targets in this thing, right? I mean, all previous terrorist attacks were more or less just mindless attacks on the general public – designed to do what?"

"To spread fear and terror among the general public," said La Vonn.

"Exactly, but while everyone is shocked and scared, the effect dissipates rather quickly, why?"

"Because the people who are killed are ordinary everyday folk, not famous people or world leaders," said Chico.

"Right, so if you want to generate terror that lasts a lot longer, you hit the famous people, hit the leaders, the politicians – hit them where it hurts."

"Yep, clever strategy," said Paul. "Between us, the people are expendable; leaders are not. Politicians with power in their hands will react. Mind you, if word were to get out that the reaction was greater when politicians were threatened rather than ordinary people, that's not good for politicians. But that's a longer-term problem. The people can't vote them out until the next election. An assassin can vote them out tomorrow."

"Right," Maria responded, "but while they are trying to force them to react and look scared, the magnitude of their demands surely makes it impossible for them to be met."

"Perhaps," said Mike, joining the conversation for the first time.

"Go on, Mike," said Maria, "you've probably had more experience on this thing than anyone."

"Well," he continued, "to my mind, there has been a strategic change here. Whoever is running that organisation now is not a mindless spread-blood-in-the-streets terrorist. This shows cunning, strategic planning and stealth. No statement made until eight people had been killed, including three prominent leaders. Who knows how many more they plan to kill? As far as I can see, they may have already achieved their goal. I've met with some senior politicians myself, and believe me, they are terrified! I wouldn't rule out the possibility of concessions being made. I mean, I don't expect our faceless man's terms to be met in full, but I doubt he does either."

There was silence around the table for a few moments and then everyone seemed to resume speaking at once.

Eventually Pete was heard above the din. "You know, the man may have a point. I mean look, I'm not sure if this guy is telling the truth or not, but he or his people have managed to avoid detection now for almost two months, despite being chased by the strongest and most sophisticated law enforcement agencies on both sides of the World. I think our political masters may realize this also and possibly make some moves."

"And what should we do until then?" said Chico.

Mike shrugged. "I guess the only thing we can do is what we do best – keep looking. If it makes people feel any better, I feel our man from last night has exaggerated his strength. I could be wrong but I'm still sticking to my "one killer" theory."

There was a general hush around the room and he wondered if he was incorrect – for a terrifying moment he imagined that the organisation had clones in every country; but he immediately dismissed the thought.

"No," he said, "it has to be. These killings were carried out by one very clever guy acting on instructions from an organisation; which one, we did not know, precisely, but now there is little doubt as to who his backers are. And one other thing, again, in my view: there is no longer any need to look for a pattern – we never found one because there wasn't one, and there won't be, because this is just terrorism. But it is precisely targeted terrorism; that *is* the pattern. The man said that they would strike at random but the targets are specific – they are the elected leaders or politicians of countries who have troops or bases in Arab countries. He also said they would continue to strike and I, for one, believe him."

"Interesting thoughts, Mike," Maria agreed. "But I still think the demands are impossible and the organisation must have known they would never be acceded to. Even in the extremely unlikely situation that say the U.S., Britain and the other NATO powers agreed to withdraw from the bases, their Arab allies would surely place them under enormous pressure to stay. Oil supplies would be quietly mentioned and it wouldn't happen, or at least surely not enough to satisfy the demands? So where does that leave our organisation and its faceless terrorist? Free to continue his murder and mayhem?"

"Perhaps," he responded, "but the whole landscape over there is changing. Many of the U.S.'s former political allies have been overthrown. For sure, many of the main ones are still in place, but with Egypt, Tunisia and now Libya having changed regimes, and severe pressure in Syria and Bahrain, the whole dynamic has changed. A side effect of this is that Al Qaeda has actually lost some of its influence, so this may well be an attempt to win it back."

There were deep sighs and nods of agreement all round. Just then, Maria's secretary entered and whispered something into her ear.

"People," she said, "We gotta take a few minutes for this." She took a remote control from the table, keyed a button and a large screen descended from the ceiling at the top of the room. A further touch of a different button dimmed the room's lights. The big screen came to life and a podium came into view. On the front of the podium was a dark blue plaque, which read "Seal of the President of the United States of America." The President was introduced and stepped to the podium. He was grim-faced and pale, yet the set of his jaw was firm and determined.

"My fellow Americans," he began. "America does not respond to terrorist threats. America does not respond to terrorist's demands. America will not be forced by a few mindless people to be swayed from the work we are doing to make our nation more secure for all our people. We are of course aware of public disquiet, of public concern. Let me assure you that all of our defence and law enforcement agencies and those of our allies are working full time on this threat. I am confident that it will be identified, ruthlessly pursued, tracked down and eliminated. I have spoken with our NATO allies this morning and they are as one with the United States of America. I would ask for people's patience, perseverance and co-operation at this time. Our country has been threatened many times in the past but it has never and

287

will never bend to the threat of evil. Let me assure you that once again, America and her allies will prevail. Thank you."

"Wow," said Maria, "strong stuff, huh?"

The atmosphere in the room was so heightened that many people felt like standing up and applauding. However, they checked themselves. Words were fine and could be inspiring but it was they who were the ones the President had referred to when he spoke about ruthlessly tracking down and eliminating the threat, and right then, they weren't exactly sure how they were going to achieve that. Still, the President's broadcast had given them a boost. They noted that he had made no direct reference to what had been demanded or hadn't deemed the threat worthy of a reply. But it was very real and until they tracked it down, no one was safe.

They broke for more coffee and then Maria took brief reports from each section head and agency representative. Eventually, at around midday, they broke for lunch. Afterwards, Paul, Mike, La Vonn, Chico, Pete and their colleagues trooped back to their offices and did what every policeman everywhere has done for hundreds of years when they have no leads – they painstakingly began going over all the paperwork again. It was amazing; no matter how many times you reviewed a document, you could miss something; a vital clue, a link to take you somewhere else that would lead you to something that could give you a breakthrough. Mike wasn't one of these guys who felt that the answer was always there, it was that you just hadn't found it yet; but in the absence of anything more concrete to work on, he was prepared to give it a try.

Chapter 28

Martha Slaughter was worried as she shuffled around her old frame house in the countryside north of Charleston, doing her last few chores to ensure she left the place spick and span as usual. She knew that neither she nor her husband were getting any younger. She knew his sight had been getting progressively worse but he had insisted he could see fine and had again refused to go to an optician. Judging by the way he walked into things or moved about unsteadily, she doubted his eyes were as good as he claimed. But John was stubborn. She would have preferred if they didn't travel this year but as usual, John had insisted. "We've been going south every summer straight for over forty years, woman, ain't gonna change now."

And she knew what he meant. It was one of their favourite family rituals. Every summer since their courting days, they had headed for the warm beaches of Florida. After they married and the girls came along, it was their favourite time of year and they looked forward to the trip with ever increasing anticipation from Easter onwards. "How many days to go Mom?" "How long now Mom?" She wiped away a tear as she remembered and saw again, in her mind's eye, the little girls in their summer dresses as they danced excitedly around John's big old Buick anxious to be off. She thought for a moment that she had even heard the echo of their shouts and squeals of girlish laughter. And perhaps she had; maybe this scene was forever preserved in her memory in such a way that it allowed her precious glimpses of the past.

But that had been many years ago. The girls had long since married and moved away. Arlene was in California and Melanie in Fort Worth. They visited on occasion but not often enough.

Perhaps John was trying to recapture the golden years when the four of them were inseparable – the girls would play for hours in the surf and the sand, only coming in for supper when they were exhausted, despite Martha's constant pleas and scolds.

She reluctantly withdrew from her reverie and tried to concentrate on her packing. Not much to put in the old Buick now; just a suitcase for each of them. No struggling to accommodate the girls' bicycles or dolls or the hundreds of toys and games that they had always insisted on bringing with them. John had never complained or never refused either. The amount of stuff he managed to squeeze into the trunk of that old car was amazing. Plenty of space in it now.

She decided she'd go check on John. He spent a lot more time sleeping these days but insisted it was just napping; the man still couldn't face the onset of advanced years. Right now he was napping on the porch, "just getting in some shut eye ahead of our trip, ma'am." But she knew better and this year she was going to insist on them stopping at least once on the journey to rest. John had a sense of pride in doing the entire trip without an overnight or even a break, barely stopping for coffee and to use the rest room. Egged on by the excited entreaties of the girls, she had been a willing party to it in the past but not now.

She gently squeezed his hand and he jerked awake.

"Shucks, must of dozed off there, woman. Hey, look at the time, we'd better get moving. Do you have everything you need?"

She raised her eyebrows and shook her head. She had always packed for all four of them, and she still did for herself and John. Even if his eyesight had been better, he wouldn't have known where to find anything anyway. He'd always been an outdoor man, working from dawn till dusk on his farm; anything that transpired inside the house was a complete mystery to him. She had loved it that way always, each of them to their own particular skills, perfectly complementing each other and never getting in each other's way.

"Just about finished now, Dad. Say, you wanna fire up that old tin can?"

"That's no tin can, woman, that's my Buick!"

It was a favourite routine they played and it softened her heart to hear his strong voice once again, just like old times. He followed her into the bedroom and began rummaging in a drawer.

"Can I help you, sir?" she said.

"Nope, just getting my piece."

"Oh, now, John, there's no need to do that. You know you don't have a permit to carry a gun any more and well, there's so many highway patrols and I mean, it's illegal and..."

"Woman," he said, "you know I don't go nowhere without my thirty-eight. Too many lowlifes out there and no one will ever say John Slaughter didn't protect his family"

She sighed and gave up. He was slow at the best of times, but the thought of him trying to shoot a gun was positively frightening. Still, it had never come to that, so if he was happy, she'd go along once again.

"Well that's me packed honey; let's get ourselves on to that highway."

Marian Turner was spending a few days at her Beverly Beach retreat. She too had yet to declare her hand in the Presidential race but since the demise of Senator Carter, she had become the frontrunner; at least in the media speculation. She was 46, dark-haired, attractive, bright, intelligent, married with two kids, and she had an absolutely immaculate background. No skeletons in Marian's cupboard, no matter how thoroughly they looked. She was another right-wing conservative but the way things looked, that was what America seemed to want right now, and she was ready to seize her moment.

Funding might be her one problem, and this was part of the reason she and John, her husband, were taking a few days out. They had invited some serious heavy-hitters to the Beverly house for 'private discussions'; in other words, to pitch for funding. It was close enough to D.C. to allow people to drive there relatively quickly but still far enough away to get well out of the big city.

John was a wealthy man, but there is wealthy and then some. If you are going to run for the highest office in the land, you need enormous financial backing, and with the transparency now required and the limits these days on individual campaign funding, it was becoming even more difficult to launch a major campaign. They had decided a strategic approach was required so Marian, John and their closest and most trusted advisers had repaired to the lakeside house to kick-start the process.

They came up with a three-stage plan. Firstly, a list of potential key campaign contributors was compiled. Her advisers would cold-call these people during the daytime and if a serious prospect was identified, Marian herself would come on the line if they felt it was required. In the evening, a mix of those who had already agreed funding and some folks from whom they needed support were invited to dinner. The mix worked a treat and the commitments were flowing in – the money would follow, she knew.

By Friday morning, they felt they were almost there. They hadn't raised enough money to mount the campaign, not even close, but they reckoned that the strategic people who had come on board would influence other's attitudes and they would soon have a domino effect. They had been very relaxed during the few days. Security had been a consideration, and all visitors had to be thoroughly searched and vetted, but it was routine. Since the terrorist attacks, anyone remotely connected with the Presidential race had been given a round-the-clock guard by the Secret Service. This was an unprecedented move at this stage of the campaign. But out here by the lake, they felt safe; at least, a lot more so than in the city. No one could get within half a mile of the place, and given its location, with sea frontage and a view of the woods to the rear, they reckoned it was pretty secure.

It was a beautiful balmy August morning so they decided to have a late breakfast on the patio. Dinner the previous evening had run very late. A steel magnate from Pittsburgh and a paper manufacturer from Baltimore had been there. Heavy funding commitments had been achieved, but the amount of cognac that the guys put away had made John distinctly seedy this morning. He joked that before the campaign was over, he was going to do serious damage to his liver. Still, for Marian, he would do anything. He was crazy about her and their marriage had lasted solidly for twenty years. It wasn't just Marian who was squeaky-clean – she knew for sure that they wouldn't find any skeletons in John's cupboard either.

"So who's on the phones list today, hon," he yawned as she poured him another glass of orange juice.

"Mainly west coast industrialists, some Silicon Valley people, but relax, darling, no one who can make it here for dinner tonight. This evening is for you and me. We have the Dobsons and the Craigs tomorrow night, then back to D.C. Sunday."

She placed her hand in front of her eyes to protect herself from the glare.

"You OK, hon?" he said.

"Sure, I'm gonna have to bring some sunglasses out here. It's just the sun's glare got in my eyes."

"Ah OK, but the sun doesn't come from…"

John Turner dived across his wife, bringing them both crashing to the ground just as the coffee pot on the table above them exploded into a thousand pieces. Next, a flowerpot shattered, followed by a window. They were under sustained attack.

Security personnel in flak jackets immediately flooded the patio. John stayed down, covering his wife, who was shaking uncontrollably.

"Over there," he shouted, "in the woods – that tree towards the front."

The security detail immediately responded with heavy fire towards the woods and half the men took off after the assailant with the remainder staying to protect the Turner family.

John had sensed something was wrong. The sun rose in the east. They always had breakfast facing the woods with the sun at their back. Sunglasses had not been required – there had been no glare. All of these thoughts had flashed through his brain in the micro-second that he realized the glare was actually the reflection of the sun off something metallic. He was almost inclined to dismiss that, but then he had seen the man and the horrible truth had dawned on him.

Under the guard of their security personnel, both John and Marian crawled back into the house through the shattered patio doors. Both were deeply shocked but had suffered only a few superficial cuts from the broken glass and other debris. They were ordered by the Secret Service security detail to stay down and out of sight until they were sure the danger had passed. John suggested they go to his den and one of the guards offered to make a fresh pot of coffee. He held her close and she clung tightly to him.

"John, I've always owed everything to you, you've always been my rock, the one I can depend on. Now I owe you my life. You really have no idea how much I love you right now."

"Hey, no sweat, honey, and I love you too; and you know what? We are gonna fight this thing. If that was the mystery assassin out there, well, we gotta be the first to have beaten him and that's gotta be a good omen. Hey, we're going places, babe – together."

"I sure hope so, John," she said as she shivered involuntarily.

"That's a definite, honey. Hey, let's have some of that coffee."

After their initial barrage of covering fire towards the woods, the team advanced slowly and carefully to the spot from where they assumed the shots had been fired. But they found no one. A later forensic examination would find no brass, but would find footprints leading back through the woods to where a car had been parked. The would-be assassin had surely been operating on the very limit of his range, as the trees were well over half a mile from the Turner's house. Still, he had managed to hit his assumed target, or would have, if her husband had not acted so quickly.

Comprehensive enquiries in the surrounding area yielded little. One guy thought he had seen a silver car emerge from the woodland track shortly after he had heard the shots fired by the security detail. He had not gotten a license plate. As to make and model, he couldn't be sure, but he reckoned it was "one of them Japanese imports." Tire tracks were vague, as the entire area was bone dry, but from the vague patterns that could be discerned, it was verified that the tires could well have come from a Japanese import; in fact, from any of about two million of them.

John Turner had seen the man seemingly resting against the tree as he took aim, but he could not give a description. For a start, the distance was far too great and the man had been wearing a baseball cap and dark glasses, or at least John thought so.

The forensics would, once again, have been a total waste of time, but for the slight traces of blood found on the grass in the area around the tree. The forensic boys painstakingly followed the trail all the way back to where the car had been parked, but there was no more of it. It appeared that the man had taken precautions to ensure his wound did not leave any evidence. Perhaps he had bandaged it temporarily with a handkerchief or something. Closer examination of the grass showed some of it had been torn, suggesting he had wished to remove all traces of the blood. The miniscule traces were carefully bagged and preserved and immediately sent to D.H.S. for analysis.

Back in D.C, it was almost time for lunch and the team was going through what little evidence they had again when their mood suddenly received a massive boost.

The door burst open and Paul's deputy, Bob Weitz, burst in and declared, "Hey people, listen up, looks like our assassin has tried again; only this time, he didn't get his man, or in this case, his woman."

Everyone began speaking and asking questions at once and Bob explained what had happened, and the key element; a blood sample was on its way by high-speed police escort.

Walker was back on I495 listening to the radio. That had been a close shave, but not as close as the police might have thought. He had had lots of time to gather up his brass and make good his escape. He had plenty of time left, too, to get the documents he required for Katya. But he had a few more calls to make before he headed south.

Chapter 29

The machine clicked into top gear immediately. Every hospital, clinic and medical facility was alerted. Every doctor, nurse, and former or present medical official was tracked down and warned discreetly, or as discreetly as was possible, to be on the look out for a wounded man who was around five feet nine. Even veterinary surgeons were included in the search! It was always likely to be another needle-in-a-haystack search, as the net had to be cast very wide. They started with D.C. and the State of Maryland and then expanded outward to include every medical facility from Pittsburgh to Philadelphia to Richmond. When they began to run out of places to check, they expanded the search to all pharmacies and drug stores where people came to buy dressings for wounds.

There were a number of inherent flaws in the process. First of all, they did not know how badly the man had been wounded. Given the small trace of blood, it was obviously not arterial so would probably not require urgent medical attention. Second, if the killer were as experienced and well-planned as he had appeared to be up to now, he might well have his own medical kit and would be able to administer self care. Thirdly, even if he were not, he would be highly unlikely to go to a recognised medical facility where he might have to explain a gunshot wound. He might well have a contact with medical training; an ex-doctor who had been struck off for malpractice, or whatever. The possibilities were endless and the search was incredibly wide-ranging. They would require a lot of luck if they were to make a breakthrough on this front – but they had to try.

Le Vonn and Chico had every guy in the department out on the streets squeezing every snitch they knew and calling in every

296

favour they could think of to try to get a line on someone who may have gone to a medic. Their counterparts in every other city in the catchment area were doing likewise but no one had heard anything so far.

The blood sample had been sent for initial typing and ultimately DNA analysis. It was frustrating for everyone but all they could do was to sit and wait and re-examine and re-analyse what they had. Mike was working on an enormous database that he had compiled from the D.H.S. and F.B.I. computers, which tracked all political assassinations and known hits for the previous fifteen years in both the U.S. and abroad, where records had been made available. He was looking for hits where a silenced weapon had been used, but there were any amount to choose from. In some cases, the suspected killer had been identified but not apprehended. Some of these suspects appeared a number of times. Many had then been killed themselves in reprisals by organised crime or by other hit men hired by an unknown person or persons. Some had disappeared, presumed either killed or retired. A depressingly small proportion had been caught, and even with those, most were caught for other offences, but had been suspected killers. He had looked at hits from New York to Nicaragua and from Cuba to California. Occasionally, patterns emerged, but rarely led anywhere as there were numerous murders with a question mark in the column for 'suspected killer'.

He had been working on this for two days now without a break and he was just about ready to give it up. He decided to take a break and called Wendy to see if she was free for an early dinner.

"Sure am, where you fancy?"

"Well, how about the half-pound burger at Stetson's?"

"Stop, my mouth is watering already!"

"OK, catch you there around 6.30."

The bar was crowded as usual, with happy hour patrons crammed into every corner. After a short wait, he managed to secure two stools at the bar. He sat on one and draped his jacket over the other and ordered a beer. Wendy arrived and gave him a look, a hug, and then a deep kiss. He almost swooned with pleasure.

"You know, despite working on that friggin database and getting nowhere for the past two days, I'm excited. I've got a good feeling, like we're really close."

She regarded him slyly and gave him the slightly confused look. "Excited? Good feeling? I should hope so."

"Ah Jesus, sorry, I was thinking too much about the case again. I mean, that just goes without saying."

She punched him playfully on the arm; "You're so easy to rile, you big Irishman. I'm only kidding, but you know something – you'll get a big opportunity later on to show me just how excited you are," she said as she flashed her eyelashes at him again.

"Wendy, if you don't cut that out, I'm taking you home right now!"

"Yeah, right – promises, promises. I think we had better get a burger into you first. You may need your strength. Anyway, sorry Mike, what's with the case?"

They ordered burgers and beers and he briefed her on the latest developments from that morning and the follow up searches that were ongoing. She tilted her head to the side again in that way that drove him crazy, but, serious now, she said, "If his profile fits the one you've been feeding me up to now, and I think you've got that right, he either won't seek medical help or he'll have some lined up that's not traceable."

"So, which is it?"

"I'd favour the second option. He's a very careful planner and although he seemingly acts alone, I'm not so sure. I've got a feeling he's had some help. He's got to, if you look at where he's been. It's a moot point anyway but I'd say he's got to have some contacts everywhere he operates. Like, how did he get a gun in Poland? He could have got it elsewhere in Europe and carried it in, but that's risky. Even if he did, that means he had to have had a contact there too."

"I know, but the police forces in Poland and half the rest of Europe have called in every favour, including offering immunity to known arms dealers, and they drew a blank. OK, in fairness, that was a long shot as immunity today could mean arrest next month, but still, we didn't get a whisper."

"Right, but back to my second option. The guy is a specialist, a craftsman; well, a marksman, right?"

"Yeah, go on."

"Well, was there any sign of him limping back to his car today, or any sign he was wounded?"

"Well, I wasn't there but I don't think so, why?"

"That suggests that he wasn't wounded in either his torso or his leg. Think about it – a bullet in the torso would have produced a lot more blood and hampered his movement. Same for a wound in a leg. We can certainly rule out a head wound. What does that leave? His arms. Bullet usually goes straight through, right? The wound can be messy but not fatal and can be bandaged up, allowing him to get away relatively quickly. But he's a marksman, right? So his most important assets are his eyes and his arms – he couldn't take a risk that his arm might be permanently damaged or impaired, so he's got to have it seen to, right?"

Mike's reply was to lean over and kiss her on the lips.

"You know, you're wasted in real estate babe."

"Ah, come on, I'm sure the heads at D.H.S. have worked that out."

"Well perhaps, but I suppose they were checking every medical facility anyway."

"So, right," she continued. "We know who he is working for so get Paul's people to check on any dodgy Arabic doctors for starters." Mike smiled.

"I think they are checking on everyone who's ever done first aid, whether they're black, brown, white or yellow."

"Yeah, of course, and anyway, it might be a bit too obvious. If he had someone with medical expertise tucked away, you'd have to assume the guy would be far too terrified to contact the police."

"Yep, you would, and where does that leave us? Back at square one again?"

"Possibly, but here's a thought; a long shot, maybe, but see what you think. Paul's people have got huge resources on this one, right?"

"Absolutely; you name it, he can get it."

"OK, right, and presumably Capitol P.D. know the names of all the dodgy medical people around town? Now, he's been operating all over, but three of his hits have been in the D.C. area so chances are that if he has a medical man that he's right here."

"I think I know where you're headed babe – let me guess, the guy is too scared to tell the police so we give him a helping hand – we go through his trash. If we find a match, we put serious heat on the guy to give us a name, right?"

"Yep, why not try it?"

"Yeah, why not? It's as good as most of the other hare-brained schemes I've been listening to for the past month."

Mike decided to make a quick call to Paul to see if the theory was feasible. He pulled out his cell phone just as their burgers arrived.

"Hey buddy, I was just about to call you, we've got happy days here"

Mike felt the hairs stand up on the back of his neck.

"What, you've found his doctor?"

"No, but we've got the quickest result we've ever got on DNA analysis, and you know what, blood from the crime scene today matches Alfonso's toothbrush."

"Jesus, the friggin toothbrush, I'd almost forgotten about it, fantastic."

He briefly described Wendy's theory and Paul said they'd get P.D. to try to run it. Mike turned around and punched the air with delight.

"Told you we were close babe; well, we just got closer still."

Spencer Nichols would have been a disappointment to his parents, if his parents had been around any more to see how he had turned out, or the depths to which he had sunk. He had been a diligent student all through high school; not brilliant academically, but always interested in medical science and generally making people better. His love of animals and his efforts at rescuing strays and nursing them back to health was legendary. His parents had been proud when he had graduated high school and had been accepted to the medical faculty of George Washington University. He ultimately graduated U.W. with first-class honours. He did postgraduate studies at the world famous Johns Hopkins Medical School in Baltimore, and eventually specialized in neurosurgery; or to be precise, neurological microsurgery. He was recognised as a brilliant young surgeon with finely honed skills. He had pioneered techniques such as endoscopic endonasal surgery for pituitary tumours, chordomas, and the repair of cerebrospinal fluid leaks. There were very many people walking around today who would have been paralysed or at least partially handicapped but for Spencer's delicate skills.

However, somewhere along the way, Spencer had discovered alcohol. He had drunk beer at college, but probably no more than most of his peers. But that was fine when he was with his fellow students. He had a brilliant and finely-tuned mind but as so often happens, he was deficient in other ways, most notably in social skills. He was not a good mixer and found female company difficult. Alcohol had calmed him and after a while, it became his constant friend. He had been careful not to use it at Johns Hopkins or later when he specialized but as time progressed and he hadn't met that special girl, he began to feel more and more isolated. His few friends settled down in their own lives and poor Spencer took refuge in the bottle.

He was aware that alcohol was the worst possible thing in the extraordinarily delicate job that he performed, requiring at least twenty times more precision than an airline pilot, he reckoned, and airline pilots were checked regularly. But no one checked surgeons, and a good mouthwash and a few breath mints usually got him through. Over time, living alone and going from work to his depressing apartment wore him down. He was seen as a loner so people left him alone. If they had only known.

The inevitable eventually happened. A young girl was admitted for the removal of a non-malignant tumour in her neck. It was normally a routine operation, even though the procedure was very close to her spinal cord. But Spencer was drunk, and a job that he could normally do almost with his eyes closed turned into a disaster. The girl became paralyzed from the neck down; Spencer was suspended indefinitely, and eventually struck off. The girl's parents won a $50 million lawsuit against the hospital. There was no way back from there. Everyone in the medical profession and beyond now knew and referred to him as the fifty million dollar man. He was finished as a physician.

He sank into depression and had almost drunk himself to death when he was arrested one night for starting a fight in a bar and was thrown in the can to dry out. The judge eventually offered him probation if he agreed to go to rehab. He did, and there he met Clara, a fellow alcoholic. She was the best thing that had ever happened to him and he had regretted that he hadn't been lucky enough to meet her before his career took a downward spiral. But at that stage Clara had been going through her own personal hell.

They had both been dry now for over five years and they led a good, if simple, life. Clara waited tables at a diner but even with tips, she didn't make enough to keep both of them so Spencer was obliged to practice illegally. He was well known as a 'fix-up' man for the city's criminals who couldn't risk using regular medical facilities for fear of being picked up by the cops. With sobriety, his medical skills were still perfect, and in a very short time, he acquired a reputation as the best in the business. In fact, some of the crime bosses used joke that Spencer's stitch-up jobs were better than what you would get in a regular hospital.

He rarely knew his clients and he knew better than to ask. One great thing about them was they always paid cash so there was no need to make recoveries from Medicaid or Medical Insurance. Neither was there any need to pay insurance premiums, keep records or pay income tax. On the downside, he had to be on call 24 hours a day, seven days a week; but to be fair, his clients usually respected his privacy and rarely bothered him late at night unless it was an emergency. Most of the criminal underworld knew of Doc Spence, and that was in itself a protection.

So when the man in the dark glasses came to his door in the early evening with a flesh wound, Spencer barely looked at him, but cleaned and dressed his wound, gave him an anti-histamine injection, some painkillers and sent him on his way. The man

302

never spoke apart from to ask what the fee was. Spencer asked for $200. The man offered $500 and put a finger to his lips. Spencer assured him that there was no need and that his privacy would be respected and his visit would remain confidential. But the man insisted, shoved the money at Spencer and departed.

Interestingly, Spencer had had a call-out from the P.D. earlier in the afternoon, asking him if he had seen or treated a man with a gunshot wound. At that stage, Spencer hadn't, so his denial was genuine and convincing and the policemen went on their way. He had promised to inform the police if anyone turned up later, but he had no intention of doing any such thing, regardless of what the man had supposedly done. He had his reputation to protect. If word got out that he had 'ratted out' a client, his business would more than likely cease. He would also be very lucky to avoid a far worse fate. The people that he dealt with did not give you a smack on the wrist or a warning. They played for keeps – surely the cops knew that! So he had treated the man quietly and expertly and sent him on his way.

Spencer's trash was collected on a Friday but Capitol P.D. couldn't wait that long so when Spencer and Clara were sound asleep, dark-suited forensic officers quietly went through his bin, carefully extracting any material that looked remotely related to medical treatment. The same procedure was followed with a number of others, who were suspected of providing covert medical attention, across the city. The 'evidence' was carefully bagged and sealed and returned for examination. Their initial task was to find a blood match. Unfortunately the blood found at the crime scene out at the lake was O+, the same as 35% of the population, so they knew this would be a lengthy process. However, the work was spread out and every laboratory made itself available throughout the night – they were pulling out all the stops on this one.

At around 08.30, they got it – a full DNA match. At 08.43, they went in. Spencer and Clara had been sleeping late but were awoken by the sound of their front door crashing inwards. A second later, the men were in their bedroom; serious, mean-looking guys in dark fatigues, wearing helmets and flak jackets.

303

The man who seemed to be in charge said, "Freeze, F.B.I." but these guys didn't look like what he imagined federal law enforcement officers might look like. Perhaps the world had changed.

Spencer and Clara did, literally, freeze; trapped in their bed in abject terror as a half dozen submachine guns were trained on them.

"OK, Spencer, here's the deal. Listen carefully because I'll only say this once. We need to know the identity of the man you gave medical attention to yesterday afternoon. He came to you with a gunshot wound. Don't even think of denying it. Don't even go there because I've got six guys here with awful itchy fingers, and they could blow you and Clara away in an instant. It's called collateral damage, Spence. You with me?"

Spencer felt a trickle of moisture run down his inside leg. Jesus, where were the friendly neighbourhood cops that had called to him the previous afternoon? He was, quite literally, terrified, and these guys were American law enforcement officers!

"But, but, but," he began.

"We don't want no buts, Spence," said the leader, and one of his cohorts pushed his weapon closer to Spencer's chest. He thought he was going to have a heart attack. His pulse must have been close to 200. He was bare-chested and dressed only in his boxers. He felt exposed, vulnerable, and thought he was about to die.

"No, wait, wait, for Christ's sakes wait! I swear, I absolutely swear, as God is my judge. I never saw the guy before. I have no idea where he got my name. I didn't ask. I don't ask. I never ask. I just do my job and ah Jesus, you gotta believe me." He broke down, sobbing uncontrollably.

"OK Spence, I'm not sure if we believe you but you know, either way, we gotta take you in; and believe me, it won't be no picnic. You are going to a bad place man so if you can recall anything about this guy, anything at all, you better give it up and quickly."

"Look, he was medium height, stocky, sallow complexion, sort of dark-skinned and he wore dark wrap-around sunglasses. I mean, I didn't see his face. I mean I didn't look at his face. I never look at their faces. It's sort of understood. I mean, it's too dangerous."

"OK Spence, we believe you, sort of, but you're still going down man. You've got two minutes to get your clothes on or we take you the way you are. Oh and Spence, change your friggin shorts, will ya? Don't want you stinking out our SUV, do we?"

"But for what? I ain't done nothing except give a guy medical attention."

The leader laughed heartily. "You ain't done nothing! Man, Spence, you are the world's last great innocent. OK, how about aiding and abetting a fugitive, accessory to murder after the fact, maybe even conspiracy to commit murder? And that's just for starters. Man, there's enough stuff here for the D.A. to lock you away forever."

"Wait, stop it." They were the first words Clara had uttered since the guys had broken in. She too had been frozen in terror, but now she seemed to gain strength from somewhere. "Stop this now," she screamed. "We are all Americans here so please act civilised. I may have some information that can help you, but I sure as hell ain't gonna give it to you sitting here in my nightgown. Get the fuck out of my bedroom and take your goons and your guns with you. I want five minutes for me and Spence to dress and we'll meet you in the kitchen."

The leader exhaled loudly and thought about his options. "OK, ma'am," he said, "whatever you say, but we'll be right outside."

They slowly filed out of the room but not before thoroughly checking for any escape routes or concealed weapons. They found none.

"Clara, baby, what do you mean information? Jesus, I'll be killed if I say anything."

"Nothing Spence, just fucking nothing. Jesus, do you realize who these people are? Do you realize who they are looking for? Will you for fuck's sake grow up and just go and wash and put some clothes on!"

They met in the kitchen, on cue, five minutes later. The atmosphere had changed considerably and one of the team had even made a pot of coffee. Clara poured herself a cup, dumped in some milk, took a deep breath and started.

"OK, I accept your apology for the rude intrusion to my home this morning. I know who you guys are and I know who you are looking for. I may be able to help you, but you've got to drop this crap about sending my husband away to prison. Spencer is not a criminal. He's a very kind, conscientious medical man who would never refuse help to anyone. Yes, he does medical procedures without reporting them, and I know that is technically illegal, but everyone's gotta make a buck."

"I'm sorry ma'am, but right now, Spencer is but a minor detail. Whether he's sent away or not is immaterial and I doubt anyone would give a toss either way. I can't give you any guarantees anyway, certainly not without knowing what information you have."

"Look, do you want the information or not? I'm not prepared to help you unless you drop this ridiculous charade about my husband being put away forever."

The man went outside and came back within a few minutes accompanied by three pleasant-looking men in dark suits. The first man asked politely if he could sit down and Clara agreed. Spencer had sat through the entire conversation with his mouth open, seemingly in a daze.

"Ma'am, I'm Paul Lincoln, Homeland Security," he said, offering her his I.D. "The commander here tells me you may have some information which could help us. Let me assure you that the criminal we are pursuing poses a most serious security threat to the nation, and any help you could give us in apprehending him will be greatly appreciated. In a word, ma'am, if we catch this guy, it won't really matter what your husband has done. At least, we will do our utmost to keep him out of it. Ma'am, I know we've never met before, but please trust me. This is Pete Stewart from F.B.I. and Mike Lyons from MI5 in Britain. Both these men are witnesses and will vouch for me."

Clara took a sip of coffee and considered briefly, looking from one man to the next. Then she rose and touched her husband briefly on the cheek.

"Don't worry, Spence," she said. "You'll be fine. You are far too innocent and too open and too trusting. You had to be protected." Her husband stared at her in total confusion. She went to the corner closet and from the top shelf extracted a small loose-leaf notebook. She flicked through it until she came to the page she needed, then tore a separate page out of the back of the notepad and wrote on it. She came back to the table and placed the piece of paper face down on the worktop.

"Mr Lincoln," she began. "I'm trusting that you and your people will now leave me and my husband alone and will not bother us again. I tell you absolutely honestly that I have no more idea of who my husband treated yesterday than he has, but that's the guy's licence plate."

Chapter 30

It was a Toyota Camry, the most popular car in America. The licence plate showed that it was registered to a Mr Jason Harper, who apparently lived at an address out in Chevy Chase. It was a common enough surname, but the house was also registered to the same man. A comprehensive check revealed, however, that the Jason Harper who appeared to be the owner of the vehicle and the property had actually been killed in action in Iraq in 2007. A quick drive-by in an unmarked vehicle verified that the Camry was parked in the driveway.

One of the biggest police operations ever mounted began to move quietly into place. An outer ring comprising hundreds of officers took up position a full block away. Heavily armed, flak-jacketed and helmeted SWAT teams converged on the area from all sides. Mike and Paul were again, officially, observers.

There's enough firepower here to take out a city, Mike thought, and they are only going up against one man. Still, better to be safe than sorry and God knows, he has escaped so often. He felt an excitement, an adrenalin-fuelled high, coupled with the anticipation that soon their quest would be over.

Heat-sensing equipment had been brought in and it showed that there was definitely a person in the house. The individual had been upstairs when they had first shown up, presumably sleeping late, and had subsequently come downstairs. Right now, the person was in the kitchen to the rear of the house, presumably having a late breakfast. If the guy had been shot, he'd be taking it easy. Why not? It fit the pattern perfectly. They'd get him before he left, if he intended to leave at all today.

It was a quiet neighbourhood, mostly inhabited by young couples, some married with children. Judging by the absence of cars parked in front of houses, it was assumed that most were gone to work in D.C. or elsewhere. Some would say a burglar's dream – nobody in the house all day and the street quiet – but burglars and cops knew different. These were mainly what burglars called 'plastic houses', meaning that their owners were mortgaged and borrowed to the hilt and could only keep afloat by constantly charging stuff to their credit cards. There was no cash or valuables in those houses; hence they were largely left alone. In the street in question, the houses were generally well-maintained, with the buildings in good condition and the lawns and flowerbeds very presentable. The street was lined mainly with oak trees, which were showing the first hint of the onset of autumn.

The house itself was a modest, colonial style, two storeys over a basement. It presumably had a living room, dining and kitchen downstairs with three bedrooms and a bathroom above. The basement would be used for laundry, the heating boiler and for storing junk. While it looked traditional, it had probably been built in the 1970's, when the timber-frame style of construction had come back into fashion. Exhaustive checks revealed that there were only two doors; one at the front and one at the rear. There was no exterior access from the basement. The Camry was parked out front, and according to the heat sensor monitoring man, the engine was stone cold and had not been used that day.

To mount an assault operation on a place like this took time and planning. While SWAT teams are always on alert, constantly practicing and ready to go, they do like to get it right first time and not to encounter any surprises. If they have to go in urgently, they'll go, but if they have time, they'll take it. Only logical, Mike thought. No point busting in there half-cocked and starting a fire-fight where people could get killed. He didn't dare to say it, but there was also a possibility that the perp could get killed, and they would not want that. There was a lot of information they needed from this guy, and they needed him to be secure, fit and healthy to question him. SWAT teams orders were to apprehend the suspect, preferably alive and without resorting to firing their weapons. They were then to disarm and immobilize the subject and prevent him from harming himself.

After what seemed like hours but was only in fact about forty minutes, the advance team moved into position. Mike thought they looked like the same guys that had hit that medical guy's house earlier, but he couldn't be sure as they were unrecognizable behind their helmets and gas masks. The leader was giving final instructions over the radio and Mike, Paul, Pete and all the team had headsets to listen to the assault.

"OK guys, one more time; heat sensors tell us the guy is still in the kitchen. No 1 breaks the front door, 2, 3 & 4 go in, in Delta formation. No 5 breaks the back door, 6, 7 & 8 follow in Delta. 9 to 12 secure front windows. 13 to 16 secure rear windows, understood?"

Each team acknowledged in sequence. The team leader then spoke again. "Back-up team 3 stand-by out of sight at the front. Back-up team 4 stand by out of sight at the rear. Nothing gets by you, ya hear? When we move in, you follow us rapidly. Team leaders please acknowledge."

Both team leaders acknowledged. What the mission leader did not state, because he didn't need to, was that he was designated No 2 in Team 1, which effectively meant he would be first in the door.

At this stage the lead group had moved up close to the house stealthily and the team leader's voice over the headphones had dropped almost to a whisper.

"OK, please confirm positions in reverse sequence?"

"Roger that, rear windows secure and in position."

"Front windows secure and in position."

"Rear door team in position."

"Check, front door team in position and on my say-so, we attack – on the count of three; one, two, three; go, go, go."

The front and back doors splintered and disintegrated inwards simultaneously. Three men dived through the front door and three more through the back. The house was actually open-plan so both teams of three converged on the man sitting at the breakfast table. He had dropped the coffee cup he had been drinking from in shock but he very quickly took in the situation and then calmly placed both hands above his head. Although they were fairly sure there was no one else in the house, the back-up teams had already filed through to secure the upstairs and the basement. Particular care was taken to look for booby-trap devices or tripwires but none were found.

The man who had been seated at the table was read his Miranda rights and told he was under arrest for murder. His hands were secured behind his back with handcuffs but the officers took particular care not to disturb the dressing on his right fore-arm.

During a subsequent search of the house, four false passports were discovered, or rather, legitimate passports, but all in different names and all bearing the man's photograph. A Glock pistol was also found hidden in the basement whose markings matched those on the bullets that had killed Senator Carter. Explosive devices were found hidden under the basement floor. None were active but all were capable of effective operation. They finally had their man.

Chapter 31

The terror was over. The sense of relief was palpable. The news networks and the newspapers were actually complimenting the police and joining in the sense of patriotism and community and togetherness that the crisis had engendered. For once, there were no recriminations, no "what took the police so long to catch the guy" etc. The man who had been apprehended had generated such a sense of terror across two continents in such a short space of time, seemingly with impunity, that people were just glad that it was over and grateful to the men and women who had risked their lives to bring him to justice. The naysayers and the hindsight merchants would have their day in time but for now, all was congratulations, handshakes, backslaps and compliments. This was despite the fact that the man had been rushed into custody in a sealed police van and had not been seen since. The media had been denied their "perp walk" when the suspect had been arraigned but no one was complaining. This was far too important a drama to be played out in front of the world's media.

The President had called Maria Gonzalez to thank her personally. She had asked his permission to record the call so that she could play it back for all of her subordinates and colleagues and the President had readily agreed. The new British Prime Minister had called Mike to offer his congratulations, which he had accepted, reluctantly, but had made it quite clear that it was on behalf of the police forces of several different nations that had assisted in the manhunt.

"It's amazing," he said as he lay with Wendy in her D.C. apartment. "All this celebration and congratulation – all down to your idea of searching through the guy's trash cans."

"Ah, I'm sure the guys would've gotten round to it eventually," she replied modestly. "Anyway, how is the interrogation going? I mean, I know you are not directly involved but have they got anything at all from him as yet?"

"Well, there's the thing. Guy hasn't admitted anything or denied anything. In fact, he hasn't said word one!"

"Has he asked for a lawyer?"

"Yeah, well, sort of. The guy doesn't speak – at all – to anyone. He's been thoroughly medically examined and was co-operative. He hasn't resisted anything up to now and we have him for what, three days? When we told him he was in big trouble and he needed a lawyer, he motioned for a pen and paper and wrote the name of an obscure advocate whom Paul's guys are having difficulty tracking down. The guy may have skipped town or he may just be on vacation. We don't know. The smart money says he does not want to be involved, regardless of the publicity it might generate for him."

"What happens if the lawyer doesn't show up? I mean, where does that leave the perp?"

"Well, we've anticipated that and we asked our man – we are calling him Mr Harper until we confirm his identity – if he wants a state lawyer, but he just shook his head. Paul's people seemed to think he was initially in shock but he has gathered himself together since and seems to be very strong-willed."

"Well, he would be, wouldn't he? I mean, if he's managed to work his way halfway round the world and committed all those murders, he must have nerves of steel, apart from a heart of stone."

"Yeah, he does. I mean, F.B.I. and D.H.S. have brought their top psychology people in to look at the guy and they cannot read him at all. Communication is nil and I don't just mean verbally. He doesn't speak, but his body language is silent too. He gives nothing away. He's like a man of stone."

"So what are they planning to do?"

"Well, some were recommending a Guantanamo-type detention with far more intense interrogation, possibly with psychological intimidation. But the chiefs say no. This may only strengthen his resolve. They don't think he'd have any problem with torture, either physical or mental. They say he may well have been through it already or may have had training in how to build resistance to it."

"So, you have no idea if he's the only one, if there's a cadre of them, who hired him or them, or what they were, or are, planning? Sorry Mike, I know you haven't. I was just thinking aloud."

"I know, Wendy, I know. Look, to be honest, we really have very little information. The strategy right now is to just keep feeding the media the line that the man is being questioned and hope that the lawyer shows up. I have a hunch he will and I also think our suspect will speak when he does."

"So, right now, today, what you planning to do?"

"Oh, let's see, we could walk in the park, visit the Smithsonian or we could just have breakfast and come back to bed?"

She punched his arm. "I meant work-wise but hey, come on old man, it's early, in fact it's only 07.30. If you get your ass in gear, we've got time for all three!"

Walker was having breakfast at home in Orlando with his wife and two daughters. The doorbell rang and Cindy got up to get it.

"You've got lots of visitors, honey," she said, "and so early too."

"Bring 'em on in, dear," he said, "the more the merrier."

Four men entered the room, all dressed in suits and ties.

"Hi, Carl," said the Senator, but then he turned and half his head was missing. "Ah ha, fooled you there," he said.

Then the three councilmen appeared to have changed into casual clothing and set down their golf clubs. "You ready for a game today, Carl?" said the Mayor. "And hey, today we're playing for keeps."

Walker realized that all three men were dripping blood all over his beautiful tiled floor. He was horrified and tried to scream but he couldn't, and his wife and daughters were laughing heartily.

He called out and awoke with a start, realizing he was dreaming. It was OK; he was fine. But he was on a train. He must have dozed off. Then the ticket checker came and asked to see his

314

ticket. The man had a British Rail uniform on, complete with cap, but there was something wrong.

"But you're not supposed to be checking tickets," said Walker. "You're the Prime Minister."

"Still have to make sure everyone buys their tickets, don't we sir? Ah, a Prime Minister's work is never done," said the P.M.

Walker searched for his ticket but there were no pockets in his jacket and his wallet was missing. "I'm sorry sir, I seem to have mislaid it."

"Come now sir, we've all heard that one before; failed to purchase a ticket, did we sir? And what's this here? Oh, a rifle; now, we shouldn't be carrying this, should we sir? Gentlemen, if you could just assist me here," he said, motioning to a group of heavily armed policemen behind him and to the side. Walker made to escape but then the P.M's head exploded, covering him and the surrounding passengers in gore. No one seemed the least bit put out. In fact they all kept laughing uproariously. Even the P.M, whose head had disappeared, laughed loudly. Only Walker cried out.

He awoke again in a lather of sweat, heart beating rapidly, chest pounding. Then he saw the four walls and the locked door and he knew where he was. He lay back in frustration. Fuck it; he realized he'd finally been caught. He had to figure a way to get out but right now he didn't seem to have the strength. He fell back into a deep but troubled sleep.

Mike and Wendy had, just as she had suggested, a very full day. Being aware that it could actually take you an entire lifetime to see all the exhibits in the Smithsonian, they decided to concentrate on a part of it they thought was manageable – the National Museum of American History. Having got there, they quickly realized they'd have to compartmentalize their viewing even further as the Museum had over three million artefacts.

Mike had never been one for visiting museums per se but he had to say he was awestruck. Being a lover of travel and generally being on the move, he was immediately lost in the Transportation section, exploring modes of transport from Rails, Roads and Waterways to Air and Space. He explored locomotives, coaches, buggies, wagons, trucks, motorcycles, bicycles, and automobiles — from the earliest to the most modern. He was like a kid again and Wendy indulged him fully.

After four or five hours, they were both beat so they got take-out coffee and went for some fresh air. They strolled along Constitution Avenue and sat for a while in the President's Park, looking towards the White House.

They sat in the glow of the warm afternoon sunshine. There wasn't a cloud in the sky and the air had that lovely, early autumn feel, where the oppressive summer heat has dissipated but there was only a slight breeze and still enough warmth in the air for it to be pleasant without a hint of chill.

"You know, I could really get to like this city," he said.

"Aha, so have the plans to see the rest of the U.S. been put on hold?"

"Oh no, not at all, I really do want to travel around your country, but I was thinking maybe I could use D.C. as my base."

"Oh, were you now, Mister? So, let's see, you'd jet off or drive off or whatever and wander and maybe come back to see the little woman once in a while, eh?"

He laughed loudly. "You're hilarious. I mean, you're thinking too many moves ahead of me. I haven't made any plans yet."

"Ah yes, but that's what you were thinking, wasn't it?'

"Absolutely not," he said, looking into her eyes. "How much of the country have you seen? Why not come with me and we'll explore it together?"

"Hmm. Ok, sounds tempting, but what about work and dollars and cents? I mean, we can't just take off, can we?"

"I don't see why not in all honesty. I mean, I'm semi-retired." She reached over and placed her arms around his neck and kissed him long and deeply.

"Thank you," she said. "Do you know, you are just so, so romantic. That is what I love about you."

"That's all?"

She punched him again. "Well, there might be one or two other things, but that's all the compliments you're getting today, Mister! Hey, come on," she glanced at her watch, "we're going to a celebratory dinner with Paul and Barbara, remember. I've got to do my hair and change and get ready."

"Ok," he said, kissing her lightly on the forehead. "I've got a feeling I'm gonna enjoy tonight."

They had reservations at The Palm in Dupont Circle, which apparently had the reputation for some of the best steaks and seafood in the city, if not the entire country. Having always been a relatively casual diner, it was the first time Mike had put on a jacket and tie to eat since he had come to Washington. His first impression was that it was well worth it. Wendy looked stunning, even managing to look more beautiful than he had imagined. Barbara also looked gorgeous as indeed did most of the clientele of the place. The furnishings were luxurious without being over fussy. The ambience could certainly be described as classy!

Greetings, congratulations, hugs, kisses and handshakes were exchanged before they each sat to choose an aperitif. In due recognition of what they'd all been through over the previous weeks, Paul ordered a bottle of Cristal and all agreed it was appropriate. Menus were delivered and perused. Barbara went for the crab salad to start, followed by the lobster. Wendy went for the reverse, starting with the lobster bisque, followed by Alaskan king crab legs. The men both went for the crabmeat cocktail, followed by fourteen-ounce filet mignons.

Barbara proposed the first toast. "Can I say well done to you guys, but this toast is to our new-found friends, Mike and Wendy." They clinked glasses and drank with deep satisfaction. A wine list was proffered and bottles of Californian Red and White were ordered.

Paul then began, "Sorry to bring up work again so soon but this thing is still around and you know, it's probably on our minds anyway?" They all nodded in agreement. "Well, I'm just thinking, I mean, what do we do with this guy? He could be potentially our greatest source of intelligence on this organisation and what they are planning, or he could be worthless, merely operating under orders. I mean, he may not even know who is running him."

They sat in silence for a few moments, then Wendy ventured, "I think if he is who we think he is, he's got to know lots. At least he will know who *he* was going to try to hit next; that is, if we assume he was operating to a schedule."

"Yeah, but you'd have to assume that whoever was running him or whoever his contacts were, are long gone. They couldn't take the risk that he'd grass them up. But yeah, he may be able to enlighten us in other ways. What do you think, Mike? I mean, your people have lots of experience of taking in suspects over there."

"I don't want to sound like a party pooper or whatever you guys call it but from what I hear, I think you could take this guy out to Guantanamo or wherever for six months and get nothing from him; that is, unless you find the key – you know, you need to find what will unlock him. You may well have something he needs or something that will persuade him to talk, but I don't think any form of torture will get you results. They sure as hell didn't with us."

"But how do you figure that?" Barbara responded. "I mean, no matter what amount of remission he gets or whatever deal he strikes, he's still looking at either the death penalty or life imprisonment."

"On the face of it Barbara, you are 100% correct," Mike said, "but that said, there are lots of people walking round in Ireland today, some of them even elected politicians, who were in the same position twenty years ago as our suspect is now."

Wendy responded, "Are you seriously suggesting that someone would let this guy go as some part of a peace deal? I mean, that's preposterous, isn't it?"

"I don't want to upset anyone or to say Mike is right," Paul said, "but these are strange times we live in. Let's say our man is a believer, willing to fight to the death, willing to martyr himself for the cause – then we won't get anywhere with him. But if he's a mercenary, and he may well be, and let us say he was able to deliver us some of the top people in his organisation, who can say we won't deal with him?"

There was silence around the table as their starters arrived. After they had eaten a little, Mike resumed.

"Sorry if I sound a little cynical, ladies, but I'm afraid that's the way the world works. If this man were to give us a lead which might save hundreds if not thousands of lives, why shouldn't we deal with him?"

"But what about all the people he killed and their families, and in the case of the leaders, their people. Surely they wouldn't stand for it?" said Barbara.

Mike raised an eyebrow and Paul nodded. "Again, it's a valid point Barbara, but sometimes families and even entire peoples don't have a say. If it's expedient and necessary, a way is often found."

"It's true," Paul agreed, "and the passage of time can change everything. For example, there are people the world over who were regarded by many, including governments, as terrorists in their younger years who are now highly respected and in some cases even revered Heads of State."

"Come to think of it, I know, you're right, but anyway," Wendy interjected. "Tonight is not the night for this discussion. This is a night to celebrate. I know you guys have been working round the clock for God knows how long, so tonight you relax; cheers and well done!"

"To be fair, I think thanks may be due to you too, Wendy," said Paul. "This is a team effort here."

Everyone agreed and glasses were clinked again. A truce was called after that and the women spent the rest of the night chatting about Washington and where to go and where such and such could be got, whereas the men spoke about sports – given the transatlantic difference, the discussion involved all types, but usually those involving a ball of some description. Desserts were ordered and they finished with coffee and cognac.

Walker was free again. The previous incarceration must have been a dream. He was on his motorbike heading out to the wetlands. He turned the bike in to the usual place at the mailbox, but when he got to the clearing, the cabin was gone. In its place was a railway station; but how could that be? There were no train tracks out here. This was a wilderness. He went on to the platform but lost his footing. Suddenly, his parents came into view and he relaxed.

"Come on son," said his dad, "up you come, you can do it, you know you can." But he couldn't – no matter how hard he tried; he could not raise himself up.

"Come on, young man," said his kindly old grey-haired mother, "sure you're strong; it's no bother to you." But then he wasn't on the platform at all but on the track and a train was coming into the station – fast. He heard the train whistle but it sounded like a beep rather than a shrill sound. His parents reached down for him but the train guard pushed them away and the train closed over him; and then there was only darkness.

Chapter 32

The lawyer showed up on Monday afternoon, trailing clouds of smoke and TV cameras. He had apparently been out of town on vacation and had his cell phone switched off. He had, of course, seen the coverage on the TV news, but had never dreamed that it was his client who had been arrested; or at least that was what he had said to the waiting news media whom he had hastily assembled outside Capitol Police Headquarters. He had returned to his office this morning to a mountain of messages from the police, and had immediately set to work. Yes, of course his client had been accused of serious crimes, but this was the U.S.A. and his client was innocent until proven guilty. He promised that he would defend his client to the fullest extent allowed by the law and he felt confident of the outcome. But first of all, he needed to meet with his client. He promised a more detailed statement later, after the meet.

The lawyer's name was Victor De Costa. He was roughly forty-five years old and was usually an advocate of small-time criminals of the house-breaking, theft and minor drugs offences variety. He would have thought himself slightly above those lawyers who worked the free legal-aid scheme. No, he represented criminals who could afford to pay for his services. He was short and squat with slightly receding hair, but his dark looks, jet-black hair, and perfect white teeth made him not unattractive. He tended to smile a lot and no doubt he would be honing that smile to perfection in the weeks and months to come. This would be a serious chance for Victor to make the big time – this would be his fifteen minutes of fame, but who knew? It might be a lot longer. This was the break he needed to make it into the big league.

Victor had some form in that he had previously represented two Yemenis who had been suspected and subsequently accused of conspiracy to cause explosions. Even though D.H.S. were sure of their men, the evidence was somewhat thin and De Costa could probably have got them off if he had put his heart into it. A compromise was reached and the two men were quietly deported back to Yemen, with a permanent ban on ever entering the U.S. again.

"So, it appears that Victor is the lawyer du jour retained by the organisation," said Paul, as they drove to Police H.Q. to rendezvous with the team and meet with "Harper's" lawyer. De Costa had been given an hour with the suspect in private.

"It's ironic, isn't it," Mike responded, "given their supposed wealth, that they would use lawyers of the calibre of this guy, Victor de Costa. Perhaps it's indicative of the lack of regard in which they hold their people."

"Yeah, I suppose if you have an organisation that trains martyrs, why would you need to hire expensive lawyers to defend them? I mean, they're expendable, sorry to say – there's lots more where they came from."

"But not this guy, surely. I mean, we don't even know if he *is* a member. My hunch is that he isn't. He's a paid recruit, a mercenary if you like, and he would surely merit better than this."

"Right, but follow the logic – if he is a mercenary, surely he'd be on some serious bucks for what he's just done and he could afford to hire a better lawyer himself, not just the one the organisation provides?"

"Yeah; makes me wonder, Paul, makes me wonder."

"What, you having doubts? I mean, we've got DNA matches here and in Italy. We've got the pistol that killed the Senator. We've got his travelling kit and explosives hidden in his basement, and the I.T. guys have found a shitload of heavy stuff on his computer; everything from bomb making to gun websites and terrorist tips. I mean, what more do you need?"

"That's just the thing, Paul, it's too perfect. For a guy who covered his tracks meticulously over two continents, he appears to have gotten very sloppy, no? Or is it that we've got better? I dunno. You know, even though it all fits, how do I say this; even though all of it fits, some of it doesn't."

"What parts of it don't fit? I thought we had open and shut here, man."

"The lawyer for a start. We've a guy who's been halfway around the world staying in hotel suites that cost up to a thousand bucks a night. He buys top-of-the-range armaments and abandons them. He travels first class – at least on the few occasions that we managed to ascertain where he had travelled."

"Right, I get it, so why would he ask for a two-bit lawyer who costs what? Maybe $150 an hour? He could hire guys who cost ten times that."

"Then maybe I'm just looking for flaws. Perhaps the guy really *is* a fanatic, who spends the organisation's money as required to maintain his cover and achieve their aims but cares not a jot for himself. I mean, once he's caught, his cover is blown anyway. He's no longer any use to the organisation. In fact, he's better off dead, so he can tell no tales."

"Yeah, it's plausible. But I still think you got something there, buddy. Let's talk about it again afterwards." He pulled to the curb. "For now, let's see what Senor De Costa has to say for himself."

Victor De Costa was all smiles and white teeth and gold chains and rings and he reeked of cigar smoke. All he lacked was a cocktail glass in his hand, thought Mike. He was seated at the table with Paul, Le Vonn and Pete. They were accompanied by the Deputy District Attorney, Marvin Adams. Paul handled the introductions.

"Well, I guess," De Costa began, "you could say this is unprecedented, no?"

"You can say what you want to the press, sir," said Le Vonn, "but here in the real world, we've got your client on some heavy charges and he's going down fast."

De Costa raised and spread his arms wide. "Ok, ok, first things first. Gentlemen, let me assure you that you are making a big mistake here. My client will be pleading not guilty to all charges and I will be mounting a most vigorous defence."

"So he speaks, does he?" said Pete. De Costa ignored the remark.

"My client will speak when he needs to speak. Right now, he's been accused of crimes that he had no hand, act, or part in committing, and he chooses to exercise his perfectly legitimate right to remain silent."

Paul ventured, "Would your client be prepared to speak to us under certain circumstances?"

De Costa laughed loudly. The smile rarely left his face and now it was in full bloom. "I ain't got an idea. Whaddya mean anyway, certain circumstances? My client is innocent, full stop, so I don't see what you got to talk to him about. We're not talking deals here gentlemen, we're gonna go all the way on this one."

Yeah, so that you can have your name in lights, thought Mike. Meanwhile your client gets the needle after a valiant defence fails utterly, but hey, the lawyer is still standing and he's gonna make his fortune on this one. Despite his personal feelings for the lawyer, he decided a conciliatory approach would best serve their purpose.

"Mr De Costa," he began. "Forgive my intrusion. As Paul said, I'm MI5 on special assignment to the investigation. We seem to be miles apart here. Pardon me if I state that I assume it may be of use to you to fully defend your client and to prolong the process."

De Costa smiled again.

"But, without asking you to reveal your defence strategy, can you give us any indication of how in God's name your client is going to defend himself? I mean, the evidence is overwhelming, so I'm trying to help you here."

De Costa smiled again and considered. He was smart but not too smart. Mike was playing to some extent to the man's ego.

"Look," the lawyer said, "I'm gonna tell you guys no more than I'm gonna tell that bunch a goons out front when I leave here, but what I'll be saying is that my client is innocent; he has no knowledge of the crimes of which he is accused. He did not commit those crimes, nor has he any knowledge of who did."

Mike weighed this. Would the public believe De Costa? Probably not. Surely they'd see him for what he was – a self-serving lawyer seeking his day in the limelight. But then he could be wrong and the last thing they needed was public disquiet or confusion.

The Deputy D.A. had been quiet up to now. "It may seem a strange question, sir," he said to the lawyer, "but can I ask you to reveal your client's full name to us? I mean, it's pretty obvious that it isn't Jason Harper. We found several passports in the house which fit your client's description, but as of now, he's still the mystery man."

De Costa considered. "OK, his real name is Wade Johnson, which I'm pretty sure was on one of those passports you found?"

"Ah, come on, Victor, you hardly expect us to believe that?"

"Look, Mr Adams, I'm a lawyer right? I ain't a friggin genealogist. The guy comes to me and asks me will I be his lawyer if he needs assistance. He tells me he's Wade Johnson, so gimme a frickin break here!"

"OK, let's call him Wade for the moment."

Paul decided to keep going now that they had the man talking. "How does your client explain the fact that his blood was found at the crime scene?"

"He don't, he says you guys must've planted it. Swears he's never even been in the district, claims he wouldn't even know how to get there."

"Yeah, right," said Pete, shaking his head, but trying to play the lawyer for as much information as he could. "And I suppose he has a plausible explanation for the gunshot wound he received out there too?"

"You bet he's got an explanation. He says he was mugged." De Costa raised his hands. "Yeah, right, I know I know. But hey, here's something; he says he was walking home to his place two evenings before you guys picked him up. He's just walking up his driveway, minding his own business, right, when he suddenly gets hit over the head from behind. He's got the bruise on his head to prove it. He says he was knocked out cold and doesn't know how long he was out. He says when he woke up, he'd a wound in his right arm that was bleeding heavily. He still had his wallet but his cash was taken. He patched it up best he could but next day, it had gotten worse so he figured he'd better go to see Doc Spence".

"So why did he go to the quack Doctor to get it stitched up? Why didn't he just go to a regular clinic or emergency department?"

"Who the hell knows? Ah look, these guys, you know – they live on the edge, on the margins. I mean, look, don't ask me how the gun was in his basement or what he was surfing on the net. I only represent the guy. I don't know what sort of shit he is mixed up in and I really don't want to know but I'll tell you one thing. I believe him on this, or else he's a hell of a liar. Look, anyway, I can't sit round here talking to you guys all day, I've got a press conference to attend, so if you gentlemen would excuse me?" He smiled the smile again and got up to leave. "See ya in court, Counsellor," he said to Marvin Adams, as the smile beamed.

The meeting broke up and everyone filed out. Mike quietly followed the lawyer as he made his way to the rest room. He joined him as they were both washing their hands.

"Mr De Costa," Mike began, "might I have a quick word?"

The lawyer considered briefly again. "Ah, OK, sure buddy, shoot, but can you make it quick?"

"Certainly; you understand that my colleagues in there have to be, shall we say, a bit more formal or circumspect with you?" De Costa nodded. "Well, perhaps I can be a little more off-the-record. You strike me as a tough guy sir, if I may say so; but at the same time, a hardworking, honest to goodness, home-grown patriotic American?"

De Costa actually blushed. "Well, I wouldn't say that. I mean, being a lawyer means you gotta play the odds, you know what I mean, but yeah; I love my country, I did my time in the forces. There wasn't any war on at the time but hey, had there been, I was ready. What you driving at anyway?"

"I think you know, sir. This case or this investigation has caused an enormous amount of public disquiet, fear, and the very thing it was meant to create – terror. It would probably cause consternation if the public were now to get the wrong impression, you know?"

The smile was back. "Aha, so I got at least one guy who's prepared to accept my guy's plea of innocence, but you don't want me hogging the airwaves with it, right?"

"I didn't say I accepted your word on anything yet, sir. I was merely appealing to your better judgment."

"Hey look, what's your name again; Lyons, is it? Yeah, now you listen, buddy. I might not be your five-hundred-buck-an-hour, thousand-dollar-suit lawyer, but I ain't stupid. If I go out there shouting about injustice and my client's innocence, I know I'm gonna get boiled alive! I can read the public mood too man, so for now, we'll take it slowly – put our toe in the water and see where it leads. But hey, I'm gonna tell you something for nothin – you and your buddies in there better get moving because unless I'm really reading this one wrong, it ain't over yet."

Chapter 33

This time, he was on the highway. He had the Camry in cruise, or thought he had, when suddenly it began to gain speed. He watched the needle pass through 80, then 90, 100, up past 110 – he pressed the brake but the car kept moving even faster. He tried to disengage the drive but the gear lever was stuck. He was swerving in and out of the lanes trying to avoid other cars. He risked another quick look at the speedometer; 120 mph. But a Camry couldn't go this fast, could it? His momentary glance at the dash forced him to lose concentration and he didn't see the Mack truck in time. He cried out in horror as the vehicles impacted and awoke in sheer terror, again totally bathed in perspiration.

His parents were there again, sitting in chairs this time. His father got up and came over to him saying, "Hey, you awake, Mister?"

It took him a few seconds to take in his surroundings.

"But, but, you're not my old man," he said.

"No, I sure as hell ain't son, but I sure am glad to see y'all awake."

The old lady who had been seated next to the old man now came and took him by the hand.

"Oh, we were so, so worried about you, son. How are you feeling? Better?

Walker was still totally confused. He seemed to be in a bed in a room somewhere with little or no natural light and he was wired up to some monitor. Perhaps that was where the beeping had come from. There were intravenous tubes going into both of his arms. He tried to speak but his throat was like sandpaper.

"Wait, wait," said the old lady. "Drink some water. There now, you'll be fine, son."

He could not remember when last he had been called 'son'. He was in his late fifties, for Christ's sakes. Still, these folks sure were old enough to be his parents. He took a deep draught of water and cleared his throat.

"I thank you very much for your care, ma'am, but would you mind telling me who the hell are you and where in God's name am I?"

"Oh Lord in Heaven," the old lady began, "we plum forgot about that. It's been so long, you see. I mean, five days now. Sorry son, I'm Martha and this here's my husband John. You see, we was on the highway heading south for our vacation, like we always do, and, well, I no sooner hit the road but I settle down for a nap, ya know, after all that packing and all. John always drives and he's steady as a rock but Lord have mercy, he must have just nodded off for a second and didn't see that mighty tailback on I95."

Walker remembered nothing but he was beginning to deduct by now that he must have been involved in an automobile accident of some sort. He took another sip of water and swallowed deeply. "Sorry ma'am, can you be a little more specific?"

"Oh sorry dear, I do go on. John, maybe, you could explain?"

John looked decidedly sheepish and contrite but offered, "Well, my sincere apologies, son, no question but it was my fault. I must've just dropped to sleep for a few seconds at most. Next thing I know, I hear this absolutely horrendous crash and I've rear-ended your Camry. Course, me and Martha was belted in and we didn't get a scratch. That old Buick, she's done built like a tank and she barely got a dint in her front fender; but man, that Camry sure folded like one o' them concertinas, so it did, I tell ya. You didn't seem to be too badly hurt but you sure hit your head one hell of a bang. Doctors here have diagnosed severe concussion."

Bits and pieces began to come back to him and he vaguely recalled travelling south on I95 after his second little trip to D.C. But his memory was fuzzy. He couldn't remember how things

329

had gone, or even where or why he was headed south. He decided to play it cool for the moment.

"Ma'am, sir, thank you again for your concern. Did one of you say I've been unconscious for five days?

"Yep, you sure have been," said Martha.

"And have you folks been here all the time?"

They glanced from one to the other, and then John spoke. "Well, I gotta level with you, son, we was really worried about you. I mean, I've driven that highway for over forty years and never even had the slightest shunt but man, last thing I'd want, either of us would want, is to hurt a fellow human being, and, well, we wanted to be here when you woke up. The doctors said you would wake up 'cept they didn't think it'd take five days. Ah shucks, we've been fine though, we've been sort of covering night-time in shifts and we spend most days here together."

"Well, that's mighty kind and caring of you, sir and ma'am, and I thank you for it."

"Least we could do son, seeing as t'was our fault y'all ended up in here in the first place."

The door opened and a very pleasant nurse in a blue and white uniform entered. "Hey, he's awake," she said. "How are you feeling, sir?"

"Well, apart from a slight headache and an almighty thirst, fine, actually. When do I get out of here?"

"Oops, not for me to say, sir. Doctor will be here this afternoon; you'd best speak to her. I guess we could do with a little brightness in here. Cover your eyes for just a moment sir, this may hurt a little." She drew the curtains back and sunshine flooded the room. He flinched at the sudden bright light but gradually his eyes adjusted. "That better?" He nodded. She took a chart from the end of the bed. "One very important question, sir," she smiled, "what do we call you? You had no I.D. on you and we didn't want to break locks on your briefcase or personal baggage so we've been calling you Mr Camry."

Walker forced a smile and motioned for another glass of water, allowing him time to assess the situation. Surely the police were involved if he had been in an auto accident? Highway Patrol? Local police? State police? Shit, where was his car? Had they searched it, found the hidden compartment beneath the rear seats? Probably not; why would they? He was just an unfortunate citizen caught up in a minor auto crash. He wasn't suspected of anything, was he? And anyway, the Camry was registered to – whom? He finally remembered. He drank his water and cleared his throat.

"Sorry nurse. You can call me John, John Robinson," and he offered his hand.

"Well, awful nice to meet ya after all this time," she said, pleasantly.

"Nice to meet you too nurse," he said with a smile, "and what can I call you?" She was very pretty, and if circumstances had been different, he might have – no; he cast the thought from his mind.

"Oh, you can call me Amanda, and I expect you'll also want something to eat."

"Absolutely," he said, only now realizing that he was totally famished. "Whatever you've got, Amanda, any type of food really, whatever you'd recommend."

"I think we'll start you on something light, John, coming right up." She sashayed out of the room.

"Hey, you know you missed all the big news these past few days?" said the old man. 'We could put on CNN for you if you like but I guess it's sort of died down now. You know, they finally caught that feller that was shooting them politicians all over the place. Caught him red handed in D.C. they did."

"Well, did they now? And about time too. Gee, I'm sorry I missed that." He was too! At least that part of his plan had gone according to schedule.

The events of the previous week were now coming back to him rapidly and each realization dawned on him with greater trepidation. Did the police track down his John Robinson persona from the car's registration? Did they find his Atlanta lock-up? That would prove to be a dead-end. Did someone dig deeper? He decided if nothing had happened in the five days he was in here, he just might be OK. He decided to take it slowly.

"Sorry folks, did you say my car was a write-off?"

John Slaughter smiled. "Ah, hell, no man; I mean, she folded like she's probably supposed to, I don't know with those new foreign cars, but don't you worry bout that at all now. We done got her fully repaired for you and she's sitting right out there in that car park. It's all paid fer, too; least we could do in the circumstances."

'Why, thank you again," he said. Things might just be looking up here.

"Oh, and this is a private medical facility and that's all paid for too," Martha added proudly.

"Oh, I can't accept that," he said. "I'll be happy to reimburse you folks."

"Nope, can't do that," said John, who looked down and shook his head.

"You better tell him John," Martha said, touching her husband gently on the arm.

Walker waited, unconsciously holding his breath. Slaughter seemed to notice.

"Oh, might as well git it over with," he began. "But hey, nothing for you to worry about, Mister; no sirree, nothing at all. You see, I hope you don't mind, but we didn't call no police or highway patrol to the scene because, well, cause, you know, I'm an old man and..." The man seemed to struggle to speak. Martha touched him gently again. "Well, you see," Slaughter continued, "an old man like me, if I was to report this, I'd lose my license for sure, and at my age, can't ever see me getting it back; and you know, Martha and me, that's our only way of getting around these days. Don't walk so good no more and that old Buick, well, it's like a part of me, you understand?" The man had tears in his eyes. Walker nodded. This was getting better.

"Well, the hospital here, like ya know, they gotta notify someone, so we just done told them to notify our own local Sheriff, but he ain't gonna say nothing; and sir, I mean, if you can find it in your heart to forgive us folks, I hope it don't upset yer too much?"

Walker was so relieved he could have kissed the man. You beautiful old bastard, he thought, what a break to catch. What was this? A combination of Murphy's Law and the luck of the Irish?

To have everything go just according to plan only to then be rear-ended by a crazy old buzzard; but then the bonus – one who didn't want to involve the cops? Way to go, he thought! He thanked his lucky stars and everything else besides. He looked at John Slaughter, who was still looking at the floor. The man slowly raised his head, looking at Walker for a reaction.

Walker winked. "Hey, I've never been one myself for undue procedure or involving cops when you don't need them. I'm sure those guys have plenty other things to worry about." He extended his hand and Slaughter took it firmly.

"You got yourself a deal, sir," he said. The relief in John and Martha's faces was visible. Martha took his hand in both of hers firmly.

"May God bless you sir," she said. "We'll never forget this."

"It's nothing at all, ma'am, and thank you so much for watching over me."

"Well, I'm sure you're gonna want to get something to eat, and after that you'll need some more rest so we'll leave you be for now."

"Thanks, again ma'am," he said, then it suddenly dawned on him as his brain cleared a bit further. Everything *had* gone well in D.C. but now he realized why he had been driving south – Katya! He had paid $5,000 to get her a passport and had sent it registered mail to Sandy Lane. He had also booked a flight for her to Miami, and she had been due to arrive – when? He'd been out for five days; Jesus, two days ago!

"Sorry ma'am, before you go, do you know what happened to my cell phone?"

Martha's face fell. "Sorry, John; I'm afraid it got smashed in the accident," she replied sadly.

"Not to worry, how about my laptop?"

"Well all your stuff is in that there locker and I think it's OK but we ain't been near it. We done touched nothing, John."

"That's OK," he said. "Can you just pass it to me as I need to catch up?"

"Of course you do. So sorry for our manners, we really plum forgot, we've been so long looking at you there."

The old man passed him his laptop, which was still in its case and seemed intact. He asked the man to plug in the mains lead as his battery would surely have expired by now. The old couple made their apologies and left. Walker booted up the PC and checked for Wi-Fi . He opened his contacts file, then plugged in his head phones and double clicked his Skype icon. He went to "Call Phones" and punched in Katya's cell number. Christ, he was supposed to meet the girl in Miami. Where was she? Would she have betrayed him? He cast the thought from his mind the instant it came. No, she wouldn't – she had too much to lose and a lot to gain; and anyway, he had long since established that she was the loyal type.

The number dialled through and she answered on the second ring.

"Hallo?" she said cautiously.

"Katya, it's me. So sorry, I got delayed. I mean, I've been in a slight auto accident, but it's OK, I mean, I'm OK now."

She burst into tears on the other end. "Oh Jesus, I've been so worried about you; I thought, I mean, sorry. Oh Jesus, I'm just so relieved, but where are you? Can I come? Can I help? I mean, can I do anything?"

"No, no, it's fine, I'll be out of here in a day, but where are you? I mean, did you have any difficulty getting in or what?

"I am just fine, my darling. I had no problems in Miami. All those stamps on that passport you got me seemed to do the trick. I'm sure glad they didn't ask me about any of them, though, as I mean, I did a bit of research, but nothing detailed."

Walker laughed. "You did just great Katya, but where exactly are you?"

"Oh yeah, sorry, I didn't say. I'm in a motel close to the airport. I figured I'd stay here a few days anyway and just prayed that you'd eventually show up."

"Ok, just stay right where you are and I'll come get you in a few days. Don't worry, I'll be there."

"Sure I will, but please be careful."

"Of course, Katya, of course I will." He suddenly felt very tired but at the same time, an idea came to him. "Katya, I've just been thinking. You have an international driving permit, don't you?"

"Sure do, hey, you want me to come get you?"

"Well yeah, it might save – I mean, I gotta rest up probably another day or two, so if you can rent a vehicle down there and come north on I95. I'm – Jesus, where the hell am I? Hold a minute." He reached for the nurse call button just as the girl wheeled in a trolley containing cereal, toast, some preserves and fresh coffee. Nothing had ever smelt as good.

"Sorry for the delay, kitchen's off duty at the moment. I think this is all we should try for now John," she said. "We'll see how you're feeling later on for maybe a light dinner?"

"This looks fantastic, Amanda, but sorry, just one more question if I may; where the hell am I?"

She laughed heartily. "Sorry, John, we've been so used to having you here, we forgot you were unconscious when you came in. You're in the Colleton Medical Center in Walterboro." Walker frowned. "Oh sorry," she said, "it's in South Carolina. Man, you really were out of it, weren't you?"

"Yep, I guess I was. In fact, last thing I remember is cruising on I95 but I think it was in Virginia!" Amanda left and he returned to his headphones.

"Katya, you still there?"

"Loud and clear, where am I headed for?"

"Well, it's straightforward. Just get on to I95 and head north. Take the Walterboro exit and then call me. Ah shit, no, my phone was totalled. OK, try to find the Colleton Medical Centre in Walterboro, shouldn't be too difficult for a bright girl like you."

"I'm on my way, you get lots of rest and I'll be there before you know it and hey, I love you." He heard the slight break in her voice as she said it. Oh shit; she meant it. This girl was in love! What could he do?

"Love you too, Katya," he said.

He ate his late breakfast and had a brief nap. He was almost afraid to fall asleep lest he was out for another five days, but he need not have worried. This time, the dreams were more pleasant. As he was back on food and drinks, the intravenous tubes were disconnected and the doctor pronounced him fit and healthy, although advised him to take things easy for a while. Now that his schedule had been interrupted, he would have to start planning again, so he intended to do just as the doctor recommended.

Katya arrived the next morning and he was discharged. John and Martha Slaughter were there to see him and were overjoyed. Despite the mishap, they were determined to continue on their trip to Florida. Martha assured them she would never nap in the car again and would keep a close watch on old John. Heaven help the other road users with that pair, thought Walker. Still, they had managed a trouble-free run for forty years, so who knew?

The Camry had been fully repaired and was where they had parked it. A discreet check showed that nothing had been disturbed and everything was still in place. The only thing that had been disrupted had been his schedule, but that could always be changed. He now had to decide whether to continue using the Camry or to use Katya's rental. Why not? It had worked in Europe. Still, that was a minor detail.

He had left his mark in Walterboro for sure. They would certainly have taken his blood and other samples in the hospital but it would only have been for medical purposes. There had been no police involvement, and even if there had been, they would have had nothing to compare the samples with. He was still in pole position; still the man. But hey, don't get too cocky – you just never knew. Who would have thought that *he* would have been taken out by an old couple almost in their eighties?

He smiled to himself and Katya caught it and smiled back. She had booked a double room in the Days Inn and they had just made love in it. They had had a leisurely dinner and had relived some of their blissful times on the cruise and their whirlwind meeting of only a few short weeks ago. He kissed her tenderly and held her close. After a while, she drifted off to sleep. Walker, having slept for five days, was suddenly seized with a surge of energy. He decided to resume his planning.

He slipped out of bed and padded to the desk where his laptop had been set up. While he waited for it to boot up, he took stock of his situation. He had never had any intention of killing Marian

Turner or her husband. In fact, she wasn't on his list. If he had intended to kill her, she would be dead and he would not have been detected. He had in fact been aiming for the coffee pot when the husband had dramatically knocked his wife to one side. He had inadvertently helped Walker as by clearing the bodies out of the way, he had cleared the line of fire, allowing shots to be fired which shattered the window and the flower vase.

As he was at least a half-mile from the security detail, and the world record for half a mile is around two minutes on a track, he reckoned he easily had three minutes before anyone arrived at his position. Given his reputation and the expected caution that would be shown by the response team, it would be at least five before anyone arrived. He had already left the trickle of blood and he was fully camouflaged, so he just quietly slipped away. He couldn't be sure if anyone would see the silver Camry. It was unlikely but just in case, he had switched plates to match the one in Chevy Chase anyway.

The guy he had set up was an Al Qaeda sleeper. The Bahraini had done his research and knew that Walker liked back-up on jobs. Therefore when he had given him the list, he had also provided a second one, with a list of names, addresses and code words to allow him to approach some of his operatives in the cities where the hits were due to take place. Walker had thought long and hard about back-up, but in the end had decided not to use them; too unreliable, he felt. The Bahraini was unlikely to have given him his top people anyway. But he needed an edge, something in reserve to allow him a bit of breathing space to continue his mission. He felt he needed a 'straw man'.

Walid Al Samri, a.k.a. Jason Harper, a.k.a. Wade Johnson, was it. The guy had assumed the identity of a man who had been killed in Iraq, so he wouldn't be cooperating with any police investigations. He'd be doing his best to keep a low profile. Walker had raided Walid's house on his first trip to D.C. and had stolen a toothbrush and picked up several hairs and tiny skin particles. These he had liberally left in the various hotel rooms he had stayed in, thinking that if by some remote chance police had found out that he had stayed there, that they would build up a database of DNA samples, assuming them to be his. However, given the cleaning regimes in the hotels, he couldn't be sure that any of them had ever been discovered. The toothbrush must have been, though, unless the Italians were more inefficient than he thought. But the blood was the key.

He had mugged poor Walid the night before he fired at Marian Turner. He waited in the shadows and socked him as he approached his front door. When the guy was out cold, Walker shot him in the arm, again using the silenced weapon, but was careful only to wing him, lest the man bleed to death when he was out. A small sample of blood was easily acquired and he was home. He figured Walid wouldn't get medical help straight away, if at all. But if he did and if the police were looking for a guy with a gun shot wound, bingo! Walid *had* gone to a Doctor and the set-up had worked perfectly, except...

Damn the Slaughters anyway. He'd had a perfect plan hatched for his next hit – it would have been out of sequence, but who knew or cared? The Bahraini had said he didn't; the order was not important. He'd also created a window of opportunity for himself that would have given him three, maybe four days at least of free operating time, maybe more. His stay in Walterboro had surely blown that at this stage.

But don't be too despondent, he told himself; perhaps it was still there. The police really needed an arrest on this one and he had given them one on a plate. Walid wouldn't talk, of that he was certain. They could send him to Guantanamo for six months and they would not get one word from him. Would the Bahraini provide him with a lawyer? It was unlikely. Would the Bahraini twig to what Walker was at? For sure he would, and for sure he would approve. The man would probably laugh heartily. His people, particularly the likes of Walid, were expendable – the cause was the thing.

Maybe the investigation would just stop with Walid. After all, the evidence was overwhelming. The suspect wouldn't talk. The police were under enormous pressure to apprehend the killer. He had just provided them with one. The set-up was perfect. Perhaps he still had his window after all. He accessed the internet and commenced plan B.

Part 4
September

Chapter 34

They left early in the morning, Katya driving the Camry. He had taken it out for a spin the previous evening just to ensure all was well and it had seemed as good as new. In a quiet rest area off the highway, he had thoroughly checked the compartment beneath the rear seats and found all to be in order. There was possibly a very slight risk in taking the Toyota but he felt it was balanced by the ability to store what he needed in it without detection.

They had parked Katya's rented Honda in a long-term parking facility. He had toyed with the idea of taking two cars for back-up but decided, on balance, that multiple vehicles weren't needed on this one, and they might even complicate things. There was also the option of returning the vehicle to the Hertz facility at Walterboro but that might leave a trail also. He had just introduced Katya to the Slaughters as Katya, not identifying her as a friend, wife, daughter or lover but he was confident that they wouldn't be saying too much about either of them.

So really, they were both free to travel and explore as much as they wished. Katya was still on cloud nine after her whirlwind drive through Europe, her cruise across the Atlantic, her time in Barbados and now, a new country – and hey, she was a citizen of this place! At least that was what her passport said and she had entered the country on it without any difficulty. To be precise, the name on her passport stated Katherine Robinson – nice touch that, he thought. For the moment, they would be Mr and Mrs Robinson – a touch corny perhaps, given the age difference? Naw, hang that; you could find couples of all ages together nowadays.

It was amazing how she trusted him. She had said that she loved him and he strongly suspected that she did, but at the same time, she was far from stupid. When she had asked over breakfast that morning where they were headed next, he had replied north and she had accepted this without query. He added that he had some more business to do that would take a couple of days and it would be really nice if she drove him again.

She didn't ask him what the business was, where it was, how long it would take or what she was expected to do, apart from drive. She just smiled, touched his hand and said, "I'd love to drive you man, wherever you wanna go, just tell me. You have no idea what you have given me, you know that? I mean, I know I said this before but you really are the first man, the only man, who has ever cared about me."

"Thanks Katya, that's so kind of you to say that but I need to thank you too."

He wondered again. She was bright, intelligent and she must know that it wasn't all one way and that he had in fact, used her greatly. Still, he supposed that to take her out of the life she had been stuck in was probably the key, not to speak of the first class travel. He had also given her – how much at this stage? Approximately $50k. Yeah, peanuts to him, but let's retain some perspective here; it would probably seem like a fortune to her.

Now, leaving morals aside, were she to betray him, what would she face? An uncertain future for sure; the money supply would dry up and she would be identified as an illegal alien who had entered the country under false pretences. Perhaps if she gave them the big prize, D.H.S. might do something for her on the visa front, but there was no certainty in that – she might just as easily be deported. In any event, given her background, she would be naturally cautious when dealing with anyone in authority.

No, he had nothing to worry about from the gorgeous Katya, other than the fact that she had perhaps fallen in love with him. Christ Almighty! He had forgotten all about Cindy. Shit, was his brain working at all? Had the concussion done more damage than he thought?

He gave Katya another $2,000 and asked her to head into town to purchase two i-Phones and to spend the remainder of the cash on phone credit. When she returned, he called the Lake Mary house. There was no reply. He then called Cindy's cell but was told she was out of coverage. He tried the ranch in Nebraska and was mightily relieved to hear she was still there.

There was also relief in Cindy's voice. "Hi Carl, hey, we've been a bit worried about you. Gee sorry, the girls have been having so much fun we decided to stay a few more days. I called the house and your cell but couldn't get you."

"Gee, that's fine Cindy, stay as long as you want honey; you know I love to see you and the girls having a good time. Sorry, but my cell got damaged but I've got a new number now. I've got to stay up north another few days anyway, so you can get me on this." He gave her the new number and he relaxed.

It was amazing. Cindy never seemed to question him either. When he said he was away on business, she accepted it fully, never querying what he was up to or never seeming to be particularly worried either. Mild concern, perhaps, but she seemed to think he'd always come through. Well, he would, wouldn't he? Did he really inspire that much confidence? Perhaps he did? Or did she know the real story but kept quiet? No point worrying about that now.

Maybe it was because no matter where he had ever been, he had always showed up eventually, usually smiling at the success of whatever his latest venture had been. And why not? He was the man! But was he totally immune to the pain and suffering his trade caused? No, he wasn't. He shivered involuntarily as he recalled the nightmares of the previous week. Would he be like this for the rest of his life? Would his victims revisit him in the dark hours before dawn?

Katya seemed to sense his discomfort and reached over to touch his hand.

"Maybe you need a little more time to rest, you've been through a hell of a lot. You might need a few days of complete relaxation?"

"Naw, I'm fine, headache has disappeared so I'm good to go. In fact, this is how I relax, long distance driving does it for me."

"Yeah, I sort of guessed that but you just chill totally today and leave the driving to me, deal?"

"OK, deal." They high-fived and he hit the dial on the radio. Alan Jackson was telling him that the whole world had gone singing country music. Perhaps it had, but he had his doubts. He settled down to chill, just as she had told him to.

This time it was Mike who showed up at Paul's place at 6.30 in the morning. Paul appeared at the door, bleary eyed and enquired what was happening.

"Oh, nothing much, just couldn't sleep. I was gonna bring us some take-out coffee but I figured you'd do a far better brand right here in your own kitchen."

"Right on man, give me a minute to get this machine going."

They sipped the dark Colombian in silence; black for Paul, lots of milk for Mike, no sugar for either. Paul eventually broke the silence.

"Still bugging you, eh?"

"Naw, I just couldn't sleep and I fancied some of Barbara's delicious homemade blueberry muffins."

"Hey, pardon my manners, man. I think she made a fresh batch last night." A quick search discovered the sweet confections and both men tucked in.

"No, seriously," Mike began, "why do I keep getting the feeling that we've been had here? I mean, the evidence is overwhelming. OK, we haven't got him on all the killings, but there's enough to suggest he was involved in them all; and yet, somehow I don't buy it."

Paul chewed on a muffin and considered. "You've got a point for sure. I mean, as we said, the guy doesn't leave a trace of evidence for weeks but then seemingly gets sloppy. For sure you can say that Marian Turner's husband's sharpness saved her life and put the first real dent in our man's plans. But why then would he stay around D.C. and use his car, even parking it out front for all to see?"

"Conversely, you could argue that he was wounded, confused, needed medical attention, which he thought he could get without detection and then slip away until he was ready to make another run. I mean, by all accounts, this guy has been living at this address for months although neighbours saw little of him. He's been driving that Camry and the tire tracks out at the golf club could have come from a Camry."

"Yeah, you're right. Now you know you've just made the argument for standing down the task force and that's been done as of yesterday. Maria has released everyone to either catch up on other duties or to take a well earned break."

"Difficult to blame her. You've got a suspect in custody; there's been no further activity so she can't expect her people to keep on it. Still, the guy just doesn't fit the picture we imagined for someone who carried out all those assassinations. And then there's the lawyer."

"But what else do you expect him to say? I mean, we weren't privy to the conversation he had with his client and they did speak for an hour. Look at it from the point of view of the suspect. If he pleads guilty, he gets a quick trial and either gets the needle or life in prison. From the lawyer's viewpoint, he gets what, maybe one or two press conferences, his client pleads guilty and in a couple of months, everyone's forgotten about him and the whole incident. So, they only have one option – to plead not guilty to everything and to try to engineer this massive police conspiracy based on the huge pressure we were put under to produce the perp."

"Yeah; you know, you're probably right. Lawyers lie all the time, don't they? Well, it's their job to defend their clients, regardless of their crimes."

"You wanna ride into the city with me Mike? I mean, I know it's a Sunday but this is a hell of a big week. Unfortunately I'm not one of the ones that Maria has told to take a break. We've got some very serious intelligence on some guys up in The Big Apple and you know, with the tenth anniversary of 9/11 coming up there, we've gotta be super paranoid. The lock-down up there is gonna be something – from what I've seen, a mouse would have to be highly skilled to get in there next week."

"Gee, sorry, I'd forgotten all about that. You plan on travelling up there?"

"I'm not sure yet; depends on how the back room work goes over the next few days. Why? You wanna come?"

"The thought had occurred to me alright and as I don't seem to have any shadows to chase this week, I might as well."

Paul smiled and clapped him on the shoulder. "OK, let's hit the office first and see what gives. Give me ten minutes to take a shower and I'll be right with you."

As usual, Katya made excellent progress and by mid afternoon they were on the outskirts of Richmond. Rather than go all the way to D.C., he decided to get a motel here and maybe even use it as a base. They were only an hour and a half from the capital and he could go back and forth to do his research and planning. He asked Katya to look for a fairly big motel with outside access as usual, or a hotel that was big enough to be impersonal.

They eventually settled for a suite at the Country Inn, just off I95. It was somewhat isolated, with only a McDonald's or a Burger King nearby to eat in but it was ideal for the highway and if they wanted a proper meal, they could always drive into the city. Anyway, they would have plenty of time to eat after all this was over. He was already fantasizing about where he would base Katya; or maybe he wouldn't base her anywhere at all but let her go free to find her own level. She had served him well and he had developed a fondness for her. Was it love? No, probably not. Regretfully, he was too far gone, too hard-bitten, too used to life's nasty side to enjoy the innocence of falling in love. Yet despite it all, he was not cynical and still strongly believed in the concept – it was just unlikely it would touch him; that was all.

When he thought that he had at one stage considered quietly disposing of Katya, he felt a twinge of guilt. Had he really been serious about it or was it just an option? Don't fool yourself, he thought. Never fool yourself; always be brutally honest. That's why he was as good as he was. So, would he have killed her? Definitely, although he had never killed unless it was absolutely necessary for his own protection. He had regretted the death of the guard in the Wilanow Palace more than all of the others. When it was work, he had the ability to distance himself, not to see the targets as real people. But the guard was different; he had only been doing his job and he had been hopelessly outmatched.

The Country Inn was perfect; close to Washington but not too close; remote but accessible; comfortable but impersonal and so close to the highway that if they needed to, they could be in the wind in minutes. That was one of the things that fascinated him about this great country; the highway system. Its arteries sliced through the countryside and were in many ways its lifeblood. Almost everything that was produced anywhere in America travelled the highways before it was consumed. The continuity and efficiency of the system allowed for rapid and, in many cases, same day delivery throughout the country. But it also allowed free, unfettered travel throughout the nation for everyone. In an hour, you could be in a place where no one had ever heard of you or knew your name. In a day, you could be lost forever. The UK and Europe were different. No matter where you went, there was always the possibility you would be recognised or discovered, despite the large population. It was probably just a matter of scale, but whatever; it suited his profession admirably.

Mike and Paul and the team had spent the day viewing covertly obtained video footage of the New York suspects and analysing phone transcripts in an effort to ascertain whether the suspects were innocuous or deadly serious. There was no doubt that something was afoot as the guys appeared to be taking great precautions when they met and seemed to be using a number of different addresses. This might just be a group of people visiting each others apartments but the videos suggested otherwise and the transcripts, although translated from Arabic, also suggested code words and caution. Farouk, their Arabic language expert, was suggesting a possible covert incursion to one of the apartments when they could ascertain for sure that there was no one at home. He held back on recommending a full raid as there was no guarantee that they would get the right people and they then risked driving the others into deep cover.

Mike had asked how they mounted covert raids or incursions but was given a vague answer which basically told him that they never took place, or at least they were not carried out by the police or D.H.S. personnel. But there were smaller groups out there, he knew, they had even had them in the UK back in the day. Usually funded under some obscure sub-heading in the Home Office or the Foreign Office, they were always highly trained, well-chosen and fiercely loyal. But if something went wrong, the authorities would disown them completely; and it had happened. That was part of the risk you took to protect your country, and there was many a man or woman buried without military honours, who had shown as much or even more bravery in the field than those who were given the full treatment. But they would have wanted it that way, and the people who really mattered to them knew, and cared.

"Your heart's not in this, is it man?" Paul startled him somewhat as he took a seat opposite. Mike smiled.

"That obvious, huh? Sorry, I guess our conversation of this morning is playing on my mind and I still get the sense of unfinished business."

"As I said, you may be right. Can you do me a favour?"

"For sure, name it."

"Well, I'm gonna be tied up here with this New York scare, but the more I think about it, I'm convinced you've got something. Can you keep working on it and ignore all this crap?"

"Well, to be honest, I'm really doing just that. Actually, I was just about to call Wendy to get some dinner anyway. Any chance you and Barbara can join us?"

"Ah gee, dunno." He glanced at his watch. "Yeah, it's only six o'clock. If we get finished here at a reasonable hour, we'll join you for dessert or something later. Where you headed, by the way?"

"I'm not sure; I'll text you when we decide, OK?"

They were back in casual dining mode so they agreed on James Hoban's Irish Restaurant and Bar in Dupont Circle. She drank Guinness while he stayed with Coors and they shared baskets of wings, chicken tenders and fries. It was football night – every type of football as the new season had just started in both the English Premiership and the American N.F.L. The place was packed with revellers. They made small talk and watched some of the football but she knew it was still on his mind.

"OK, come on out with it. You're still not happy with this thing, I can tell."

"Well, Paul and I spoke this morning about chasing shadows and you know, that's what I feel I am doing right now. Ah, I dunno, Wen. I mean, maybe we have the perp. The lawyer is probably just ramping it up to get publicity, and the guy is probably guilty as hell."

"Have you ever considered that there might be a dichotomy or confusion here?"

"What do you mean confusion?"

"Well, consider this: You say your suspect is guilty as hell, right? But guilty of what? From what I've heard, he does seem guilty but maybe not of the crimes you've been tracking him for."

"Yeah, I have considered that, but given the evidence, we can hardly have a case of mistaken identity."

"Well have you considered that he may not have committed the murders but may have been an accessory in some way?"

"We have but that doesn't explain the gunshot wound or the fact that his toothbrush turned up four thousand miles away."

"Have you thought about the possibility that he may have been set up?"

"Yep, sorry hon, been down that road too and if he was, it's gotta be the most elaborate set-up ever."

"Hmmm, perhaps, but we have said all along that our assassin is nothing if not thoroughly professional and he plans for every eventuality."

"True, he has been and you know, that's the very point I was discussing with Paul this morning. The way he was caught so easily, it's just not him. I don't buy it. OK, perhaps he was wounded and not thinking straight, but it's too far a leap for me; it's totally out of character with his previous behaviour. It's almost as if he was waiting there like a sitting duck."

"Ahem, well, I do seem to remember some girl suggesting you search trash cans. I mean, he may not have anticipated that."

"Ah jeez, sorry, yeah, of course, but either way, it just doesn't seem like him to hang around D.C."

"Well, he hung round the night he killed the Senator, surely? I mean, he could have left the city but it's unlikely, isn't it?"

"Yeah, perhaps you're right, maybe I am chasing shadows. Maybe I should just give it up?"

"No, no Mike, I'm not saying that at all, just trying to tease it out and see all the angles. No, I really think you've got something so hold on to it for a little while at least."

They ordered more beers and another basket of wings and suddenly Paul was with them. "Sorry guys, Barbara's on baby sitting duty, she can't make it tonight."

Mike pulled over a stool and signalled the barman for another beer.

"You've been over it again man, I can tell by that guilty look on your face!"

Mike made to protest but Paul waved him away.

"No, no, only kiddin. Hey, I asked you to keep on it, I've got doubts myself."

Mike nodded in acknowledgement. He then took a long draught of beer, drained the bottle and called for another.

"OK, let's go over the facts again and this time, just for a moment, let's assume that the guy we have in custody is a patsy, OK?"

Paul and Wendy agreed.

"So, he's been active on what, five occasions, on four of which he's killed a total of eight people, right? Seven politicians and a security guard. Now why, on the one occasion that he fails to kill, does he get caught? Well, the initial answer is that he doesn't, you see; he actually gets clean away from the site of the attack, only to be caught having breakfast the next morning. Doesn't make sense. Wait." He signalled for them to hold a moment. "It doesn't make sense unless the whole Marian Turner thing was a setup. Perhaps he meant to kill her, perhaps he didn't, but either way it doesn't matter to the setup."

"Hey, I'm with you," said Wendy. "So he's careful not to contaminate the scene apart from the blood which he plants but which is not his own." She was warming to her theme. "The gun he could have planted any time. The websites were probably the guy's own doing and caused him to be the patsy in the first place."

"The toothbrush?" Paul enquired.

"Well, that's the bit that required the cunning plan, said Mike, "and our man is definitely cunning."

350

"It's definitely a plausible scenario, I'll give you that; but you said yourself, he's been active five times and killed on four occasions. Why would he set a trap now and not before? I mean, what does he have to gain?"

"Jeez guys, that's obvious," said Wendy. "He gains *time!* He's the subject of the biggest manhunt ever mounted. OK, he's managed to evade detection, but he must be feeling the heat. If he can set up what I think you guys call a "straw man", he takes the heat off himself and buys some time."

"Yeah, go on, I follow," said Mike. "Time to do what, you think?"

"To plan his next move without having to look over his shoulder. Assuming that it *is* a setup, and that he's done it now and not after his previous hits, he must be planning something big."

All three looked at each other in horror.

"The 9/11 commemoration," said Paul.

"Perhaps, but I don't think he's a guy for the big symbolic statement. He has always gone for the easy target. By all accounts, it isn't gonna be easy up there. He's not political, just doing a job so no, I don't think so, unless he knows something about New York that none of you guys do."

They all suddenly looked up at the screen where the football had been interrupted for a news flash. The volume was raised as the newscaster announced, "Suspected assassin Wade Johnson, whom police arrested for a string of political killings one week ago and who has been refusing to speak to police, has today dramatically indicated his intention to change his plea to guilty of all charges. We now take you down town to the offices of Johnson's lawyer, Victor De Costa, who is about to make a statement."

You could hear a pin drop in the bar. The entire place watched with rapt attention. De Costa came to the bank of microphones. The smile was still in place but it didn't seem to be as wide or as beaming as heretofore.

"Ladies and gentlemen," he began. "My client, Wade Johnson has spoken with me again today. He has been under enormous pressure this past week and has pleaded his innocence. However,

351

he has told me today that he has now had qualms of conscience. The whole thing has become too much for him and he wants to admit his guilt to all the charges."

There was uproar and questions were fired from all sides. De Costa raised his arms and pleaded for quiet, explaining that he had not finished.

"I must at all times respect the wishes of my client, and therefore I intend to enter his plea of guilty when the matter next comes to hearing. I will make no further statement at this time."

The uproar continued but a cowed Senor De Costa walked away.

The announcer returned, "Well, dramatic news from down town this evening..." The TV returned to the football and everyone started to speak at once, except the three who were frozen in silence.

Mike eventually ventured "Well, that's sure blown our theory out of the water, hasn't it? We were chasing shadows after all. It just shows you never know, do you? So hey, come on you guys, not so despondent. Have a beer and celebrate. Well done."

They touched their glasses but there was a certain hollowness about their celebration.

In the Country Inn, Walker was sitting on the bed watching CNN. He had spent most of the previous evening surfing news websites trying to gauge the mood. Whether the manhunt had really been stood down and whether the police had really believed that they had got their man? Tonight, he kept switching round the various TV News Networks searching for similar indications. When the newsflash came through, he almost fell off the bed in shock. Fortunately, Katya was in the shower. He could hardly believe what he was hearing and the smile just kept getting broader on his face. When he saw the demeanour of the lawyer and compared it with the man's earlier broadcasts, he picked it up straight away. That was one scared dude, he thought.

"Thank you very much Mr Bahrain" he shouted, "you owed me that one. Way to go, yes!"

He even broke with his security routine and called room service.

"Hey, can we get a decent bottle of champagne up here please? Moet & Chandon will do fine, thank you ma'am."

Katya emerged from the shower with her long hair wet, wrapped in a skimpy towel.

"Hey what's this I hear about champagne?"

"It's coming right up baby, and you know something? Come right over here, my sweet girl. You look good enough to eat."

Chapter 35

Mike had spent a sleepless night trying to figure it out. The decision by Johnson to change his plea to guilty far from convinced him; in fact, if anything, it made him even more apprehensive and hardened his resolve. It just didn't fit. Somewhere, there was a mental pebble grating under a doorway and he couldn't let it go until he found where it was lodged.

Paul wasn't stupid either and they had all noted the changed demeanour of the lawyer the previous evening. As Johnson, or whatever he was calling himself this week was held in solitary, the inference had to be that someone had gotten to De Costa, who had presumably been instructed to tell his client that he was changing his plea. Their muted celebrations afterwards had told their own story.

The problem would be convincing everyone else of their reservations. The people at D.H.S., F.B.I., Capitol Police and elsewhere were as enthusiastic as *they* were but everyone liked a nice tidy ending and it looked like they had it.

Even if they could convince people of their fears that they might have gotten the wrong man, the problem was what to do next; Mike's "chasing shadows" theme kept recurring. If their hunch was correct, the assassin was too clever by half and he was planning something big; the problem was anticipating what it was and then taking measures to prevent it.

That was an awful lot of ifs to consider but nonetheless, Maria was sympathetic to their views when she met both men the following morning. The demands on the head of any police or indeed government law enforcement department are always great and never cease. For the head of D.H.S., multiply that by any number you like. Since the commencement of the War on Terror, each day brought its own new demands and concerns and suspicions and priorities. The United States was a hell of a big place and difficult to protect at the best of times. When most of your key staff had been employed full time on a major terrorist threat for two months, other areas were bound to suffer and you never knew where the next threat was going to come from. Maria's problem right now was her and her team's need to apply almost total concentration on the following week's commemoration in New York City.

That tied up Paul and most of his people but she was prepared to allow him stay involved with some of his team providing backup and Mike was going to continue to work it full time. Maria agreed to open doors for him as required. The question was which doors and where? As a first shot, all agreed that a trip to Ground Zero to check out any possible threat there was probably as good a place as any to start.

Trying to second-guess an assassin had proved impossible up to now. Trying to anticipate his next move when you weren't even sure he was out there was likely to prove even more difficult. But they had to try; and maybe he was going to attempt something in New York. If he did, it would certainly provide a huge coup for his employers and would seriously embarrass the country and its security forces.

After the previous night's champagne celebration, both of them had fallen asleep easily and Katya had slept late. But Walker had been up at 04.00 exploring possibilities, hacking websites, looking at potential opportunities, surveying locations and routes. The problem was that he had to more or less start from scratch. He had had a great opportunity fully researched and planned for a couple of days previously when, if everything had gone to plan – and it had – the police would have been thrown off guard and he would have been able to strike. Still, the Bahraini's intervention might extend his window.

For a while, he couldn't figure it out. He'd surfed two hundred websites and hacked half as many data bases. He was bone tired but he kept at it. Thoughts came and went and jumbled through his head. He was lost in his own world in cyberspace, his fingers floating over the keys at hyper speed. It was in there somewhere, he knew, and if he kept looking he'd find a way in.

The man could not stay locked up indefinitely. Everything was in cyberspace if you looked hard enough. He knew people were obsessed with recording things and writing things down. In the old days that meant reams of paper and hundreds of inaccessible notebooks and ledgers. But in the modern era it meant computers and computers were connected to databases and both were connected to telephones or data lines which were connected to the internet; so everything was potentially in cyberspace. No matter how secure an event was planned to be, some people *had* to be told in advance, and people recorded things everywhere; on their i-Phones, on their laptops, on Facebook and Twitter, they sent e-mails, they told friends and friends recorded things. The amount of communication out there was mind-boggling – and dangerous in the wrong hands. The trick was to find the information you needed in the vast web of cyberspace. You just had to look hard enough; but, of course, it helped knowing where to look.

Again, he forced himself to relax – he had time, what was the hurry? Perhaps if he lay low for a few months, the police would think they really did have their man and he could slip back into the game? But no, that had never been his way. Once he had a task, he had to see it through. His whole being wouldn't be able to relax until he did. Anyway, he *was* in the game, and no one had a clue who or where he was. But he wouldn't rush too much; he would be cautious; he would wait for his opportunity and it would come. It always did if you waited long enough.

Around 09.45, after almost six hours straight staring at the screen, he thought he had something – it was just a hint, but that was all he needed. A quick cross-check on scheduling, positioning and deployment on several other databases which he hacked into with consummate ease confirmed that he was on to something. Checks on other databases revealed more information and his excitement built ever further. Something out of the ordinary was going to happen next Tuesday; they just didn't say what, exactly, but that did not worry him. He had his start point and he was confident that with some fine-tuned searches, he would very soon have a reasonably good idea.

He next got a fix on location. Google Maps and Global Earth gave him ground detail and City Hall was kind enough to provide layouts of the buildings. Hmm; promising, he thought, checking out the angles; not ideal, but possible, and it didn't involve flying or driving half way across the country. Now, the crucial factor – time. Did he have enough? It was Monday morning. He had potentially eight days to plan; well no, realistically four or five. The area would probably go into shutdown mode over the weekend, or perhaps not. Either way, he had to assume he had five days maximum. It was plenty really. He had often had less time in foreign, far more hostile places and had accomplished his mission smoothly. This would be a bigger challenge, but he would adjust his plans accordingly.

By about 10.15, he felt he was ready. He downloaded what he needed to his printer, placed the plans and maps in order in the folder and gently woke Katya.

"Hey, morning sweetie, fancy some breakfast?"

She yawned and stretched and gave him that lovely satisfied smile.

"Nothing I'd like better. As you Americans say, I could eat a horse!"

They both showered and changed and hit McDonald's. They got take-outs and decided to eat on the go. Katya drove again and as soon as Walker finished his breakfast McMuffin and coffee, he fell fast asleep. He had set the sat-nav for her and asked her to wake him when they got to Pennsylvania Avenue.

She was as good as her word. He awoke, stretched and drank in the sunshine. It was a beautiful fall day in D.C. and he had a good feeling about this one. He asked her to pull in to the curb for a few moments.

"OK, I gotta take about an hour here to check something out. How good is your sense of direction?"

"Ah, I'd say not bad, I've been driving since I was about 14 and I'm a quick learner."

"Good, so can you drive around the city for an hour or so and familiarize yourself with some of the landmarks? It might be useful for later. Hold on and I'll tune the sat-nav to give you a sort of commentary on where you're going. If you get lost, no sweat, just keep driving and if you get completely lost, pull over and hit the reset button – it'll bring you right back here. You got it?"

"In one. See you in an hour."

"Hey, that's my girl, take it easy."

He spent the hour walking briskly, careful not to dwell or loiter or draw attention to himself. It was another beautiful sunny, day so the wraparound dark sunglasses were appropriate. He was very conscious that this entire area was teeming with high-resolution state-of-the-art digital video cameras so he was careful to play the tourist when it was appropriate, taking multiple shots when he could. It was unlikely that he would need them but he prided himself that his research had to be thorough. Katya returned after precisely one hour and he was glad of the cool air-conditioned interior after an hour in the hot midday sun.

"Where to now, boss?" she joked.

'Oh, I think we'll let Marcy decide. What do you think?"

"Ah, our satellite lady. Whatever you say."

Walker keyed in another destination and pressed start. The computerized voice in the system instructed them to drive for 400 yards and then to turn right. As they set off, Walker mounted a miniature video camera on the dash and asked Katya to drive slowly, at or just under the limit. He connected the camera up to his laptop and digitally recorded the route, at times changing the camera angle and at other times asking Katya to pull over while he panned the device around 180 degrees.

When they reached their destination, he asked her to drive back into the city by a different route, still videoing their progress. When they got to the city, he keyed in the destination again and they returned via an alternative route, again following the same procedure. Each journey took them almost half an hour. Once, when they reached their destination a third time, Walker got out and disappeared for an hour and asked Katya to get a take-out as they were both hungry. After eating, they returned for a fourth time by another alternative route, this time parking in a different lot with Walker again getting out to conduct further checks.

Eventually, satisfied with his day's work, he asked her if she was tired or if she was ok for the drive back to Richmond. She laughed at the thought of being tired and protested that she had been sitting on her ass all day! It was now just after 6pm and traffic was quite heavy on the capital beltway before they got back on 95. He tried to study his notes from the morning and his video footage but, exhausted from constant concentration, he eventually gave it up and slept all the way back to the Country Inn.

She nudged him awake gently when they arrived at the motel and he awoke with a start. "We're home" she said.

"Ah, sorry Katya, I haven't been good company."

She smiled again, that smile, and shook her head. "You are great company, my darling. You're here with me, that's all the company I need, all I'll ever need."

He kissed her tenderly. "Ok, we've been eating take-outs all day and I must stink from all that perspiring in that sunshine. Let's go shower, and you put one of those pretty dresses you got, and I'll take you out for a proper dinner."

"Sounds like a date. Give me half an hour."

They had dinner in "The Hard Shell", which was advertised as the best seafood restaurant in town. Walker would have to say that it certainly lived up its billing. They shared a mixed platter of oysters, clams, shrimp, mussels, crab legs, and lobster, and he ranked it with the best he'd had. They washed it all down with a Chablis Premier Cru. Katya raved about the place saying she had never eaten anywhere or anything remotely as nice.

"You've been through a tough life, dear, and you deserve to be pampered a little," he told her. "You stick close to me and you'll see lots of places like this, I guarantee it." She smiled then, a warm, genuine smile, and took his hand in hers. If she had any idea what he had been up to that day, she never said. In fact she made no comment whatsoever about the day. For all she cared or commented, he could be an engineer surveying the place for road works, but of course he wasn't and she surely knew that by now. She seemed to have a finely-honed instinct for knowing what he wanted to talk about and what was off-limits. It was almost as if she knew there was no point asking as he wouldn't be able to tell her anyway; or was it more than that? She was clever so did she know what he was up to now? But he'd been down that road already and was satisfied that whether she did or not, she'd be loyal.

Neither of them could handle dessert so they made a quick exit and were in bed sound asleep by 11.30. Walker had alerted her that the next day would be even busier.

-----

228 miles north, Mike and Paul were having steaks in Keen's on west 36th St in Manhattan. They had touched down in J.F.K. late in the afternoon and had had only a brief run thru of the planned security arrangements. They were due at Ground Zero at 08.00 the next morning to meet with the N.Y.P.D. and Paul's own local people. The city seemed relaxed and comfortable again, just as Mike had remembered it from many years before. As someone had said, the towers were gone but the spirit lived on. New Yorkers were a proud people, proud of their city and its heritage, but the wounds inflicted in September ten years previously had gone deep, tearing the heart out of the city and robbing it of thousands of its brightest and best people.

Paul had been assigned to the city briefly after the attacks and remembered a tough time. "Ah jeez Mike, it was weird, ya know? I mean, the world changed that day. For months afterwards the nation was on high alert. Many New Yorkers lived in fear. Life in this city, which had always been so vibrant, felt sad and strained. This was the place that had always claimed it had everything; all human life was here. But for many months, every time people heard sirens or a plane overhead it would send a jolt through them. I'm not saying people lived in fear, because New Yorkers would be too proud for that, but many people lived on high alert; maybe some still do and for some others, only the passage of years has helped the feeling to subside."

Mike nodded. "Yeah; well, I can imagine the very last thing they'd want is for something to ruin the anniversary, but from the overview of what we've seen this evening, that's highly unlikely."

"Yep, there's a huge construction boom in this city right now. It's stronger than it ever was and people are vigilant. It's almost as if they're saying, you can attack us once but you won't get away with it again. Crime is at an all time low and the civic spirit here is remarkable. It's like a model for other cities to follow. There's an enormous amount of empty or half-finished construction sites but every square inch of them will be searched time and again before the anniversary and you can bet every single vantage point will be manned on the day."

"So I guess it's a non starter for our man; that's if he's still out there, huh?"

"Well, you never know, but we'll see in the morning and make our plans then."

"Yep, I guess it's best to hold our fire for now."

Tuesday morning, Walker was on his laptop at 04.00 running some more checks on websites and databases to fine tune his search. He triangulated the information from a number of sources and was happy with the results. This was good to go, provided he put in some serious preparatory work and if the location suited. He had studied two potentials briefly the previous day. He would conduct more intensive research today.

He called Katya at 06.30 and they were both showered and in McDonald's drive-thru by 06.50, and on the highway by 07.00. He spent the journey reviewing the videos, sometimes discarding pieces, sometimes zooming in on key areas and all the while making copious notes. He began to feel the surge of confidence again. Every time he did this, he realized why he had never been caught – because he considered all the angles and covered all the bases, and then he covered them again. He felt he was almost like an artist at work on a fine painting. A delicate stroke here, a minor change there, gradually creating a masterpiece that would function perfectly. Although, in his world, it was unlikely that he would ever get the chance to stage an exhibition.

"You wanna go straight to yesterday's location?" Katya asked when they approached the city.

"Yep, park in the second lot we used yesterday, but if you like, go and explore down town again or go shopping, because I'm gonna be some time. I can call when I need you to collect me."

"Great, downtown here we come. You sure I can't be of any more help, though?"

"Katya, you are a fantastic help, believe me. If I had to do this on my own, it would take me twice as long; but no, everything is fine. All I need is a driver who's fresh and alert. I'll handle the rest."

"Ok, gotcha. See you later." And she was gone.

He noticed that Katya had made no comment whatsoever about the fact that his appearance had changed completely from the day before. Instead of a shirt and jeans, today he wore a dark navy three-piece suit, white button-down shirt and red tie. Yesterday's wraparound sunglasses had been discarded and replaced with slightly tinted traditional framed spectacles. Yesterday, he'd had about four day's beard growth. Today he was clean-shaven. Yesterday, his hair had been wild and poorly combed. Today his hair was slicked back and coiffed to perfection. While he wore no material disguise, to the casual observer, it was two different people. Today he would pass for a lawyer or a businessman. Yesterday he could have been mistaken for a blue-collar worker. He even affected a different gait; yesterday a casual slouching walk, today brisk and business-like.

He had taken his laptop in its case and he went for coffee at the coffee shop in the little strip mall on the corner. From there, he had a clear view of where he believed his target would be, and a view of two potential places from which to make the hit. What he could not see were the two other potential sites where his intended target would also likely be present.

He took his laptop off hibernate and called up the plans of the two buildings. One was a fairly standard sixteen-storey office block. The other was a commercial building with a builder's providers, a drug store and a pet shop on the ground floor, and associated offices on the second. The plans indicated that the remaining six floors were apartments that were entered through a courtyard with a locked entrance gate. He had already done a number of projections on the laptop using estimated heights to try to ascertain his lines of sight from various parts of the building to his target areas. The problem was that he was working with estimations and these would be no good on the day. He needed to be precise; needed to know exactly what vision he would have from each potential vantage point, and to achieve that, he had to gain entry to the buildings. Not a major difficulty under normal circumstances, but this was a long way from normal.

As far as he could see, there was security on the office block. In the other building, he couldn't just walk into one of the businesses and ask to go upstairs. Neither could he break into any of the apartments. First he had to gain access to the courtyard. Even if he managed that, then there may well be a concierge to be bypassed. Not impossible, and he had gained entry to far more heavily guarded installations in the past, but it was a problem to which he needed to work out the optimum solution nonetheless.

His first step was to Google the apartment building to see if it had any units for sale or to rent; no such luck. He then doubled-checked the websites of most of the city's main realtors to make sure that they didn't have a unit on offer. None of the commercial realtors was offering space in the office block either – maybe he was out of luck today?

He changed tack and checked the list of businesses in the office block. He came up with a lawyer's office on the third floor rented to an Ernest P Madison, dialled the number and asked if he could make an appointment for that afternoon? He could. Well, the appointment was for his mother, a Mrs Appleton; yes, Mrs Dorothy Appleton. A simple family matter needed to be attended to, and Mr Madison had come well recommended. The guy sounded like he could do with the business and readily agreed to a meeting at three p.m.

Next he called Katya's cell and gave her a precise list of items he wished her to purchase for him and where she should acquire them. He told her there was no hurry – she had three hours at least. It was still only 11.00.

He ordered more coffee and kept working his laptop. He was one of about a dozen others availing of the free Wi-Fi and the bottomless cup of coffee that the place advertised. He sipped his coffee and examined his options. He was into building No 1. That was good but he needed at least one alternative, perhaps two. There were other buildings down the street that offered possibilities but from his research, none of them offered views of all three target areas, and none of them appeared to have sufficient height.

On impulse, he decided to try something with the apartment block. Finishing his cup, he paid the waitress and tipped her and walked briskly out the door, waited for the light and walked across the street. He turned left and started to walk around the block. The courtyard to the apartments was reached through an alleyway that appeared to be a dead-end. He needed to survey the area on foot to ascertain if there was an alternative. He turned right and right again, now approaching the building from its rear, all the time keeping it in his line of sight. When he turned the first corner, he felt the pavement rise steeply, and realized he was on an incline. When he reached the second right turn, the ground levelled out again. The apartment building was still to his right but then he realized he was in luck.

There was a side entrance to the apartments, which, due to the sharp incline, accessed the building on either the second or third floor. There had to be, he thought. He had missed it on the plans presuming it to be a window. The courtyard entrance was downstairs and was accessed by vehicles, but surely not everyone in the building had a car?

He briskly walked up to the doorway and noticed his second piece of luck – no concierge. Well, it did look like a relatively low rent block. It being mid-morning, there was very little chance he could slip in as someone was exiting, so he scanned the list of doorbells, looking for what he hoped might either be single ladies or widows. He only chose apartments with even numbers as the plans had indicated that they were the ones that faced the street. He found a Ms. Crowe and a Mrs O'Sullivan. There were also a Mr and Mrs Hough and a Mr and Mrs Fletcher who might have potential.

He decided to try Ms Crowe first. There was no reply after three rings so he hit Mrs O'Sullivan.

"Hello, how can I help you?" A frail, kindly voice.

"Good morning ma'am, I'm in the neighbourhood today to talk to people about God. Would you have five or ten minutes to talk with me today?"

"Ah no, sure I know all about that, sonny, sure I'm a practicing Catholic. Ah no, sorry now but sure you'd be wasting your time on me."

"Of course ma'am, thank you ma'am and sorry for bothering you today."

"Ah, not at all son and the best of luck to you."

He next hit Mr & Mrs Fletcher. There were twenty other potentials but he didn't like the look of them; they were unlikely to suit his purpose today. He was running out of options here.

"Good morning ma'am, I'm sorry to bother you, but would you have ten minutes to talk about God with me today?"

There was a pause. He was aware that each apartment had a video link and that the lady was probably studying him so he smiled. It must have worked and he heard a buzz as the door opened.

"Sure, why not? Come on up, son, and we'll have some coffee anyway."

Her apartment was No 54, on the fifth floor and it had a perfect view of all three sites. The old lady was high up so she enjoyed the view and didn't bother with net curtains. He relaxed and spoke to her at length about the Lord and the Bible and how to save her soul. She spoke about her deceased husband and admitted that she worried because Walt hadn't always been the straightest, what with some of his business dealings and all. He stood up and asked her to talk about him in detail while he walked round and studied the view, pretending to look to the heavens for guidance while all the while working out angles and trajectories. At the same time, he tried to absorb what the old lady was talking about.

She spoke at length about Walt and despite the old man's failings, she had clearly loved him very much. He assured her that from what she had told him, he was positive that Walt had really been a good man at heart and that he was certain he would get his heavenly reward. That made her feel even better and she made him more coffee. In fact, she had made him several cups and would have talked to him all day. The lady was obviously lonely and he felt a small pang of guilt for using her as he had. Still, he seemed to make her day and when he eventually pleaded that he must leave to continue the Lord's work, she seemed most pleased and thanked him profusely.

During his walks round her apartment, he had at one stage surreptitiously taken what he assumed were her apartment keys and had taken a photo of each on his i-Phone. It might be difficult to get precise matches cut, but he'd get them done near enough to allow him to enter, or to be more precise, Katya would. The apartment setup was perfect. Now all he had to figure out was a way of getting the old dear out of the building and himself into it next Tuesday. It would be a shame if he had to harm her in any way. No doubt there would be security on the building but he'd find a way round that too. When he departed, she asked him to call again and he assured her genuinely that he would. A lot sooner than you think, ma'am, he thought.

He met Katya in the parking garage at two o'clock and collected the purchases. He had deliberately chosen this particular lot because he had noticed it had no security cameras. She made no comment while he efficiently transformed himself into Mrs Dorothy Appleton in less than fifteen minutes. The way he did the hair and applied the make-up did evoke a comment, however.

"You know, this is just, what do you say, unbelievable!" she laughed. "I mean, it is like being with a completely different person. How do you do this so well?"

He shrugged. "Years of practice, probably."

He dumped his laptop on the back seat, took the slightly used handbag she had brought, donned the horn rimmed glasses, and tottered off. He was wearing the sensible heels she had bought for him with the rest of the outfit in one of the second-hand charity shops. No point going in with all new clothes. Too likely to stand out and attract attention, or worse, suspicion.

Mrs Dorothy Appleton signed in at the security desk at 2.30. Her name was in the book and the assistant thanked her and told her she was in good time. Dorothy replied that at her age, time was plentiful so she wouldn't mind the wait.

She took the elevator to the third floor but did not go directly to Mr Madison's office. Instead, she took another elevator to the sixteenth floor. She worked her way back down again, catching glimpses of the street-facing offices as she passed those with either open doors or those that were glass-fronted. From what she could tell, the view was every bit as good up here. But there was no need to go to the sixteenth floor. The fifth would be fine and it had a vacant office with a flimsy door lock that could probably be opened with a paper clip. She wondered why it hadn't been advertised to let with any of the realtors. But not to worry, gaining access to the office would be easy once access was obtained to the building.

Dorothy then proceeded to Mr Madison's office where she gave him details about her situation and her concerns about her late husband's estate. She was troubled because well, her son was putting her under pressure; but no, her son was a good boy. It was that witch he had married that was causing all the trouble, forcing her boy to force his Mamma to hand over the estate. It wasn't fair. The estate was hers. She was an old lady and she had to take care of herself in her declining years, so she couldn't hand over control; what would Mr Madison advise?

He paused, seemingly giving the matter grave consideration. She could see from his expression that she was boring him to tears but he was polite and enquired gently as to the size of the estate. Dorothy informed him that she wasn't too sure. Well, there was the town property and the lake-side house, then her late husband's investments, but these had probably lost some value in that darn recession and anyway, she knew nothing of that side of things. He had always handled their finances.

She could see the dollar signs light up behind Madison's eyes as he suggested politely that perhaps she might like to retain him to go through it with her and to place a proper value on the estate. Oh now, that would be most kind she assured him. Wait, could she come to see him next Tuesday as she would be in the city again that day? With great disappointment, he informed her that he could not meet her on Tuesday as the building had to be vacated that day for "infrastructural repairs". Would Monday suit? No, unfortunately, the building was closed on Monday also.

He could meet her on Wednesday or even this coming Friday if that was OK? She checked her diary and assured him that Friday would do fine. Same time as today? Splendid; she assured him that she would bring all her documentation with her then and hopefully he could make some sense of it. He wisely didn't even mention the subject of his fee. The man thought he was in for the long haul on this one. How wrong he was!

Dorothy thanked the man profusely and assured him that she would be fine getting downstairs. No, she didn't need a cab, her daughter-in-law was collecting her. She winked at Madison as she said this and he winked back. Clever old bird after all, he thought.

That was it; he had an in – to both places. He might have to spend the weekend in the office block, but that was a minor detail. Right now it was a question of deciding the optimum position. He had taken numerous shots on his i-Phone from both buildings and would feed them into the laptop later. Right now, he was exhausted and just needed to chill. He flopped into the passenger seat of the Camry and asked her to just drive.

"Katya, I really don't know what I'd do without you, thanks again. Head for Richmond please, I'm gonna chill. Maybe find a service stop along the way where I can resume being a male again."

She giggled. "You just relax, your super driver is here."

It had been a good day and he had achieved more than he had expected. Still, having accomplished phase one, gaining access, his problems were only starting. While the place might be relatively deserted now, it would be thoroughly checked over the next few days, and come next Tuesday, it would be crawling with security personnel. But that was a problem for tomorrow. Right now, he'd enjoy today. Within minutes he was sound asleep.

Chapter 36

Wednesday morning would be spent rechecking, revalidating, recalculating. He would go over everything in minute detail, reviewing each location, entrances, exits, alternative routes, backups. He'd look at every relevant section of video over and over again. He would play the entire drama over and over in his mind. Then he'd disassemble it, reassemble it, adjust it, make contingency plans, and run through the entire thing again. He'd compile a list of what he required right down to the finest detail.

After three hours, he was more comfortable; he felt he had a grasp of how it would play. He had originally thought the timescale might be too tight but after his detailed research – both manual and electronic – during the previous days, he was confident that time would not be an issue. Anyway, he felt he had to take the chance – he had to strike when the opportunity presented itself. He might not get another one as good as this for weeks, and who knew what would happen in the meantime? He had been reasonably lucky so far; some dead ends, but he had caught a few breaks also, and he was well on schedule. The final plan would not involve luck and would leave nothing to chance.

He still didn't have a precise fix on timing and it was unlikely that he would get it. People might be quietly informed about a visit, but timing was always a last minute arrangement. No one would know, probably not even the man himself. The minders would have the final say there. Still, if he was in place well ahead of schedule, he could wait. He was good at waiting; he'd been doing it for most of his life. He considered the possibility that the whole visit might be cancelled at the last minute due to some crisis but that was a risk you took. If it was, it would be back to square one next week, or the week after, or whenever he could pick up another lead.

He had decided they would not go to D.C. today. He needed to play everything out in his mind many more times yet and he needed peace and quiet for that. Besides, turning up in the same place in the same car three days running was probably pushing it, even if he had looked completely different on the first two days. He was half beginning to regret not bringing Katya's rental but on reflection it might have just complicated things. For a start he would have had to drive one of the vehicles and while he normally loved driving, he needed the travel time to study and plan and most importantly of all, to think.

He had been formulating the germ of a plan in his mind for a little while and thought it was worth a try. But for this he needed Katya. He had hardly spoken to her since the previous evening but she knew he needed to concentrate so it had not been a problem.

He suddenly surprised her by looking up and asking, "How are your acting skills, baby?"

"Well," she pouted, "it depends on who's asking me, and what role I'm required to play; but I'd say pretty good."

He laughed. "No, not that sort of acting, you little devil, I mean straight acting." He gave her a telephone number he had acquired from the normal online directory service, and a list of instructions, almost a script, which he had already prepared and printed for her.

"OK, seems straightforward enough. Can you give me a few minutes to familiarize myself with it?"

"For sure, take all the time you need."

After a few minutes, she was ready. He dialled the number on the computer and they both listened on speaker.

Katya began, "Hi there, is that Mrs Fletcher? I hope you don't mind me calling you today? My name is Cathy and I represent a company called Super Save Supermarkets. You may have heard our advertisements – we call ourselves the SSS, providing super service for shoppers everywhere. Firstly, I wanna say, this is a genuine market research call and we got your number from the phone book. Would you have a few minutes to speak to us today and maybe answer some market research questions?"

"Why sure honey, you go right ahead, I got all the time you need."

"Gee, that's great, ma'am. Well today we're cold calling people to check out if it would be worthwhile opening an outlet in your area, so I just need to ask you a few questions about your current grocery shopping habits; is that OK?"

"Go right ahead, honey."

Katya then ran through the list of pre-prepared questions, such as where did the lady usually shop – in small shops or supermarkets? What was her average spend? Which was more important to her, quality or price? Would she consider changing to SSS if they were located close to her and could guarantee quality of service and good value? Etc. The lady gave long, thoughtful, detailed answers and seemed prepared to stay on the phone for as long as Katya wished. He had read her correctly – a kind but lonely old lady. Katya finished the questionnaire and thanked Mrs Fletcher profusely.

"Well Mrs Fletcher, that seems to be all. Thank you so much for being so helpful to us today."

"Why, not at all, honey."

"Oh, and one more thing, Mrs Fletcher. Not everyone whom we call is as cooperative as you, so we offer a little incentive to people. Every person who participates in our survey gets entered into our Super Savers Draw for two tickets for a week's holiday in the Caribbean."

"Why, that's very kind of you honey, thank you very much."

"No, thank *you*, ma'am. Now we've got about fifty girls making calls so there's gonna be a lot of folks in that draw but you've got as good a chance as any, so thanks again and the very best of luck."

Walker again felt a small twinge of guilt at deceiving the old lady but he could not stop himself from bursting out laughing.

"Jesus babe, you were brilliant. You're a natural born actress."

"Hey, come on, it was only a phone call."

"But it was so bloody good, I almost believed it myself."

"Ok, I'm just glad I can help you, even in a small way."

371

"Oh, you've been a big help Katya, believe me, and I can assure you, there's no aspect of this one that's small."

He had decided that they would move today. Impersonal or not, any more than three days at a remote motel might just attract attention. Again, the risk was slight but it was as easy to move a bit further on up the highway. It would also cut down on travel time to the city. He had asked Katya to get him a take-out breakfast and to pack the few things he had brought with him. He also assigned her the task of finding an alternative motel nearer to D.C. and to drive them there. She enthusiastically set about her tasks and again seemed pleased to have something to do and to be able to help. It appeared to be in her nature to help people, particularly if they were kind to her.

She was packed and ready to roll by 11.00. They had prepaid for the room and had paid for any room service as it came so there was no need to check out. She packed everything into the Camry and told him they were ready to go. His only contribution to the preparations, apart from taking a shower, was to unplug his laptop, carry it to the automobile and plug it into the car's power output point. She let him be as he continued with his work.

After less than an hour, she pulled off the highway and parked. He had been concentrating so hard he had barely noticed their progress. He did a double-take as he initially thought they were back where they had started. Then he saw the location sign over the door and realized that Katya had chosen another, almost identical Country Inn, but this one was in Woodbridge, right on the outskirts of D.C. He had asked her to pick a place which would again be anonymous but where they might be able to spend a little longer than three days. This was perfect as they would just seem like a normal couple visiting D.C on a budget and staying in the outskirts where the hotels were just as good but the rates were more reasonable.

They had spent Tuesday at Ground Zero being briefed on the security arrangements for the following Sunday. Incredible precautions were being taken. Mike felt Paul's initial comment was right on the money: not even a mouse could get through and to even try, he would have to be a very brave mouse.

Yet he could not help feeling they were missing something. He sometimes had a sixth sense for this type of stuff and he had this strong perception that they were looking in the wrong place. He remembered back in the UK that many times when they were following up leads, the answers were often in the exact opposite place from where they were looking. If you were dealing with ordinary thugs, it was one thing, but when you were dealing with terrorists, they were usually intelligent, whether they were believers or mercenaries. They all tried to think one or two steps ahead of the authorities, so you had to constantly try to visualize where they would go next or what they would attempt.

As they used say in MI5, the Irishman had a nose for it, or a sort of sixth sense. A lot of police work was drudgery, checking and rechecking, following up on potential leads, chasing tips, seeking linkages but there was often a need too for inspiration – to make that quantum leap, to think outside the box or, as in this case, to get inside the mind of the killer.

He had, at this stage, more or less dropped all pretence that the poor sucker in custody back in D.C. was their man. Yes, he was probably linked to the terrorist movement, and he was possibly a sleeper, and he may have been planning all sorts of mayhem, but Mike could just not see him for the assassinations of the past two months. No, there was another guy out there and he was planning something; he knew; he could feel it; he could sense it; but what or where was the baffling part.

He was able to relax but he was still a deep thinker. It was no great leap to think that the assassin might have a go at the President, but it was unlikely. The last U.S. President to be shot was Ronald Reagan, gunned down in the street along with several of his advisers outside the Washington Hilton by John Hinckley in 1981, when he had only been President for 69 days. Despite his advanced years, Reagan survived the attack, even famously giving an interview on a stretcher on the way to hospital where he had quipped, "Who's minding the store?" Hinckley had been declared insane but subsequent information came to light showing that he had gotten close to the former President Jimmy Carter on a number of occasions.

This seriously embarrassed the authorities and prompted a complete review of security. It had always been tight but now it was totally nailed down like never before. You just didn't get near the President any more. Everyone who met the man would have been thoroughly vetted. When he travelled, it was in an armoured limousine, and there were usually a few of them so an assassin might have to take out three cars and even then he wouldn't be sure if he had succeeded. The man might not be in any of them. When the President appeared in public, there were rarely press releases beforehand unless it was a big event that everyone knew about. Other appearances, while they might have been planned for weeks or months, were only confirmed at the last minute and timing was never verified in advance. There were no lines of greeters shepherded behind rope lines, like in Reagan's time; or were there?

But wait, this was the official line, wasn't it? This was what the White House and the Secret Service wanted people to believe. Was the truth different? During the lunch break, he had a few minutes and decided to do some research. He started to look at where the President had been over the previous four months. Christ, he'd been around a hell of a lot. He supposed elected politicians were no different the world over. Jesus, the man had even been to Ireland and had drunk beer in a bar with the locals! Surely they couldn't have checked out all the patrons or verified their neutrality? And then there had been street walkabouts and public speeches on podiums.

OK, the Secret Service did ensure every access point was thoroughly checked; even going so far as to order that all the sewer and other manhole or access covers in the vicinity were welded shut. They inspected all buildings within firing range of where the President was appearing, and they positioned their own men on the rooftops of those buildings during the visit. But was a lot of this cosmetic or done for effect? He didn't think so, but ultimately there was no such thing as total security. The man was democratically elected and he had to show his face to his electorate on a regular basis, particularly when he was up for re-election in just over twelve months. This was what kept the Secret Service men and women and people like Maria Gonzalez awake at night. Apart from political attacks or possible assassination attempts by terrorists, there were thousands, maybe tens of thousands, of looneys out there. Most were harmless. A few, like John Hinckley or Mark David Chapman, were not.

"I guess we're more or less all done here," said Paul, thanking the N.Y.P.D. personnel and his own guys. "You OK with this, buddy?" he said to Mike.

"Yep, I think the guys have it locked down tight. I don't want to tempt fate by saying it, but this is as secure a set-up as I've ever seen so I don't think you'll have any problems here."

"That's sure kind of you to say, sir, and thank you for your advice," responded John Cranfield, a senior analyst with the N.Y.P.D.

"You're welcome, and you all have a good day on Sunday."

They were driven back to J.F.K. and caught the shuttle back to Washington.

"I don't think we've got anything to worry about up here," said Paul. "Maria's just come back to tell me we've stood down on those guys we were monitoring for now. Oh, don't worry, we're gonna keep them under observation, but our people think their current capability is pretty much nil. They seem to be just agitators or talkers. That, America can handle. Lord knows we've got plenty of 'em. It's the doers we gotta worry about. Hey, I'm beat. You mind if I catch some shut-eye on the way back?"

"Sure man, you go right ahead."

As Paul dozed, Mike booted up his laptop again and revisited some of the stuff he had downloaded on Presidential visits, walkabouts and the general security surrounding them. Now, if I were a hit man, he thought, would I want to go up against that lot? Certainly not, but could I find a way around them? Possibly, but he needed to look at it from a practical point of view. You could only learn so much from a website.

They landed in Ronald Reagan on time, and were picked up and driven to the city. Paul wanted to collect his own car to drive home and Mike was meeting Wendy for dinner. As they drove, Mike ventured, "Look, you know how I feel about this thing; it's like a bug I can't shake. I'm really no good to you here right now but I need to ask you a favour; a big one."

375

Paul shrugged. "Just name it, buddy."

"Could you get me on to the President's security detail? Just as an observer, or an adviser or whatever term is expedient?"

Paul whistled. "Phew, that is a big one. Straight answer is, I couldn't do it, but Maria might be able to. You really think our boy is gonna take a shot at the top man?"

"To be honest, I don't know what I think. He may even be playing us or playing me, but I don't think he set that guy up just for fun and I can't think of anyone bigger he'd be planning to take a run at."

"Yeah. You know, you're right, but the man is fully protected, locked down tight, or so the Secret Service boys tell us." He could see Mike's raised eyebrows. "You think different, huh? Yeah, you could be right. A lot of that is just sort of inter-agency banter, and I mean they have lost Presidents and had them shot at before."

"Look Paul, as I said, I don't know what I think right now. I mean, there are a dozen, two dozen other prominent people he could take a shot at and we'd have no warning but if he is planning on the big one at some stage, he may not have a better time to do it than right now. Plus, I know this may sound crazy but I've got a sort of a hunch, a feeling, call it what you will. Guys back in London used to call it a nose for trouble."

"Yeah, you're right man; Jesus, the more I think about this. Look, I've been so caught up in this thing and then going straight to the New York issue that maybe I can't see the wood for the trees. Let me talk to Maria. I'm sure she'll still be there when I get to the office, and I'll see what I can set up. Let me call you on your cell later, OK?"

"You got it."

There was a noticeable change in atmosphere in D.C. There probably was elsewhere too. He'd spoken to Alan yesterday and he'd told him a lot of the tension had lifted in the UK. also. Mike had been circumspect, and had not revealed his suspicions about the suspect being held in custody, but Alan had gleaned enough from his tone to realize that the scare was not over. Yet the media were saying it was, and that was where 90% of people took their cue.

Perhaps it was best. The economies of the western countries that had been under attack had been shaky enough beforehand, and the fear generated by the assassinations had reduced economic activity even further. People were not spending money or going out to enjoy themselves as much; or in some areas, not at all. Many were obsessed with what had been happening, and the News Networks, which would normally be only briefly scanned, had been watched 24/7 for the latest developments. He shuddered to think what the impact might be if the assassin struck again, regardless of whom the target was, and people suddenly realized the threat had not been neutralized at all.

He met Wendy in Stetson's again and gave her a brief overview of what had gone down in New York and how he'd been thinking. He was verbalizing it in his own logical way when he realized that there were tears in her eyes. He took her in his arms and held her close.

"Oh honey," she began, "I've spent my entire life looking for someone like you. Look, I know it's your way and I wouldn't ever want to try to change that but will you please, please, just for me, promise to be careful."

He held her close again and promised that he would. It was the first time he had seen tears in the eyes of his bright, smiling, beautiful, happy girl, and the fact that they were for him almost broke his heart.

At precisely the same time, at the Country Inn in Woodbridge, Walker took a break from his constant studying of his maps, notes and the data on his computer.

"Hey Katya, I think it's time we called Mrs Fletcher again and gave her the good news," he said.

"Coming right up". Katya came to the computer and he dialled the number again.

"Hi, is that Mrs Fletcher?"

"Yes, who is this?"

"Oh hi, Mrs Fletcher, this is Cathy here from SSS. Remember we spoke earlier when I did the survey with you?"

"I sure do honey, I thought it sounded like you."

"Well, Mrs Fletcher, brace yourself now because the good news is that you are the winner of our fabulous prize of a week's holiday in the Caribbean."

"Oh my Lord, oh honey, thank you so much, this is really wonderful, what do I need to do?"

"Well, not a lot ma'am, but first we need your full name, and we need to verify that you and your travelling companion have current valid passports."

"Oh Lord, my travel companion, of course; why, that will be my sister Iris. I've only got one sister and she loves travel. Oh, this is so exciting. Oh and my full name is Thelma Fletcher."

"OK ma'am, can you get the numbers of your own and your sister's passports, and I'll call you back for them in say twenty minutes?"

"Certainly I will, and you sure can, honey; sorry, I mean Cathy.

'Thank you, Mrs Fletcher. So, just to confirm: you and your sister will be collected by limousine and brought to Reagan International. From there you'll fly to Barbados where you'll stay for a week at the Sandy Lane resort with everything paid for and that includes all meals, drinks and use of all facilities. In addition, we are gonna give you $5,000 in spending money.

"Oh my word, I've never won anything in my life before. This is just fantastic. Thank you so much Cathy. I'll go get the passport numbers now."

"That's great, ma'am. Oh, just one thing; the holiday is pre-booked from this weekend, so will you be ready to travel this coming Friday?"

"Are you joking, honey? That gives me two whole days to pack. For a prize like that, I'd go tonight if I was asked."

"That's great, ma'am, call you back in twenty."

Walker hugged Katya and punched the air with delight – he was in! It was Wednesday evening.

Chapter 37

Mike's cell phone buzzed as he was taking a giant bite out of his burger. He saw from the digital display that it was Paul.

"Hi, hold a second, man," he said through a mouthful of ground beef.

"Right buddy, here's the deal. First of all, Maria shares your concern and is really appreciative about this, so here's what she's arranged: tomorrow morning at 08.00, you go to an address on Pennsylvania Avenue, I'll text you the precise details. You're meeting a guy called Trent Jackson. He's a big guy but he doesn't bite. Now he's also a good friend of mine so give him my best. He's Secret Service and he's in charge of the top man's detail for the next week. He's been told to facilitate you in any way possible and he's aware of your background and your concerns on this, ok?"

"Perfect, just perfect; I really appreciate it"

"No sweat man, you've already been fantastic on this and we really appreciate what you're doing. You know, depending on what gives here or what you come up with, I might just be joining you later."

"Ok, thanks again Paul, I'll be in touch."

He checked his watch. It was only a quarter to eight.

"Right, Paul's arranged it so don't worry about me. I'll be in good hands. Anyway, I'm never really in the front line on these things and from tomorrow, I'll be in these guy's hands just as a strategist or an adviser."

"Yeah right," she said. "Adviser my ass. I know you, Mr Lyons, and I know what you'll do and won't do."

"Wendy, I'll only do what I have to do. I mean, there's gonna be maybe a hundred or two hundred guys in the detail so don't worry."

"Ah, yeah; ok, sorry. Look, I know you'll be fine, but you know?"

He held her close. 'Yeah, I know; me too."

Early on Thursday morning, he met up with Trent Jackson. He arrived armed with two large Styrofoam mugs of coffee and offered Trent one as an introduction.

"I like your style, man. I was just about to get some from the canteen but their coffee sucks. This is good stuff."

Mike immediately knew what Paul had meant when he said that Trent didn't bite. He was a huge man, at least six feet, seven inches, maybe a bit more and was built like a tank. He was African-American and he reminded Mike of a tall actor whose name he couldn't quite recall at that time of the morning. Trent had a ready smile that showed flashing white teeth, and where Mike came from, he would have been classed as one handsome dude. He closed the door and dropped into the seat behind his desk. He must have been over three hundred pounds, but Mike could not detect an ounce of fat on his frame.

"Have a seat man and I'll run through where we're at with you. Maria gave me the heads-up on where you've been at with the investigation, and she says you feel there might still be a threat, particularly to our man?"

"Well, it's like this, Trent," Mike began. He ran through the events of the previous two months in detail, down to his concerns about the "straw man" and why he might have been set up. Trent listened intently, not interrupting but making an occasional note on a legal pad on his desk. When Mike finished, he was silent for a time and sat back, sipping his coffee, thinking, and running through the scenario in his mind. When he eventually spoke, it was with his mighty brow furrowed.

"You know, Mike," he began, "that's a hell of a story, and you're absolutely right to bring your concerns to us. We probably get a hundred threats a day to the Commander in Chief. Now, most of these are just cranks, but we do occasionally get a serious one which forces us to act. Sometimes we call in our other colleagues in D.H.S. but this time they are already on the case. I gotta say, though, that this is about the most serious threat I've heard for some time. The problem is, what the hell can we do about it? I mean, how do you anticipate what a guy like that is likely to attempt and when?"

Mike thought before he replied. "Well, I don't wish to be negative, so I'm not going to suggest we keep the man under wraps, although that's what the French and the British did with their leaders after they had been attacked."

"Oh man, you know if I had my way, he'd never leave that big house across the street." Trent chuckled. "But unfortunately it doesn't work like that. This is America, the greatest democracy on earth, and the people want to see their leader."

"Yeah, I understand, but is there any way we can sort of announce he's gonna appear somewhere but then withdraw him at the last moment, or divert him to appear elsewhere? It might force our man to show his hand."

"Oh sure we can, in fact we do that all the time. If there's a realistic threat, we cancel. If there's a potential threat, we relocate or reschedule or change the route. The programme we give out ahead to participants ain't always the one we follow and sometimes the man himself doesn't know until the last minute but he never complains. In fact, he's very appreciative of what we do and never causes us trouble. I mean, the man can take advice."

"OK, great, it's good to know we've got some flexibility. I mean, I've no intention of changing anything or even recommending changes right now. I just want to make sure we're all on the same page here."

Trent sighed. "Oh, we are, man, we are, but even with the best will, there are some things that we can't change and we just gotta muddle through with and hope for the best. I know that may sound like heresy but it's the truth. No one can be protected all the time unless you lock them away in a box. And right now, we've got a particular problem. Next year is re-election time and the man is under pressure in the polls. He's also being criticized from all sides. I mean, I've protected four Presidents, and I ain't just saying this because he's of my race, but I've never seen such

381

attacks on this office holder before. The things he's been accused of are unreal. I mean, from day one, he's been subjected to intense scrutiny and criticism on everything he does. No allowance was made for the fact that our country was on its knees economically when he took over. Our standing in the international community was at an all time low because of our involvement in various seemingly futile wars. Now, look at where America stands today compared to three years ago. Anyway, sorry for going on. You've probably guessed I'm not just his minder but his biggest fan." Trent laughed loudly, but there was truth in what he said, and he passionately believed in it. Mike liked this guy; he felt he could do business with him, felt a kindred spirit.

"You know, Trent," he began, "I gotta agree with you. But all we can do is try to keep him safe. Getting re-elected is his problem. I guess I understand now, though, why he's been out in public so often, meeting people, pressing the flesh. Even if he wanted to, which I'm sure he doesn't, he couldn't lock himself away and just come out when guys like us deemed it safe."

"You got it spot on, man. That ain't the American way and never will be – fine for tin-pot dictatorships but not in a democracy, no sir."

"Right. So can we look at what he's got planned until say, the end of next week?"

"For sure, but you gotta understand, this can change and there's some locations or appearances I may not be able to tell you about yet; but don't worry, you'll know in good time." He swivelled his computer mouse and double-clicked on the icon marked "away games."

It had only taken Walker five minutes on the computer to arrange the holiday the previous evening. He had already pre-booked the flights and the accommodation at Sandy Lane in anticipation so all he had to do was confirm the reservations. He booked the limousine pickup for 5.30 on Friday evening. Katya would call beforehand with the air tickets, the hotel vouchers and the spending money. Mrs Fletcher's sister would already be at her apartment so both ladies would be collected together.

He hoped that the lady had no other relatives or friends whom she would ask to keep an eye on her apartment. Just to be absolutely sure, he had Katya ask her about this when she called back for the passport information and had enquired if she needed someone to feed a pet or to take care of the place. Mrs Fletcher had said that they were very kind to ask but she had no need. Neither was she worried about a break-in as the apartment was on the fifth floor and there was good security on the building.

On Thursday morning, he asked Katya to drive him back to the location to complete his final preliminary checks. He was dressed down completely again, wearing jeans and sneakers and an old "make love – not war" T-shirt. He wore a large string of beads around his neck and affected a dark brown wig, braided at the sides and decorated with cheap jewellery. He looked every inch the ageing hippy and about as different from his Tuesday persona as it was possible to be. He put away the laptop this time as she drove. It was only a short distance and he wanted to go over everything again in his mind.

He would have from Friday evening until Tuesday morning in Mrs Fletcher's apartment to set up, rehearse his moves, and go over them again and again. He already knew the area like the back of his hand; he knew every route in and every route out. He couldn't be sure which streets would be closed off, but he was taking no chances; he would have Katya meet him in a safe place where he would be certain traffic would be moving normally. He was familiar with the building layout, but by Tuesday, he would know every door, window and broom cupboard in it. He would have three full days to work out his optimum shooting angles. It was almost too easy so he would go over everything again until he could do it blindfolded. There would be lots of police and security and there would only be one of him but that would not be a problem. He would be invisible. He would be well away before they had even figured out where the gunshots had come from. He needed an edge and he had it!

He couldn't believe his luck. Perhaps it was payback for the unfortunate encounter with John Slaughter's Buick. Jesus; he had been out for five days. What the hell, he'd survived. He had probably had hits where he was in position for longer periods in advance of the mission, but right now, he couldn't recall any. There would be security personnel crawling all over the place from the weekend but he didn't anticipate them being a problem. It would have been nice to still have the option of the other building as a backup but as he could not be in two places at once, he decided to burn his boats there and go with Mrs Fletcher's apartment only. He, or rather Dorothy, wouldn't therefore be keeping the appointment with the lawyer on Friday afternoon.

He needed to cover his bases so he took out his iPhone and made a brief call to Mr Madison explaining that his Mother had unfortunately been taken ill and would have to cancel her appointment on Friday. No, she didn't wish to reschedule just then but she would be sure to call Mr Madison just as soon as she felt better. He thanked the lawyer politely and hung up.

Katya dropped him off today three blocks from the location and headed back into the city. She would collect him later three blocks in the other direction. Today, Thursday, would be his walking day. He would carry out his final optical check of the area, the roads in and out, the exits, the entrances, the streets, roads, alleys and the sidewalks. He walked the routes that he would use on foot and committed them to memory. Then he chose alternates. He noted where the traffic lights were and memorized their sequences. He stepped the walking distances and recorded, then memorized them. He probably already knew all of them by heart from his detailed studies of the large-scale maps of the area, but he needed to be certain. He carried a shoulder bag and if anyone had stopped or queried him, he had a supply of flyers printed up advertising a series of upcoming concerts by obscure bands. It was all legitimate and he had checked it out thoroughly on the web. In the event, no one bothered him and he didn't need to hand out a single flyer. He even managed a coffee and a cupcake at the coffee shop on the opposite corner to where he would be situated, to consider it from that angle. No one gave him a second look.

After five hours of walking and often retracing his steps, he was content. He strolled to where he had agreed to meet Katya and she arrived right on time, not before, not after. That's my girl, he thought. Once again, he didn't bother with the laptop. He just sat quietly and closed his eyes, absorbing everything into his mind, surveying mental pictures, then filing them away. He concentrated until they reached the hotel. Then he smiled at her and she knew he was happy. He was ready to roll.

They looked at the schedule for the next ten days and tried to assess potential weak points, where there might be an exposure. Trent regarded the schedule and began.

"OK, we've got no movement until New York on Sunday, but you reckon that's locked down water tight. Monday he's meeting Arabs and Israelis to check progress in the peace talks; that is, if there is any," he added cynically. "Afterwards, we've got a news conference on the Middle East talks to be held on the White House lawn, weather permitting. You don't suppose our man's got himself a White House Press Pass, do you? I mean, I've heard guys say they're scarcer than hen's teeth. Other guys say things a lot worse." He roared with laughter again.

"OK, I guess we can forget about Monday. What we got Tuesday? Oh yeah, the schools."

"Right; look, this is under the heading of 'stuff you gotta do' or stuff you gotta be seen to be doing in election year. It's a sort of back-to-school thing. He's presenting prizes to students who were best in class last term. Great publicity shots, beautiful kids, multi-racial model school."

Mike's senses visibly heightened.

"Hey, don't worry. I guess we can discount the pupils as they're little kids huh? Now, every teacher and every worker of any description who's gonna get within fifty yards of the man has had their backgrounds checked back through three generations. All right, I'm joking, but they're all clean as a whistle. Any black marks at all, or even suspected marks – they're out; don't get to meet the man."

"OK. Where's the school located? And hey, looks like there's more than one school. What's the idea?"

"OK; well, the school is in Laurel, which is basically an outer suburb of D.C. It's a short trip up 295. There's really only one school, but it's sort of divided in three parts. We've got elementary school for really little kids, then we've got Middle

School or Junior High for slightly bigger ones, and then we've got High School for teenagers. It's all basically the same complex, but two of the sections are on opposite ends of the block and the High School is across the street.

"OK, and he's gonna use the limo to travel between the different sections?"

"That's the plan, although you never know. I mean, if it's a sunny day, he may walk; but don't worry, we've got it covered. There are, let me see, two high buildings in the area, but unless you're very good, they're out of range."

"Trent, our man *is* very good. I hate to say it but he's outstanding."

Trent raised his hands. "Sorry. Yes, I know, I know, but look here. We ain't taking chances. All buildings have already been thoroughly searched and will be again on the day. The buildings will be patrolled during the visit and all non-essential staff will be evacuated. All personnel in the office block have been given two days off. Traffic will be stopped for four blocks in all directions."

"Is there not any way we can cut it down to one location and bring all the kids together for the presentation?"

"Possibly, but the PR folks want as many photo opportunities as possible. It really don't make much difference anyway in that the man is gonna be exposed for the same amount of time. It might even be better if he keeps moving?"

"Yeah, maybe you're right. I might take a run out there over the weekend if that's alright?"

"Absolutely, whatever you want. Sorry, let's look at Friday." Trent groaned. "Shit, I know, I know, this one has risk written all over it, but." He spread his arms.

"I appreciate the man doesn't do things without having a good reason, but does he have to play golf, and does he have to play at *that* course? Sorry, I'm not getting at you Trent. I guess this has been looked at?"

"You got that right. Ah, look, it's a veteran's thing. Very important to show solidarity with the troops, particularly right now when he's under attack from all shades of right-wingers."

"But why play golf with them?"

"There'll be a lot of influential people there, Mike. Ah, look, I know the place is big and exposed but it will be crawling with both civil and military security and we'll be watching the angles."

"Yeah, presume you've noticed the number of high buildings overlooking the area. Same procedure as at Laurel, yeah?"

"You got it. We'll need a lot more personnel but we can't take chances."

"Right, so when you guys are down in The Big Apple this weekend, I'll take a look at both locations if that's alright?"

"For sure, we'd love you to. You've got my driver at your disposal from tonight and he'll take you anywhere you wanna go and get you access when you get there. Anything you wanna comment on, feel free. If we can make it more secure, we'll do it. If you consider something too risky, we'll promise to look at it."

"Excellent, sounds like a plan. Pleasure dealing with you, Trent. You have yourself a good weekend down there."

He raised his eyebrows. "Yeah, right. You too, man, mind how you go."

She knew by now that they would be apart for a few days. He was planning on taking over Mrs Fletcher's and she guessed she would be staying on at the motel even though he hadn't said. He apologized for neglecting her over the previous few days as he had been very busy. In fact, he had been concentrating so intensely that they had hardly spoken, but she hadn't complained.

Tonight he took her to dinner at Dixie Bones Barbeque. They ate ribs with baked potatoes, washed down with beer. It was a real down-home place, with local bluegrass music playing in the background, and she absolutely loved it. They ate pecan pie for dessert, had more beers, and then struggled back to the motel where they made love long into the night.

Chapter 38

Many of the team had been in position all weekend, casually dressed and quietly blending in with the surroundings. The stereotypical image of Secret Service personnel in black suits with dark glasses and earpieces, speaking into the cuffs of their jackets, didn't always hold true. The modern-day agent dressed as appropriate for the occasion. The guys in the suits were the visible image of the Service, appearing when the President, or one of the numerous other American dignitaries or visiting foreign heads of state that they protected, had a public engagement. But there were thousands of other personnel who did the back-up work; checking the layouts, clearing the ground, making the environment safe in advance of what was usually a brief appearance. Planning could go on for weeks, or sometimes months, if it was a foreign engagement. It involved numerous meetings with local law enforcement, civic groups, business people and ordinary citizens, and basically anyone who was in any way connected or discommoded, or just needed to be informed. Much of the work was routine and was done unseen, but none of the people doing it were under the slightest illusion that their task wasn't important. On the contrary, they were aware that it was vital to the security of their nation and its Commander in Chief.

They walked and ran and jogged the area all weekend and most didn't even attract a second look. It was a heavily populated area and to the casual observer, they were just folks out enjoying their weekend. But they were watchful all the while, trying to pick up any evidence of unusual activity; something that just might be out of place, something that had been moved, something that didn't fit, something that was there that should not have been. They had all studied high-resolution maps and photographs of the area in advance so they knew what to look for.

They found nothing. Everything was as it should have been. All the sewer and communications access points had been welded shut the week before, and would be double-checked ahead of Tuesday. Access to all roofs in the area was sealed and would only be accessible to their own officers on the day.

In addition to the jeans and sneakers brigade, a very visible team had checked out every room in every building for two city blocks in each direction. Particular attention had been paid to the higher buildings that offered a view of the schoolyards. The large block where Mr Madison had his offices was deserted, apart from two rent-a-cop security personnel on duty at the front desk. The building had been thoroughly searched and all entrances and exits sealed off. The two guys at the front desk were now twinned with two Secret Service men and the same configuration would be in place until late Tuesday afternoon. The atmosphere was relaxed and friendly and the men related well to each other.

In the apartment building, similar searches had been carried out. Because the building was residential, it could not be fully evacuated, but a lot of people were still away on holiday so the few people in residence were mainly old folk and retirees, some couples and some singles. All were very eager to please and most were of the generation who were anxious to cooperate with the authorities. Each resident was interviewed and asked about their plans from the weekend until the Tuesday. A list was compiled of all in residence. Backgrounds were investigated discreetly but all checked out fine. There was no concierge, but in a similar setup to the office block on the opposite corner, two Secret Service men set up a temporary desk and checked people in and out. Far from being discommoded at being asked to sign in and out, the residents were cheerful about it and were grateful for the additional security.

The schools themselves had been searched numerous times, and scanned with metal detectors and patrolled with sniffer dogs to detect any possible hidden explosives. Again, nothing had been found. A final check would be undertaken on the Tuesday morning and the team who carried out that search would then remain in situ until after the visiting party had left.

Mike had visited the Golf Club on the Saturday and hit Laurel on Sunday morning. Trent's driver, Raul, was as good as his word and facilitated full access, introducing him to everyone and making him feel an integral part of the team. There was some gentle ribbing about an Irishman advising them on how to carry out security checks but Mike made it clear that his primary function was to observe and learn. If he had any recommendations they would come later.

In the event, he didn't as he was hugely impressed with their professionalism and thoroughness. He also detected an almost vocational zeal about most of them. They fully understood what their role was and they took it deadly seriously. They were polite but tough – you wouldn't want to mess with any of these guys.

Mike had effectively moved full time into Wendy's place and Trent had agreed to pick him up from there at 06.30 on Tuesday morning. A full briefing had been planned for 07.00 in the school gymnasium. He was surprised to see that Paul was also seated in Trent's Lincoln. He jumped in and the four men set off.

"Hey man, Maria gave me the morning off so I decided I'd go watch some real police in action," Paul joked as he handed Mike a tall Styrofoam mug with a green and white Starbucks logo.

"Thanks, man. Jeez, does anyone in this country make coffee at home? You guys seem to permanently run on take-out coffee."

"Yep, I suppose we do," Trent mused, "but as they say, there's an awful lot of coffee in Brazil, so I guess someone's gotta drink it. Now, speaking of take-outs, we're not expecting any trouble today man but the motto is always to be prepared, so keep this little baby under your belt." He handed Mike a standard D.H.S. issue Sig Sauer P229 pistol. "You ever fired one of those before?"

"Nope, but I wouldn't worry. I've shot similar. I'll figure it out."

Both Trent and Paul carried similar weapons. In fact, D.H.S. had officially adopted Sigs and issued them to all personnel. They were found to be more reliable, less prone to accidental discharge due to their longer trigger pulls but capable of manoeuvrability at close quarters and with a complete repeat strike capability. Mike examined the weapon and found that it contained a full twelve-round magazine – well, it would, wouldn't it? These guys don't mess about, he thought.

The 07.00 meeting was brisk, business-like, but routine to Trent's team. It was obvious they had done this many times before and many were hardened veterans, some even going back as far as Nixon. Wow, that's eight different Presidents, he thought. Who am I to tell these guys what to do?

Trent spent the morning visiting the various units, checking and rechecking that all was in place and locked down, all the while in touch with all units by radio. Paul and Mike accompanied him at times, but also wandered around on their own. The buildings had all been rechecked and sealed off. Locks had been placed on doors and windows. Agents were in position on roofs with binoculars constantly scanning the surrounding area for even the slightest sign of any unusual activity. There was none.

Walker was seriously chilled. The set-up was perfect. All he needed was for the visit to go ahead as planned. He had been aware of the activity over the weekend and viewed this as a positive sign. He had been politely asked about his plans and had been requested to allow access to the apartment twice already by polite young men. He had readily agreed. The silenced rifle had been disassembled and hidden in the framework of Mrs Fletcher's overstuffed armchair, which he had sat on during the searches, assuring the young men that they were no trouble at all and were not discommoding him in the slightest. There was no way any of these young men were going to request a senior citizen to vacate her favourite chair.

At around eleven that morning, the doorbell buzzed again and he slowly made his way to answer it. He glanced in the mirror as he approached the door. Brilliant, he thought, one of your best ever. Even Mrs Fletcher would have difficulty believing that she wasn't looking at a mirror, or hadn't suddenly grown a twin.

He opened the door and greeted the men. There was a very tall, well-dressed African-American man with an earpiece, and a slightly smaller but also tall, broad-shouldered white man with a neutral expression.

"Sorry to bother you again ma'am," said the very tall man, "just carrying out some final checks."

"You come on in and go right ahead, son," she said. "I'll just sit here and stay out of your way."

The African-American went through the apartment thoroughly, looking in each room, opening closets and even checking for false partitions or ceilings. The white man stayed in the living room and spent most of the time looking out of the big picture window.

"Great view you got from up here, ma'am," he said.

"Well, sure it is, son, and when you get a clearer day, you can see right the way over to the big park in Fort Meade. And because it's fifth floor, it's a great relief at my age; you know, no need to worry about burglars, huh?"

"Aye, you're right there, ma'am. It would be a brave burglar who would scale those walls."

Walker was well practiced at not showing heightened senses so he remained deadpan, but there was something about this man that struck him as familiar. He wasn't an American, that was for sure. He detected a slight Irish accent, although he knew from it that the man had not spent all his life in Ireland. He studied the man again from the corner of his eye. He rarely if ever forgot a face. Could it be? Surely not, that guy had been British, hadn't he? And that was a long time ago. But it was him, wasn't it? A bit older, but wearing well, still fit. Yes, it was the driver, matey, from the bungled London job all those years ago. But what the hell was he doing here? The answer was obvious – Jesus, he's looking for me!

The Americans must be worried if they were getting the Brits to help them, he chuckled inwardly. But of course the man wasn't British at all; there was no mistaking that soft southern Irish accent, even after presumably spending years in the UK. Yes, it was him.

Walker's mind took him back to a day many years before in a London Park. The young bobby had done well; very skilful behind the wheel and eager, but not clever enough. The boys had been listening to the open band police radio also and knew the ideal place to intercept. That was the beauty of Kelly's M.O. There was always a backup plan if you got in trouble on the main one. Nine times out of ten his hits worked like clockwork, but you had to be prepared for when one didn't. Most of the time, his Principals provided the backup but he hadn't trusted these young fanatics on this one. Anyway, he didn't need them because he had Katya, and he was being paid more than enough to organise the backup and pay for it himself.

The Irish man checked that the window locks put in place by the Secret Service over the weekend were still intact, and thanked "Mrs Fletcher" for her cooperation. Both men pronounced themselves satisfied and left.

He waited about a half an hour and then began to mobilize. He first put on a pair of plastic surgical gloves. He changed back into the hippy outfit, T-shirt, jeans and sneakers and neatly placed the Mrs Fletcher persona in the kit bag he had recovered from the frame of the armchair. He took out the disassembled rifle, quickly reassembled it and then ran through a series of checks to ensure it was fully operative. A quick text to Katya confirmed she was in the city and would rendezvous at the agreed time and place. He wasn't really concerned that she wouldn't show, but he checked anyway. He would be taking whatever clothes he had worn. He would leave the rifle, as it would only slow him down. There would be no prints on it anyway. He had eaten and drunk frugally over the few days and all that was left in the refrigerator was Mrs Fletcher's. He had kept the apartment spotlessly clean and he was confident there would be little if any trace evidence. He had already put the bedclothes in the washing machine that morning.

He then crawled across the carpet and set to work on the picture window. He concealed himself behind Mrs Fletcher's floor to ceiling curtains at all times, lest he be seen by the rooftop spotters. It was a sunny day, and with the glare he had observed when viewing the building from the coffee shop, it was highly unlikely, but he wasn't taking chances. Not when he was this

393

close – he was operating out of sequence on his list, but the two remaining targets would be routine compared to this one. In fact, he had already formed draft plans for both of them. There would no doubt be a massive manhunt after this hit but he'd covered the bases so he was not in the least apprehensive about being detected.

First, he used the glasscutter to carve a neat little square out of the bottom corner of the window. It was about four feet up from the floor and had a generous windowsill where he could rest the weapon. He then used the rubber suction tool to extract the piece of glass, which he lowered carefully to the floor. The muzzle of the gun fitted perfectly into the slot, allowing him enough movement to swivel to all three locations. The gun was camouflage green, almost the exact shade of the curtains, so by now, he thought, the chances of being spotted were nil. He withdrew the weapon and carefully placed it on the ground. He didn't need to look out the window again. After four days, the view was imprinted on his brain. He returned to Mrs Fletcher's armchair and settled down to wait.

Mike and Paul were now at the other end of the block walking through the elementary school playground.

"What you think, bud, wrapped up tight, yeah?" Paul enquired.

"Seems to be; I think we must've walked the entire area by now. Trent's got a hell of an efficient team here. Can't be totally secure, but he's got it pretty close."

"Right, so what do we do apart from making a nuisance of ourselves?"

"I don't know, I think we're cool here. The only real possibilities are that office block and the apartment building at the other end of the street, but they're fully covered. I've been in both and they seem to be buttoned up good but maybe I'll just hang around one or other of them. What do you think?

"Why not? I'll take the offices and you take the apartments, deal?"

"Fine with me. Let's go." When they reached the end of the block, each went to opposite sides of the road.

"Stay in touch," said Mike.

At 1.20 p.m., Trent – codenamed Big Daddy – spoke into his microphone to do a final check.

"OK, all ground units, final check before we give the go-ahead. Units one to twenty, please confirm in sequence."

"Unit one here, all quiet."

"This is Unit two, Roger that, nothing happening here either."

Each unit reported quiet and normality.

"OK, roof spotters, this is Big Daddy; please report in sequence?"

"Roof man No 1, negative on any signs of activity."

"Thanks Roof man No 1, I copy."

They ran through the sequence again and then he checked with his people back at the school. At 1.28, all units had reported and were coordinated.

Trent took out his cell and hit the digit 5 which called a pre-programmed number. The phone was answered on the first ring.

"Yo, Big Daddy."

"We're good to go here. Bring the man on. I repeat, this is a go."

Chapter 39

The motorcade left Pennsylvania Avenue at 1.32.pm, slightly ahead of schedule. It was a lot smaller than usual but still contained two large, fully-armoured Cadillac limousines, or 'beasts' as they were known in the Secret Service. The designation referred to a combination of their power, strength and manoeuvrability. They reportedly had eight-inch-thick armour, tear-gas cannons and Kevlar-reinforced tyres. The engine size and power were not known, and for security reasons, most of the other details remained confidential.

Several police vehicles preceded the beginning of the motorcade. These cars and motorcycles drove ahead to clear the way for the main party. They temporarily blocked traffic at intersections and smoothed the path for the oncoming official cars.

Next came the official part, preceded by two Secret Service cars. They were followed by what was referred to in the business as the "secure package." In the event of an emergency, the secure package would break off from the rest of the group. This always included two limousines, and was heavily guarded by local law enforcement and the Secret Service. All cars would be driven by experts in defensive driving techniques.

The next part was made up of vans and large SUVs transporting White House staff members and selected members of the press. At the rear was a communications van that recorded the President's movements, an ambulance, and additional police vehicles. As usual, all the vehicles were surrounded by motorcycle outriders.

It was an awesome sight for a visitor or a tourist, but D.C. residents often complained about the constant traffic disruption and felt the number of vehicles was showy and overkill. Those closer to the protection detail knew better. Every vehicle in the motorcade played a vital role and the last thing any of them were there for was show. Initially slow in the city streets, the group picked up speed when they hit 295 and they would arrive on schedule.

The elementary school got out at 2.30 and the Principal, whose mail Walker had hacked, said she expected that the prize giving would be just after two o'clock. He was in place just after 1.30 and was relaxed but totally focused. It would be simple, really; two small squeezes on the trigger and the job would be done. The sun was now to his left and actually enhanced the quality of light in the target areas, making the task even simpler.

Despite himself, he felt his pulse quicken marginally. This was The Big One! He thought of the mayhem and the recriminations this would cause, but abstractly. It wouldn't really affect him. He didn't live in that world, hadn't for a long time. He continued to remain focused but he allowed his mind go where it wanted to.

When the deed was done, he thought, automatic instincts would take over with the Secret Service and the police, and that instinct was to protect the others in the Presidential party and the general public. So the natural tendency would be for the cops to move to the centre, where the incident had occurred, and for the public to run in the other direction. In the confusion, he would quietly slip away. He had one small bag and it was ready at the doorway. Some of the agents might guess where the shots had come from, but with no sound, people would become disoriented. In his experience, they always did. There might even be mass panic, a stampede to safety – all the better for him. The Secret Service boys would know what had happened alright but their sworn duty was to protect the Presidential party – apprehension of the suspect was a secondary consideration. Mind you, there was the Irish guy, but hopefully he would be at the other end of the street with the group.

He thought of his employers. He knew now why these people were paying him so much money to do what he did. Their strategy was to demonstrate that no one was safe, not even the most powerful man on earth. If you could get to him, you could get to anyone, regardless of the level of security; and it was true. Unless people lived in an underground bunker 24/7, they were vulnerable, and even if they did, he would still probably figure out a way of getting to them. For years, these guys had just detonated bombs and shot people at random to spread terror, but the effect soon wore off. If they could show that they were capable of taking out the top man, they would surely be effective beyond their wildest dreams.

He thought about previous assassinations. Everyone who had been alive at the time, including him, remembered where they were when John F. Kennedy was shot. Many people felt that his death had set America back at least a generation, maybe more. What was certain was that the assassin that day in Dallas, whoever he had been, had changed the course of history. Kennedy had been America's most charismatic leader, many would say, ever. His loss was a tragedy from which it took the country years to recover. The current man, many had claimed, had as much, if not more, charisma and presence. He was more than a President, more than a leader; he was a ground-breaker and a true statesman. There was no question that in the next few minutes Walker would alter history, but he wore it lightly.

Hell, people still talked about Lincoln's assassination and that was 150 years ago! Ask any kid who had shot him and they would all tell you – John Wilkes Booth. But there was also a subtle difference, which the terrorists would play for all it was worth. Both J.F.K. and Abe Lincoln had been taken out by fellow Americans. If things went to plan, no one would know precisely who had been the assassin on this one, but they would sure as hell know who he was working for. Imagine the frenzy and the terror you could spread if the President were taken out by foreign terrorists. Everyone would want to invade everywhere, chasing invisible or non-existent enemies – many thousands would be lost in pointless conflicts, eventually leading to the same confusion, disillusionment and disaffection that followed 9/11, only this time descending to chaos and complete disruption, perhaps even the breakdown of western society as they knew it.

Yes, this was a concentrated, professionally organised effort to undermine both the leaders of the western world and their security services, and to spread fear and terror throughout western society; and he was its instrument. Did he want to be the man who changed the course of history?

Oh well, it was too late to pull out now. He thought again of the massive manhunt, but dismissed it. They had never found who had really killed Kennedy, and it for sure wasn't Oswald. He had been active for over two months now and they had not come within a country mile of apprehending him – and they wouldn't, not as long as he kept his cool and stuck to his plan. It was just another hit – just another day's work.

He caught a flurry of activity out of the corner of his eye. Yep, here they were. Now; relax, focus. First opportunity would be the short walk from the limo to the Elementary school. Shouldn't be a problem, as he would surely pause to be greeted by the Principal and whatever other dignitaries had been wheeled out.

The cavalcade rolled to a stop in front of the school and a dark-suited Secret Service Agent opened the door. He caught a flash of colour to the right, and realized it was the children lining up to greet the President. This wasn't the way the Principal said they had scheduled it. The man was supposed to be met by the V.I.P.'s and then proceed to the classroom. But of course, he realized; it was a sunny day and this was an ideal photo opportunity for TV and news media.

He aimed the rifle and pressed his right eye close to the telescopic sight. The man was reaching down and handing something to a little girl of about six. Ah Jesus, even he couldn't take the man out doing this. He couldn't do that to little kids. In his mind's eye, he saw his own little girls. OK, he decided to stand down for now. Given the beautiful fall day, it was odds on the man would walk to the Middle School anyway so from this angle, aiming downwards, he'd get him easily crossing the street. If he used the limo, there were two further locations and both were closer.

Mike was in the third floor lobby with the Secret Service agents.

"All quiet, guys?"

"Going like clockwork; another ten minutes and we're outta here."

He noticed a middle-aged man sitting at a small table to the side and wandered over. The man had a clipboard with a list of names and he was ticking them off as he worked a landline telephone.

"Hi there; nice day for it, huh?"

"Yep, sure is." The man extended his hand. "Hi, we haven't met. Name's Arnold Schmidt. I'm the Building Superintendent."

"I'm Mike Lyons, I'm with these guys."

"Yup, I know. I'm going through our list of residents calling everyone in the building to remind them of tomorrow evening's residents meeting – it's just routine."

"Sure, mind if I take a look?"

"Not at all, be my guest."

Mike briefly scanned the list. It was neatly set out floor-by-floor and seemed in order. He was about to hand it back when something struck him.

"Oh hey, not being critical, but you left out Mrs Fletcher on the 5th floor"

"Naw, I didn't. Mrs F's away on vacation for a week. She left last Friday."

"You sure?"

"Absolutely, she won some competition for a trip to the Caribbean. She left Friday last with her sister."

"But then, who's up in-?" He felt his stomach hit the floor as realization dawned in an instant. "Aw, sweet suffering Jesus."

He didn't wait for the elevator but hit the stairs three at a time. He felt the burn of adrenalin as he hit each flight. He had started from the third floor lobby so he reached the fifth floor landing in seconds. He pulled the Sig and cocked it. He dashed, panting, to apartment 54 and in one continuous movement struck the door lock with his heel. It burst inwards in a shower of splinters.

There was no old lady now. Instead, there was a man lying over the armchair with his eye to the sight of a rifle pointing through a small hole in the picture window. He took the pistol in a two-handed grip.

"Freeze, right now, drop the rifle and don't move a fucking muscle!"

The man nonchalantly dropped the rifle and spread his arms.

"So you figured it out. Fair dues."

"Jesus Christ, Kelly?" Mike swayed slightly as the shock of who he was seeing dawned.

"Aye, John P. Kelly at your service, matey, long time no see, eh? Well done, matey, you got there eventually. Ironic, isn't it? What? Never thought it would come down to this; never thought it would be a fellow Irishman that would collar me. And to think that all these years, I thought you were a Brit. But of course you really are a Brit; what we used call a west Brit. I come from the same place as you do, boy, but you're a fuckin turncoat, a collaborator; I might have known."

The accent was back now, as if he had never left. He edged towards the table.

"Stay where you are, you bastard." Mike tightened his grip on the trigger.

"Come on matey, you and I have far more in common than Brits or Yanks."

Mike struggled to maintain his composure. "I said, fuckin stand where you are! We have nothing in common."

But Kelly was hyper. "Come on laddie, I've got your number – forced emigration, right? Had to police the Brits because the Paddy's wouldn't accept you, right?"

Mike said nothing but Kelly persisted. "Come on son, what's it to you? We're the same people – fuck these guys. They're the ones that forced us to be what we are – screwing the lifeblood out of us for generations. Remember the auld sod. Come on!"

"We all had choices, Kelly. You made yours – I made mine."

"Aye, we did, but you came from the peaceful part of the island – we had it much tougher where we were brought up, me boyo."

401

"Look, shut the fuck up. Whatever you did in the past is past; we have peace now, no thanks to you, and even if you had a difficult upbringing, which I know for a fact you didn't, that doesn't justify flying halfway round the world assassinating people."

"Ah, but I'm good at it mate, that's why. You're obviously good at being a copper and good luck to you, but I'm good at what I do; so I do it and fuck you." Kelly had been edging ever closer in imperceptible movements.

Mike tried to take out and thumb the radio Trent had given him earlier but he couldn't seem to get a response. Where the hell were the guys from downstairs? Trying to alert the main group to move the Chief, most probably.

"Just fucking stay where you are!"

"Arra stop, you'll not kill a fellow Irishman, no matter what I've done."

It suddenly registered with Mike that in all the years he had spent in the police and in anti-terrorism, he had never killed a man. He had discharged his weapon many times and had wounded a few but he had never killed. He hesitated for just a microsecond, seeing himself back in Ireland as a young man, forced to emigrate because there were, yet again, no prospects in his own land. He quickly banished the thought but a microsecond was all Kelly needed.

He lunged at Mike and knocked the pistol to one side. Mike dived for the weapon, assuming a defensive position as he anticipated Kelly would do the same. Instead of a scuffle, he recovered his pistol in an instant and swung it back towards where Kelly had been – but the man was gone.

Down on the street, utter confusion reigned. The President was safely back in his limousine speeding towards the White House so the main threat had receded. The word was that there was someone in one of the buildings at the end of the block, but no one was sure. Mike tore back downstairs and hit the lobby. The two agents were still there, both on their radios. The Building Superintendent seemed in shock.

"Where did he go?" Mike shouted.

"Where did who go?"

"The bastard who was in 54, he ran this way. Ah shit, there's another exit, the bloody fire escape."

He dashed to the back of the building. This was the Achilles heel. The fire escape could not be locked for health and safety reasons, but it was supposed to be covered. But when he reached the entrance, there was no one to be seen. They must have assumed it was harmless because it was at the back, he thought.

The fire escape was Kelly's escape route and he knew precisely how many steps in each flight and how many it took to reach the ground. He came down it two at a time, efficient but careful not to trip, and leaped the final few steps. As he hit the bottom, he charged straight into Paul, who had been alerted by the guys at the desk and was running hard to cover the back. Both men crashed heavily to the ground in a tangle of arms and legs. Paul shouted "Freeze," but he did so before he had time to cock his gun – an old trick, that, which Kelly had used himself in the past.

Kelly rolled and swivelled in one quick movement. His Glock coughed twice, catching Paul in the abdomen. In the same movement, Kelly was up and running towards the alley. He was winded but he was ahead. A quick glance showed no one behind him – yes, he was the man!

Mike arrived seconds later to find his friend bleeding profusely. He was as white as a sheet and was only breathing fitfully.

"Ah Jesus, Paul." He fell to his knees and tried to staunch the flow of blood. Paul pointed towards the alley.

"Go, man, go – I'm fine, he's… few… seconds… ahead…"

The two agents arrived. One of them thumbed his radio.

"Man down, man down, medics, quick, rear of the apartment building."

Paul had slipped into unconsciousness.

"Keep him breathing and stop the haemorrhaging," Mike panted. "Fuck you, Kelly, you bastard," he screamed and took off towards the alley.

Kelly had to run through a web of back alleys and side streets and lanes, but he was running as freely as if he was in his own back yard. He was in sneakers but his pursuers, if there were any, would not be. He knew that the streets around the school were all closed off to traffic, but he also knew exactly where he was going whereas his pursuers did not; the benefit of research. He hadn't achieved his goal today, but he'd have another chance.

He was panting heavily as he rounded the last corner. There was Katya, exactly where he asked her to be and the rear door was open. Oh you gorgeous little beauty he thought. He dived in and shouted, "Drive, baby drive, go, go, go!" It had been a close shave but it was only four miles to I95 and he'd be home free.

Mike chased through the back streets and alleys in a seemingly fruitless search. He headed to where he felt traffic would be flowing normally, but he was operating on pure instinct. He might have been going the complete opposite direction to where Kelly had gone for all he knew.

After what seemed like an eternity, but was really about two minutes, he came to a cross street where traffic appeared to be flowing normally. There was no sign of Kelly, no sign of anyone. He sighed in despair and was about to turn back in disgust when he heard a slight screech of tires to his right.

About three blocks up, he caught sight of just a flash of a silver vehicle turning right. He wasn't 100% sure, but it looked like a Camry disappearing around the corner. A Toyota Camry, going at high speed. The significance hit him like a punch in the gut and he put it together - that's got to be it – a fucking Camry. That's what the bastard's been using. He raced to the light and flashed his ID to the first vehicle in line.

"Sorry, ma'am, police in hot pursuit. I need your vehicle, please, right now."

He must have looked plausible because the woman jumped out in fright leaving the keys in the ignition.

He gunned the motor and did a U-turn back in the direction the Toyota had gone. It had been travelling at fairly high speed, and Christ, there must be ten thousand of them in this city, but he was gonna give it one right go. He realized he had no light or siren so he was on his own. He had no backup so he manoeuvred his cell phone from his pocket and did the only thing he could – he dialled 911.

"Emergency, police please." He was put straight through.

"Please state your emergency and your location sir."

"My name is Mike Lyons; I'm on Special Assignment from the U.K. with D.H.S. I was assigned to the President's detail this afternoon and I have reason to believe I'm now in hot pursuit of the man who attempted to assassinate him."

"Is this a – no – oh shit; hold on sir."

It took a few seconds and several switches but he was eventually put through to Trent. "Mike, I've heard. Where are you? What you driving? What's our perp driving?"

"I've no idea, don't know these streets; wait; hang on, I'm just turning on to Staples Mill Road, and the Staples Mill Shopping Plaza is on my left. The suspect, but I repeat, only a suspect, is at least two blocks, maybe more, ahead in a Silver Camry; no licence plate as yet but I'm gonna keep this line open so I'll update you as we drive. I have a hunch our man's in that car but it is only a hunch. I'm not sure, repeat, not 100% confirmed."

"OK man, we copy you. Don't worry, we ain't gonna go shooting up the vehicle but we're putting up road blocks all over the place and we've got air support coming in so within ten minutes this whole area is gonna be gridlocked anyway, I mean shut down. Only problem is that our man may be heading to Interstate 95 or 64. If he hits either, we may lose him in the spaghetti so try to stay close. We'll try to intercept, soon as you get us a plate."

Mike wondered about the wisdom of that strategy as Kelly could always stop and escape on foot again. He appeared to be superbly fit and while Mike was also in shape, he wasn't sure he could outrun him. Opening fire in a built up area was not an option. He also knew that Kelly would have backups and ways out and fall-backs all over the place. That was the way this guy had always operated, and was probably why he had survived for so long. If he were allowed to reach one of his boltholes, then they'd lose him again, perhaps permanently this time.

He made the turn but couldn't see a Camry. Ah shit; it was hopeless, wasn't it? The guy had over a full minute start on him. A long straight stretch opened up in front of him but his man could have turned off anywhere, couldn't he?

Yes but he hadn't. He thanked God for American grid systems and long straight streets and avenues. About three blocks up, he caught sight of a silver Camry. He suddenly realized he was speeding, and looked to see what he was driving. A Subaru Impreza. That would explain it. Now, all he could do was to try to keep in touch and hope Kelly didn't know he was following him.

He eased through the traffic and got to within four or five vehicles. The Camry was proceeding cautiously, seemingly careful not to exceed the limit. He got the plate and relayed it to Trent. As he edged ever closer, he tried to make out the driver but it was difficult in the sunshine with tinted glass.

He eventually got up close and pounded the steering wheel in frustration. Wrong bloody vehicle! The driver was a woman! With great weariness he picked up his cell phone.

"Trent, hold it. Vehicle is being driven by a lady. Ah shit man, it was just a hunch; looks like it didn't come off this time. You can stand down. Sorry bud."

"That's OK Mike, we're still proceeding with road blocks throughout the city, so can you give us a full description of the assassin?"

"Yeah, for sure." He relayed the description of how Kelly had looked at the apartment block, but his heart wasn't in it. Who knew what Kelly looked like now? The man could be having a makeover as he spoke. Mike remembered that he had had a reputation for disguises; his impersonation of Mrs Fletcher that morning had sure fooled Mike and Trent, and God knew how many others.

They were just coming up to the confluence of I95, I64 & I195, and the Camry headed up the ramp. Mike, heavily despondent, just followed. He thought of Kelly's penchant for disguise and then it hit him like a hammer blow. Shit; the man's M.O. had always included a driver. Maybe, just maybe, but no; the lady driving the Camry didn't seem to have a care in the world and drove nonchalantly. She seemed to know exactly where she was going as she expertly manoeuvred through the labyrinth of overpasses, underpasses, intersections and interchanges. She eventually chose I95 south. Mike followed but at a safe distance. He didn't really know where he was going but he didn't have anything better to do just then so he'd keep on it.

After a few miles driving south, he noticed a figure emerge from the back seat of the Camry and swing over the seats into the front. The man kissed the lady and they seemed to engage in animated conversation. It was Kelly. Gotcha, he said quietly, got ya; and this time, you won't even see me coming, mate! He grabbed the cell phone. Shit, the connection to Trent had broken. He hit redial. No signal, out of coverage! How the hell could he be out of coverage when he was still in the middle of Washington? He threw the phone on to the seat and cursed all cell phone providers. He tried again – still no signal.

He looked at the gas gauge in the Subaru. Almost empty – thanks, lady; nice car, but it would be nicer if you had put some gas in it for me. He had a decision to make and very soon. Kelly and his lady could be driving all the way to Florida and it looked like he was gonna go about another ten miles before he ran out of gas. He thumped the wheel again in frustration. He could try to run them off the road but that was risky. Forget about the movies. It doesn't work like that. He was as likely to kill himself as them, or disable his car and let them get clean away, so it wasn't an option. Besides, while his car was faster, theirs was a lot bigger. He could stop at a service station and try to call Trent from a pay phone to alert him but that was also risky. It could take a while to intercept someone on a highway as big as 95, and in the meantime, Kelly could have switched cars. In fact, Mike was surprised he hadn't done so already.

In the end, nature intervened, or so it seemed to Mike. Either Kelly or the woman needed to use the bathroom. They pulled into a service stop and parked right beside the restrooms. Both jumped out and headed in that direction. Mike slowly eased to a stop about six car lengths away and slipped quietly out of the vehicle, easing the Sig out of his waistband. But just as Kelly reached the rest room door, he wheeled round, aimed the Glock squarely at Mike and fired twice.

He fell heavily but managed to roll away out of the line of fire, putting the car between him and Kelly. The bastard had obviously seen him in the rear view mirror, or maybe it had been the woman. He was bleeding profusely but it was only his left shoulder so he still held his weapon. Kelly came running across the car park to finish him off but he took cover, held the Sig steady and fired. Kelly tripped and fell and the Glock clattered to the ground.

A huge Mack truck was just entering the service area and it sounded its klaxon loudly. Kelly ignored the truck and dived for his weapon, but this time Mike was up and ahead of him.

Leaning over the Subaru, he called out, "Freeze, you bastard. No more chances, Kelly. Move a fucking muscle and I swear I'll blow your head off."

The truck driver jumped down from his cab and ran for cover or help or both.

Kelly relaxed visibly, sat up, and raised his arms. "OK, mate, you got me; fair cop. I'm going nowhere."

"Right, just very slowly; face down on the ground, hands behind your back."

"Now, is that any way to treat a fellow countryman?"

"Just shut up and fucking do it!"

Kelly made to lie down but in the tiniest fraction of a second, he dived for the Glock. He was fast but this time Mike was ready. In the split second, Mike saw, not the deprivation Kelly had referred to, but a peaceful land, open to all comers. Then he thought of Paul and his beautiful family, and Dave Mortimer, and all the other innocent victims; and he pulled the trigger and then pulled it again and Kelly lay still. He slumped to his knees, weak from his own wound. He had never killed a man in his life before but he felt sure he had now.

He struggled over to Kelly. Miraculously, the man was still breathing. He shouted at one of the truckers, "Hey, get in there and call 911, I got a wounded man here." The man disappeared at high speed. He bent over Kelly. He tried to staunch his wounds but blood was pouring from his chest.

"Not for me, laddie, not for me," he coughed.

"Hang in there, medics are on the way."

"No, too late. What's… what's your name?"

"My name is Michael."

Right, Michael, I'm…" He struggled and coughed up more blood. "Codes."

"What? No, don't try to speak. Save it."

"No, my jacket, here." He pointed to his chest. "Bank codes…. millions… use it right; use it for the old country…" He was fading fast. "Use it to make sure they never… they never produce another bastard like me. Promise me."

"OK, I promise you, but hang in…"

But he was gone.

Mike collapsed back against the fender, exhausted.

There was a persistent ringing noise, which he couldn't place, but then he realized what it was. His cell phone signal had returned. He struggled up and reached into the car to answer, stumbled, and felt his head swim from blood loss. It was Trent.

"Hey man, sorry we lost you. Where the hell are you?"

"I'm not really sure, Trent. Some rest stop on I95 South, but I need medical attention. Got shot in the shoulder but hey, it's OK, man, it's over. It's finally over."

Someone must have called 911 because the medics were there within minutes and he was stabilized. There was no hope for Kelly so they placed a blanket over him and placed him on the green grass margin. Ironic, Mike thought. As he was being placed in the ambulance, he noticed that the Camry had disappeared.

Epilogue

The meeting was held in the usual suite in the Gulf Hotel. The members of the Council arrived, as usual, covertly. The Bahraini was somewhat apprehensive. The airwaves had been full of the story of the failed attempt for the previous days. These men did not take failure lightly. As usual, there was no agenda and no papers. The Saudi opened the meeting.

"I would like to propose a vote of congratulations to our dear friend, Sheikh Khadira," he ventured. The vote was carried unanimously.

"You did well, my friend," said the Egyptian. "We didn't achieve all our aims, but thanks to Sheikh Khadira's bold strategy, we are strong again and we have shown that we can strike right at the heart of the enemy."

"Tell me," said the Afghan, speaking for the first time and addressing himself directly to Abdullah, "can we assume that there are more of these men of which you speak, and which you retained?"

Abdullah cleared his throat. "Indeed there are, my friends, and I am sure they can be persuaded to work for us."

"In that case," said the Afghan, "I propose that we make the funds available to allow you to continue on this path."

The proposal was agreed and the Bahraini thanked them and smiled graciously.

Katya had driven the Camry to the next town and abandoned it. She was careful to wipe it down fully before she left – she had learned well from him. She had the remainder of the cash in his briefcase, almost half a million bucks. She also had numerous prepaid credit cards with limits she could only guess at. She had thought about keeping the car – it was registered to John Robinson, and she was now officially Katherine Robinson driving her late husband's car, but the police would surely have gotten the licence plate so she decided wisely to leave it. She had his laptop, and while she wasn't brilliant with computers, she thought she would eventually figure out how he accessed his offshore accounts.

She was a little sad that he was gone as she had developed a deep affection for him. When she had told him that he had been the first man who had cared for her, it had been the truth. But she had had a tough upbringing and was wise to the ways of the world. He had been kind but she knew too that he had used her. Yes, she was a little sad, but she was young and she'd get over it and love again.

She caught a Greyhound to Walterboro, picked up the Honda and drove it back to Miami. After that, she wasn't sure where she would head. America was a big place, and she had her whole life ahead of her and lots of money to enjoy it. She missed him but she would be fine now.

Two weeks later, a very distraught lady called to the Lake Mary Police Department. She had arrived back from Nebraska a week before to find her husband missing. After initially thinking he had just been delayed, she had reacted with shock and horror when a likeness of someone who appeared to be him was flashed across every news media outlet in the country identifying him as the man who had carried out a failed assassination attempt on the President.

Deep down, she had always suspected something was not quite right with the way he did his business, but in her wildest nightmares, she had never suspected anything like this. The Police Chief was gentle and sympathetic. He saw her in his private office and confirmed her suspicions. She collapsed into the chair and sobbed uncontrollably.

In the late afternoon, Mike and Wendy sat on a bench by the Veterans Memorial in Constitution Gardens. He had his arm in a

411

sling and was still quite weak. He had been very quiet during the previous days and she had let him be.

"How's Paul?" she asked.

"Well, thank God he's out of the ICU, but it will be some months yet before he's back. He lost a hell of a lot of blood and almost died. Maria told me it was touch and go when he was brought in."

"Yeah, I've been speaking to Barbara and she was really scared."

They sat in silence for a time, watching the people identifying some of the names on the wall, of a loved one, a son, a daughter or maybe a friend or neighbour. They watched the leaves swirl in the light breeze. Most of them had fallen now and there was a distinct chill in the air.

It was Wendy who eventually broke the silence.

"You've been very quiet. Is everything ok?"

"Ah, sure honey. There's always a down period after the high of solving a major case, or when you finally apprehend your suspect, but apart from all that, I never like to see loss of life, any life."

She touched his hand.

"Who was he?" she said.

He exhaled and considered.

"Oh, just someone from a long time ago; a guy I should have caught when I was much younger, but more naïve. God knows how many lives might have been saved if I had, but there's no point going over that now. He was from my own country, but from a different tradition. He was probably a product of his time, a guy who believed in something but then lost his way, went bad, took the wrong path. Then he found he was good at it and made it his profession."

"They're saying in the media that police in Florida have apparently found evidence linking him with dozens of assassinations. He seems to have operated for years."

"You know, Wendy, I don't think we will ever know what crimes he committed. He was the best at what he did, but what he did was evil and he seemed to have no problem living with it. That I cannot accept. But I think it may have been his ego that

412

eventually got him caught. He knew he was good, but he didn't just want to be the best, he seemed to need to prove it to himself all the time. I mean, the jobs he took on over the past three months were outrageous. Perhaps only he could have gotten away with them."

She ventured, "Maybe he wanted to be recognised. I mean, he lived most of his life in the shadows. He was the best at what he did, but he could never advertise that."

"You know, you're probably right. We all like to be recognised for what we do well. But, as I say, I don't condone the death of any man, but you'd have to say the world is a safer place without guys like Kelly."

The crowd around the monument had thinned now to almost a trickle. The pale afternoon sun had long since departed. The breeze had freshened and there was a hint of rain. The light had faded earlier today and the evenings were beginning to close in. She shivered involuntarily in the slight chill. He wrapped his good arm around her and said, "Come on Wendy, let's go home."

Author's Biographical Note:

Liam Flood is Irish. He has spent most of his life working in the Aviation and Retailing industries, based in Ireland, Hong Kong, the Middle East, Ukraine and Russia. He now works as a business consultant and spends his time between Ireland and Russia. He is married with two adult children. This is his first novel. He has also written many business papers over the years and a non-fiction book entitled, "Russia in the 21st Century".

Lightning Source UK Ltd.
Milton Keynes UK
UKOW050622110412

190471UK00002B/2/P